How Perfect Is That

A NOVEL

Sarah Bird

Pocket Books

New York   London   Toronto   Sydney

Pocket Books
A Division of Simon & Schuster, Inc.
1230 Avenue of the Americas
New York, NY 10020

First Pocket Books trade paperback edition July 2009

POCKET and colophon are registered trademarks of Simon & Schuster, Inc.

For information about special discounts for bulk purchases,
please contact Simon & Schuster Special Sales at
1-866-506-1949 or business@simonandschuster.com.

The Simon & Schuster Speakers Bureau can bring authors to your live event. For
more information or to book an event contact the Simon & Schuster Speakers
Bureau at 866-248-3049 or visit our website at
www.simonspeakers.com.

Manufactured in the United States of America

10 9 8 7 6 5 4 3 2 1

ISBN 978-1-4391-2308-9

Rave reviews for Sarah Bird's comic triumph

How Perfect Is That

Winner of a 2008 *Elle* Readers' Prize and
featured in the 2008 *New York Post*
"Required Reading" list

"A scorching sense of humor."

—*The Austin Chronicle*

"Pure wicked fun . . . "

—*Kirkus Reviews*

"Ms. Bird's wickedly good grasp of social satire couldn't be finer."
—*The Dallas Morning News*

"A rollicking, laugh-out loud funny story. . . . Highly recommended."
—*Library Journal*

"A fried Twinkie of a book—crunchily witty, creamy-hearted and shockingly delicious."

—Janet Fitch, author of *Paint It Black*

"A scathingly funny look at red state high society. . . . Hilarious."
—Will Clarke, author of *Lord Vishnu's Love Handles*

"A laugh-out-loud addition to Bird's long line of estrogen-fueled dramedies."

—*Publishers Weekly*

"A very funny book . . . with the pace of a screwball comedy."
—*Houston Chronicle*

"Smart, sardonic satire and irresistibly irreverent irony."

—*Booklist*

"A fast-paced, fun story. . . ."

—*Palm Beach Post*

. . . and to the Republic

"What I'm hearing, which is sort of scary, is they all want to stay in Texas. Everyone is so overwhelmed by the hospitality. And so many of the people in the arena here, you know, were underprivileged anyway, so this is working very well for them."

—former First Lady Barbara Bush,
after meeting Katrina evacuees
at the Astrodome, September 5, 2005

Bill Moyers: *What happened to the moral compass?*
Thomas Frank: *It got demagnetized by money.*

—*NOW*, July 9, 2004

The awful thing about life is this: Everyone has his reasons.

—Jean Renoir, *The Rules of the Game*, 1939

"*. . . the only way not to think about money is to have a great deal of it.*"
    Affluence, unless stimulated by a keen imagination, forms but the vaguest notion of the practical strain of poverty.

—Edith Wharton, *The House of Mirth*, 1905

This I set down as a positive truth. A woman with fair opportunities, and without an absolute hump, may marry whom she likes.

—William Makepeace Thackeray,
Vanity Fair: A Novel Without a Hero, 1848

CONTENTS

Pemberton Heights   1

Seneca House   63

Cast Out   221

PEMBERTON HEIGHTS

Kippie Lee Teeter

Requests the honor of your presence at
a garden party, une fête champêtre,
a ladies' luncheon.
Call it what you will, this event
wouldn't be complete without *you*!

April 3, 2003

One o'clock until the cows come home.
7 Hargrove Lane
Amuse-bouches & other delectables

Catering by **Blythe Young's**
Wretched Xcess

Event Coordination Extraordinaire

April 3, 2003

FOUR-FIFTEEN in the morning is the perfect time to catalog the one commodity I am still rich in: regrets. I keep trying to pare that lengthy list down to a manageably brief inventory of everything I failed to acquire during marriage to a scion of one of America's wealthiest dynasties. Over the past few months, I have smelted a King Solomon's mine of lost swag down to the few basics I most regret either not obtaining or not hanging on to:

1. A husband
2. A home
3. A Pap smear

I've added and removed "4. Children" from the list several times. Currently, they are off.

Recently I've also started to regret christening myself Blythe Young. I chose the name at the end of my sophomore year at Abilene High School. It was a decided improvement over the one my mother had saddled me with, Chanterelle Young. I was tired of being taken for either a stripper or, far worse, exactly what I was, the daughter of a trailer-trash tramp of a mother too stupid to know that in her single, solitary moment of maternal lyricism she had named her only child after a mushroom.

Eighteen years later, however, instead of blithe and young, I feel burdened and every day of my thirty-three years. What I am is divorced, desperate, and currently clinging frantically to a very tenuous toehold here in Bamsie Beiver's historically significant carriage house. Although Bamsie redid the main house in meticulous turn-of-the-century detail for maximum "authenticity" and "tax benefits," my abode never received such tender ministrations. Renovations on the carriage house appear to have started and stopped once the horse turds were swept out.

The sky lightens to a clotted gray signaling that no matter how much I might wish otherwise a new day is dawning. I brace myself for the next item on the chronic insomniac's agenda: an elaborate road trip revisiting all the points in my life where I took disastrously wrong turns. First up, the prenup. I put the prenup on hold, since it is more than a wrong turn; that damned prenup is its own entire journey of the damned with an itinerary drawn up by my former mother-in-law, Ilsa She-Wolf of the SS, known more generally as Peggy Biggs-Dix. Peggy ruined my life. Without her I would still be Mrs. Henry "Trey" Biggs-Dix the Third, mistress of Pemberton Palace. I would still be sleeping on Frette sheets, numbered like works of art, thick and dense as deep sleep itself. I would still be breathing in air that smelled of lavender, eucalyptus, and the kind of clean that only generations of really dirty money can buy. Without Peggy, I wouldn't be where I am now, huddled in Bamsie's dank carriage house, staring down bankruptcy.

Bankruptcy? Who am I kidding? I was bankrupt when I married Trey. I believed he would rescue me. But his succubus of a mother sliced my oxygen hose and left me gasping on the ocean floor. No, it is what lurks beyond bankruptcy that is so terrifying. I forbid myself to burrow any farther into this rathole. My future will be decided today. So, although the lengthy list of things I would rather be doing than coordinating Kippie Lee's garden party would lead off with "Anything" and finish up with "Gum surgery," I have no choice. One, just one, just one healthy check, will keep me alive long enough to regroup and come back to fight another day.

In another city. Under another name.

Kippie Lee's check is my last, rapidly fading hope for staying out of debtor's prison. The words "debtor's prison" fill my mind with images from *A Rake's Progress*. Wastrels in powdered wigs despoiling themselves at the gaming tables. Blowsy slatterns in mobcaps with beauty marks painted over syphilitic sores. Grand ladies in Marie Antoinette wigs amusing themselves by gawking at the debt-maddened lunatics imprisoned in Bedlam. The vision is highly motivating.

It is do-or-die time. I have to get that check. Failure is not an option. *Semper Fi.*

Already imagining I have Kippie Lee's check, I prioritize my list of creditors into Vultures and Jackals. Vultures—my unpaid employees, the IRS, inattentive suppliers—won't attack until I've stopped moving. I can let them wait. The Jackals, on the other hand—Sprint, Visa, American Express, MasterCard, Loan Sharks 'R' Us—are already nipping at my hindquarters with their massive, wildebeest-thigh-crushing jaws. This pack will have to be seen to first. I plan to scatter precisely enough dollars in the path of the Jackals to make them unlock their cruel masseters and release my gluteals. That will give me some breathing room.

Thus bolstered, I struggle to clear my mind so that I can get a bit more sleep. Instead, the hamsters on their wheels turn even faster. They pull me back, all the way back to the day when I met Henry "Trey" "Tree Tree" "Double T" Biggs-Dix the Third. Back to the beginning of the end.

I met Trey shortly after the dot-com bubble burst and I was in financial free fall owing to the first incarnation of Wretched Xcess Event Coordination Extraordinaire going belly-up. Wretched Xcess was not just the name of my business but the encapsulation of an entire zeitgeist as manifested in Austin, Texas. That was a heady time when too much was never enough and the clever boys in the backward caps, Teva sandals, and cargo shorts could not burn through their venture capital fast enough. Excess, that's what my clever boys wanted and that's what I provided.

Drunk with the rest of the country at the vast money kegger thrown by the venture capitalists, I expanded to meet the needs of my ever-more-demanding clientele. Though the Bubble Boys were still padding around in flip-flops, they could tell their Beluga from their Ossetra. And, in every case, they wanted the Beluga. They also wanted the titanium chafing dishes, the Baccarat crystal, and the tablecloths with a four-digit thread count embroidered by French nuns that I felt forced to acquire. High-end all the way. Leveraged to the max. *That* was when I should have worried. But I had fallen under the spell of my bright boys. We were rewriting the laws of trade and were all going to retire by the age of thirty-three. Thirty-four at the latest. Working was for chumps. We would float together forever on the bubble that had already lofted us so much higher than we could have ever dreamed.

And then?

Pop.

A bubble. Yes, I could have dealt with a bubble. But did it have to be filled with deadly swamp gas?

We all fell. Just some of us, weighted down with titanium chafing dishes and tablecloths heavy as rugs, hit significantly harder than those who'd pulled rip cords on parachutes in varying hues of gold. Or who'd simply moved into Mom's garage. Mom's garage was never an option for me, since my mother, Vicki Jo, was herself living in a garage. Griz's Hawg Heaven Harley Garage to be exact, owned by her "old man."

Vicki Jo keeps in touch by sending photos taken while she is "riding bitch" on the back of a chromed-out Harley-Davidson, piloted by Griz himself, whom Mom proudly describes as "a 1%er Outlaw Bandido thru and thru." In most of the photos, my mother is hiking up her top to reveal the bouncing maternal mammaries tanned to a rich, beef-jerky brown. I have to give Vicki Jo this: She has great tits for a woman her age and could almost pass for the thirty-nine she claims. At least when her very inconvenient thirty-three-year-old daughter isn't around. As for Griz, imagine a circus bear riding a motorcycle. Now stick a Nazi helmet atop its sloping head, give it a wallet on a chain, and there you have my mother's paramour.

Yes, my mother is a biker chick. Vicki Jo warned me early and often that mothering was not her "bag." My father had promised to do all the raising if Vicki Jo would handle the birthing. Mom couldn't help but feel she'd been welshed on when her husband died of a heart attack shortly after "the kid" was born. Making the best of a bad deal, my mother got a "shitty-ass, monkey fuck of a job" with the phone company and grudgingly kept me in sneakers and Clearasil for the next sixteen years with periodic memos that this wasn't "the tour" she had "signed on for" and that "we all got to float our own boat in this world." The instant I turned sixteen, Vicki Jo informed me that the "gravy train" had stopped and that her "me time" had begun.

Mom's answer to "What happens to a dream deferred?" was to move to Myrtle Beach, home to a very active biker scene and purchase a wardrobe of leathers, cutoffs, halter tops, and bandannas. Vicki Jo looked upon my childhood as an annuity and felt that every dime she'd put into raising me should have been accumulating interest and be available for withdrawal at any moment. The last time she hit me up for a loan so that Griz could get a valve job before the big Suck, Bang, and Blow Rally, she had been peeved that I was broke.

"What happened to that rich dude you married?"

"Being married to me didn't make him one penny less rich."

"Goddammit, don't tell me you signed a prenup?"

"Okay, I won't."

"What's that monkey fuck's name? Me and Griz are going to pay a visit on his sorry ass."

"Ethan Hawke."

"Gimme the son of a bitch's number."

"I'll get back to you on that."

I don't mention my mother much. All right, I don't mention my mother ever. It isn't that I'm ashamed of her. Or, okay, it isn't *just* that I'm ashamed of her; I fear the response if I tell the truth. Maybe illustrate it with a snapshot of Mom, riding high behind

Griz, top hiked up, tan Mommy muffins exposed, big drunk grin on her leathery face. I fear that my confidant will look from the photograph to me, then back and say, "Ah, that explains it." Because all my mother explains is the obvious: Girls who aren't born rich have to work what the Lord gave them a lot harder than girls who are. We have to work it a *lot* harder. That is *all* my mother explains.

April 3, 2003

6:00 A.M.

I AM STILL wide awake when the radio alarm clicks on. I half listen to a story about some superhero file clerk shooting her way like Rambo out of an Iraqi hospital. With an impossible to-do list, I jump into the shower and have just started sudsing up with the last of my Bulgari Thé Blanc shower gel when Trey calls out to me from the next room. My heart stops. I can't make out exactly what my ex-husband is saying, but he uses the earnest and heartfelt tone he puts on when he's trying to sound earnest and heartfelt. And/or get laid.

I'm saved. The hope of being rescued from having to perpetrate Kippie Lee's party makes me giddy with relief.

"Trey?" I trill, stepping naked from the shower, ready to jump into whatever reconciliation/farewell-fuck scenario he might be playing out. I open the door, imagining how dewy and soft-focus I look in the cloud of escaping steam, and behold an empty room. On the radio, President Bush is telling an audience of marines at Camp Lejeune that their brothers in arms have "performed brilliantly in Operation Iraqi Freedom."

I consider it cruel and unusual punishment that the leader of the free world sounds exactly like my ex-husband. Though I know that this bitter disappointment gives me every right to a minibreakdown, I cannot allow myself such a luxury. I cannot hurl myself onto Bamsie's lumpy bed and sob my heart out because no one is coming to save me, because no one was *ever* coming to save me. No, today I have to be a warrior, and I have to gird myself accordingly.

I appraise my wardrobe and consider the critical choice of what to wear. This day, more than any since the divorce, I have to establish that I still belong on Kippie Lee's side of the social divide. I zip past my Marc Jacobs, my Anna Suis, my Prada. I need more armament than they provide to make it through the coming ordeal. I need the closest thing I have to true haute couture; I need the suit of lights. I pluck out my shimmering Zac Posen gold duchesse satin suit. Just putting it on recalls the exquisite feeling of all the fittings I managed to finagle. A garment custom-fitted by Zac Posen with nine additional arcing darts undulating between hand-finished French seams is like wearing an all-access backstage pass.

Shoes? The Christian Louboutins, of course, with their ultra-exclusive sliver of red on the inside of the heels. I want to broadcast class, not go *Sex and the City* with Jimmy Choos. I want to get paid, not laid. But which ones? Are the berry peep-toes accessorized with a Swarovski crystal the size of a golf ball too much? I think not. I slip them on and check the effect: intimidatingly prosperous. I can pull off anything in my twinkling shoes and the suit of lights.

On the radio, Bush signs off. "May God bless our country and all who defend her. Semper Fi."

Did our president just say "Semper Fi"? The very words I'd been thinking to myself just moments earlier?

It is as if George W. Bush himself has blessed my mission and promised that everything would turn out fine. What could possibly go wrong?

April 3, 2003

II:00 A.M.

*A*H, PEMBERTON HEIGHTS, *the creamy white filling squirting out of Austin's exclusive Tarrytown Twinkie.*

The image calms my jittery nerves as I pilot the Kia Sedona minivan that has replaced my beloved Escalade toward the street where Trey and I lived not so very long ago. I am about to switch off the radio and concentrate on dodging crippling grief when the word "Enron" pops out at me. I turn the volume up.

I have to stay current on the Enron situation for that rare occasion when one of the ladies wants to talk about something other than Italian glass tile and who's had work done. Since the consensus view on Enron among Kippie Lee's group is "government witch hunt," I need to collect further evidence of big government's attempt to throw sand into the gears that power free enterprise and the American way. But the only news on the Enron front today is that indictments naming the participants in a gaudy array of fraud schemes will remain sealed for another month.

Drat.

I turn the radio off and brace myself. Kippie Lee's gigando manse is directly beneath Pemberton Palace where I lived high on a hill above them all during my short marriage. It is bad enough rattling onto my old street in a minivan, but even worse is having to arrive without backup, since I can't afford to hire minions for any but the barest minimum of essential hours. Consequently, I am all by myself when I step up to the front door of Kippie Lee Teeter's titanic French Provincial. The Teeters tore down not one, not two, but three houses to construct their Xanadu. Petitions started circulating the day the foundation was poured to ban such McMansions forever from Pee Heights in particular, and the whole precious 78703 zip code in general.

I plaster on a glittering smile, pinch my cheeks, then ring the bell. Surrounded by chafing dishes and cans of Sterno, I force myself to forget all the times when I was greeted effusively as a cherished guest, a friend, an equal. No, let's be honest; when I was married to Trey, when I was *Mrs.* Henry "Trey" Dix the Third, I was better than Kippie Lee, better than any of them. They sought me out, a treasured addition to the guest list. When asked, "Who's coming?" my name would be the first one a hostess coyly dropped. Like many a divorcée before me, though, I learned to my eternal sorrow that it was never *my* name they were dropping.

It was the illustrious Dix family name with its magical White House links being dropped. And in Austin, Texas, in 2003, the third year of the reign of our former governor, it is all about White House links. Austin Republicans had suffered through more than thirty years since they'd last had a Texan in the White House. And that one had been a—shudder—Democrat. For three decades Rs had watched their city kowtow to every D who ever tossed a bluebonnet seed onto the side of a highway with Lady Bird. Now is their time to ride the glory train, and they are all highly determined to get their tickets punched.

Kippie Lee certainly is. Apparently, back in Midland, Laura Bush used to babysit for her. Or maybe Laura was her godmother or camp counselor, I can't recall. Whatever the feeble connection with the First Lady, Kippie Lee has somehow managed to enshrine it in Xanadu and leverage them both into total social dominance of Pemberton Heights.

I ring the doorbell again and consider Kippie Lee's dubious White House connections. Laura Bush's true inner circle claims that since Kippie Lee wasn't even born back when they were giving hand jobs in Midland, she is a rank pretender. That hasn't slowed Miss Kip down. She and the coven cherish the few tenuous Bush connections they have and desperately seek out new ones. No one was sought more desperately than my ex, Trey Dix the Third, since the Dixes and the Bushes go way, way back. All the way back, in fact, to the Jurassic period when the petroleum that both their families' fortunes were built on began forming. This meant that for the brief, shining duration of my marriage, I too was a White House connection and the Zero Three-ers cultivated me like a hothouse orchid.

My skin prickles as I wait at the front door, now more Jehovah's Witness than hothouse orchid. I feel a laser beam of attention skitter across my back and turn to see who is staring at me. As usual, there are no actual human beings on the street other than a couple of yardmen. When I look up, however, up to my former home, Pemberton Palace, perched above the neighborhood majestic as a potentate on a throne, I find my former mother-in-law staring down at me. Peggy Biggs-Dix's nickname, the Iron Chancellor, never seemed more apt. A bulldog in pearls and a summer frock, the sun glints off her iron-colored hair and the iron-colored lenses of the binoculars she holds to her eyes.

I feel her up there gloating and punch the doorbell furiously. Still no one arrives to rescue me. I press my ear to the door and hear furious whispering, most of it coming from Kippie Lee. But when Graciela, the live-in housekeeper, finally opens the door, the Kipster is nowhere in sight.

"Miss Blight, can you go to the back?"

"The back? The service entrance?" I am certain I've heard wrong. Kippie Lee was one of my stalwarts, one of the women I called my Flying Buttresses because they had supported me so solidly when my marriage crumbled. Actually, the marriage imploded more than crumbled. One day Trey and I are doing a mat Pilates class together, the next a lawyer, *a lawyer,* is telling me that my marriage is over. In the immediate aftermath of that bombshell, Kippie Lee poured endless glasses of Pinot Grigio and agreed that Trey was a Dix in more than last name.

And now this? Asked to use the service entrance?

There could be no more definitive signal that I have officially plummeted from Up- to Downstairs. I hide my shock and humiliation and chirp out with more pep than a Texarkana girl rushing Kappa Alpha Theta, "Not a prob!"

Feeling Peggy's vulture gaze drilling into me, I drive the little minivan around to the back of Gigando Manse and consider the deep irony of my demotion to Downstairs: I was never really Upstairs. Not on paper where it mattered. Not after the Dix family's team of carrion-eater lawyers slid that prenup under my pen.

The tears I will not allow to fall make Pemberton Palace look wobbly and long-ago, like something out of a misty fantasy. Fantasy has always been my stock-in-trade. It's what I built two careers on: event coordination and photography. Some would say that my last incarnation as Trey's bride was little more than a canny career move. All I have to say to those slanderers is: "Check out the prenup." Would that I had been half as calculating as I am accused of being. And would that such calculations had occurred before I signed that damn prenup.

As I scuttle back and forth unloading foil-wrapped trays, flowers, and rented polyester tablecloths, I see the silver lining in this service entrance cloud: I am sheltered from the Iron Chancellor's rapacious gaze and, even better, Kippie Lee won't be monitoring the supplies that financial necessity has forced me to lay in. I am stuffing the evidence of my cost cutting into the trash when our hostess herself appears in the kitchen.

"What's that?" Kippie Lee asks, stopping me from shoving the trash compactor closed.

I whirl around, making sure that the sunlight catches the Zac Posen in just the right way. "Kip-Kip! Wow, you look amazing." Amazing is what most of Kippie Lee's crowd think she looks. With her long straight expensively bleached hair and long straight fastidiously starved body, K.L. has always modeled herself after fellow Tejana Jerri Hall. She has whittled herself away, however, to the starved, hanging-on-by-a-thread look of a fellow sister in desperation. Her doll-baby-bright, blue eyes glitter a little too intensely; her size 1 Pucci frock hangs a little too loosely. Kippie Lee appears to be in the crisis phase with a straying husband when she is in danger of giving him what he wants and making herself disappear altogether.

I point to her shoes and squeal, "You got the Chanel croc heels! I was so going to get those exact heels."

Kippie Lee tips her left shoe from side to side, examining it as she recalls, "God, they made me wait, like, two months before . . ." She catches herself and stops suddenly; my feint into friendship has failed. Once again all business, Kippie Lee yanks open the compactor, and her mouth drops in horror as she reads the name on the wrapping I was trying to hide. "Sam's Club?" She points to the trays of food waiting to be presented to the cream of Austin society. "This is what you're going to serve?"

"No, no, of course not." I pirouette to shield the trays of Sam's taquitos I'd planned to slip through customs as Petites Tournedos Béarnaise à la Mexicaine.

"Blythe, you promised me a true fête champêtre, a classic English garden party. The menu we agreed upon was amuse-bouches to include, but not to be limited to, mustard-seed-crusted tuna loin with an herb-coconut sauce and quail stuffed with goat cheese."

I hold up a finger to silence Kippie Lee and furiously punch numbers into my cell phone. "Guillaume, bonjour. *Comment va avec les amuse-bouches?*" I pause, nod thoughtfully, and throw out an occasional enthusiastic, *"Bien, tres bien!"* as I listen to the dead silence of a dead cell phone whose bill I haven't been able to pay in months.

I snap the cell shut and announce triumphantly, "My staff is putting the finishing touches on the tuna loin even as we speak."

"Are those . . ." Kippie Lee snags a flower from one of the buckets I bought from a street vendor on the way over. "Carnations?" She might as well have asked, *Used toilet brushes?*

"What?" I squint with irritation at the flowers. "Oh, damn, Les Fleurs du Mal messed up my order. Don't worry, I'll get it sorted." I purposely say "sorted," not "sorted out." Dropping the occasional Anglicism—"one off," "brilliant," "chuffed"—has a nice distancing effect. I work my thumbs and forefingers frantically as a pachinko player as I simultaneously punch a text message into my phone and juggle to keep the dead screen out of Kippie Lee's sight.

"Blythe, you promised masses of peonies and lilies, and many sets of the Dix family antique Royal Winton china in the coveted Dorset pattern. And croquet. You said there would be croquet."

I can recall nothing about this Victorian fantasy I apparently painted, though I do like the croquet flourish, and answer smartly, "A staff member just called to say he has secured the precise croquet set used by HRH and that he is on his way right now to set it up. I'll check to make sure he has it."

Before I have a chance to make a pretend call on my pretend phone about the pretend croquet set, K.L. begins manhandling the smudge pots I picked up at Family Dollar, then spritzed with Glade. "These aren't your signature votives." Masses of votives in colors and fragrances that harmonized with masses of flowers used to be the signature element of Wretched Xcess events. In plummier days, when Trey's lobbying clients were picking up the bills, the votives had been soy-based marvels compounded with my own signature fragrance.

"Kip-Kip, if you had given me the advance we agreed upon I could have—"

"You know I wanted to, but Hunt put his foot down."

Now we are on very thin ice indeed. The major reason that poor Kippie Lee is hosting this or any other party is to silence the rumors regarding trouble here in the starter castle. Rumors about how Hunt Teeter, Miss Kip's philandering asshole of a husband, has been getting the kind of cleanings from his nubile young dental hygienist that left Happy Rockefeller a widow. Unfortunately for K.L., though, if you want to throw a big the-marriage-is-fine party, El Hubbo has got to put in an appearance. Ominously, Kippie Lee had not been able to wrangle Philandering Asshole into making so much as a cameo. In the end, she was forced to settle for this, the all-gal-pal weekday garden party.

"Well, without an advance—"

"Duncan and Cherise told Hunt that they were not completely in love with what you did for her opening."

"Duncan and Cherise Tatum? The Tatums were *mad* about that event. I perfectly matched the food to Cherise's remarkable show of button art. Cunning pieces. Little button men holding little button hearts out to little button women. Button dogs lifting button legs on button fire hydrants. Button girls chasing button butterflies. I picked up the motif perfectly and served a complementary buffet every bit as fanciful. How perfect was that?"

"You served Eggo waffles, Necco wafers, pepperoni kebabs, and circles of bologna on Ritz crackers."

"Yes! Wasn't it inspired? Buttons? Circles? Circles of life, circles of friends, circles of food. They adored it."

"They stopped payment on the check."

"All right, Kippie Lee, I'll level with you. A few Wretched events might have been the tiniest bit less than flawless after . . ." I pause before going on to identify the Damocles' sword hanging over K.L.'s head. ". . . the divorce." Waiting for a gush of sister feeling to well up, I blink back tears that I don't have to summon so much as simply stop fighting for one second. "Well, a woman really finds out who her true friends are."

Kippie Lee takes a second to imagine all her friends drinking Belmontinis at the Belmont without her and a few drops of compassion do actually moisten her arid expression. I push this tiny opening. I'd heard that even though Hunt Teeter's firm had made one fortune on legal prestidigitation when the venture capital money flowed to the dot-commers, then another fortune when it was rerouted through bankruptcy court, his wife's extravagance was rumored to have been the final straw, the one that caused him to stray. What Kippie Lee's three-teardown Xanadu had ended up tearing down was her marriage.

I decide to play that card. Sniffing, I go on bravely, "I guess, though, what I miss most is my house. My home."

Kippie Lee puts her hand on her mouth, suppressing the horror that rises at the thought of losing the house that cost her so much.

"I mean, of course, I could have stayed on"—I raise a born-again finger toward Pemberton Palace—"up there. But it brings back too many memories."

Kippie Lee places a hand on my arm.

Bingo! The buttress is flying again. This is my opening; I have to scoot through it while I can. "At least George and Laura have stayed on my side."

"The Bushes?"

"Yes, we visited them so many times at Kennebunkport. Gathering of the clans, all that. Forty-one and Junior." I press my index and middle fingers together to symbolize the closeness between Trey's father and the forty-first president of the United States. "Bar wants me to do something clambakey for her this summer when the whole gang gathers. You didn't hear it from me, but . . ." I glance around the empty kitchen and Kippie Lee leans in. "Bar hates Peggy. Loathes her. When Bar was doing fund-raisers for Planned Parenthood back in the Texas years, Peggy was on the board, and it got so bad that Bar had her banned."

"Really?"

I nod affirmatively.

Kippie Lee drags herself back to the matter at hand, though with considerably less vehemence now that I have again reestablished my White House–insider status. "Okay, but the votives?"

I look down and pretend once more to read a message on my cell phone. "Jean-Philippe just texted. The votives are on the way, Kips." I turn my nervous hostess around and give her a gentle push. "Now, you, my little goddess, all you have to worry about is making yourself even more fabulous than you already are. Scoot, scoot, scoot."

Kippie Lee leaves and I slump onto a hammered-copper bar stool. After sitting for a moment, I notice that I can't catch my breath and that my hand resting on the two-inch-thick textured-glass countertop is trembling with a palsied rattle I cannot control. With a macabre syncopation, my right eye starts twitching. I put my twitching hand against my twitching eye and feel my spastic colon tick like a time bomb.

Pausing only to grab my silver Fendi hobo, I rush out. I'm cracking and have to find sanctuary before the meltdown. Thank God for K.L.'s adoration of Texas's first and still most glamorous celebrity-socialite, Becca Cason Thrash, who has thirteen powder rooms and two bedrooms in her twenty-thousand-square-foot Houston home. Thirteen to two. The ratio mesmerized Kippie Lee, who believed that it held the secret to earthly happiness. When she tried to duplicate it, however, her husband put his foot down. "What the hell do you think we're running here?" Hunt had demanded. "A potty-training academy? Four is the absolute maximum number of crappers I will allow."

Kippie Lee split the difference and went for eight powder rooms, and Hunt went for Marigold, the comely young dental hygienist. He'd first been attracted to Marigold because she smelled like Dove soap instead of all the "froufrou crap" his wife had specially compounded in some Swiss laboratory. The affair turned serious when Hunt asked Marigold where she wanted to go for a weekend getaway and she answered that the redfish were running in Rockport. After that, Hunt stopped caring about powder rooms. Or Kippie Lee.

Whatever toll those powder rooms had exacted on the Teeter marriage, I am glad to have such a wide choice of hideouts. I duck into the first one I come to.

"What the—?"

"Oh, sorry, boys, my mistake."

I quickly back out of the media room, where I have accidentally burst in on Kippie Lee's son, Hoot, and several of his middle school chums from St. Stephen's enjoying a sprightly double feature of *Good Will Humping* and *Glad He Ate Her.*

Resetting my compass, I make my way to the largest powder room, the one with a small fireplace, lock the door behind me, and collapse onto the lid of Kippie Lee's Toto UltraMax toilet (same brand the Pi Phi Bulimia Queens use for all their heavy-duty flushing needs). Once seated, I have serious doubts whether I'll be able to stand again. I can usually put on a good front. A great front. It's how I've survived for the past year since Trey and his mother's death squad of lawyers pulled the plug on me. But the constant humiliation of serving women whom I used to entertain in my home and who used to entertain me in theirs has taken a heavy toll.

I can't hold back the tears any longer. I start crying and cannot stop. I am coming unglued and all I can think about is what a great story this is going to make: The day the caterer locked herself in a powder room and refused to cater. I can hear Kippie Lee bestowing the details of my collapse like party favors.

And guess who the caterer was?

Who?

Blythe Dix. Well, Blythe Young now. The family made her give up the Dix family name.

No.

Yes.

So why wouldn't she come out of the powder room. Was she high?

"No!" I startle myself by speaking this fierce defense out loud. But it is the truth. I am not high. Not at this exact minute anyway. I wanted to do this event with no chemical amendments. And not just because my supplies are running perilously low.

Keeping up the pretense that I am simply helping friends out with their parties for the sheer fun of it is exhausting, but I have no choice. The instant that the 78703 zip code discovers that the Dix family has totally disowned me and that whatever gossamer ties I might once have had to the White House have been severed, I will be tits up. When they realize that catering is not just something I am doing to fill the time between spinning classes, but the one activity standing between me and starvation, I will be most definitively hosed. When they twig to the fact that I have moved out of Pemberton Palace and into Bamsie Beiver's carriage house not because the Palace "brings back too many memories" but because I was "tossed out on my ass without a dime," I will no longer be of any use to them whatsoever.

The gossips in my head start twittering again. I imagine them zeroing in on my deepest, darkest secret: "I heard that Trey took her to the cleaners in the divorce."

My answer—which the Pemberton Princesses must nevereverever hear—is, *I wish*. I could have managed the cleaners. But Trey Dix the Third and his family of wolverines weren't content to just take me to the cleaners. No, they took me to the taxidermist. I have been gutted but have yet to be stuffed and stitched back up.

"Get a grip," I order myself as I splash water onto my wrists from Kippie Lee's cobalt blue vessel sink etched with dancing nymphs. But no grip arrives. The past year of living on nerves, Stoli, and speed have done me in. I dry my hands on a monogrammed guest towel and study myself in the mirror. I wish there were someone around, someone male with tons of money, to admire how sexy my navy blue eyes look when they are swimming in tears. How puffed up all the crying has made my lips, how uncontrollable sobbing has plumped my skin the way long bouts of vigorous sex do.

Instead, outside the powder room's sculpted glass door, I hear the distant echoes of Kippie Lee having the mandatory preparty nervous breakdown, then, ominously, the staccato clacking of Chanel crocodile pumps draws closer. A shadowy form appears at the door. I don't worry. Kippie Lee's Southern-girl "niceness" which, at its most basic, consists of an aversion to making scenes, will protect me from anything truly dire.

Kippie Lee pounds on the door. "Blythe? Are you in there? Blythe, come out. We need to talk."

The words "need" and "talk" in the same sentence always mean someone—lover or employee—is going to get the ax.

"Little busy in here, Kip-Kip!" Again that indomitable Kappa Alpha Theta pep.

"Blythe, I'm serious."

Kippie Lee's dominatrix tone tells me that I might have miscalculated. That this far west of the Mississippi sufficient pioneer-gal grit may have entered the mix that a Texas girl *will* make a scene. I hold my breath and pray that there is still enough of the belle in Kippie Lee that she won't break down the door.

Kippie Lee leaves and I relax. Unfortunately, the clack returns a moment later followed by the unmistakable snick of a black AmEx card sliding between door and jamb. I am outraged. Kippie Lee is breaking in. Violating the sanctity of the powder room. This I had not expected. Resigned as a prisoner being led to the gallows, I am almost grateful that the jig is finally up. I am so deeply, deeply tired. Whatever steep descending step in *The Rake's Progress* comes next, it can't be any worse than this.

And then the cavalry arrives.

"Miss Keeply," Graciela calls out. "They are here. *Los otros.*"

My minions have arrived.

"Miss Keeply, they want to know where do you want them to put the tables?"

With an irritated sigh, Kippie Lee removes her card. "I'll be right there, Graciela."

Before I can crater again, I give myself a stern talking-to. Have I forgotten that Chanterelle Young, born and raised and got the hell out of Abilene as soon she could, is more of a Texas gal than the whole lot of them? Grit? Try growing up in a double-wide a block off I-20 with a Dairy Queen for your country club and the boys' JV football coach for your secret boyfriend when you were barely thirteen. Grit? I have more grit in my craw than a Rhode Island Red. The Dixes and everyone else in Zero Three might have reduced Blythe Young to baking humble pie and serving it to them on doilies, but by damn they will never force Blythe Young to eat it.

I give my nose a definitive blow, then power-flush the Kleenex down the Toto. I have had my moist moment and now it is over. I will hide out while the underlings set everything up, then if I can just hang on until the guests arrive, it will be smooth sailing from there. Kippie Lee will never make a scene in front of guests. I can safely emerge and throw the absolute best garden party for her my limited means will allow. A party good enough, at any rate, to get that one lifesaving check. In order to accomplish this mission, however, in order to step out of this locked bathroom, I must become a different person. A person with the hide of a rhino, the morals of a hyena, and the metabolism of a hummingbird.

So, once again, circumstances dictate that I reenlist my old defender to effect the necessary Jekyll/Hyde transformation. I fetch the Fendi bag and remove a thirty-two-ounce commuter cup with CODE WARRIOR printed on the side. The Warrior entered my life during the early days of Wretched's first incarnation when I had to do the work of ten to meet the demands of my bright dot-com boys. With no one other than myself to depend on—as usual—I was forced to devise a secret formula to keep fluid, electrolyte, and psychopharmaceutical levels stable.

And now, exactly as it has been since Vicki Jo Young gave birth to me thirty-three years ago, it is Blythe Young against the world. Just a girl who never had family money or even a My Little Pony lunchbox when all the other girls in third grade had one, doing what she has to do to survive. And right now, she has to do some Code Warrior. I take all the fixin's out of my purse and mix up my proprietary blend of Red Bull, Stoli, Ativan, just the tiniest smidge of OxyContin, and one thirty-milligram, timed-release spansule of Dexedrine. I shake, drink, sit back down on the Toto UltraMax, fasten my safety belt, and wait for the g-forces to blow my cheeks back.

My friend Stoli hits the jangled synapses first, smoothing the way for her buddies Ativan and OxyContin to do their jobs. Desperation, mortification, regret, and panic melt away before the Warrior's might, exposing the bone-deep exhaustion that lies beneath, and I nod off for the first bit of real sleep I have had in weeks.

Moments later, I wake with my heart thudding in a full-blown panic attack. The spansule has dissolved and Code Warrior's Dexedrine shock troops have hit the beach. My jugular vein is throbbing; I am grinding my teeth and snorting like a bull about to charge. My thoughts cascade past at a frightening speed. I am hurtling through time and space on a psychic luge sled and fear I might throw up.

Perfect. I have become precisely the person I must be in order to face the cream of Austin society.

April 3, 2003

1:30 P.M.

Holding my breath, I tiptoe out of the powder room. Over the roaring of blood pumping maniacally through my ears, I notice that the Teeter house is completely quiet. Guests have arrived, cars have been parked, and all the college boy valets are relaxing beside the circular drive. A happy twittering emanates from the backyard. I was out longer than I thought; the party is under way.

I peek out at the Teeter grounds. An acre of manicured St. Augustine unrolls perfect as a pool table beneath the artful twists of venerable live oak trees. Against the green, all I see is pink. Pink skirts. Pink jackets. Strappy pink sandals. Pink lipstick, pink nail polish. And tan. Lots of bronzer. Many trips to the spray-on-tan guy. Apparently all the wardrobe and makeup consultants got together and decided: pink and tan.

Threads of black and white and buttons of silver dart through the pastel, stitching it together into the ideal party ensemble. My minions, bless them, in their black pants and white shirts have stepped into the breach. They bustle about, tilting silver serving trays toward guests. And what guests they are, a calculated blend of Old Austin stalwarts—the women K.L. grew up brunching with at Tarry House right after church every Sunday of her life—together with a smattering of Dellionaire spouses and a shrewd court-jester sprinkling of Austin's more presentable artists and writers.

But, ah, the jewel in the crown. I see Kippie Lee has scored the big one: Lynn Sydney Locke. Lynn Sydney swept into Austin a few years ago, dripping with money from two highly remunerative marriages, and took over the town. She is the avatar of New Austin, the one who upped the ante on Kippie Lee's Old Austin crowd. With her arrival, the ultimate was no longer scooting up to Salado for a dress from Grace Jones. It became trips to New York for Fashion Week. With Lynn Sydney's ascension the big name "gets" for a dinner party ceased to be Lady Bird Johnson's great-niece and became art critics flown in from Las Vegas, any member of the Bush family or administration, and, the prize himself, Michael Dell. As for brunch at Tarry House, once Austin's Bright Young Things began eating Roquefort sorbet and Beaujolais summer truffle risotto, well, it just came to seem sad.

Most threatening to Kippie Lee and the Austin Old Guard, however, is that Lynn Sydney is thinner, better dressed, and, worst of all, has a better house. At least that was the verdict of *Architectural Digest* when it celebrated the minimalist marvels of her house's microscopically exquisite two thousand square feet in an article entitled "The End of Austintation." The famous architect-writer raved about the house's "subdued palette and commitment to spareness." Kippie Lee's friends comforted their upstaged queen by claiming, "It looks like a cellblock. A bomb shelter. A bunker." The writer extolled the "spatial ambiguity" of Lynn Sydney's house, and the friends, as threatened as Kippie Lee by this challenge to the McMansion aesthetic, hissed, "She put the damn bathtub in the dining room. That's not ambiguous, that's mental illness!"

Kippie Lee's Old Austin crowd whispered among themselves about how "nouveau" and "arriviste" Lynn Sydney and her ilk were. And then they did everything in their power to be as much like the chic newcomer as they possibly could.

At this very moment, in Kippie Lee's backyard, the ladies gather around Lynn Sydney and chirp at her, frantic as baby birds in a nest begging for sustenance from the one who has the power to fly away; the one who needs them so much less than they need her. Even Lynn Sydney's wardrobe choice speaks of that freedom: Lynn Sydney is wearing jeans.

Though the jeans are True Religion, and her top is a vintage Pucci from Decades in LA, amid all the carefully chosen designer pink, Lynn Sydney's outfit is a statement whose dismissive meaning the ladies cannot mistake. Still, with the arrival of the closest thing Austin has to a celebrity-socialite the party seems launched, and I take one of the very few full breaths I have been able to suck in since the divorce.

The breathing part of my program ends abruptly, however, when I see Lynn Sydney answer a call on her cell. She turns her back on the princesses of Old Austin and speaks to the unseen caller with a noticeable increase in animation. A second later, she is waving hurried good-byes. With the departure of its most glittering guest, Kippie Lee's party falters.

This is not good.

I retreat to the kitchen, where party machinery is in high gear. Amid the aubergine La Cornue range, the double Miele dishwashers, the assorted Sub-Zeros, my staff is a domino blur of white and black as they nip about loading up trays with all manner of Discontinued and Clearance food items that I have previously tucked into cunning sachets of phyllo dough.

"Hey, Blythe, what are you doing back here?" In her hasty escape, Lynn Sydney has cut right through the kitchen.

"Just, you know . . ." I wave vaguely toward the kitchen.

Lynn Sydney takes my equivocation for polite reticence and shakes her head with sympathetic understanding. "Tell me about it." She holds up her cell. "That's why I told Siobhan"—she names her children's Irish nanny—"to call and rescue me. I can talk about backsplashes for just so long, then I have to escape. Is that a Posen?"

Lynn Sydney examines the jacket's lilac organza lining, nodding approvingly as she feels the hidden stitching. "Did you get Zac to custom fit this?"

I nod modestly.

"God. Major score, bitch. Who did you blow?"

Before I can answer her attention is diverted. "Are those Sam's taquitos?" Lynn Sydney helps herself to a double handful. "God, I would kill for a DP."

I hand her one from the refrigerator, and through a mouthful of Dr Pepper–moistened taquito, Lynn Sydney says, "Your ex-husband hit on me the other day."

"Why does that not surprise me?"

"He's kind of cute, but so not my type."

So not your price range. Lynn Sydney is through with family money controlled by terrifying mothers-in-law. Her current suitors are all self-made gazillionaires.

Her phone rings and Lynn Sydney checks the number. "This one's for real." She purrs, "Hey, boo," into the phone before mouthing to me, "Call. Okay?" as she rushes away.

When I turn back to the party, I behold a massively unsettling sight: Kippie Lee and her henchbitches, no doubt miffed by Lynn Sydney's departure, are conducting a little consumer research in the middle of the parklike grounds. They are quizzing one of the minions, Juniper, and poking suspiciously at the hors d'oeuvres polka-dotting her silver tray. I suck my breath back in.

Oh Jesus.

It gets worse: Now they are sniffing my "pâté."

Shit.

Now, *now!* they are rubbing it between their fingers. My "secret ingredient" is not going to stand up to that kind of pointy-nosed scrutiny.

It's your own fault, I want to scream at K.L. I might have been able to make real pâté if I'd had a decent advance. Kippie Lee and Philandering Asshole left me absolutely no choice but to go with the only extender I could afford—Crisco. They should thank me, all those bony society babes. At least their husbands should. Not a single one of them couldn't do with a little lard in the can.

Damn.

Now Kippie and company are subjecting my "polenta" to laboratory analysis. Even from this distance, I can make out eyebrows struggling to fire Botox-frozen nerves into expressions of doubt and puzzlement.

Oh God. They've started in on my *mousse en bombe.*

Enough! I want to scream. So mistakes—prenup, prenup, prenup—were made? So corners were cut? So the polenta I am serving may or may not be Cream of Wheat enlivened with the magic of sunny yellow popcorn seasoning? So the *mousse en bombe* that my staff is unmolding at this very moment might be more familiar with brown Whip 'N' Chill than thirty-dollar-a-pound Belgian chocolate? So the watercress sandwiches may or may not contain St. Augustine clippings? So the Copper River salmon gravlax is really catfish freshened a bit with the most artful injections of Red Dye Number 2? Who in this crowd of the sucked and tucked can possibly object to a bit of freshening? Who?

When Kippie Lee spits out a bite of watercress sandwich, I see my hostess emerging as a leading candidate. Unless decisive emergency action is taken, all will be lost. I regret the necessity that is being forced upon me, but necessity it is.

From amid the chaos in the kitchen, I spy my secret weapon. "Sergio!"

Sergio hastens to my side and whispers, "Jes."

I stole Sergio from Antoinette of Antoinette's Let Them Eat Cake the instant I saw how Sergio's velvety Venezuelan lashes and gigolo-white teeth tended to mesmerize even the most rabidly sniffing and poking of society matrons. Thank God, Sergio is in the country illegally, and his employment options are limited. Those lashes and teeth are all that now stand between me and utter ruin.

Sergio, ah, my sweet Sergio, he knows what his master's business is and he is eager to be about it. I grab the American Spirit cigarette he is smoking, suck it down to the filter, and toss the butt into the in-door ice dispenser of the Sub-Zero.

"Here." I yank a tray of phyllo surprises away from Olga, a double-jointed modern dance major with classical ballet training from somewhere in the former Soviet Republic. Olga is highly effective with male clients, but a dead loss to me at this estro-fest. With one snap of the wrist, I pop all the ersatz hors d'oeuvres into the trash, shove the tray into Sergio's capable hands, and then I utter the words that are the equivalent of turning the keys to begin a nuclear launch sequence: "Kir Royales."

Sergio nods knowingly. Swiftly, he sets up the souvenir champagne flutes etched with the words MAZEL TOV, STUIE that I pilfered from the last of my high-end bar mitzvahs. I dive into the Sub-Zero, where I've stowed an arsenal of champagne bottles carefully salvaged from glamorous events back in the day—Cristal, Veuve Clicquot, Dom Pérignon. The glittering names overwhelm me with nostalgia for the lost paradise of the Internet bubble. Back then, I served the Dom. Magnums, fountains, sprinkler systems of the Dom. I push aside the gilded memories of my boy geniuses and pull out the bottles which I refilled earlier with an amusing little Sauterne from the handy eighteen-liter box. A quick glance to make sure no nosy parkers are about, then I palm an Alka-Seltzer into each bottle for precisely the right amount of methodoise effervescence.

"Jew wan me to pour?" Sergio asks.

When the memento bottles have ceased foaming, I nod. "Yes, pour."

Sergio works quickly, filling the glasses, a tiny strainer deftly employed to sieve away telltale flecks of the *plop-plop, fizz-fizz.* Speed is of the essence. The vintage must be only barely thawed if taste buds are to remain properly numbed. When the glasses are all topped up to MAZEL TOV level, Sergio glances at me. No words are needed. I peek to the left, to the right. The coast is clear. I nod.

In place of the prohibitively expensive crème de cassis liqueur I would have been sloshing about in cushier times, today I am pouring a more modestly priced decoction of one part Welch's grape jelly diluted with two parts grain alcohol, then misted with a tincture of the secret ingredient that Sergio—dear, loyal, brave Sergio—smuggled across the border at Piedras Negras in his boot for me: Rohypnol.

"Date rape drug" is such an ugly term. And so far from my intent. All I seek is a bit of fuzziness, not the full nonconsensual coma. Besides, I have worked out a precise formula using myself as the guinea pig. I'd spent many a night—though I can't recall exactly how many—experimenting to determine the safest, smallest dosage possible. After all, that boot heel only holds so much. All I want is to make sure my clients have a good time. It's all I've ever wanted.

And once Sergio fans out with his most Royale of Kirs, I can guarantee a good time will be had by all. Kippie Lee's ladies' luncheon will be remembered or, more precisely, forgotten, as the event of the season. Everyone will agree it was a smashing affair because, in the grand tradition of all the absolutely best times of anyone's life, no one will be able to recall a single thing about it. Kippie Lee will have her triumph over Philandering Asshole. A few less-than-perfect party details such as the whiskers on the "salmon" will fade away, and a happy hostess will write the check I need so desperately. The kiss of the Roofie is now all that stands between me and redemption.

Sergio flips open the compartment in his boot heel and hands me the vial. I swiftly set about crowning each Kir. Using an eyedropper, I meticulously titrate a dose into each glass large enough to blur a few less-than-perfect details but small enough to maintain check-writing consciousness. When each flute has been fortified, I pass Sergio the first tray and entrust him with the vital mission: "Get one of these down our hostess's throat. *Stat.*"

Sergio heads out holding the tray before him like a frantic intern Code Bluing with his crash cart. He runs a broken field pattern through a line of lady dipsos who hold trembling hands out toward the receding cocktails. Sergio breaks for the end zone, flutes of violet bubbly tilted toward Kippie Lee; her best friend, Bamsie Beiver; and the rest of their inner circle: straight-shooting Cookie Mehan; the ethereally beautiful Paige Oglesby; Paige's shadow, three-time Westwood Country Club women's doubles tennis champ Morgan Whitlow; and Missy Quisinberry, who, I fear, does not drink.

I can live without Missy, she is known for never having a good time anyway. Kippie Lee is the only one who absolutely must accept the kiss of the Roofie.

I stop breathing and pray silently.

Then . . . yes!

Miss Kip reaches a hand out toward Sergio's tray. Sunlight

dances across the diamonds on her tennis bracelet and over her nails frosted with one of OPI's new Asian-influenced pinks, Whole Lotta Seoul. I allow myself to hope that the monolithic row of dominoes tottering above my head, waiting to squash me like a bug, might be stayed. She picks up a flute and—

"Uh, 'scuse me?"

The voice behind me, aggrieved, postadolescent, does not bode well. The domino slabs creak ominously. I turn and find a full-bore mutiny in progress. My helpers, my little crewmates in their uniforms of white and black, have put down their trays and are glaring in a way that couldn't make me feel any more like Captain Bligh if they'd all had scurvy and knives between their teeth.

Their Mr. Christian is Juniper, a junior at UT in American studies. She glowers at me through black-frame glasses. Two-inch-long pigtails bristle above her ears. I had assumed that Juniper with her liberal arts major understood that she was preparing for a life of poverty. I'd even hoped that, coming from such a known hotbed of Marxism, Juniper might extend me a bit of working-class solidarity. Her first words reveal that I have missed that bet.

"You promised you'd have checks for us at the start of this party."

Olga and Doug, the employees who've been with me the longest, step forward to back Juniper up. Olga, I had expected Olga to turn on me, but Doug? Doug and I have history.

I decide that my best defense here is a good offense. "Those trays are not going to pass themselves, Juniper." I sniff haughtily.

The traitors exchange looks of eye-rolling exasperation. Too late I recall just how well haughty had worked for Captain Bligh. Juniper stiffens her yoga-limbered spine. "You still haven't paid us for the last two parties. My tuition for next semester is due."

"Tuition? Juniper, I'm living in a *carriage* house."

Doug, looking a bit flushed, dives in. "Yeah, but your carriage house is right around the corner in this ritzy neighborhood."

"*Et tu*, Doug?" I say more in sadness than anger. Long ago, in a kingdom far, far away, Doug had been one of my bright boys in a backward cap. He'd used his bag of venture swag to set up

patiopaversbymail.com and to finance some truly remarkable parties which Wretched Xcess coordinated. He had, ultimately, stiffed
me on a huge job when his company went Chapter 11. Unlike all the
other boy geniuses who'd bailed on their debts, however, Doug is
still trying to make good by working off what he owes me. He
hasn't made much of a dent in the balance. Not on what I pay.

I am forced to remind him, "Doug, you used to live in Pemberton Heights, too."

"I haven't been able to afford Oh Three for a very long time,
Blythe. You know that. I scaled back." There is an unmistakable
note of censure in his voice.

"Doug, you of all people must understand that I *have* to live
here. I *have* to live among my clientele. Now that I'm a divorcée,
these women would forget me in a heartbeat if I didn't show my
face. I represent everything they dread most: the wife who lost her
job. They *want* to forget me. They *want* to forget that they can be
fired. Doug, I *have* to keep showing my face. I *have* to live in Pemberton Heights."

Doug sounds almost sad when he says, "Blythe, I feel you,
I really do. But you gotta pay us."

I address my crew, "Look, guys, I don't know how to make this
any plainer to you except to say: I have not had a Pap smear since
before the bubble burst."

Even more annoyed than usual, Juniper shakes her head. "What
did she say? Pap smear? Is she having a stroke?"

"Pelvic exam," I clarify. "Can't afford one. That is how bad off
I am."

Juniper squints her eyes in intense irritation as if there were
bees in her head. "I don't care about your, your twat! Pay us!"

"I will do what I can, I promise you that. If it means that I have
to live in the little minivan, I will pay you, all of you. Justjustjust,
please, finish this one party."

They seem agreeable enough then a whisper reaches me.
"Coke-addled cunt."

"What? I heard that, Juniper. I heard that and I'll have you all know that I am offended. Deeply, deeply offended. Because you are wrong."

I rush in to buttress my position, prove my point, gain more moral high ground on my accuser. "I am not a coke-addled cunt. It has been more than a year since I've been able to afford to addle myself with even the most anemic, baby laxative–extended line! This!" I hold the Code Warrior cup high. "This bargain-basement buzz is all I can afford!" My stirring summation to the jury does not meet with quite the surge of sympathy I'd hoped for.

Juniper's head jerks up and her beady eyes narrow to gun-turret slits behind her glasses. "Pay us." Her demand has a fatally non-negotiable ring to it.

Am I that dead that even the Vultures are now moving in?

My head swims and I fear I might be infarcting. "Drink." I rasp out the word, clutching my chest. "Must have something to drink."

I yank Kippie Lee's Sub-Zero open, grab a pitcher filled with a glistening beverage in a ruby-colored Kool-Aid hue, and chug a giant mouthful before realizing it is hummingbird nectar. Fearing that spraying the mutinous band with red sugar water might not be the best play at this critical juncture, I spit the sugary slurry into Kippie Lee's farmhouse sink.

Outside the window above the sink, I spy a tableau that eases my defibrillating heart. Sergio, my trusted liege, my loyal vassal, my savior, is, at that very moment, coaxing a flute of forgetfulness toward Kippie Lee's overcollagened lip bills. With the tip of a brown finger, he taps the glass past her critical regard, beyond the point where she can scrutinize each and every little speck of foreign matter floating behind a past client's name.

"Blythe, don't pretend like you're having a heart attack. We won't be put off by your cheap theatrics."

"Juniper, shut up for a minute, okay?"

"We will not be silenced by—"

I press my hand over Juniper's mouth to quiet the little Norma Rae so I can concentrate fully on watching Kippie Lee's formerly weak chin, firmed now with a dimpled implant, tilt slightly upward, bringing with it that slender tube of violet oblivion, that vessel of carbonated amnesia. Up, up, up it tilts. Kippie Lee's preternaturally pouty mouth opens, exposing the unearthly blue-white of excessively bleached enamel. Then the glycolic-peeled column of her neck undulates. Only when I witness the first big swallow heading south, down toward the Silicone Hills below, do I lower my hand from Juniper's mouth and announce, "Yes. Yes, I will pay you. In fact I am going to collect from our hostess at this very instant."

Speed is of the essence. I have to get to Kippie Lee while she can still sign a check but before she begins talking to her new best friend, Mr. Tree. I stride with all the crisp professionalism I can muster out of the kitchen, through the backyard, and straight into an IRS agent.

How do I know the intruder is from the IRS? It is not just that he is the only male mussing his Thom McAns on the Teeter lawn that tips me off. It is not even the beige Ford Focus parked in front of the manse or his Men's Wearhouse suit with its Jerry Garcia tie stab at individualism. No, the big tip-off is that the agent, plump and pasty as a deadly mushroom, opens his jacket and flashes a badge with the name JENKINS and the letters IRS embossed on it.

No one gets audited anymore. One in a million. They've got Enron to worry about. Don't worry. They'll never come after you.

That's what my accountant, Chester Milt, told me. Unfortunately, in recent months, Milt also offered this same opinion in a sneering tone on several libertarian radio talk shows along with choice comments about the general incompetence of the "Internal ReveNUDE Scurrilous." Milt then went on to inform listeners of their sacred duty to dismantle "the closest thing we've got to a Nazi Gestapo" by refusing to pay taxes. Shortly after Milt made the big time via a phone interview with Rush Limbaugh, the IRS swore a fatwa on Chester Milt and all his clients. They needed a high-profile conviction and they needed it fast. I fit the bill perfectly: a former member of the Dix family who'd been cut adrift from their powerful protection. The IRS could appear to be going after a fat cat with no fear of any political repercussions. Hence, I moved up very high on their Most Wanted List.

Agent Jenkins asks, "Could you point out the caterer?"

"Caterer?" I blink several times and shake my head as if puzzling out the meaning of the word. "Oh, yes, caterer. Actually, I believe that Kippie Lee did it all herself. She's an absolute wizard in the kitchen, our Kippie Lee is."

Jenkins looks around suspiciously, fixing on the abundance of seventy-dollar manicures that give the lie to the presence of any "kitchen wizards" among the pampered group.

"Yes, I'm looking for"—Jenkins checks a document that has the unsettling look of a subpoena or bench warrant and reads off the very last name on earth that I ever want to hear spoken by a representative of the United States Internal Revenue Service—"Blythe Young."

Thank God, it has been months since I have been able to talk my face guy into so much as the merest prick of Botox on credit. I can wrinkle my brow in utterly convincing puzzlement and answer, "No. No one here by that name."

"We have it on good authority that she's here."

"Sorry, I'm best friends with Blythe and I happen to know that she's out of the country. Borneo, I believe. Possibly Kathmandu."

"I spoke with her former mother-in-law, Peggy Biggs-Dix, just moments ago, and she assured me that Blythe Young is here."

Curse that bitch.

"Oh goodness, the dear old lady's care provider must have let Mrs. Dix wander out of her sight. The Alzheimer's, bless her heart. Was she dressed?"

Beefy Agent Jenkins casts a suspicious glance at my grubby, sawtoothed nails and asks, "Where's the kitchen?"

I point the agent toward the outside door of Kippie Lee's media room, hoping that Hoot's double feature might hold his interest for the few precious minutes I need.

When I turn around I notice that the minions all have their noses pressed against the kitchen windows. I try to subtly wave them back to work, but the mutineers remain frozen at the window, pointing frantically. Finally catching their drift, I slowly turn to face what they are pointing at and find Kippie Lee wobbling about and muttering, "I feel all floaty."

I see now that it was a mistake to use myself as a guinea pig in the drug trials. Clearly, I should have made adjustments for the amateur. Kippie Lee lists heavily to starboard and I rush to her side. *Too late.*

Like a tipsy debutante attempting the deepest of curtsies, Kippie Lee sinks slowly onto the thick, green mattress of her ultraluxuriant lawn and passes out cold, completing the starburst pattern formed by her four already unconscious friends, Bamsie, Cookie, Paige, and Morgan.

My panicked gaze finds Sergio's. He shrugs in his winsome way, an apology for poleaxing our hostess, whose next check is now far more likely to be written to a crack neurologist than it is to Blythe Young.

In the next instant, Agent Jenkins emerges from the media room blinking and unamused. The first celebrant he approaches is the disastrously abstemious Missy Quisinberry. Standing upright over her fallen friends, wearing a look she doubtless learned in her Old Testament Bible Study Group, Missy lifts a long, bony finger and points it, deadly as a Smith & Wesson. The agent follows the damning index, and his double-barreled gaze settles on me.

Some spasm of residual manners combined with a vestige of guilt causes me to smile and wave with a cringing sickliness.

I reflect that it is in just such sticky moments as these that character is tested. I call upon my girlhood heroines, those icons of courage and moral clarity, who have always guided me through life's toughest tests. I consider what Marie Curie, Margaret Mead, or Florence Nightingale would have done in such a situation as this. In the end, though, I decide that my best model in this particular test has to be the plucky Wilma Rudolph, who overcame polio to win three Olympic medals, and I tear ass out of Kippie Lee Teeter's garden party.

April 3, 2003

FIND YOUR STILL and quiet center. Fully inhabit this singular moment in time." Wasn't that what Lakshmi Pettigrew, my ashtanga yoga instructor at AbsSolution, was always telling her students? I careen onto Exposition Avenue, then perform a few select pranayama breathing exercises to keep from stressing about being hunted by the IRS and feeding controlled substances to currently unconscious clients.

The breathing doesn't do much to get me into the singular moment, since the moment I am currently inhabiting seems to be one that will lead directly to federal penitentiary. Thank God, I have managed to retain possession of the Code Warrior. I take several chugs and my friends Stoli and Ativan quickly set about smudging out tension faster than any ten Hindu sages. So efficient are *mis amigas* that I have nearly forgotten I am on the run from the IRS when I glimpse a beige Ford Focus approaching in the rearview mirror. Who would have thought that a bureaucrat could move so fast?

I cut a sharp left across traffic and a horrendous *thunk* from the back of the van causes me to wonder if there is an anvil loose. As I whip the minivan through a maze of turns, I long for my Escalade, lost now to the repo man, though I was very careful never to park it twice in the same spot. I could really use Barry, my OnStar concierge, right now. I wish I could dial Barry up and quiz him about the extradition policies of various foreign countries as well as

maximum penalties for not paying taxes for how many years? I
don't want to know.

How could I have found the one CPA who preached tax evasion? on the radio? I have to admit that one way to locate such an
individual might have been to ask everyone you knew for the name
of the most "easygoing" accountant around. "Easygoing" would
have been fine. "Fomenting revolution" is not working.

One more bubble—that is all I need. That would really put
me on my feet again. As the oil barons used to say around the time
crude plummeted to fifteen dollars a barrel, "Please, Lord, send me
just one more boom and this time I won't piss it away." Well, the
barons got their boom, all right. Or installed it in the White House.
Whatever. I am no Bolshevik. All I want is my second—okay,
third—chance. Give me one more boom and I promise I will not
piss it away. Or snort, or swill. Or buy shoes and titanium chafing
dishes. Or sign prenups. Especially not sign prenups.

A Bruce Springsteen song about debts no honest man can pay
runs through my brain.

That's it. I *am* honest. I will, metaphorically, sing the Boss's
poignant lyrics to Agent Jenkins and throw myself on his mercy. I
will explain how the situation snowballed out of control until the
only possible way I could get through my life was on a river of
Code Warrior. Surely the Enron debacle must have stretched the
grading curve a little. What are my paltry thousands in comparison
to their millions? Billions?

I decide to surrender. Swelling with righteousness, I focus on the
clouds of pink blossoms haloing the redbud trees that line the street.
I note the banks of daffodils turning their sunny yellow faces up to
greet a newborn world. With prison now a certainty, I force myself
to fully inhabit this singular moment of golden yellow, free-world
goodness. Unfortunately, it also happens to be the same singular
moment in which I pass a covey of cyclists. So European, so *Lance,*
in their stretchy caps with the tiny brims, spandex riding shorts
padded in the seat like a baby with soggy Pampers. Unfortunately,

this singular moment is also inhabited by a landscaping truck loaded with pallets of sod approaching in the opposite direction.

I skid off the road, transforming at least one sunny bank of newborn daffodils into a mustard-colored tire track. The mysterious object in the back hammers the cargo area like a bowling ball in a fifty-five-gallon metal drum. The mystery is solved when the next abrupt correction in course causes the side door of the van to slide open and my Chef's Choice Professional Meat Slicer to rocket out, landing directly in the path of the cyclists.

I whisper a prayer of apology to the universe as the cyclists jam on their brakes and execute face-plants of varying degrees of difficulty.

Bumping back onto the roadway proper, I *get* that this might not be the perfect moment to find my still and quiet center. Or to surrender. This might, in fact, be the perfect moment to double back and strip my house of all pawnable possessions that have not yet been repoed before the long tentacles of the IRS attach suckers and liens to them.

I swear that if I am allowed to survive this one extremely sordid episode, I will make reparations, massive offerings, generous donations, alms for the poor in perpetuity. I squeal around and head south, passing the spandexed cyclists sprawled around my meat slicer.

Along with panic and fear, a soggy tide of doubt, moral qualms, and bottomless regret wells up. I fight it down with more Code Warrior. Memories of the Zac Posens, Pradas, Marc Jacobs, and all the other designer apparel waiting for me in Bamsie's carriage house are also soothing. If a woman is forced to leave a marriage with nothing but the clothes on her back, those would be the clothes to leave with. All I need is an Internet connection and I'll make a fortune selling my finery on eBay.

I have no time to lose. No time for regrets. No time to stop and secure the side door of the little minivan. I have to accept that the stack of flyers I printed up in the most eye-catching of neon hues is fluttering out the open door like a dazzling cloud of butterflies.

Any other time, I would have worried about leaving a trail of neon evidence emblazoned with my name, address, and three phone numbers, none of which is currently working. Compared with tax evasion and unlawful delivery of drugs, however, a littering charge hardly registers.

Against all logic, a deep calm seeps through me as I reenter Pemberton Heights. Some would call it the scene of the crime. But what crime? The crime of a few event coordination missteps? Or the crimes I committed as Mrs. Trey Dix, wife of one of the state's most powerful lobbyists, when I supplied tenderloin up front while, around back, Trey provided legislators with powders, pharmaceuticals, trips to golfing meccas around the globe, senatorial letters of recommendation to West Point, private audiences with the pope, girls—both professional and nonaffiliated—and, most crucially, big juicy cuts into the biggest and juiciest deals that ever made their way through the Texas state legislature?

Here's what I will tell the IRS on my day of reckoning: *I could not have been more blind. I suffered under the delusion that the not really really rich have about the really really rich: I believed that since they have so much, they wouldn't be petty.*

To my sorrow, I learned that the really really rich are not like Evel Knievel, who, when asked why he was jumping the Salt River on a motorcycle, answered that it sure wasn't for the money. That he wasn't going to eat any better or dress any better or live in a better house. That he already had enough. What I learned is that in Dix World there is no such thing as "enough."

Agent Jenkins, I will say, the really really rich, like my former mother-in-law, the She-Wolf, and her spawn, want not only theirs but yours as well. Yours and your children's for the next umpteen generations. That's how they got really really rich. They didn't get it by being exceedingly nice and always waiting their turn. They rig the game so they get everything in perpetuity and we, the peons, get just enough to stay alive and keep working for them. It's the perfect host-parasite relationship except that a tapeworm will never make you feel like it's your fault for wasting away. As I said, I am no Bolshevik, but that's the game I was a victim of and that's how it's rigged.

That is what I will say on my day of reckoning.

I deliberately avoid Pemberton Palace and head east toward Bamsie Beiver's carriage house. The plan is to nip into my squat, clear out anything worth pawning or ingesting, and be gone before Bamsie returns. Before sneaking onto my street, however, I check to make sure that Bamsie's black Range Rover is nowhere in sight, that the coast is clear. On my way to the Beiver residence, I pass stately homes with their accompanying stately vehicles out in front. The Tatums' navy blue Jaguar. The Quisinberrys' cream-and-chocolate Rolls-Royce. The Oglesbys' silver Benz. The IRS agent's beige Ford Focus.

Shit! Shit! Shit!

My foot is on the accelerator before the words "stake" and "out" have time to wrinkle my cerebral cortex. I blast by the Focus. Luckily, Jenkins isn't in it. I spot him on the porch of the carriage house, nailing something to the front door. A fresh cloud of flyers printed with my smiling likeness blows out the back door. I regret now having chosen a photo that played up a certain resemblance I bear to a younger, slimmer, generally much hotter Martha Stewart. Felonious panderer to the moneyed class is an unfortunate note to be hitting at this precise juncture.

Not until I emerge safely from Pee Heights do I notice a blinking on the minivan's dashboard that turns out to be a low-fuel light. I have no money and I'm running out of gas. A big swig of Code Warrior helps to calm my thrashing heart.

Think. I have to think.

Clearly, my lam time will be limited. I must go to ground. Locate a safe haven, shelter in the storm. But where? The answer pops into my head and I reset my compass for the Elysian Fields of west Austin far, far away from the Oh Three zip code, for the world of Dellionaires, spindly brainiacs who managed to hang on to their bubble gazillions. Thankfully, there is almost no cross-pollination between them and the family money/billable-hour serfs of Pee Heights. So it is safe to head for the one place big enough and remote enough to house my Bedlam of anxieties: the Pyramid House.

April 3, 2003

3:45 P.M.

I ALMOST NEVER DO THIS, but at that very singular moment, I have absolutely no other choice. When the fuel gauge needle drops into whatever color is below orange and the cursed minivan begins choking and sputtering, I pull over and carefully dab the back of the van with mud, paying particular attention to the license plate area. Then I coast on fumes into an undercapitalized mom-and-pop station not yet equipped with credit card readers and other troublesome security devices. I execute a nimble fuel-and-flee, limiting myself to the few dollars' worth of gas I can pump before Mom starts shrieking and Pop retrieves his shotgun from under the counter.

"I'll pay you as soon as I can!" I yell out the window, already too far away to be heard or hit.

I swoop along the hills high above Lake Austin on 2222, a road with a perfect roller coaster of numbers for a name. A couple of sips of Code Warrior and I am blissfully at one with what nature remains, shoved in between the bumper crop of robber baron mausoleums that sprouted during the money kegger years along what had once been a winding country lane.

The horse knows the way to carry the sleigh!

I effortlessly maneuver a maze of turns that delivers me to the hugest piece of cheese a poor little mouse like myself can imagine: the Pyramid House. I gaze fondly up at the site of so many lavish affairs and recall the many times in palmier days when I led a convoy of caterer's trucks up to this very residence.

The Pyramid House is a nearly life-size replica of one of the smaller pharaonic tombs built by gaming magnate Turk Lord and his trophy wife, Blitz, with the help of a platoon of the finest masons that could be smuggled across the Rio Grande. The official cost is given as twenty million, but insiders always poke thumbs up at least eight or nine times, bringing the actual total closer to thirty million. The Lords built their house high above the banks of Lake Travis to celebrate the success of Turk's first massive multiplayer online game—Sand!—in which teams of grave robbers battle gangs of mummies to be the first to plunder the tombs of the pharaohs.

I remember my clever boys in their backward caps waxing enthusiastic about how realistically the mummies' windings flapped as they attacked marauding grave robbers. If only my boys had been half as good at plundering in real life as they were in the virtual realm I wouldn't be sitting behind the wheel of a minivan. Sadly, in the end, the only sure way for the clever boys to make money proved to be off of the other clever boys.

When the Bubble Bucks were rolling, though, they rolled higher at the Pyramid House than anywhere else. When Sand 2! was released, Wretched was hired to supply lobster kebabs and truffle couscous for five hundred. For that event, I had all the boys on my staff dress in authentic muslin slavewear that bore an unsettling resemblance to giant diapers. The diaphanous Cleopatra costumes I designed for the girls were a big hit, though, with the geekazoidal gaming crowd. I rented a dozen camels from the San Antonio Zoo to use as mobile serving stations. The camel toting kegs of Courvoisier was the most popular dromedary of the night.

The days of Courvoisier by the keg seem long ago as I pilot the minivan up the steep hill. But my eye is not on the vast hummock of hand-quarried limestone; no, I am focusing on the very cozy guesthouse off to the side. If I can just hole up there for a month or two, out of sight, out of mind, I am certain I can find a way to save myself.

A truck from A Moving Experience, specialists in transporting museum-quality furnishings, blocks the drive. I am not surprised to find Spree Winslow supervising the unloading of fabled pieces of furniture. Spree is an interior designer. Or what is it Spree is calling herself now? A design curator? Something that conveys Spree's lockjawed steeliness and talent for snaking high-demand items away from major museums for her clients. Spree has moved out of the price range of mere Old Austin Tarrytowners. Tapping into the Gates-esque fortunes of the very, very few who rode Austin's techno-bronc to the buzzer, Spree Winslow is the Dark Mistress of New Austin. For example, she has managed to mind-control the Lords into believing that their inner Lords can be expressed only by the furniture of Art Deco master Emile-Jacques Ruhlmann. So Spree was dispatched to scour the Continent for Ruhlmanns and other furnishings worthy of the Pyramid House. Outmaneuvering several museums and a private collector in Singapore, Spree has acquired a truckload of "important pieces."

"Don't bruise the pores of the amboyna wood!" Spree shrieks in the native Brooklyn accent she uses on anyone not paying her fifteen percent commission. Spree keeps her clientele intimidated by whispering to them in a Boston Brahmin accent. Also by being better clothed, coiffed, shod, bejeweled, and skinnier than anyone she deigns to work for. Strike that. Work *with*.

Intent upon the vault-size item swaddled in thick layers of quilted blankets being edged down the gangplank, Spree does not notice my approach. One of the movers stumbles the tiniest bit and Spree comes unglued.

"Be careful! This isn't a dinette set from the RoomStore! The Victoria and Albert Museum wanted that piece! That is a genuine Emile-Jacques Ruhlmann Art Deco cabinet worth three-quarters of a million dollars!"

"Spree, did you say that your commission is ten or fifteen percent?"

"Blythe Young, what the hell are you doing here? I thought you'd moved back to Abilene." Spree never wastes a particle of charm, to say nothing of basic human decency, on any transaction she isn't getting a chunk of. It does cheer me a tiny bit, though, that I still rate the lockjawed whisper.

"You're looking well yourself, Spree. Is Blitz around?"

"Turk and Blitz are helicopter skiing in Norway."

"This time of year? Odd. How long will they be gone?"

"At least a month. After Norway, they're going to do the Snowman Trek in Bhutan. Then they'll be attending the Kalachakra performed by the Dalai Lama."

"A month? Are you sure? Hard for me to imagine Turk taking that much time off from his empire."

"What are you doing here? I heard you'd gone out of business."

"Really? Actually, I just wrapped an event for Kippie Lee Teeter. Garden party. *Saumon en croûte. Une bombe gelée.* Baskets of violets on all the tables. Chamber group. Very elegant. Kippie Lee adored it. It was sort of a rehearsal for the event I'll be doing for Laura at the ranch in Crawford."

Spree bares her perfect little teeth in an unconvincing imitation of a smile and states flatly, "Blythe, leave now."

I understand Spree's hostility. In her place I would be hissing, spitting, and casting the evil eye because I am breaking so many precepts of the Swami Code.

That's what we are, Spree and I, Swamis. It takes a tremendous leap to jump from the ranks of caterers in panel trucks with tinfoil trays of rice and beans to event planner; from interior decorators working on commission at Rooms To Go to curators of a private furniture collection; from nothing to what Spree has. To what I had and have lost my grip on: full Swamihood.

The blessed state of Swamihood is achieved only when no party, no garden, no wardrobe, no diet, no interior design, no flower arrangement, no massage, no facial, no manicure, no Botox injection, no lipo, no laser peel, no pet training, no haircut, no highlight, no low light, no yoga, Pilates, spinning, personal training, or therapy session is considered quite right unless it has been sanctioned by a bona fide Swami.

We both understand that I am violating the first of the Swami commandments: I am thy Lord, thy Swami, thou shalt have no other Swamis before me. The presence of another Swami casts doubt on the divinity of both, leading to confusion and heresy. As a Swami who has seen better days, whose high-priced judgments are now in serious doubt, I am a living reminder that Swamis might not have all the answers. That their very expensive opinions might be fallible.

"Are they here?" Blitz Lord skips down the limestone steps. "Are my Ruhlmanns here?"

I give Spree a look that says her lie about the Dalai Lama has been officially entered in the *Swami Grudge Book,* then I turn all my attention on Blitz Lord. Blond hair, white teeth, tan skin, blue eyes, Blitz could be a *Sports Illustrated* swimsuit model tomorrow if it paid a fraction of what being married to Turk Lord does.

Blitz started off as Turk's personal trainer, which gave her that most dangerous of all powers, permission to touch. Why wives ever allow husbands they want to keep to go to a trainer, dental hygienist, facialist, or anyone other than a barber with hair growing out of his ears is beyond me. And a massage "therapist"? Start dividing the artwork right now. Anyway, after Sand! hit big, Turk (then known as Marvin) ditched the first Mrs. Lord—the only female in three states who would talk to him during his Dungeons & Dragons years—and married Blitz. She turned out to be a great acquisition. Especially after being retrofitted with new, even perkier tits, puffy lips, and rumors of a tightening "down there."

Blitz leans in close to hear Spree's refined whisper. "Not only does Aunt Spree have your Ruhlmanns, Petunia, but many, many other goodies that will transform the architecture of your life."

Blitz claps and bounces about on aerobically perfect calves. "Tell me! Tell me!"

Happily for Spree, Blitz Lord is the ideal client: insecure with tons of social aspirations. An eager student, she parrots every Swami opinion planted in her buttermilk blond head as she tries to throw off trophy wife status and work her way into the heart of Austin society. Her current push consists of giving giant donations to the Platinum Longhorns. Though membership is typically reserved for actual graduates of the University of Texas, a sufficiently large gift of Sand! dollars has made Blitz, a graduate of the Elixir Institute's Six-Week Personal Training Certification Program, into an honorary Platinum Longhorn. I am certain, though, that the Plat Longs' steering committee, composed of Zero Three alumnae such as the Kipster herself, Bamsie, Cookie, and most of the other henchbitches, will never allow a "nouveau" trophy wife outside of the Zero Three zip code to do anything more than write gigantic checks.

Spree begins the inventory. "Well, there's a fabulous Scalamandré armchair, a to-die-for nineteenth-century Burmese Buddha, an absolutely gorgeous chandelier from a Mogul palace in Gujarat, which I heard Susan Dell coveted mightily, and—"

"Blitz Lord! Look at you!" Cutting Spree off, I squeal in the high-pitched tone audible only to dogs and Texas women. "You look great!" Of course Blitz looks great. It's her job. Blitz fends off the cyber sluts who swarm around her alpha-geek husband with marathon running and a live-in personal trainer/chef. She looks especially radiant today with a tan freshly sprayed on by someone who knows his anatomy.

I ignore Spree's ovary-shriveling glare and push on. "Spree told me all about the Ruhlmanns. She knows what a hugehugehuge fan I am of Ruhlmann's work and insisted I come out for a quick peek."

"Oh. Cool." Blitz's enthusiasm, subdued though it is, assures me that the sound of the drums beating out the news from Zero Three that Blythe Young is a pariah has not yet reached the Pyramid House. It is only a matter of time, though. Blitz is already giving me "the look" that asks why I am still present. "The look" is the canary dying in the mine shaft, which reminds the Swami that she is not really just one of the girls. Behind "the look" are the words *You may go now.*

Luckily, Blitz cannot utter those words. They are too overtly Upstairs for a good middle-class, suburban American gal whose only experience with "help," before Turk Lord upgraded her from personal trainer to wife, was the guy from Orkin who came to spray for cockroaches once a year. I have to connect with Blitz and connect fast if I am to have any hope of Kato Kaelining myself into that snug guesthouse.

As Spree rhapsodizes about the "pieces" she has acquired, I ransack my mental Rolodex for that one core concern that will immediately bond me and Blitz. Religion? Charitable cause? Political affiliation?

No, I have to go deeper. Guesthouse deep. Husband? Children? Schools! Yes, that's it! Schools are a surefire connection point. Always good for at least half an hour about how the client is not *really* a private school person, but, God, they are praying that little Max and Lucy get into St. Stephen's. Or at least St. Andrew's.

Schools? Children?

What am I thinking? Children pale beside The House. Copper guttering, butler's pantry, wine cellar, farm sink, outside shower, panic room. The anthropology of The House swirls through my head. I feel as if I am taking a final exam I have forgotten to study for.

Screw The House.

I'll never trump Spree in that arena. If I have any hope of getting into Blitz's hideout, I have to play my one ace in the hole: I am thin.

"Blitz," I interrupt, "you really do look great. Have you dropped some ell bees?" Fat Talk, the universal female bonder.

"God, are you kidding? I'm a total blob. But you, *you* look great."

"Are you kidding?"

"No, seriously. What are you doing?"

I think it best to keep my own special program of speed, Eve cigarettes, Code Warrior cocktails, and financial suttee, all combined with a hummingbird metabolism I did nothing to deserve, to myself. "*I'm* the blob here." I pinch the few micrometers of flesh on my belly and shake them despairingly. "I can't get rid of this no matter what I do."

"I know!" Blitz wails sympathetically. "I just can't get the definition I want in my abs. *I'm* the blob. *You* look incredible. Are you training with anyone? Because you seriously look great."

Great? Me? I make Kippie Lee look Rubenesque.

The stress of the past year along with an increasing reliance on my friend Code Warrior has turned me into the size zero all my former friends dream of becoming. Does it matter that what flesh there is on my body is pure fat? That I have the muscle tone of a tsetse fly and the cholesterol of a German butcher? That I haven't had a period in months and my libido is a memory? No, none of that matters. I am a size zero teetering on the edge of disappearing from the face of the earth altogether.

"Better than that," I exclaim. "I have this brilliant new nutrition program that will amp up your metabolism and cleanse your system. I would love to share it with you."

"Yes! Yes! Yes!" Blitz bounces about enthusiastically.

This causes Spree to grumble like a bull walrus intimidating a rival poaching on his harem. "Blitz," she whispers, forcing her client to lean in close. "When working with pieces of this stature one has to consider one's obligation to posterity. I'm beginning to wonder if the Victoria and Albert might not show more respect for the Ruhlmanns."

I have to admire Spree. If a Swami has the cojones to pull it off nothing works better than a schoolmarmish knuckle rapping.

Blitz comes to heel immediately and with a new snap in her voice tells me, "Blythe, could you just zip up to the house and share your program with Jade?"

"Jade? Your personal chef?" *Blitz Lord is handing me off to the cook?*

I feel as if I am drowning and begin to tread water frantically. "I love those sandals!" I exclaim, pointing to Blitz's Vera Wang ankle straps. "I saw them at Last Call for forty percent off."

"You did? Did they have the ones with the cutouts?"

"I almost got them! Are they cute or what?"

Ah, yes, nothing the seriously rich like better than a bargain—nine-hundred-ninety-five-dollar sandals for six hundred dollars? Get two!

As I engage Blitz with other secrets of the discounted and knocked off, Spree begins to seriously worry me. From the way her eyes are twitching and the guttural clicks she is making deep in her throat, I fear that Spree is about to pounce, sink her incisors into my neck, and shake me until my neck breaks.

Did Spree's hairline always hover that far above her ears? I remember then what I'd heard on the Swami grapevine: Spree has had some work done. That puts things in a different light entirely. It is no safer to come between a mother grizzly and her cubs than it is between a Swami trying to pay off a face-lift and her client-mark. I will have to step up the program. And fast. I pray that Blitz Lord has not heard that my White House connections have been cut off.

"You know who else loves Last Call?"

"Who?"

"Well, obviously, I can't name names, but let's just say they don't have a Last Call in *Washington, D.C.*"

"No!"

"And let's also just say that someone is coming to town very, very soon and wants to do a girlfriends' day that includes some fun and fabulous new ladies in addition to the old standbys *from Midland.*"

What bigger jackpot could I dangle in front of a baby climber like Blitz than the opportunity, for the rest of her life, to offer firsthand opinions about how much work the First Lady has or has not had done? For Blitz this fantasy shopping trip would be the equivalent of a place on the steering committee of the Platinum Longhorns.

Catching on fast, Blitz asks, "And if these 'new ladies' are generous contributors?"

"A place could practically be guaranteed."

"When? How?"

"Oh, it'll have to be very last-minute, of course. Secret Service. Heightened security. Sweep the room. Secure the perimeter. All that."

"Of course."

"I mean, I probably won't have much more than half an hour's notice. If that. And, of course, the only way you can be included will be if you come with me. So that will mean that once I get word I'll have to drive out here to pick you up, and by the time I drive all the way out here—"

"You've got to stay here! In the guesthouse!"

Jackpot! Five cherries in a row.

"Oh, well, I don't know. This *is* my busy season and—"

"Please?" Blitz beseeches. I love being besought.

"I just don't know. It might be a week before I hear from her. Maybe two. Even as long as a month. Month and a half."

"We don't care, do we, Spree?"

Spree? We? We Spree?

"Why, no," Spree purrs in a voice like one of the perfidious Siamese cats in *Lady and the Tramp*. *We are Siamese, if you please. We are Siamese, if you* don't *please.* "It'll be a big slumber party."

Blitz squeals, "Yes!" She claps her hands like the giddy Pi Phi she might have been had she gone to UT instead of doing the Personal Training Certification Program with graduate work in snaking Turk Lord away from his wife while helping him get his Dorito roll under control. "Yes! You and Spree can both stay in the guest-house."

"'Both'?"

"Yes! Didn't Spree tell you? She's moving in. There's plenty of room for both of you, though."

"Spree is moving in?" I begin to recall word that Spree's girl-friend of the past eight years had cleaned out their joint account, stolen their child-substitute dog, and left town with her qigong instructor. There is no way to parry that level of desperation. "To your guesthouse?"

"Yes! We're doing a total rethink on the cabana area. Spree has some amazing contacts in Cuba. Great prerevolutionary pieces."

There is not a hot chance in holy hell that Spree Winslow and I can ever share any space smaller than the Astrodome. Badgers in a box. I prefer my odds with the IRS.

"Yes, Blythe," Spree says in her purring Siamese way. "Do join us. Blitz is really into the Beaux Arts influence on Cuban furniture makers of the late teens and twenties. She thinks they're absolute Rembrandts of rattan."

God, Spree is good. As far as Blitz knows, Rembrandt is a tooth-whitening product, but that doesn't stop the little parvenu from beaming at this encomium to her taste.

With my ship sinking and the last lifeboat filling up fast, I panic and try a bold and innovative approach: the truth. I have no choice but to lay my cards on the table and make common cause with this sweet, middle-class girl who was a Swami herself not so long ago. "Blitz, I need a place to stay. A place all to myself for just a few days, a week, maybe, a month at the outside."

Spree and Blitz are both speechless. Blitz blinks and her hand reaches out as if feeling for a bellpull that will summon the right servant to deal with the annoyance standing before her. Or to yank the lever of a trapdoor that will shoot me into oblivion.

A smile spreads across Spree's tightened features, causing tension lines to tauten in the odd and unnatural places of the lifted.

Well, why shouldn't she smile? Spree has beaten me and she knows it. In my desperation I have broken so many rules of Swami-hood that I can barely count them all. But the number one precept of the Swami Code that I have violated, the bedrock that the whole house of cards is built on, is this: *They* must always believe that *they* need *you* more than *you* need *them*.

In the final sign of my total defeat, Blitz implores Spree with a glance to handle this icky situation.

"Blythe, come on," Spree's whisper is so low she looks like she's lip-synching herself. "Blitz has so much on her plate now, what with positioning the Ruhlmanns and the cabana rethink—"

"And hosting Lance's Livestrong fund-raiser."

"That's right." Spree gives Blitz a comforting pat on the shoulder. "How could I have forgotten the Livestrong? Blitz has more on her plate than any human should ever have to deal with."

"And," Blitz adds in a tone of overwhelmed despair, "we still haven't found the right couch."

Finding the right couch. I am sunk; lives have been dedicated to the pursuit of finding the right couch.

"As you can see, Blythe, additional houseguests at this point are simply out of the question. I mean, how much can one human be expected to deal with? Right, Blitz?"

Blitz nods, sad but brave, all puppy dog eyes and burdened nobility.

"Spree, gosh, you know what? I think you and I just might be able to share the guesthouse after all."

"Gosh, Blythe, *you* know what? I think I'm going to need a blank canvas mentally to really be able to work through all the major, major issues Blitz is facing here."

At that moment Spree is doing what I have just failed to accomplish: maintaining the fiction that the only truly important problems in the world are the clients' problems. Although Spree has just lost her girlfriend, her dog, and can't pay off her plastic surgeon, she is pretending that the question of whether to position the Ruhlmann step cabinet on a plinth base in the conservatory or the library overshadows any trivial problem she could possibly be facing.

That is the Swami Code. And I have broken it.

April 3, 2003

N UMBED BY my humiliating defeat, I ramble aimlessly through the swankier west hills neighborhoods until the quitting-time caravan of service vehicles sweeps me into their eastward migration back toward town.

I play Lakshmi's tape again. Her serene, knowing voice soothes me. "Let worries, anxieties, melt away. If your child received a thin envelope rather than a fat one from the school of his or her choice, simply know that the universe has another, a better, path for your child. Also know that my partner, Dorsey Hedges, is available for consultation on college application essays."

A pang of longing for the rarefied anxieties of the upper classes pierces me and I ache for the life of endless pampering I was once a part of, even if I was a part of it only in the way that ball moss is a part of a live oak tree.

"Let go of all appointments. Let go of all DIS-appointments. Let go of all stress. Let go of all DIS-stress. Float on a warm ocean of well-being. Allow a sense of serenity, of the rightness of your place in the universe, to flow over you."

Why had I never noticed before how perfectly Lakshmi's Om Shanti philosophy aligns with the Republican Party platform?

For one blissful moment, I imagine I am back at the ultraexclusive health club I used to belong to, AbsSolution, laid out on a sticky mat next to Kippie Lee, Bamsie, Cookie, and all the rest of *le tout* Austin.

Then I am rattled back to reality by trucks—lots of trucks—shaking the little minivan as they barrel past. Glaziers' trucks with ziggurats of glistening glass. Landscapers' trucks pulling trailers loaded with mowers, cans of gas. Remodelers' trucks with ladders, red rags tied on the ends, hanging out the back. Chemical trucks hauling tanks of pesticide and fertilizer for the perfect green, chinch-bug-free lawn. There are vans, too. Carpet cleaner, mobile pet washer, chimney sweep, rain-gutter cleaner, FedEx, UPS.

From their perches in the beds of pickups the day laborers, mostly Mexican, mostly illegal, watch the exodus. As silent and accepting as brown Buddhas, they stare back at the caravan, monitoring it without ever making eye contact and drinking Lone Stars from an eighteen-pack.

Tiny vehicles advertising maids, both Merry and Molly, slide past. Saturns, Ford Festivas, they are stuffed like clown cars with impossible numbers of women, mostly brown, all exhausted.

A replacement army of vehicles many times stronger than the one heading east surges west toward home. The Lexi and Mercedes are piloted by crisp professionals who remove jackets, loosen ties, talk into phones. They are returning to homes where the beds have been made, toilets sanitized, carpets cleaned, lawns mowed, fire ants massacred, panes replaced, tile regrouted, express packages delivered, and dogs washed.

The purposeful energy of the homeward-bound depresses me as I meander back toward town. Then a true clown car zips past, a purple VW Beetle with a magnetic sign on the side reading OOPSY DAISY, CLASSY CLOWNS INC. BIRTHDAYS, SPECIAL OCCASIONS. Oopsy's face is still painted geisha white with a tipsy, Joker smile in a toddler-terrifying shade of red. She pulls off a Raggedy Ann wig, scratches her head, sags back against the seat.

I wonder how much Molly Maids pays. How would I look in an orange wig? These dismal questions send me searching for the Code Warrior cup. One healthy slug and I snap back out of reality. With God as my witness, I vow, I will one day earn my rightful place again in the caravan. East or west, labor or management, I no longer care. Just, please God, not northeast to Huntsville Prison. This *Gone with the Wind* moment puts a bit of snap back in my garters but provides nothing in the way of an actual plan.

Think, think, think.

As I struggle to come up with a way to save myself, the rolling hills along 2222 flatten out and give way to the city. Instead of a plan, my old pal, bitter regrets, pays a call. When was the last time I had an actual friend rather than a client, a contact, or a connection? Someone I could go to now in my hour of need and say, "Hide me, I'm on the lam from the IRS, and the DEA is probably not far behind"? When did my entire life become one snarled web of networking, of cocktail chatter, and squealing at the well heeled about the weight they'd lost while shoving silver trays of hors d'oeuvres at them whether as the wife of Trey Dix the Third or the sole proprietor of Wretched Xcess? Even, or maybe especially, while married to Trey, I made no true friends. The women who'd welcomed me into their houses were never real friends any more than Trey turned out to be a real husband.

I already know the answer to my question, "When was the last time I had an actual friend?" I have known it for a long time: Millie Ott.

Oh God, no, not her, not that.

For Millie Ott means Seneca Falls Housing Co-op, the unthinkable boardinghouse where Millie and I were roommates when I was a UT coed ten years and several incarnations ago. Besides being a run-down dump, Seneca House has another fatal flaw. I struggle to recall what it was that I'd heard about the place, but I can't pull anything up from the data files. Whatever the problem is, it has been caught by my mental spam filter. No matter, my Rolodex is a wonder of nature; I will I *must* think of something better than Seneca House.

Suddenly, I realize that I have been framing my quest entirely wrong. I'm not asking for a favor; I'm answering a prayer. The people I know live their lives for guests. Literally. They buy houses with guest rooms, great rooms, massive effing dining rooms. They all stand ready to extend hospitality to platoons—battalions!—of guests. Guests that, in almost all cases outside of the in-laws they don't want anyway, never arrive. I, Blythe Young, will be the guest who will justify the tens of thousands of square feet they bought, clean, pay taxes on, and never use.

As I drive past the Pee Heights mansions, the names swirl through my brain: Kippie Lee Teeter, Cookie Mehan, Bamsie Beiver, Missy Quisinberry, Paige Oglesby, Morgan Whitlow, Cherise Tatum, Mimi McNaughton, Lulie Bingle, Fitzie Upchurch, Noodle Tiner. For various reasons—friend of Trey; does business with the Dixes; out of town; stopped payment on check; suffering from Rohypnol-induced comas—I have to eliminate them all.

I dig deeper, descending into the second tier of possibilities: the big-dog owners, the Volvo drivers, those with no live-in help whatsoever. As I am scraping the bottom of that barrel for candidates, the van sputters.

Grim reality intrudes. I have exactly enough fuel to get to one place and one place alone: Seneca House. This is a bitter pill. Once again, life is leaving me no way but the hard way. I wish I could remember what it was that I'd heard about the dump. Whatever it is, it couldn't be worse than prison. Could it?

Though I really don't want to face Millie again for a number of reasons—okay, I have snubbed my old roommate ruthlessly for more than a decade—I am starting to accept that Millie is my last hope. Or, at least, the only one I can reach on the teaspoon of gas I have left. Millie was never the grudge-holding type. In fact, Millie Ott was always relentlessly kind, thoughtful, and generous. (Also exceedingly overweight. The last time I saw her she must have been tipping close to two hundred pounds.) Millie will surely take me in. If I can make it to my old boardinghouse, I am certain she will let me lie low long enough to refuel and strike out for greener pastures.

I cross the Great Divide of Lamar Boulevard and enter the gravitational field of the Forty Acres, Longhornland, the University of Texas. Immediately, I am sucked into the land of the young, of those required to wear backpacks on the upper half of their bodies and some form of denim on the lower.

Coeds throw sticks for mutts romping about the leash-free zone of Pease Park that runs beside Shoal Creek. Bare-chested college boys, their shirts tucked into the back pockets of shorts hanging off hip bones and drooping down to calves, hurl Frisbees at chain-link cages. The streets become congested with cars, bikes, bodies as I approach the campus.

I turn off of Twenty-fourth onto Nueces Street. Not that I am in any position to pay the slightest bit of attention to omens and signs, but I do note the Spanish translation of *nueces:* "nuts." I follow Nuts Street and glide on fumes to the front of Seneca House. Before I can switch off the ignition, the van shudders to a gas-starved dead stop. The place looks exactly the same as it did when I walked out ten years ago. Seneca House is a dowdy dowager painted the drabbest of olives, a home that had been regal at the turn of the last century, now fallen on hard times.

The prospect of throwing myself on the mercy of Millie Ott, a friend I lost touch with years ago, exhausts me. All right, "lost" touch might not be entirely accurate. I might have purposely *buried* touch. I might have never returned phone calls, never answered letters. I might even have pretended to be the maid once and told my old roommate that "Mees Joong" was out. It is possible that, over the years, I might even have walked out of a store or two if I saw anyone who remotely resembled Millie.

Maybe I am a social-climbing swine, but a person doesn't move up from being Caterer to the Bubble Boys, to society photographer, to society event coordinator, and, finally, society wife, by playing Frisbee golf in Pease Park. That is never going to pay the bills. Social-climbing swine, yes, that is part of it. But with Millie, there was always something more. Something that has kept my old roommate in my dreams and my thoughts all these years. Something that still causes squirmy feelings of guilt whenever I think about her. I brush away such pointless reflections; they are sapping what precious little energy I have left.

Needing to clear my head, I try a visualization exercise that Lakshmi often had us practice. Closing my eyes, I inhale several cleansing breaths that send positive *prana* in warm, sunny yellow waves rushing through me. It washes my mind of all worry and anxiety as I focus on the God within. I breathe out cool blue negative moon energy through the soles of my feet. Warm yellow waves lap against cool blue ones. Yellow. Blue. Yellow. Blue. The polarized energies strobe through my brain.

"Blythe? Blythe, is that you?"

I wake to find a puddle of drool spotting the Zac Posen and someone who seems to know my name tapping on the window. I search the stranger's hands for a subpoena. They are making feverish cranking gestures.

"Roll down the window!"

I pretend I am on a New York subway and stare straight ahead.

"Blythe, don't you remember me?"

I glance over at the face but can't place it even if it is a very sweet face in the unlifted, un-Botoxed, un-Restylaned way one hardly sees anymore. Sort of a Gibson Girl with the complexion of someone who's grown up in a moist and misty place that turns faces pink and cream instead of into the oxblood wallets that the Texas sun produces. But remember her? No, I am certain I've never seen this person before in my life. In any event, all the dewy innocence is making my head hurt. Code Warrior to the rescue.

Glug-glug.

"Blythe, it's me, Millie! Millie Ott?"

I roll down the window. "Jesus, you're a toothpick. What happened?"

"I lost seventy-three pounds."

"Seventy-three pounds! Good Lord. How did you do it? Sonoma? South Beach? Atkins? Zone? Weight Watchers? Sugar Busters? Scarsdale? Stillman? Caveman? Cabbage soup? Beverly Hills? U.S. Air Force? Drinking Man's? High carb? Low carb? No carb? Fen-phen? Redux? Stomach stapling? Jaw wiring?" I stop, remembering that Millie is not a client and I only speak Fat Talk when I am being paid.

"I wasn't really on any program. It was just a long, gradual process. You're the one who got me started."

"Me?"

"Of course you."

I helped her? I look for signs that Millie might be joking, strain to hear the snap of sarcasm in her words. There is none. She is serious. I want to hear more about this Blythe Young who lent someone a helping hand, but the Blythe Young who needs a hideout takes precedence. "I heard you still lived here." Actually *saw the house's phone number on caller ID when I ducked your calls* is a bit closer to the truth.

"I never left. I worked out an arrangement with the house and the alum association. I guess you could say I'm sort of a housemother."

Housemother? That sounds promising.

"Does that mean you assign rooms? Find space for unexpected visitors? Things of that nature?"

"Well, not exactly. I'm more of a . . . I guess you could say a spiritual counselor. Blythe, do you need a place to stay?"

"Would it be too much of a bother? Do any of the single rooms come with private bath?"

"Well, you know, it is the end of the semester and all. The house is full. You're more than welcome to stay in my room, though. I never took out your old bed. Left it there for unexpected guests. Like you!"

I glance up at the second-story room wondering if I even have enough energy to climb the stairs.

"Blythe, are you all right? You seem different. Are you getting enough sleep?"

"A bit. Generally between the hours of one and three."

"You're so thin."

I hoist the cup. "Liquid diet."

Millie's soft voice grows even softer as she says, "Why don't you come in for a bit?"

Millie's kindness, her very presence, makes a lump rise in my throat. I could start crying and never stop. I drag myself out of the van, weary as a castaway who's finally made it to shore. One last detail, though.

"Uh, Millie, I'm a bit particular about my little minivan. I don't want to leave it out here where it can get scratched."

Or spotted by marauding IRS agents.

Millie eyes the mud-daubed van, side doors now lumpy from their hammering by the meat slicer. "Oh sure, not a problem. Just pull it around the back."

"Actually, I'm out of gas. So, maybe, if you could . . ."

Millie recruits a couple of well-fed frat boys, and together we shove the van out of sight into the backyard. Then, with my trail covered, I take a giant step back in time and follow Millie into Seneca House.

SENECA HOUSE

Time Stops

EVEN THOUGH the last time I set foot in Seneca House was a decade ago, I would have known the place blindfolded. All the signature hippie flophouse scents are here: The dank mildew smell from the leaks in various bathrooms combines with an equatorial humidity that AC units dangling from various rust-dribbled windows do little to dissipate. Cooking aromas heavy on whole grains, tamari, sesame, recompositions of soybeans, Third World staples so beloved of kids who grow up on Pop-Tarts, then go boho the instant they move away from the automatic sprinkler systems of their youth. Having grown up on hamburger that needed to be helped and with a sprinkler system that consisted of me and a watering can, I never understood the impulse.

The tang of pesticide used to thin the ranks of the cockroach armies that permanently occupy the ancient edifice adds to the bouquet. Top notes of cat pee are supplied by the strays adopted by the PETAesque residents. Patchouli incense, cigarettes (clove, marijuana, and regular), and a piña colada of overripe bananas and low-end coconut conditioner round out the olfactory ambience.

A hulking tube of lard waddles past, and I note, "Wow, that cat looks just like Big Lou."

The animal is an exact replica of the world's fattest, nastiest cat, Big Lou, that lived at the house more than a decade ago. But since Big Lou was both ancient and headed for a well-deserved grave even back then, I know it can't be her. Still, just like Big Lou, this cat has tattered stumps where fight-chewed ears once were. And just like Big Lou, she is missing her left eye. The impossible resemblance is odd enough that I move in to investigate.

"Blythe, no!"

The cat turns from a lumbering blob into a heat-seeking streak of orange fur. Claws outstretched, she launches herself directly at my bare legs.

"Blythe, don't move," Millie orders me. "That *is* Big Lou."

I stop dead and Big Lou, her one good eye only good enough to detect motion, plummets to the earth, landing with a wet *squish* as flab hits floor.

Big Lou once sank her claws into someone's date so deeply that he ended up at the hospital on IV antibiotics. After a Big Lou incident requiring medical attention, the house would always stop feeding the cat and she'd disappear long enough for the anti–Big Lou faction to graduate and move on and a new crew of suckers to move in and start the cycle again. It was inevitable: Seneca House drew the type of resident—bookish and repressed or alienated and attitudinal—that adopted Big Lou as a warts-and-all tribute to either female or outsider power.

Once the shock of Big Lou's attack subsides, the smells hit me anew. Only now, underneath them all, I detect a whiff of something entirely new. An unsettling bass note that wasn't here before. The odor is musky and combines elements of beer, sebum, and flatus.

"Are there men in the house?"

My question is answered by the appearance of a slender fellow with skin the color of tea that has steeped too long. I would have pegged him as someone's computer science or Spanish tutor, a repairman, maybe. However, since this individual is wearing nothing but a towel wrapped around his waist, a pair of flip-flops, and a shower cap, I am not certain he fits any of those categories.

Millie, soul of charity that she is, greets him with a blinding smile. "Sanjeev, hello. You'll never believe this! This is the old friend I was telling you about."

"Not Blythe Young?" he asks. "The famous roommate?"

"The very same."

Millie's answer causes this Sanjeev person to grin and say to Millie, "And so now you are Hindu!"

The comment is so random that I can't process it.

Millie flaps her hand for him to hush up and I assume he is one of the strays and dead-enders she always used to adopt. Probably suffers from a neurological disorder. Regaining control, he bolts forward, one hand extended to shake mine, the other gripping the towel at his waist. "Blythe Young! I am very pleased to make your acquaintance." His voice has the melodious oscillations of Calcutta combined with the crispness of the cricket-playing colonial's British accent.

The hand appears clean enough and I shake it, but Sanjeev notices my hesitation.

"Sanjeev is doing graduate work in biomedical engineering. Right now he's working on a fascinating project using lapsed patents on prostheses."

Sanjeev beams as Millie describes his work.

"Did you know that prosthetic technology is still based on 1912 engineering?"

"Uh, no, I was not aware of that."

"Yes," Sanjeev adds, his accent a ball bouncing over each word. "It may be made of titanium, but the design is almost a century old."

"Mmm. Fascinating."

"Sanjeev and his group," Millie explains, "are gathering up all these lapsed patents and putting them online so if someone in India needs a hook, *voilà!* They can just download the plans and have their local lab make it up. It's revolutionary, really."

Sanjeev bows his head. "Thank you, Millie. You are very kind."

"Sanjeev also has the most important job in the house. He's our labor czar."

My hand itches for a remote control so I can fast-forward through this résumé Millie seems compelled to present.

"When you were here we called the labor czar the house manager. Remember?"

I nod vaguely. I have scrubbed all memory of the house from the bank, including that bothersome detail about this place that I still can't remember.

"See?" Millie points to a dry-erase board titled HOUSE LOVE and sectioned off into chores: RECYCLING, CLEAN FRIDGE, FOOD RUNS, COMPOST. The kitchen schedule is also posted along with menus highlighting such delectables as LENTIL CURRY and FALAFEL PIE. Yum. It is all starting to sound gruesomely familiar.

"Sanjeev is brilliant at scheduling everyone for the work they have to do around the house. This place would grind to a halt without Sanjeev. He's the brain that makes it all work."

"If I am the brain, you are the heart."

Besides noticing that attention from a guy in a shower cap makes Millie blush like a milkmaid, I observe something vastly more unsettling. Through the glass panes of the front door I spy a contingent of the last people on earth that I want to see. Actually, second to last, right behind IRS agents. All my little mutineers are out there: Juniper, Olga, Doug, Sergio.

Crap!

Too late, I recollect Seneca House's fatal flaw: My four most disgruntled employees live here. Through the glass front door, I watch them come up the steps.

I cannot face this crew. Not before I am safely dug in. "I'm not feeling very well." I point toward the only open avenue of escape, the kitchen. "Water. I really must have a glass of water. Now."

I duck into the kitchen just as Juniper, Olga, Doug, and Sergio enter. Millie fills a glass from a jug in the refrigerator. The kitchen is exactly as I remember it: a restaurant-size stove with burner rings the size of hubcaps and cast-iron frying pans big as manhole covers. Bins of seeds and grains, oats and groats.

I hear the little mutineers drawing closer and grab Millie's arm, causing her to spill most of the water. "I need to lie down." I make for the back door.

"Uh, sure, but remember, our room is that way." Millie points toward the front of the house, where the posse waits.

"I'd really like to see the backyard."

"You would? Now?"

"Yeah, you know, check on the van." I bang out the screen door.

Outside, I slap the hood, open the passenger door, and grab my precious cup of Code Warrior. "Seems to be all right."

"Okay. Then let's . . ." Millie starts toward the back door.

"How about if we go around?"

"Around?" Millie repeats softly, sounding like a clerk at a convenience store talking to a customer wearing a ski mask.

"Yeah, to the front."

We circle around and end up on the porch. After I make sure the coast is clear, I drag a very perplexed Millie inside and we head for the stairs. The shock of almost being trapped by my former employees combined with general physical atrophy leaves me breathless. When I pause halfway up the stairs for a revitalizing nip of Code, Millie studies me with concern.

On the second floor, Millie opens the door and I step into our old room. It is the same cheaply converted porch, complete with gaps in the floorboards and windows that rattle when shuttle buses drive past. But there is a very secure-looking lock on the door and the room's vantage point on the second floor will allow me to keep the street under surveillance. No surprise attacks. So, in all respects, except the pack of vigilantes on the first floor dying to string me up, it is the ideal place to lie low. I celebrate by cracking the Code again. Its pick-me-up effects manage to overcome extreme exhaustion. Millie sits on the edge of the bed and watches me pace and hyperventilate. Being tracked by those velvety brown spaniel eyes makes me aware that my own pupils are ping-ponging back and forth from Millie to the street and that, even when I request them to stop, they go right on ricocheting.

"Blythe, what's in that cup?"

"Chai. Green tea chai. Very tasty. Wanna try some?" Knowing she will refuse, I hold the Code Warrior cup out.

"No, thanks, I just finished some hibiscus mint."

"Why is your collar on backward?"

"I'm a minister."

I blink several times. Words enter my head, rattle around, but fail to cohere into units of thought. "Did you say you're a minotaur?"

"Minister. I'm a minister."

"Oh, you mean you're an *a*dminister. At the university. We call that an administrator."

"Blythe, I'm a minister."

"Like a preacher? You're a preacher?"

"Not exactly. I finished seminary but was never actually officially ordained. My 'rhetorical skills' were lacking. So, I just sort of decided that this, Seneca House, would be my ministry."

"Do they pay you for that?"

"Not exactly. I have an arrangement with . . . various funding entities." She trails off. "It's too complicated to go into right now. Blythe, come here. Have a seat."

I sit down next to her on the bed. Millie takes my hand. Millie's hand is as soft and warm as rising bread dough. "Blybees . . ."

Blybees? Was there really a time when I had a nickname? Other than Coke-Addled Cunt?

"What's going on?"

Millie's agendaless concern makes my chest constrict with the need to cry. "Are you licensed to hear confession? Grant absolution?"

"No, that's Catholic."

"Do you take some similar oath giving you immunity from grand jury summons and the like?"

"Blythe, what's up?"

The jig? My marriage? My career? Any shred of hope I ever had of not ending up pushing a shopping cart with socks on my hands, nibbling on Meow Mix?

"Tell me what's wrong."

From the Chinatown of wrong turns that is my life, I distill the essence of its dereliction and blurt out, "I haven't had a Pap smear in ten years."

Millie gives me a look that has been professionally trained not to judge.

"Millie, you want to know what the bottom looks like? This is it. You're staring at it."

"Blybees, tell me about it."

"Yes, yes. I need to unburden myself. To hash this all out. Come up with a game plan . . ." My voice echoes back to me from some spot that grows more distant with each word. My last words, "review my options," sound to me as if they were spoken by a robot in the hall.

Millie puts her arm over my shoulder. "It's going to be fine. You'll be safe here. Whatever it is, it's going to be all right. Why don't I just take this . . . chai?"

I observe Millie prying the Code Warrior cup from fingers that only feel cold and dead. I can do nothing to resist.

"Lie down."

Horizontality is such a delicious sensation that I wonder idly why I don't enjoy it more often.

"Whatever it is, sweetie, we'll figure it out. Together."

Sweetie. Together. How long has it been?

Millie's voice is unbelievably soothing. Each word is a lullaby. I try to think of a question just so I can keep hearing it. "Why did that guy in the shower cap ask if you're Hindu now?"

"Oh, you mean Sanjeev. That's kind of funny. We were discussing the whole concept of dharma and Sanjeev explained how the root of the word means 'that which holds.' I really liked the idea of a religion based on being held and imagined myself floating in a giant crystal bowl of water that contained everyone I have ever known. This explained to me why I get these odd tingly feelings when anyone in my bowl is in trouble."

"Tingly feelings?" Her voice, lulling me to sleep, is giving *me* tingly feelings.

"Sounds bizarre, I know. Sanjeev thinks it is. But it's like, no matter how far away someone is, I feel them splashing when they need my help."

Splashing? I can't follow what Millie is talking about. The point she occupies is receding into a small, shimmering nimbus of light.

I don't know if I dream or hear Millie say, "I felt you splashing. I told Sanjeev that I knew you needed help. I'd been getting the odd tingles. And he told me, 'Tingles are dharma.' That's when I said that if my friend Blythe turned up, I should probably become a Hindu. If not, I guessed I'd just go on being a crazy Christian."

Whether real or dreamed, the light blinks off, and Millie fades to black.

In the Dark Forest
of the World

Is there anything quite like waking up toxically hungover in the room one occupied in college ten years after graduation to definitively hammer home for one the full extent of one's all-inclusive loserhood? I open my eyes, discover that Millie is gone, that every cell in my body has been squashed flat as a penny on a railroad track, and that the ones adjacent to my brain have not only been squashed but sharpened to knife edges.

Careful not to move anything other than my arm, I feel around on the floor beside the bed until my fingers close around the handle of the Code Warrior mug.

Ah, bless its handy, no-spill commuter lid.

Without having to lift my head, I tilt the cup toward my parched lips. One drop, two, trickle from the lipstick-smeared opening. Then nothing. All Mama's medicine is gone.

I shove another pillow under my head and prop myself up a bit farther so I can take better stock of my dire situation. Hanging from a hook on the outside of Millie's closet door is a full-length white minister's gown. A purple stole embroidered with golden doves is draped around the neck. A banner above her small, rickety desk reads, BUT THE FRUIT OF THE SPIRIT IS LOVE, JOY, PEACE, PATIENCE, KINDNESS, GOODNESS, FAITHFULNESS, GENTLENESS, SELF-CONTROL; AGAINST SUCH THINGS THERE IS NO LAW.

Posted beneath the banner is a calligraphy rendering of Bible verses. THOU SHALT LOVE THE LORD THY GOD WITH ALL THY HEART,

AND WITH ALL THY SOUL, AND WITH ALL THY MIND. THIS IS THE FIRST
AND GREATEST COMMANDMENT. AND THE SECOND IS LIKE UNTO IT,
THOU SHALT LOVE THY NEIGHBOUR AS THYSELF. ON THESE TWO COM-
MANDMENTS HANG ALL THE LAW AND THE PROPHETS.

Okay, that is good information. Now, I am starting to get the
picture. Like the bums who have to pay for their two hots and a flop
at the Salvation Army, at some point Millie is going to ask me to
accept Jesus as my personal Lord and Savior. That is doable. As long
as I know what is coming, I can deal. And then I notice a few other
calligraphic pronouncements:

> *Enough of the pursuit of pleasure,*
> *Enough of wealth and righteous deeds!*
>
> *In the dark forest of the world*
> *What peace of mind can they bring you?*
> *Ashtavakra Gita 10:7*

And laid out in the shape of a triangle with a lotus hovering at
its top is a little something from the Buddha himself:

> *On life's journey*
> *Faith is nourishment,*
> *Virtuous deeds are a shelter,*
> *Wisdom is the light by day and*
> *Right mindfulness is the protection by night.*
> *If a man lives a pure life, nothing can destroy him;*
> *If he has conquered greed nothing can limit his freedom.*

I figure these last two entries have to do with Mr. Shower Cap. I
put my hand down and feel around until I locate my purse and dig
out all the pill bottles therein. I lick the dust from their empty interiors and wait, attempting to will myself into any state that doesn't
feel as if my nerve endings were being scrubbed with a pumice
stone.

It doesn't work. I crave a lengthy list of substances, but the only one I have the slightest hope of scoring is caffeine. From the jagged, speeded-up Code Warrior World where everything—parties, people, bicyclists, regrets, recriminations, scruples—hurtled past as if I were on a rocket sled to hell, I plunge into Molasses Land. The seconds, minutes, hours don't tick by; they haul their sorry asses along, inch by inch, across a Sahara of unmoving time.

Standing up takes patience and ingenuity. When at last I achieve verticality, I shuffle to the door and pause there to listen for the voices of my little mutineers. The house is silent. Coast clear, I shamble downstairs. Without the Warrior to absorb the brutal shocks of life, each step is a spiked jackhammer to the brain.

Downstairs, I double-check that the house is truly deserted before stepping out of the stairwell. On my way to the kitchen, I halt for a rest and sink onto the same cat-piss-soaked Herculon tweed couch that was here during my first tour. The rug that was once the grimy pink of bubble gum on a dirty sidewalk is now a uniform dirty sidewalk gray. Even the causes are the same but more tattered. A pile of leaflets litters the top of the scarred coffee table: *Democracy Is Not a Spectator Sport. Protect Reproductive Rights. No Blood for Oil.*

Check. Check. And double-check.

Big Lou demands service, bumping against my hand until I scratch between her ears. Her purr is a rumbling clatter as loud as an ancient percolator.

Seneca House is even more decrepit and shabby than I feel. It is just and fitting that I should land back where I started, at a college boardinghouse that is as close to a welfare hotel as makes no difference. Returning to this pit pretty much erases the past ten years of my life, wipes the slate clean of anything I might have accomplished in my life.

Crushing headache, nausea, and an incessant twitching in my right eyelid prod me into the kitchen. I locate a jar of HEB house-brand instant coffee and spoon half the jar into a mug that I fill with water from the house's handy regiment-size teakettle.

I toddle out, concentrating on holding the steaming cup far enough away that the smell of maltodextrin and anticaking agents don't make me heave. This causes me to fail to notice that my own personal vision of hell has taken shape in the dining room and is glaring at me with more hostility than a basket of cobras. I try to charm anyway.

"Hey, Juniper, Doug, Olga, Sergio, great to see you guys."

All my former employees, except the unflappable Sergio, gape openly. The hot pink springs on Juniper's Z-Coil shoes sproing beneath her as she oscillates in disgruntled amazement. Olga's freakishly long ballerina/model neck gooses out even farther. Doug simply tilts his head like a puzzled dog. A puzzled dog with, thankfully, friendly eyes.

Juniper, always quick on the uptake, is the first to recover. She all too literally springs into action, bounding forward on the Z-Coils. "What the hell are you doing here? In a giant flowered nightgown?"

I glance down and find that while I was out Millie has, indeed, dressed me in one of the granny nighties she used to wear when we were roommates and she was jumbo size.

Juniper doesn't give me a chance to answer. "Have you been here for the past three days since the party?"

Three days? I've been out for three days?

"We went by your place a bunch of times to get paid. We thought you were hiding until we saw your landlady dragging all your clothes and shit into her house."

No! No! No! Bamsie took my couture?

"What are you doink here?" Olga demands in a probing tone that reminds me she hails from the land of the KGB.

"I'm visiting a friend."

"Who is friend?"

"Millie."

"You're friends with Millie?" Juniper is agog, her bony features threatening to slice right out of her face. "How can you be friends with such a good, decent, kind, trustworthy, honorable person?"

"Fluke of nature?"

"God, I guess so. I mean, if there was ever an anti-Millie. Someone the complete opposite of good, decent, kind—"

"Listen, Juniper, if you don't mind, I'm really not up to an all-expense-paid character assassination at the moment."

"Oh really? Is that so? Is *Little Miss Wretched Xcess* asking for some *consideration of feelings*? Is that it? A little *recognition of basic human decency*?"

I do not like the direction this conversation is taking nor the heavily italicized reading Juniper is giving it. I attempt a brisk derailment. "Hey, you guys wouldn't even be here without me. Wasn't I the one who first turned you on to this place?"

Juniper gasps and eye-rolls her way to a response. "Okay, okay, now I get it. Stupid me. Right. The world *does* revolve around Blythe Young. That, *that*, is the piece I was missing. Oh, okay, everything is clear now."

"I'll take that as a yes."

Juniper taps her chin, pretending to think, and I brace myself for another round of nonconsensual sarcasm.

"Actually, *actually,* now that I think about it you *are* responsible for all of us living here. I mean, where else could we afford to live on the *slave wages* you were paying until you decided to pay, oh, the very cost-cutting *nothing!*"

"*Da*, this place is like gulag. Is labor camp. For you!"

"Now, Olga, come on. That's a bit extreme—"

Juniper drops the sarcasm and escalates to direct confrontation. "Blythe, pay us what you owe us. Now. My tuition is due."

I miss the sarcasm.

"*Da*," Olga chimes in. "And I nid to pay rent to lif here."

"Sergio? Doug? Would you like to jump on this dog pile? Kick me while I'm down?"

Something flickers in Doug's eyes. Pity? Shame? He shakes his head and looks away. "Not really." Juniper pokes him, though, until he adds reluctantly, "The bank is threatening to repossess my car."

"Sergio?"

Sergio shrugs and drops his velvety Latin lids. "Hey, sometimes you get the elebator. Sometimes you get the shaft."

"Guys, I'm sorry. I reallyreallyreally am, but I am far more conclusively hosed than any of you are. I have nothing. Literally not a thing."

Juniper takes the olive branch I have extended and starts clubbing me with it. "Well, I'm sorry that the trophy wife wasn't smart enough to get the trophy—"

"Trophy wife? I'm too smart to have been a trophy wife."

"Too old, more like it."

"Hey! Come on—"

"And I'm sorry that you also snorted up everything you made picking the bones of the Internet bubble—"

"Mixing our metaphors there, Juniper."

"—but that doesn't mean we're gonna bail you out just like we're supposed to work our entire lives to keep you in Depends because you bankrupted Social Security."

"Uh, Juniper, I'm thirty-three."

"Who cares? You've got that whole the-world-revolves-around-me boomer thing going, expecting us millennials or whatever to come in and clean up after you."

"Juniper, what is your point?"

"My point is, *Blythe,* you had your time at the trough. You had the bubble. You had Clinton. Now you owe us. I'm about to get thrown out of school, Olga's on the brink of eviction, and Doug is dodging the repo man."

"Try the IRS."

"You brought your troubles on yourself." Juniper's voice is disturbingly calm. "You snorted and lied and connived and conned and cheated and scammed your way into the mess you're in. You created your own hell."

This is all beginning to sound like a bad production of *A Christmas Carol* with Juniper as the Ghosts of Christmas Past, Present, and Future. Where is Bob Cratchit to counsel forgiveness?

"You owe us."

"Jes, jew owe us." When Sergio cuts me with a gaze adequate to etching diamonds, I know that the roaring in my ears is the sound of the falls I am about to go over without a barrel. This is my moment. When backed up against the wall, I always come through. I am a clutch player. I have to deliver. I have to argue my way out of this corner with dazzling rhetoric and spin the likes of which the world has never previously seen.

Or I can pretend to faint, a maneuver that has squeaked me out of many another tight spot. Unfortunately, this time, on the way down, I accidentally knock my head against the table, and the lights truly do go out.

It's Called a Conscience

JUNIPER? JUNIPER, can you hear me?"

I open my eyes to find an extremely annoying and extremely fuzzy nurse dressed in lilac scrubs grinding her knuckles into the back of my hand and calling me Juniper. I fear I've entered the Twilight Zone and been condemned to bounce a mile in Juniper's Z-Coils.

"Why are you calling me Juniper?" I demand. "Stop calling me Juniper."

The real Juniper sticks her face directly in front of mine and enunciates very, very slowly, "Joo-ni-per, you are in an examining room at the university health center where we brought you after you fell and hit your head because this is where we bring *currently enrolled* University of Texas students because otherwise it is very, very expensive to get medical care. So it's lucky you are a *currently enrolled* student and that you are entitled to medical care here at the university health center because you are a *currently enrolled* student. Isn't that right, *Joo-ni-per*?

"Juniper," Juniper continues, "here's your *student ID*." She holds a blurry ID card up to my face. In the photo Juniper is wearing her black-rimmed glasses. I touch my face and find that I am wearing those precise glasses.

"Oh, okay." I take Juniper's ID, relieved that I don't have brain damage. Noticing a breeze blowing across my lower back, I glance down and discover that I am now dressed in a pair of Olga's jeans of the low-rise sort that make sitting down a pornographic activity.

"Okay, Juniper, make a fist." A prick on the inside of my elbow alerts me that the nurse is drawing blood. "The doctor will want to do some tests. Find out why you're so unresponsive. And open your fist."

I keep my hand balled up tightly. My blood and tests. Not a winning combination. I order my corpuscles to stay in their cozy veins, but the nurse unsnaps the rubber tubing from my arm and the traitorous platelets rush into the syringe.

"The doctor will be right in." Lilac Scrubs bustles out.

The instant the door closes, Juniper snatches her glasses off my face and the world clicks into far too sharp a focus. "Great. This is just great. They're gonna do a toxicology screen and I'll have every drug known to man on my record. I should have just left you twitching on the floor."

"Twitching? I was twitching?"

"You were twitching before you fell. Shit." Juniper plops down on the rolling stool.

"Thanks, Juniper. Thanks for not leaving me on the floor."

Juniper shakes her head in disgust. "It's called a conscience. Really makes life so much easier *not* to have one, doesn't it?"

The obvious implication being that my lack thereof has delivered me to my current bed of roses. "Well, anyway, thanks."

"Okay. It's done. God, why did I ever think you could pass for me?"

"Juniper, don't worry. I'm really good in these kinds of situations. Fast on my feet. Good in the clinches. Just fill me in on your medical history."

"You don't need to know that."

"Yes, I do. I mean, maybe you're a hemophiliac or something. That would be important to know."

"I'm not a hemophiliac."

"How can I impersonate you in front of a doctor if I don't know your medical history?"

"This is ridiculous. Let's just leave right now."

"That would look more suspicious than anything. Just tell me what your last few visits were for."

Juniper's disapproving lips thin even further.

"Juniper, I don't want you to get thrown out of school for doing me a favor. *You* don't want you to get thrown out of school for doing me a favor. Tell me."

An exasperated, resigned exhalation, then, "Okay, last time I was here was to get an IUD fitted. Time before that was because I needed lower-dose birth control pills. Before that chlamydia. Venereal warts. Thought I had herpes but didn't."

"Okay, I got it. Is there a pimp involved in all this?"

"I knew it! I knew I shouldn't have told you."

"When you were working for me, did you wash your hands regularly?"

"Good-bye. Any brain damage you might have suffered would be an improvement. I'm leaving."

Just as Juniper's hand touches the knob, the door bursts open, and Lilac Scrubs reenters reading intently, mesmerized by Juniper's *Story of O* medical chart. "Because of your, ah-hem, 'history,' the doctor would like to do a quick"—and then the words, the magic words—"pelvic exam and Pap smear while you're here. So put this on with the opening to the front." She hands me a gown laundered to near transparency. "And this." A drape quilted like a giant paper towel. "You know the drill," the nurse says with obvious disapproval.

Before the door closes, Juniper rips the gown and drape from my hands. "That's it. We're leaving. Now! What are you doing? Stop taking your clothes off! Are you completely insane?"

"Juniper, I haven't had medical insurance since I left UT. When I had money, I didn't have time. I actually had an appointment with a gynecologist, but Trey divorced me before I could get in. Ever since the divorce, basic medical care has been beyond my means. A pelvic exam is winning the lottery for me. A Pap smear, God, a Pap smear . . ." My eyes actually tear up. "A Pap smear is a hopeless dream." I grab the gown and drape back. "But a girl's gotta try."

Before Juniper can finish counting the ways she hates me, I have my clothes stripped off and am back in the saddle again. Feet in the stirrups, legs in the traditional Happy Thanksgiving position, this turkey is ready to be stuffed.

"Don't worry," I assure Juniper. "We're nothing but body parts to today's insurance serf medico. These assembly-line docs wouldn't remember you or me if they'd just seen us ten minutes before for spontaneous combustion."

The door swings open. I catch a microscopic glimpse of the doctor and immediately yank the paper drape up to hide as much of my face as I can. Since the doctor's head is down studying Juniper's chart, I risk another glimpse. Her name tag confirms the awful truth: ROBIN FELDMAN, M.D., PH.D., Scourge of Seneca House.

Robin was living in the house ten years ago at the same time I was while she finished a doctorate in counseling. She used all of the residents as therapy guinea pigs. I myself had submitted to many sessions so that Robin could practice asking how I felt about whatever I'd just said. Apparently, though, screwing with people's heads had not provided Robin with enough of a career challenge, so she had gone on for a second doctorate that allowed actual penetration.

Of all the gyn joints in all the towns in all the world . . .

"So"—Double Dr. Dr. Robin checks the top of the chart for a name—"Juniper, you've had a little bump on the head."

Robin looks up from Juniper's chart.

Still hiding most of my face beneath the drape, I see an opportunity and decide to seize it. "Uh, actually, the head thing's all good. Probably just the pelvic today; then I'm good to go. Know what I'm saying? Whatever. No worries. Yo, yo, yo." I try to sound as much like an early twenties gal as I can. Juniper shoots me a frankly furious glare and makes strangled growling noises until the doctor looks her way, after which she pretends to be engrossed in a poster detailing the bones of the ear.

Robin sits on the rolling stool and zings over to the foot of the examining table. The paper on the table crinkles when she pats the spot at the very end and tells me to "scoot" my "bottom" all the way down. I insinuate my pudenda into the circle of light and warmth cast by the goosenecked examining lamp, and Robin angles it onto my panoramic vista.

Having a great time! Wish you were here!

Then she shoehorns the duck-billed speculum in and ratchets it open for the full spelunk. The instrument is freezing cold. No doubt Lilac Scrubs soaks the thing in ice water for wantons like Juniper.

Having slightly less of a great time.

Robin leafs through my outer foliage like a distracted housewife fingering a head of wilted radicchio. "Hmm, the venereal warts seem to have cleared up."

I peek at Robin over the edge of my Brawny drape and see my absolute least favorite expression: a brow furrowing into inconvenient questions. One of which pops out. "Did you have the IUD removed?"

"IUD?"

Juniper stabs a finger at her own scenic wonderland.

"IUD. Yes, yes. Removed it myself. It was"—I have no idea what an IUD is capable of and hazard—"itching?"

Not the correct answer. Robin's brow furrowing and the heat from the examining lamp both intensify as she leans in for the third degree. She checks the chart yet again, then swivels back to the sunken concavity of my belly. "Juniper, you seem to have lost quite a bit of weight." Another peek. "Quite a bit."

"Oh, thanks. You, too," I answer automatically. "What are you doing? South Beach?"

Robin peers over the top of her glasses, then back to Juniper's chart, then back to what romance novels would call the moist delta of my secret womanhood. From the delta, back to the chart, then back again to the delta. I am really not enjoying the way Robin's gaze bobs back and forth, checking the chart against the viscera splayed out in front of her. Dr. Robin is counting my rings and discovering that the tree she is examining is significantly older than records indicate.

"Maybe just a quick Pap smear, then I'm out of here?" I suggest helpfully.

"I thought I recognized that voice!" Robin yanks the drape out of my hands. "Blythe? Blythe Young, that *is* you. Why are you here? Why do you have Juniper Montroy's chart?" I recall Robin's niggling affinity for rules, technicalities, laws. "Am I examining the wrong person?" She turns to Juniper, who is pressed against the ear poster trying to assume the shape of a eustachian canal. "You're Juniper Montroy, aren't you? Blythe, how did you get in here? Are you attempting to obtain services by fraudulent means?"

"Oh, God, no!" I try to sit up, but the speculum persuades me otherwise. "Whatever is happening, and I'm not saying that anything *is* happening, Juniper had no part in it whatsoever. I stole her student ID."

"But she's here."

"Yes, but only because I threatened her."

Robin's gaze goes from my spindly physique, which has all the intimidating power of a set of wind chimes, to Juniper's Valkyrian form with its star-halfback-on-a-girl's-field-hockey-team-muscularity. Robin quirks a skeptical brow and I backpedal.

"Threatened to expose her, uh, medical history," I clarify. "Tell her parents or boyfriend or something."

Robin can buy this. Governments have been brought down with less incriminating evidence than what is in Juniper's chart. Seeing my hopes for a Pap smear fade, I grasp at a straw and ask, "I don't suppose this would be the time to mention my migraines and how well they respond to Vicodin?"

The ill-timed Vicodin request brings my reunion with Dr. Dr. Robin to an abrupt end. "The only reason I'm not calling campus police," she says by way of farewell, "is because Millie maintains that you two are still friends."

Seconds later, Juniper and I are on the sidewalk being buffeted by students with mufflers wound around their necks to protect them from temperatures dipping dangerously into the mid-eighties.

"On the bright side," I say, "although no prescriptions were written, no identity theft charges were filed either."

Juniper snatches her ID back and stomps away.

The Warm Ocean
of Petrodollars

Uᴘ ᴛᴏ ꜱᴏʟɪᴅꜱ ʏᴇᴛ?" Millie asks, holding out a tray of food she diverted from the kitchen. I have been hiding out in our room. Given Juniper's pique about the health center incident, I think it best to lie low for a while. Millie is unaccountably cheerful as she slides the tray onto my lap and helps me tuck a napkin under my chin.

"Did you know that before you came to and hit your head you were out for three days?"

"Uh, yeah, I heard." I poke at the dinner offerings: Lentils drearied even further with a greenish sheen of curry. Unpeeled carrots "steamed" to body temperature for a tepid dirt-flavored crunch. Irish soda bread streaked with salty veins of powdery baking soda. *Yum.*

"We were so worried about you."

"We?"

"Well, Sanjeev and I. I had to tell Sanjeev."

"And he's the . . . with the . . ." I pantomime shower cap.

"Yes. I can't wait for you two to get to know each other better. I've told him so much about you."

"You have?"

"Of course."

Of course? "Like what?"

"Oh, just all the fun we used to have together. Like when we planted that herb garden in the back? That was the first time I ever

86

ate pesto. Oh, and I told him about the scavenger party you orga-
nized when we all went to ritzy neighborhoods and said we were
sorority girls going through rush and we had to get everything on
our list: wine, Brie, crackers, smoked oysters, pâté. And we got it
all. That was such a fun party."

"Well, certainly cost-effective."

"That was when the house first gelled. Blybees, you could get
anybody to do anything. Sanjeev will be happy to see you up and
about. He was worried when you still hadn't come around after an
entire day. Then even more worried because your sleep was so,
so . . . troubled."

"Troubled?"

"Well, you yelled a fair amount."

"Listen, if I said anything, anything that might have mentioned,
oh, the IRS or, gosh, I don't know, Rohypnol—"

"No, you said things like, 'Leave me the eff alone.'"

"I said 'eff'?"

"No, you said the *F* word. Quite a bit actually."

"Sorry."

"Please, I'm no prude. I don't care. Sanjeev was a little startled,
however, when you told him to get his mothereffing hands off you."

"Why were Sanjeev's hands on me?"

"Well, after all the thrashing, you went completely still, so I put
a mirror under your nose. Fortunately, there was condensation, but
I was still worried. That's when I had Sanjeev take a look."

"Why?" I did not like the image of a strange foreigner in a
shower cap examining me. "Is Sanjeev a doctor?"

"Not exactly. But his father is and he grew up helping him in the
clinic for indigents that Dr. Chowdhury runs in Calcutta. Oops, did
I say 'Calcutta'? Sanjeev always corrects me about that. It's *Kolkata*
now. 'Calcutta' is the Anglicized version. Sanjeev says Kolkata probably originally meant 'land of the goddess Kali.'"

Millie notices I am squinting involuntarily in an attempt to filter
out the excess verbiage. "Oops, sorry, I'm wandering. Anyway, Sanjeev was great. He checked your pupillary response with a penlight.

Then he sort of rolled you from side to side and said, 'Good oculocephalic reflex.' Then, 'No cluster breathing. No ataxic breathing. No Cheyne-Stokes.'"

Millie repeats Sanjeev's pronouncements in a fake, deep voice, like Shirley Temple imitating Daddy. "The test you didn't like was when he ground his knuckles into the bone right under your eye socket."

"Can't imagine why I wouldn't have enjoyed that."

"Yeah, that's when you told him to take his mothereffing hands off you. Blythe, do you use drugs?"

"What?"

"Sanjeev went through your purse to make sure you weren't, you know, on anything. And there were all these empty pill bottles. And lots of them had other people's names on them."

Oops, my borrowers.

"Oh those, yeah. I was filling prescriptions for some elderly neighbors of mine. Hip replacements. Hard for the old gals to get out."

"That's exactly what I told Sanjeev. I told him that Bamsie and Kippie Lee had to be the names of elderly shut-ins. Or, possibly, the pills were pet medications. But he still wanted to call in EMS."

"Thank you, God, thank you for that. No EMS, okay? No authorities of any kind."

"Well, Blybees, I've run on long enough, time for you to eat something."

I am starved, but the thought of eating makes me sick. Even wonderful food, and curried lentils do not qualify as wonderful food. I push a hard chunk of carrot around the plate.

Millie places her hand on top of mine and I know it is time to pay up. I can't stand to go through the whole charade, so I cut right to the chase. "Would it help if I accepted Jesus?"

"What are you talking about?"

"Buddha? Shiva?"

"Are you all right? Do I need to get the penlight or grind my knuckles into your eye socket?"

"Isn't that what this is all about? Personal savior and all that?"

"You mean you think I took you in to convert you?"

"Well, maybe. Partially."

"Blythe, you're my friend."

"But I haven't been a very good one."

"You were busy. Your life took you elsewhere. Your wedding. Oh my gosh, Princess Di couldn't hold a candle to you. I'm sorry. I shouldn't have mentioned that, should I?"

"No, it's fine. The parties were the best part of my marriage and that one was a doozy."

"Blythe, I'm so sorry. When I read that you'd gotten back into catering I knew that you must have been heartbroken and needed to keep yourself busy. I mean, it couldn't have been for the money, not after being married to Trey Dix the Third."

"Oh, certainly not for the money."

"The affairs you hosted at Pemberton Palace sounded like something out of the Gilded Age. I'm certain you raised a fortune for all those causes, the museum, the new library, Reading Is Fundamental, the Ballet Guild."

I dip my head and appear modest. I'm not. I am biting my tongue so I won't blurt out that almost the only thing raised by any of my parties was my social standing. After you fly in Donatella Versace or some other name and pay for a room at the Four Seasons, a few dozen replenishments of the minibar, and rotating teams of well-endowed "masseurs," there is never much left over for the museum or ballet. "So you went to divinity school and became a minister?"

"Well, seminary, actually."

"What flavor?"

"Episcopalian."

"What made you . . . Why did you . . . Why are you laughing?"

"Nothing. It's just funny to see you so hesitant and awkward."

"Well, the priesthood or whatever, it's—"

"Weird?"

"I wasn't going to say 'weird.'"

"Just think it, right?"

Yes. "No, no. Not at all."

"Back when I was in seminary and people asked why I was going, it usually really meant either, 'Hmmm, I didn't know you were a religious nut' or, 'I guess this means that you're the person who has to help me through my existential crisis and tell me why I'm on earth.'"

"That's not it at all." *That is it exactly. And, P.S., Millie, tell me why I'm on earth.*

"Then they would expect me to argue them into believing while they held me responsible for the Inquisition and Jerry Falwell and priests and altar boys and everything else Christianity has ever done."

"How does this work? Are you affiliated with some church?"

"No, I was never ordained."

"Is that like going through medical school but not getting your license?"

"Kind of. I can't practice religion in any of the fifty states."

"Really?"

"Blybees, can't you tell when I'm kidding? But it's sort of the truth."

"So why weren't you ordained?"

"Like I said, rhetorical skills lacking. Stage fright. Can't be a preacher if you can't preach. Funny, I was just talking to Sanjeev about this—"

Again with the Sanjeev?

"—and he told me something his father taught him. Which is that, essentially, a life of faith is a life of service. Sanjeev says that ordination or no ordination that's exactly what I'm doing now. Ah well, can you trust a man in a shower cap?" She abruptly switches the subject. "Was the breakup really hard?" Millie winces sympathetically. "You don't have to talk about it if you don't want to."

Her concern makes me aware of how long it has been since anyone cared. How long I've been on my own, struggling to keep my head above water. Even, actually especially, with Trey; once his mother turned on me, I felt as if I were flailing about in a shark tank with the fins circling closer.

"How did you two meet?"

"At Trey's youngest brother's wedding. I was the photographer."

"Of course! That's great. You actually used your photography degree."

"I should have been in pharmacology learning how to sedate hysterical brides or in psychology picking up tips on getting them to accept the reality that just because this is the veryveryvery most special day of their whole entire lives does not mean that they're going to magically appear twenty pounds lighter in their photographs. Thank God for the diffusion filter."

"What's that?"

"It's God's special gift to women that makes it appear as if they were photographed in a steam bath. No crow's-feet, laugh lines, complexion irregularities, mouths, noses, or ethnic identity. For some reason, most of my subjects wanted to look like Casper the Friendly Ghost. Just two heavily outlined and mascaraed black holes in a sheet of white. Of course, that can all be Photoshopped now."

I had forgotten how great Millie's laugh was. How wonderful it was to have her listen with such rapt attention. We'd fit together this way from the first moment I walked into the room. I never had any illusions about my need for an audience. A need that Millie filled with unconditional and deeply misguided adoration. I assumed she did it partly because she was cringingly grateful that I hadn't taken one look at her jumbo bulk and immediately demanded to be assigned another roommate.

"You were always so fearless."

"Bankruptcy will do that to a person. Besides, wedding photography turned out to have a lot of hidden benefits." Like providing the perfect introduction to the anthropology of Austin society. From behind the protection of the lens, I learned names, net worth, whom to suck up to, whom to look through. And that is how I knew, when I was hired to help shoot the Withers-Dix union, just how huge a deal it was. Two of the richest, most influential families in not just Texas, but the entire country, coming together. It was a Medici moment. Officially, the bride's colors were lilac and cream, but the actual hue that every molecule of the event was steeped in was green. The kind of dark, saturated green that only marinating in oceans of money for several generations can impart. A green so assumed, so taken for granted, that it falls right out of any visible color spectrum and is perceptible only to those who've inherited the right rods and cones.

"Benefits like meeting a husband," Millie says with a look of suppressed delight, as if I'd just gotten off a very good but very naughty one.

"Actually, I only got the gig because my former mother-in-law—"

"Peggy Biggs-Dix," Millie blurts out like a child anticipating a favorite part of a bedtime story. "Wife of Henry Dix the Second, son of Henry Dix, nicknamed Uno, who was a wildcatter from Oklahoma who went bust, then made a fortune servicing the industry. Pipelines, right? I think I still have that issue of *Texas Monthly*."

"Yeah. They started with pipelines and now the family has tentacles in every sheikhdom and caliphate where a dinosaur ever died."

"Didn't the article allude to some friction between Uno and his son Junior?"

"Henry 'Junior' Dix the Second." I recall Trey's quiet, detached father. He had been a giant disappointment to Trey's grandfather Uno, whose swaggering braggadocio and questionable business practices stood out even in the bare-knuckled, boomtown oil bidness. Peggy, a connoisseur of humiliation, especially her husband's, loved to tell the story of how Uno would summon his shy, bookish son out to the patio, order Trey's father to stand in the sun, then yell out, "Well, by damn! The little turd *does* cast a shadow!"

"Uno and Junior were very different people" is all I tell Millie.

No need to go into what a relief it must've been to Junior when his father packed him off to boarding school at the age of ten. The next time Uno clapped eyes on his son, Junior had a law degree from Harvard and a hoity-toity wife from a fancy Boston family who rode him like a Shetland pony. Apparently, Peggy Biggs came with tons of class but no cash. She was the one who maneuvered her husband's rise from, essentially, a clerk in the company's sleepy legal division into the largest shareholder in the thirteenth largest privately held energy consortium in the country.

"What is Peggy like?"

"Ah, my former mother-in-law."

Peggy is so far outside of Millie's circle of goodness and light that she would never understand how certain extremely wealthy women believe that their money somehow entitles them to everyone else's as well. It isn't a logical calculation, but through force of will and access to a Rolodex that included every captain of industry as well as most of their generals and foot soldiers, Peggy somehow made it work. Driven by ambition and using family ties to every administration since Warren G. Harding's, Peggy orchestrated the favor peddling and power grabs that transformed Junior from trembling nonentity into golfing buddy to presidents and the executive hit man who convinced his board of directors that his father was a few barrels short of a gusher and had to be removed.

"Uno's dying words to the world were 'Stop her. For God's sake, stop that evil bitch.' She ruined my life. She forced Trey to divorce me."

"Forced him? Like at gunpoint?"

"No, not at gunpoint." If Millie possessed a single sarcastic bone in her body, her comment would insult me. But she is so literal and innocent that I learned early on to treat her like a visitor from another planet. So I patiently explain, "Peggy would have cut off his money."

"Oh."

A normal person would have then asked, *Didn't your husband have any money of his own?* or *Why didn't Trey just refuse and the two of you live in poverty?* Since Millie is not normal and just wants to hear a fairy tale, I don't have to answer *No,* and *I don't know.*

"Okay, back to the wedding. Tell me about how you and Trey met." Millie snuggles in, ready for more bedtime story.

"Right. The wedding. Peggy insisted on flying in this big-name photographer Chip Pinkley." Chip Pinkley was a Back East society photographer who had documented every high WASP wedding for the past several decades. Even out on the Texas frontier, full WASP credentialing was essential to Peggy.

"Anyway, Chip needed a helper and I was hired. All I was supposed to do was hand him cameras, change film, check that no little ring bearer had his finger up his nose. Stuff like that. Easy breezy. But then the legend appeared. Riding one of those motorized scooters that immediately got bogged down in the grass, and it became apparent that I was going to be immortalizing the merger all by myself."

"Well, they were lucky they had you, that's all I can say."

I shrug in agreement, remembering how, once Chip had settled in to document the afternoon light glancing off a patch of lichen, I'd had to rush around covering all the photographic bases from shots of the bride primping to the exchange of vows. Then I'd attempted to herd the families together to start the his, hers, and ours series. The scampish Dix boys, however, proved impossible to herd. "Anyway, that's where I met Trey. He was actually very nice. He tried to help me."

All I knew about Trey that afternoon was that he was the oldest of the Dix boys and something of a black sheep. After playing Margaret Dumont to the Dix boys' Marx Brothers for far too long, I was on the verge of chucking one of Chip's precious, prewar Leicas at them when Trey broke away from his fellow bad-boy brothers and asked me, "Could we have a word, Slim?" He put his arm around my shoulder, winked at his grinning brothers, and dragged me aside for a private huddle. Trey glowed with an anarchistic sense of mischief. The instant he embraced me, it was as if I'd been admitted to a charmed world where Trey and I were just a couple of bad kids, *fun* kids, mocking the pretenses and stuffiness of the grown-up squares around us.

"What did you notice about him first?" Millie asks.

"He smelled great. Like clean laundry and single-malt scotch. I've never met a man before or since who smelled better."

That was true. As far as it went. I doubt I could explain it to Millie, but what made Trey smell so good was what was missing: the stink of worry. Worry was not, had never been, part of Trey's world. Worry about anything: money, health, his future, the future of the world, feelings of others. Trey did not exude the slightest tang of worry. I snuffled up to him and sucked in the first worry-free oxygen to fill my lungs since the Internet bubble popped and the original incarnation of Wretched Xcess went Chapter 11. In fact, the moment before Trey Dix the Third put his arm around me, drawing me into his world, my major concern had been how many Cape Cod Crab Dabs I could stuff into the camera bag so I'd have something to eat the next day.

I fast-forward to our marriage and recall the utter bliss of floating on the warm ocean of Trey's love and petrodollars. I felt so safe, so protected, so taken care of. Maybe safety, protection, and being taken care of are questionable reasons to fall in love with someone. But didn't just those exact mate-seeking qualities help our Neanderthal foremothers ward off a lot of saber-toothed tigers, thereby ensuring the perpetuation of the species? Didn't they put a lot of mastodon meat in the pot? I sigh heavily.

"Is this too painful for you?" I shake my head no, and Millie asks, "What else did you like about him?"

"In a totally sophomoric, completely juvenile way, he was funny. He made me laugh."

"It may not be immediately apparent, but Sanjeev is quite funny."

"Okay."

"What happened next?"

"While I was trying to get him and his brothers together for a shot Trey started yelling like he's trying to argue me out of making him take his clothes off." I do my version of Trey's West Texas accent, "'No, Slim, no! I do not do nudity! Absolutely not! No matter how you threaten me, I will *not* pull my penis out and stick it in my mother's ear! No. That's final. What?! You're insisting, *insisting*, on a full moon over Miami? Well, I guess, if you say it's the one essential shot the bride is going to want in her keepsake album, who are we to argue? Right, guys?' And that was how I got the now-famous shot of all five Dix boys' asses lined up next to their mother's head."

It was all there in the photos I snapped that day. Peggy seated with her five roistering sons formed up beside her like Praetorian guards. Henry Dix the Second, the pale paterfamilias, conduit of the gushers of oil and gas money—diversified now into an international portfolio of collateral interests—that fueled the rollicking crew, standing off to one side, his thin lips hitched upward in a smile as fixed and distant as the Mona Lisa's.

In the first shot, Trey leans toward his mother pressing his thumb against one nostril and pretends to empty the contents of the other onto her head. In the next, he is making bunny ears behind her pewter-haired head. Then all the Dix boys assume gangsta poses, arms crossed over their white-boy chests, fingers poked out throwing gang signs. I even caught the moment when, without so much as shifting in her seat, Peggy reached around and walloped Trey with a surprise backhand that momentarily knocked the grin off his face. It wasn't Hyannis Port, but the pack of Dix boys did have a Kennedyesque aura of family solidarity, a clannishness that would protect those within its embrace no matter what crimes they committed. And Trey, as infantile as he might have seemed, somehow made the low jinks a present to me. With his winks and flirtatious gun fingers he seemed to be saying, *This is for you, baby. I'm making a total ass out of myself just for you.*

"Was he cute?" Millie asks.

Was he cute? I remember the way Trey was that day, a day as blissful and bubbly as the Veuve Clicquot he kept whipping off of passing trays and thrusting into my hand. By the fourth flute, Trey had taken command of the camera and was focusing on the bride and her attendants and I was focusing on how Trey's curly hair fizzed into golden ringlets in the dense Austin humidity and the way his broad shoulders filled out a tuxedo. Then the jacket came off and I noted some impeccable pec definition and had to wonder if there was anything lovelier than a fine-looking, fun-loving Texas man on a warm spring afternoon. And the answer had to be: *Yes, one with a monstrous family fortune.*

"Yes," I tell Millie. "He was cute."

Smell the Dividend
Tax Cuts

I SIGH. Thinking about Trey reminds me why I swore off introspection. Reflexively, I reach for the Code Warrior cup and try to drizzle out a drop or two. It is gone, really gone. And that makes me nervous. *Man with the Golden Arm* nervous.

Millie pushes the plate of vegan atrocities toward me. "Think you can eat a little bit more? Gotta get you healthy again."

Energized by anxiety, I sit up. "Health, I'm so glad you mentioned that. I don't like to talk about this, Millie, but if you must know, I'm on medication. For seizures. Both grand and petit mal. And I left my pills back where I was staying temporarily and I really, really need them." I pray that Bamsie hasn't cleared out my entire stash. Certainly the Baggies and bottles secreted in the empty Blue Bell cookies 'n cream container hidden in my freezer will still be safe.

"You want me to ride along with you to get them?"

"Actually, besides being out of gas, I probably shouldn't be driving around in the little van."

Millie's eyes crinkle to signal that she is onto my naughtiness. "You let your safety sticker expire!"

I shrug, enjoying the momentary sensation of being the scrupulous sort of person who'd be bothered by an expired safety sticker as opposed to the type who hasn't given a second thought to hurling a meat slicer from a moving vehicle into the path of oncoming cyclists.

"Don't worry. I can take you. It's on my route."

I check the clock. Perfect. It's time for the Platinum Longhorns' monthly meeting, which means that the pertinent parts of Pee Heights will be deserted and my landlady, Bamsie Beiver, will not be on the premises. I have no idea what this "route" Millie is talking about consists of, but I don't quibble. "Millie, that would be great!"

Once outside, however, my enthusiasm dims when I behold Millie's means of conveyance.

"What is it?"

Millie beams with pride. "A tandem recumbent bike. Sanjeev designed it and we built it together."

It is a Frankenstein creation welded together with parts cannibalized from other bikes and—judging from its weight—lead pipes and black hole antimatter. As we pedal down Twenty-fourth Street, Millie sits upright in back controlling brakes and steering. I'm in the reclining front seat, lying back far enough that I could be ready for that elusive pelvic exam. A lime green helmet squashes my head, my face is at the level of passing cars' exhaust pipes, a bright red flag snaps jauntily on a whippy fishing pole thing high above my head, and a sticker on the back announces to the world that RECUMBENT BIKERS DO IT LYING DOWN!! It is not possible to be any dorkier. I occupy the molten hot core of all dorkdom.

Snazzy coeds in tiny, fashion-forward, organ-grinder-monkey jackets gape in pity at me, *me*, whom *bRAVADO* magazine had once christened "Fashionista Queen of Austin's See and Be Seens." Frat boys decorating for some spring bacchanal hoot, yell obscenities, and pantomime copulation. Millie gives a friendly wave in return. I try but cannot compact myself any further or slink any lower.

We cross Lamar, then over the bridge above Shoal Creek. A pack of happy mutts romps about in the leash-free zone of Pease Park below the bridge. Millie yells down to me, "Isn't it great to be consuming calories instead of fossil fuel? To be out here, exposed to the elements, the wind whipping in our faces?"

Since the wind is currently whipping the stench of dog crap into my face, I don't answer. As we chug past the park, then up the hill into Pee Heights, I am drenched in yearning for my paradise lost. I yearn for these pristine streets so blissfully devoid of human life. In Pee Heights the only faces one ever sees outside are brown and bent over leaf blowers. Oh, occasionally you'll spot the odd walker or jogger, invariably female with a support group of other pedophiles marching toward the goal of seven percent total body fat. Male Pembies tend to get their sweating over with before dawn so they can shower, scram to the office, and start clocking the billables, churning the accounts, and clipping the coupons.

Human interaction in my old neighborhood is pretty much handled via the seasonal banner. Mother's Day seems to be the current motif. Banners with tender daffodils bursting forth and mother cats licking kitties flap from the occasional rebel front porch where they haven't been banned by interior designers. I love the banner interaction, so like e-mail with its unspoken message: *I'm a friendly, welcoming people person. Just don't ever actually show the hell up in the flesh and we'll all be fine!*

Here, amid the stately homes, the banners, the blessed Day After silence, I can breathe again. West Campus, with its hurly-burly of humanity, teeming masses clogging the sidewalks, students actually walking places, is Calcutta—oh, excuse me, *Kolkata*—in comparison.

"Turn here," I yell to Millie. I put on giant, identity-hiding sunglasses that cover most of my face. As we approach Bamsie's house, I strain my vision making certain that her Land Rover is not parked in the long driveway that circles back to the carriage house.

Once I ascertain that the driveway is empty, I bellow out, "Rudder left!" We turn sharply and are almost to the carriage house before I spy an IRS seizure notice posted on the front door.

Can't have Millie seeing that.

"Wrong turn!" I reach behind my head, grab the handlebars, and jerk hard, causing the bike to run aground and chew through a wide swath of Bamsie's xeriscaping.

"Blythe!" Millie screams as we come to a halt on the mauled greenery.

Hoping Millie will blame the petit mal thing for my eccentric behavior, I shudder spasmodically. "Sorry. We should go around the other way." *The way that doesn't involve Millie spotting that seizure notice.*

We circle back and end up hidden in a luxuriant patch of foliage. I am just about to dart into my hovel, when who should drive up to the front of the house but Bamsie Beiver.

Bamsie jumps out of the Land Rover and I am struck again by how much she looks like a very cute troll doll. Short and springy, Bamsie does everything she can to fight genetics by straightening her curly hair and wearing ridiculously high heels in order to look as much like her idol and best friend—tall, lean, blond Kippie Lee— as she can.

"Crescensio! Crescensio!" Bamsie shrieks for the gardener required to tend the xeriscape shrubbery whose main recommendation is that it requires no tending. Crescensio rushes over.

When it becomes clear that autopsies are going to be performed on every crushed leaf and blade, I ask Millie, "Do you know what would be just sososo ministerial of you?"

"What?" Millie answers.

"It would be just incredibly great if you would sort of scamper over to the little house and slither in the bathroom window that you break out with this rock. Then—"

Millie does not take the rock I try to hand her. "Why do I have to break into your house?"

"Okay, okay, I didn't want to tell you this, but there's really no choice. The IRS is after me because"—*sticky, sticky, sticky; must call this one perfectly; fit the crime to the judge*—"because of my anti-war activities."

"No!"

Bingo. Not just a victim. A martyr. What liberal could resist?

"Yes. If you don't believe me, go look on the front door. They've posted a seizure notice."

"That's horrible."

"Well, certainly inconvenient," I say debonairly. Not just a

martyr. A martyr with style. "Only because of the"—I clench
everything that will clench and grip my forehead—"seizures. So, if
you could just . . ." I hand her the rock. "The bathroom window?"

"Why can't I use the front door?"

"Well, you can except for her." I point to Bamsie, who, fortunately, is still completely absorbed in berating the gardener. "The
IRS has suborned all the rich neighbors. They're on guard. Ready to
turn me in. I can't let them spot us."

Good little liberal that she is, always up for a spot of class warfare, Comrade Millie's lips quiver, then set into a firm storm-the-
Bastille line. She narrows her eyes and asks, "What do you need?"

"Actually, if you could pretty much bring me the entire contents
of the medicine cabinet?" Millie nods and steps away. I call after her,
"And the freezer? With particular attention to any Russian potato
elixirs you might find there? And, and, and the carton of cookies 'n
cream. I am, literally, addicted to cookies 'n cream ice cream."

Millie creeps away and my depleted cells cartwheel, form pyra-
mids, and toss one another into the air for joy. Then all the joyous
frolics cease. What noise, what crack of twig, rustle of pebble,
alerts her, I do not know, but Bamsie whips around so swiftly I don't
have time to duck out of sight. She whips out her Nokia and
punches in numbers. No doubt Agent Jenkins deputized every
woman at Kippie Lee's garden party. Everything now depends on
Millie accomplishing the mission with shock-and-awe swiftness.

Unfortunately, a quick glance in her direction reveals that Millie
is not up to the task. She stands outside the bathroom, tapping at
the window with the big rock, unable to commit even the pettiest
of misdemeanors. I calculate time needed to break and enter, loot
cabinet and freezer, and wriggle back out before the agent shows
up. Rank amateur that she is, Millie will never make it. Now that
my cover is blown, there is no reason for me not to take over. I dash
to her side, seize the rock, and am about to bash in the window
when I hear the bang of a cheap, domestic car door being shut.
Agent Jenkins piles out of the Ford Focus.

"I'm feeling a lot better," I say, hauling Millie back to the bike. When she hesitates, I shove her onto the passenger seat up front.

"But your seizure medication?"

"Another time!"

Blasting out of Bamsie's driveway, we catch the agent unawares and roar right past him.

"More coal," I yell to Millie. "Pedal faster."

"This isn't safe. You're going too fast!"

In the bike's rearview mirror, I watch the agent's small car increase in size as it gains on us.

"Ramming speed." My heart banging against my rib cage, I stand on the pedals and pump for all I am worth. The agent continues to gain on us. I have nothing left to give. My lungs are on fire and my legs have turned to wood. It is hopeless. Then an instance of divine intervention: A hill, a long, steep hill, appears. Gravity, what a marvel it is. The heavy bike shoots down the hill like a luge sled at Innsbruck.

"Brakes, Blythe! Use the *brakes!*"

Still the agent bears down. The road dead-ends straight ahead.

"Hang on."

"Blythe! Turn! Turn, you—!" Millie's first-ever verbalization of truly vile cursing ends with a tooth-loosening scream as I pilot us straight into the curb designed to prevent wheeled access to the park.

Ooomph.

And we have liftoff.

I cannot imagine that the landing does any more for Millie's spine than it does for mine. The Hummeresque tank of a bike, however, doesn't miss a beat, and we tear overland, plowing though the park like a runaway locomotive. I glance behind to see the agent in his car, marooned on the far side of the curb, and I thank God for Sanjeev's Industrial Revolution–quality construction.

"The creek!" Millie screams.

I spin back around to find Shoal Creek looming dead ahead and grip the hand brakes until tendons pop. The wheels stop turning, but the bike, now a cast-iron toboggan hurtling downhill, only picks up speed. My admiration for Sanjeev dims.

"Lean," I order, and Millie, a perfect little luger, heaves to the left just enough to tip us onto the trail, shooting a dramatic rooster-tail spray of rocks and rubble into the creek below. The brakes grab and hold the instant we are on flat ground and no longer need them to avert death.

"Well, that was invigorating."

Millie slowly faces me. If we had been in a cartoon, pinwheels and symbols from the top of the keyboard would have been flying out of her mouth. Since she is a well-brought-up Southern girl and Christian to boot, she gasps eloquently, squeezes her eyes shut, and shakes her head. Hoping to put this unfortunate incident behind us, I pedal on.

A second later, we are in the leash-free zone of Dog Crap Lane. Happy pooches, the usual Animal Defense League rescue assortment—knobby greyhound, three-legged black Lab, black-tongued chow, misunderstood pit bull, several genetic experiments gone horribly awry—romp about. The jolly band catches one glimpse of the Dorkocycle and merges instantaneously into a murderous, slavering pack. Millie's terror-whitened face is at eye level with the blood-crazed curs' fangs.

Female owners shout frenzied high-pitched commands at the killer canines. "No, Xena! Bad girl!" "Martina! Billie Jean! Get back here!"

The dogs hear only high-pitched frenzy and interpret their mistresses' commands to mean *Death to the invaders! Yes! By my insane and pointless shrieking you know that I am as alarmed and outraged as you are! Kill the terrifying two-headed, four-legged, red-tailed invader! Kill! Kill! And kill again!*

I put on a massive burst of speed and leave the ravening pack in a spatter of their own doggy doo. The instant we are out of reach of the pit bull's orca array of teeth, Millie loosens her death grip on the side handles, snakes one hand up, clamps on the brakes, and brings us to a shrieking stop. She jumps up, trembling with something that I pray is not fury. My prayers go unanswered.

"You are crazy. You are a lunatic. You have been lying to me. Lying about everything. I didn't want to believe all that stuff Juniper has been saying about you—"

"Juniper! I can answer every charge. Juniper is clearly—"

"Shut up."

I do simply from the novelty of hearing such an order hurled from Millie's soft, pink lips.

"I didn't want to believe that you have really changed so much. That you really are a bad person—"

"'Bad person'? What about casting the first stone?"

"Shut. Up. If you say one more word, I'm leaving you here."

I glance around. "Here" turns out to be the end of the trail in so many ways. The rocky path comes to an abrupt halt at the foot of a rubble-strewn incline. A wisp of smoke draws my eye up to the wooded area above. Through a screen of brush and scrubby trees, I make out the orange patches of a nylon tent, the silver flash of a shopping cart, the slink of a dog tethered to a rope settling itself onto bare ground. Only gradually do several figures camouflaged by whiskers and dirt emerge. I can barely make out the hill phantoms as they shift around, poking at the thin fire, eating from a can, sleeping beneath a compost heap of old blankets.

"Here" is a hobo camp and I am one crucial conversation away from being abandoned to its tender mercies. I shut my mouth.

"I didn't want to believe what Juniper has been saying. That you cheated her and Sergio, Olga, and Doug out of their wages. That you are a drug abuser. That you left half a dozen women unconscious at your last party. That you put Crisco in the pâté."

"This all sounds so much worse than it actually—"

Millie silences me with one finger pointed up to an avenging God. "Blythe Young, you are not the person I once knew."

Well, duh.

"What happened? What happened to the person I used to know?"

As the bums above press their lips to forties of Colt 45, I fish for an answer but only come up with "Life."

"Life happens to all of us if we're lucky enough. It's what you do with it that counts. The choices you make."

"Yeah, but for some of us the *choice* of having housemates, of sharing a bathroom, of eating *Boca Burgers*"—the full range of Seneca House horrors presents itself—"in our midthirties is just not a viable option."

"There are worse things. Like lying, cheating, drugging—"

"Unless you have been dragged through the mud in a divorce court, you will never know what things a person has to do just to survive." Not that I ever made it to divorce court. Peggy's cursed prenup foreclosed even that option, but this is not the time for such technicalities.

"When does a person ever 'have' to drug people?"

"Could I just say, Millie, that however you've managed to maintain all your ethical proprieties, however you've been able to remain a moral colossus in a world where most of the breaks are handed out at birth, whatever accommodations you've made, they simply are not in my repertoire."

"I am no 'moral colossus.'"

"Maybe not. Maybe you just had normal, caring parents who sheltered you and provided for you instead of an MIA mother who threw you to the wolves."

"I guess you think that makes you a victim of circumstance."

"And you think I'm not?"

"I believe that God always gives us a way to act on our free will."

"Free will? *That's* an expensive illusion. Jesus, Millie, wake up and smell the dividend tax cuts. The game is so rigged in favor of the rich that any 'cheating' the rest of us do doesn't come close to evening up the odds."

Millie shakes her head in a sad, love-the-sinner, hate-the-sin sort of way that creeps me out.

"What do you want me to say?"

"I don't know. You're so different now. It would help to know why."

"What's the point?"

"To see if you're redeemable."

"Redeemable? That is unbelievably insulting. You should be worried about redeeming Tree-Tree Dix and his whole family. Or those rich bitches in Pemberton Heights who stop payment on checks I need to live on. Or . . . what are you doing?"

Millie is turning the bike around.

The smell of unwashed bodies, Sterno, and despair wafts down. No matter how Tough Love she pretends to be, I am certain Millie will never abandon me. Certain. Millie thrusts her foot down on the pedal and starts the contraption rolling.

Millie is leaving.

Leaving me here on Dog Crap Lane. It is a such a nightmare moment, so much the worst thing I can imagine, that I can't make myself believe it is happening. Suddenly all the hoboes lurking in the hill above coalesce into an army of depraved lechers ready to pounce upon me. They stare down with hungry eyes. I try to move, to run after Millie, but, just as in a horrible dream, I remain frozen.

One of the bums calls down in a malt-liquor-slurred voice, "Hey! Miss Millie! Where are you going?"

"I'll be back later, Curtis!" Millie yells back at the bum. "Alone!"

I unfreeze and run after the bike disappearing from view. Fortunately, the trail is a rutted mess. I catch Millie easily and make her stop. "You weren't going to leave me there? Were you?"

The preferred answer would have been a mischievous laugh at this naughty prank. Instead, Millie pierces me with a damning glance and I settle for hopping back onto the front seat. Before she can protest, the hellhounds of Dog Crap Lane set upon us, and our attention turns to protecting major arteries and favorite limbs.

At the intersection of Lamar and Twenty-fourth, we wait for the light to change. I almost ask Millie outright if I can stay a few more days. In the end I decide not to risk it. I'll just have to leech on to her for as long as she will tolerate it. The rule at Seneca House is that guests can stay as long as a resident wants them to stay. The light changes and we huff up the long, steep hill at Twenty-fourth.

It is a lot harder going back up than it was coming down. And a *whole* lot less fun.

Gravity Lost Its Hold

Over the next ten days, I slump into a lethargy of a profundity known only to French existential philosophers and tweakers after the meth lab has been busted. I haunt the house like a ghost wanting to converse with the other residents just slightly less than they want to converse with me. Most of our interactions consist of them yelling at me through the bathroom door, since the single solitary place where my body doesn't feel as if it were made of garden mulch and wire twisties is fully submerged in the big claw-footed tub in the downstairs bathroom.

Which is where I am when I recall how my problems with Peggy Biggs-Dix all started. After Trey and I met at the wedding, we kept bumping into each other at different events I'd been hired to photograph. These meetings invariably ended up with us making out in various cloakrooms, boathouses, and one particularly memorable rendezvous in a billiards room that left me festooned with a necklace of hickeys and an invitation. "Slim," Trey broke suction long enough to ask. "We've got to stop meeting like this. Wanna come to the cabin next week?"

"The cabin" turned out to be a beach estate situated on the only privately held parcel of land on Padre Island National Seashore. Trey flew us down in his private plane. The whole mob was there, all "the bros," wives, girlfriends, offspring, an assortment of attractive cousins, their attractive dates, and a drooling pack of golden retrievers forever dropping slobbery tennis balls on my foot. It was a hectic and energetic crew, with most of the tumult rotating around Peggy. I was worried about what she would think of her son dating someone who'd worked for her. But Trey introduced us knowing exactly what his mother's reaction would be: She had absolutely no recollection of having ever set eyes on me.

Trey had trailed dozens of girlfriends through the premises, and Peggy didn't waste valuable reconnaissance time profiling them unless they were "serious." Since I didn't appear to be "serious," she favored me with a smile and a warning, "Don't mind us. We're crazy. If the gossip columnists could see us now. Just regular people."

This illusion of regularness was sustained among the Dix clan through sacramental wearings of old T-shirts and ancient deck shoes patched with duct tape. Apparently, donning a tattered jersey left over from prep school canceled out ownership of private planes and beachfront estates.

Out of this whole cast and crew, I was the only one who found it odd that all the males slept apart from wives and girlfriends in "the bunkhouse." It was explained to me that when they came to "the cabin" the Dix men liked to fart and pee wherever and whenever the urge hit, and that just wouldn't be possible in "mixed company." Somehow this was accepted as a medical need up there with insulin shots.

So, I was quarantined in a harem with the all other non-Y-chromosome cases except for Peggy, who slept in the bunkhouse. That night I learned that Tree-Tree, as his family called him, had received an ultimatum from his mother: *The family needs a lobbyist. A lobbyist needs a wife. Settle down and get married or else.*

The "or else" was being unplugged from the family's financial life-support system.

"And the Chancellor will do it, too," Kayla, the new wife of the youngest brother, assured me. "Whatever the Chancellor wants, the Chancellor gets. They're all scared dickless of her."

"Is she called the Chancellor after Otto von Bismarck, the Iron Chancellor?" I asked.

The other "girls" in the dorm blinked until one of them answered that no one in the Dix family ironed. This was not what you'd call a bookish crowd.

"You do know," Kayla confided, "that Tree-Tree told the Chancellor you crewed with me back at Brown."

"What? No. When did he tell her that?"

"After dinner. She saw the way he was looking at you and started asking questions."

"'Way'? What way?"

"The way that makes the Chancellor wonder about breed lines."

Breed lines? My heart leapt.

"Just thought you should know," the newest Dix told me. "Tree-Tree's not great on giving the whole story."

Something else we have in common.

Our tête-à-tête was interrupted by a panty raid. Dix brothers, male cousins, and friends poured in the windows. Apparently, a major side benefit of the sleeping arrangements was that they conjured up old frat boy memories. This had an invigorating effect on the otherwise unexceptional Dix libido, which tended to lose focus as soon as assignations in boathouses and billiards rooms ended. Tiptoeing past the Chancellor's bedroom door and sneaking out of the house like teenagers seemed to be a big part of the aphrodisiac package.

Trey was at the head of the mob. He swept me off with a piratical fervor, spiriting me away to a secluded patch of beach where we watched feathery clouds scud past a full Texas moon that poured a boulevard of silver across the rippling waves. Double T made up for a certain lack of finesse when, my head nestled on his chest, we studied the vast and starry sky, and he shared his dreams. The Chancellor wanted him to channel his gift for socializing into a career where his talents for schmoozing and boozing would do the Dix family the most good: lobbyist at the Texas state legislature.

"But," Tree-Tree said, accentuating his Texas drawl to comic effect so that the words which followed could be taken as a joke, "I need me a helpmate or the Chancellor won't set me up. Lot of entertaining involved in lobbying. Didn't you say you used to be a caterer?"

I assured Trey that before the bubble burst I had been much more than a mere caterer. I was an event coordinator; I made dreams come true. He liked the sound of that.

That night, back in the girls' bunkhouse, I thought long and hard about how to impress Trey and, far more important, how to impress his mother. Since my success as an event planner had always hinged on tapping into the deepest, most secret aspirations of my clients, I devoted myself to parsing the Dixes.

Early the next morning, certain that I'd broken the Dix family code, I suggested to Trey that we organize a lobster boil on the beach. This involved Dix brothers hopping into their private planes and scrambling to acquire crustaceans and other Hyannis Port–type edibles. The entire clan loved the affair. Eating lobster boiled on a beach took the brothers and Dix père back to their days at East Coast prep schools and affirmed their belief that they were now America's golden family.

After all the shells, cobs, and empty beer bottles had been tossed in the fire, Trey and I snuggled in front of the blaze. As his pyromaniacal brothers stoked the flames to bonfire levels, we basked in the glow of our success. The Chancellor confirmed it with these words to her oldest son: "Well, numb nuts, for once you didn't screw up royally. This one"—she pointed a lobster claw at me, the "rowing friend from Brown"—"just might be a keeper."

Trey wrapped his arm around me possessively while his brothers yelped about PDAs, the public displays of affection frowned upon within the heterophobic family. As the brothers kidded Trey about being a "major horndog," the Chancellor's gaze, like a queen recognizing service to her royal family, fixed on me.

"You don't look like you row," she said in her preemptive foghorn voice.

I tensed my spindly biceps and said, "Been a while since college." My comment, while not an out-and-out lie, did nothing to bring the Chancellor any closer to the truth about my humble, Ivy-free identity.

"Boom Booms!" Trey hollered, changing the subject back to the family's favorite topic: drinking. The bros hustled to start concocting their preferred cocktail, shots of tequila and beer, slammed onto a bar, then chugged in one bubbly, burp-inducing gulp. A piece of driftwood served as the bar. I was crowned Boom Boom Queen for tossing back the most Boom Booms and belching the loudest.

To complete the Kennebunkport-meets-Matamoros beach fantasy, all the brothers expressed their thanks for the lobster fest by throwing me onto a blanket and tossing me skyward. Trampolined up, I soared into the night sky and gravity lost its hold on me. I froze, weightless for one glorious millisecond at the top of the arc, suspended in midair. And took in the enchanted circle below.

Their handsome faces, each smile a triumph of orthodontia, beamed up at me. In the golden glow of fire and friendship, their strong arms rose as they waited to receive me into the family. In that same instant, however, recognition registered on the Chancellor's face. She remembered where she'd seen me before, and it wasn't sculling to victory for the old red and brown. She raised her hands as if she were holding a camera and pretended to press the shutter.

The Iron Chancellor had me frozen in her sights.

Click.

Gravity reclaimed its hold, and the long descent that finally ended at Kippie Lee Teeter's garden party began.

A Simple Majority Vote

ARE YOU PLANNING to come out of there anytime this century?"
Juniper punctuates her testy question by hammering madly on the
bathroom door.

The yelling, then hammering rouse me enough to notice that
my fingers and toes have acquired the kind of wide-wale pruning
that only hours of soaking can produce.

"Could you, please, give me a minute?"

"I've already given you a freaking hour and a half!"

"Well, then, maybe you shouldn't complain so much when I try
to accommodate your schedule."

"Accommodate my schedule? Is that what you call it when
you're splashing around in the middle of the night? Get your ass
out of there!"

I bristle at the unfairness of it all. As if it were my fault that the
turn-of-the-century plumbing sounds like a pod of whales groaning
their songs across the interstellar reaches of the deep blue. I am not
entirely unsympathetic. Who wants to be awakened at three in the
morning by a pod of whales? Still, can't they make this point without hurling invectives?

*Can't they see I'm just trying to make the best of a very, very bad
situation?*

Did I collapse when my hair turned to straw? Chew my frayed
cuticles even further when my face became a dried riverbed? No, I
summoned up the pioneer spirit of the Lone Star State and I made

do. And what is my reward? More hurled invectives. Churlish complaints about using all of the house's hot water. Splenetic grumbling about the ants and cockroaches allegedly drawn by the sugar scrub applied as an emergency remedy to elbows, heels, and knees. Peevish whining about the mayonnaise deep-conditioning treatment clogging the drain.

I think longingly of the entire La Prairie product line moldering on the bathroom shelf back in the carriage house. Though Bamsie has probably confiscated that as well. No doubt, *her* skin is all plump and dewy.

Bam! Bam! Bam!

"I'm coming! I'm coming!"

Juniper bugs her eyes out at me in telegraphed fury as I walk past. My reception from Millie is no more cordial when I enter our room. She is awake and on her bed reading the Bhagavad Gita but says nothing to me when I come in. Ever since our visit to Pee Heights, Millie has frozen me out to the point that she barely looks my way anymore. In fact, I am starting to worry about how long I can hang on at Seneca House. Well, actually, given the house rules, I know I can stay on as a guest indefinitely. What I am not sure of is how long I can stand the waves of disapproval pouring off of Millie.

There is so much you don't, can't, understand. That's what I want to tell Millie. She has been sheltered. She went from living with her parents to living at Seneca House, then a few years in seminary, then back here. She has the best heart in the world. No question about that. But she just doesn't understand how the world works. She couldn't. I'll just have to lie low until Millie's grumpy spell passes.

Then, with a heavy sigh, Millie puts her book aside. "Blythe, we have to talk."

I sit up, fully alert to the breakup/firing/legal action trajectory signaled by the "We have to talk" preamble.

"Some of the residents have voiced concerns."

Ew, "concerns."

"What do you mean? All I've been doing is trying as best I can to recover from the trauma of being targeted by the IRS for my anti-war activities."

"Hmm, yes, well."

A "Hmm, yes, well" from Millie is tantamount to a *You are a lying sack of shit* from anyone else. Time to retire the anti-war scenario.

"In any case, there have been comments."

I try to look contrite as Millie lists the infractions: 3:00 a.m. baths using all the hot water in the house, olive oil cuticle soaks, stockpiling drinking glasses, unproved charges that I am eating residents' personal food and taking their magazines. I slide the copy of *Vogue* borrowed from Olga's mail slot and the empty cup of Doug's yogurt—both of which I fully intend to replace—under the covers and try to appear concerned. It is an acting challenge, since it is virtually impossible to throw an official guest out once he or she is ensconced. I recall Woo Yung, the thoroughly detestable boyfriend of an anthropology major, who lived in the house during the final semester of my first tenure.

Everyone despised Woo Yung. He lay on the couch all day, strewed dirty dishes everywhere, smoked, and stole the money we left for the paperboy. But no one would throw him out. Tolerance. That was and always has been the very cornerstone of this little liberal bastion. I know that I have not even begun to test the limits of that sacred belief. Besides, since Millie is such a moral icon, as long as I shelter beneath her angel wing, I am golden.

"So," I joke-pout. "Are you going to throw me out?"

"*I'm* not going to throw you out, but the house is another story. According to the Woo Yung Rule instituted after you moved out, any guest who stays longer than ten days has to be voted on. The question will be put to the entire house at the next meeting. We will all vote on whether you can stay. Or not. The question will be decided by a simple majority vote with a tie going to the guest. House meetings start at seven o'clock, right after dinner."

"Seven o'clock when?"

"Seven o'clock tomorrow evening. You should probably be there."

An Ocean of Nectar

THE INSTANT the door closes behind Millie, I start calculating my odds. Of the house's fourteen residents, four will definitely vote against me: Juniper, Olga, Sergio, and Doug. My former employees are champing to vote me off not just the island but out of the galaxy as well. Millie wouldn't kick anyone out, so I have her vote. That leaves nine votes that I might be able to sway in my favor. I suddenly regret those cuticle soaks and 3:00 a.m. baths.

From the nine, I eliminate house phantoms Elmootazbellah Kamolvilassitian and Choi Soon Yong. They'll never come to the meeting, since neither one ever gets home before the experimental computer science lab closes at midnight.

I am focus-grouping the remaining seven voters when Yay Bombah and Nazarite drift onto the porch downstairs for their nightly smoke-out. In their blond, white-girl dreadlocks topped with red, gold, and green knit caps and Bob Marley T-shirts, they are the house's official Trustafarians. Yay Bombah's and Nazarite's real names are Ariel and Rachel Saperstein of River Oaks in Houston, rebel daughters of the owner of the insanely lucrative Rent You Some Stuff furniture rental franchise. Though the young heiresses could afford to live anywhere, only Seneca House's utter decrepitude allows them to pretend that they are barely surviving in a Kingston slum.

I am able to complete surveillance on the ganja twins simply by opening Millie's window, directly above the porch. As is their wont of an evening, the rude girls sit in the dark on the porch and Hoover down the elephantine quantities of sinsemilla that only rich parents who love their offspring no matter what can buy. Over the past ten evenings, I have overheard enough of Yay Bombah and Nazarite's conversation to know that they would consider a house meeting so antithetical to their splifforic consciousnesses that they will never attend.

That leaves five voters I have to scrutinize: Lute, Jerome, Presto, Clancy, and Sanjeev. I need to find out everything I can about them in order to slant my plea to the jury to fit their exact demographic.

Lute proves the easiest to decipher. A deliriously handsome boy from Australia with a sleepy toddler's headful of blond ringlets, Lute favors snap-button Western shirts several sizes too small and vintage cowboy boots. I am able to gather an extensive dossier on him without ever leaving Millie's room. Sitting on my bed, I can hear quite clearly every lyric of every song Lute sings. For the first time since my arrival, I actually listen to them and learn how he feels about Operation Iraqi Freedom (against), honesty (for), girls who suck his soul dry (against), understanding the pain that a pretty face hides (for). Sincerity, the kind of sincerity that only the really good-looking have the luxury of maintaining, is the key to Lute.

Next on my list is Lute's buddy, twitchy, cantankerous Jerome, a perpetual graduate student currently writing a thesis based on a semiotic analysis of the jewelry sported by the rap singer Li'l CheeZ with the working title "Blinging It to Light." I knock on his door.

"Go away!" Jerome bellows.

I jot down "peevish" in my notes. "Jerome, hey, it's me, Blythe."

"Who?"

"Blythe Young."

"Never heard of her."

I note "No preconceptions. Good!" then use the magic name. "I'm Millie's friend."

"Oh you. The freeloading bitch who uses all the hot water?"

"The same!"

The door opens just a crack, but a crack is all I need.

"Yeah?" Jerome snarls. He is a shaggy, baggy sort of guy with a muffler wound around his neck and bagel crumbs sprinkled in his beard and across the front of his Goodwill, polyester disco shirt.

I scan the room behind him for clues. A quick peek reveals that Jerome is a collector. Stacks of old 33s everywhere, the walls a quilt of album covers with a special fondness for blaxploitation: Isaac Hayes; George Clinton; Earth, Wind & Fire. Every horizontal surface is covered with Burger King bobblehead giveaways, Scooby Doo lunch boxes, Mexican wrestling masks, and coffee mugs with dopey sayings on them like YOU DON'T HAVE TO BE CRAZY TO WORK HERE. BUT IT HELPS!

Clearly, the key to Jerome is irony, the favorite luxury of the impoverished young intellectual.

"What?" Jerome demands.

"Uh, wrong room. Sorry." He slams the door in my face. This is fine, since I have already gotten a pretty good read on him. I gather the rest of my research on Jerome and Lute sitting in Millie's room, where I can clearly hear the two argue about what to call the theoretical band that they theoretically are starting. For reasons known only to males in college, they have chosen to name the group in honor of a certain IHOP breakfast special that somehow figures prominently in their personal mythologies.

"It *has* to be *the* Fresh and Fruities," Lute insists.

"I am not fucking going to be one of those 'the' bands just because your mother had a crush on *the* Beatles."

"You are such a colossal wanker. Front your own fucking band."

At the thought of depending on his own personal stock of charisma and good looks, Jerome caves. "Okay, but it has to be singular and there have to be two apostrophes. *The* Fresh 'n' Fruity. Apostrophes," Jerome insists, "it's all about the apostrophes."

I pray that this will be enough data to allow me to play Jerome and Lute like the ancient instrument one of them was named for. Enough anyway to get their votes, which, counting Millie's, will bring my total up to three. Presto and Clancy are next. They will be slightly tougher nuts to crack. No time to lose. Back to work.

"What are you doing?"

"Oh, Millie, hey." I yank my deactivated AmEx card out of the doorjamb and stick it deep into my pocket. *Breaking into Presto and Clancy's room to gather intel* does not seem the canny reply. Instead I try "I was just going to say hi to P. and C., but apparently, they're not home."

Lucky for me, Millie is riddled by guilt for wishing that I would be consumed by flesh-eating bacteria. Like most good people, she can only handle hate in small doses before she is driven to overcompensate with niceness. "Oh pish posh," she says, laughing gently as she raps smartly on the door. "They're just quiet."

The door opens a crack. "Howdy, neighbors," Millie says.

I peer through the door at Presto, who has answered, and Clancy, who is lounging on the queen-size futon. Both have carefully tended just-got-out-of-bed hair that stands up in cute licks and swirls. Both wear black-rimmed glasses and Puma running shoes. Presto's are green and gold; Clancy's are red and white. Clancy wears an old bowling shirt with LADONNA stitched on the pocket, a 1970s Casio watch with a giant, black plastic strap, sexy, smudged eyeliner, and spring's new lighter shades for lips. Presto has on a Power Rangers T-shirt, which hugs a broad pair of shoulders, and a Hello Kitty pink vinyl belt. Again, like Jerome, irony. I get that. I get that Clancy and Presto are a couple. What I can't draw a bead on is the sex of either one. This is a handicap, but one I am pretty certain I can work with.

"Would y'all like a little company?" Millie asks.

Presto glances back at Clancy, who gives the tiniest quirk of a plucked eyebrow. "Naw, we're both fried."

"Hard day at work?" I ask. "Or school?"

"Both. Clancy is coordinating an event at Whole Foods tomorrow and I've got a huge one at BookPeople because Irvine Welsh—"

"You're event coordinators?" I exclaim. "You're *both* event coordinators!"

Presto, taken aback by my unaccountable enthusiasm, nods uncertainly.

Event coordinators! Sex is immaterial; Presto and Clancy are my kind of people. I have no doubt I can work them. "I've done some event coordination in my day," I coo to Presto. "Nothing as big as what y'all must do. But enough to know that no one really appreciates how hard it is and what's involved." Both Presto and Clancy turn their full and undivided attention on me.

I certainly do not have to fake admiration when I tell Clancy, "If you are part of the Whole Foods miracle, I worship you. I am in total awe of the team that convinced shoppers that they were saving the planet and their own souls by paying two hundred dollars for a bottle of olive oil."

Clancy looks away modestly and I encourage Presto to tell me everything.

"As I was saying, Irvine Welsh is coming—"

"The *Trainspotting* guy," Clancy explains.

"—so, of course, I want to get a big fishbowl and fill it with syringes."

"Of course you do, my darling! What a perfect way to say, 'This author wrote a book about shooting heroin.' How incredibly creative." Presto melts in the warm glow of my admiration. "I have to witness this. When does this paradigm-shifting event take place?"

"That's the problem," Presto wails, slumping into a beleaguered mass. "It's tomorrow."

I pivot smoothly and walk away. My work is done. There is no way that either Clancy or Presto will be at the house meeting tomorrow. Not with two events to coordinate. Time is short, and I don't have any to waste on nonvoters. I have one person left to research: Sanjeev.

Safe in Millie's company, I go downstairs. We settle on the flophouse sofa and Millie says, "I'm so happy you're finally taking a real interest in the house, in the residents."

"I have always been very interested in the residents."

"That's good, because there's been some talk that you, well, that you aren't really interested in being part of the house. Part of the Seneca community."

"So not true. I am totally interested in being a part of the Seneca community. That's why I want to know everything about everyone. Especially Sanjeev. Tell me all about Sanjeev."

At the mention of his name Millie's cheeks flame scarlet red. She touches them. "This damn blushing. When will I stop blushing like some English maiden from the seventeenth century? It's like having an aquarium for a head with all your thoughts swimming around for the whole world to see."

"So you've got the hots for Sanjeev."

"No!"

"That's the thought I see swimming around."

"Blythe, no, really. What you see is admiration, shared interests. Absolutely nothing more. Ever."

"Okay, fine. No hots, not even a few lukewarms. So tell me about him."

Millie gazes off, and a little smile plays across her lips as she considers how to describe Sanjeev. "I suppose, if I had to choose just one word, it would be 'principled.' But not in a preachy, self-righteous way. More a way of understanding what he believes to be right and doing that whether anyone else ever knows or cares. Like, last night, Sanjeev and I were talking about various House Love assignments and—"

"That new name, House Love, that does not sound wholesome."

"Anyway, since Sanjeev is the labor czar, he makes all the work assignments. But he's so conscientious he's always consulting with me about where I think different people would fit best. So we were talking about putting Lute on recycling even though we both know that Lute is"—Millie whispers—"lazy and won't do any assignment no matter how well fitted it is to his nature. He usually gets one of his girlfriends to do his House Love for him."

"I guess we all use whatever talents we have to serve in our own ways. You were describing Sanjeev."

"Yes, Sanjeev." Millie caresses the name, then goes into tedious detail about her last conversation with him, and I lose track of my mission. Instead of building a dossier so I can sway his vote, I find myself consumed with irritation for Bindi Boy.

This adoration, it used to be mine.

When Millie and I were roommates the first time, I would come home late from dates and she would be waiting up to hear every word. Whenever I had a wild new enthusiasm, Millie would be there dying to get on the bandwagon. If a class critique of my work hadn't been overwhelmingly positive, Millie would be there ready to impugn the professor's sanity and hold my head while I threw up tequila shots. I force myself to tune back in to the over-long recounting of her last conversation with Sanjeev.

"And then he says, 'You Christians seem to outsource your faith. We Hindus don't simply hire someone to perform our good works, then feel as if we've done our part when we toss something in the collection plate every Sunday.' Then I told him that Christians don't feel that way either. Not real ones. And then . . ."

Millie giggles. "And then Sanjeev says, 'Ah, the mythical "real Christians" I'm always hearing about but never meeting.' Kind of an insult, I guess, but pretty funny. So I reminded him that I'm a Christian and you know what he says?"

"No clue."

"He says, 'Yes, but you don't count. You're not like anyone else.' What do you think he meant by that? 'You're not like anyone else, you're a freak'? Or 'You're not like anyone else . . .'"

I know I'm supposed to fill in the blanks with subtle, nuanced interpretations of what Sanjeev might have meant just the way Millie did for me when she spent hours reading the tea leaves on my various heartthrobs, but I can't fake interest. Fortunately, I don't have to. Sanjeev bounds into the living room, and I completely lose Millie's attention.

She lights up with the sort of incandescence that my own appearances used to spark. Sanjeev wears a slate blue Members Only jacket but not ironically. His glossy dark hair is shiny as a choirboy's. He looks a lot better without a shower cap.

Taking a seat in the chair next to the sofa, he tells Millie, "We never finished our discussion about whether or not to assign Lute to recycling."

"Oh, yes, I do have some further thoughts on that."

They barely notice when I stand and motion toward the kitchen. "I've got to go slit my wrists."

"Okay," Millie chirps, never taking her eyes off Sanjeev. "I'll be with you in a minute."

I walk around the corner into the dining room to see what clues about Sanjeev I can pick up from eavesdropping on their conversation.

"You know," Millie starts off, "before we turn our attention to Lute and the recycling, I want to say that after our discussion yesterday, I dug out my old comparative religion textbook and did a bit of research on Hinduism and have concluded that we're all just trying to understand Brahman and achieve moksha in our own way."

"Oh, Millie, not you too." Sanjeev's Hindo-Brit accent usually makes everything he says sound both incredibly smart and incredibly chipper. But when he says, "Oh, Millie, not you too," he sounds sad. Sad and disappointed.

"Not me too what? I'm just saying that Hinduism and Christianity aren't that different."

"And you mean that as a compliment."

"Of course."

"You don't mean it to be patronizing and condescending to a religion that had developed a highly sophisticated theology while your lot were still painting yourselves blue."

"Sanjeev, that is the last thing I would ever intend."

"Of course. It's just that I'm so tired of all the other ones, all those cheerful Christians saturated in what they believe to be tolerance and goodwill who think they are bestowing some sort of gift by perceiving similarities between their enlightened twenty-first-century Jesus cult and the poor benighted cow worshippers of the subcontinent."

"That is not at all what I'm saying."

"So tell me," Sanjeev asks. "Beyond moksha and Brahman, what do you *think* you know about Hinduism?"

Uh-oh, the italics Sanjeev whips around "think" worry me. Millie, however, ignores the warning sign and plows right ahead.

"From what I recall when a Hindu sage lectured at seminary, Hindus believe that all religions are the same. That they all lead to the same truth. That there are many different paths, but they all guide us to the same destination."

"Oh, Millie, that is not worthy of you. You, of all people, should know that the path is everything. If you take away angels plucking harps on clouds and seventy-two virgins waiting in paradise, nothing is left *but* the path."

I do not like Sanjeev's tone of exasperation and, frankly, I do not like Sanjeev. It is also pretty clear that he is not as into Millie as Millie is into him. Which really makes me not like him.

Who does he think he is?

"Then explain it to me, Sanjeev. Make me understand."

I zone out as Sanjeev goes on about Hinduism being an "ocean of nectar." About deities with the heads of monkeys and elephants. About blue gods named Kali and Lord Krishna. About a fierce goddess who drank wine and slew the buffalo demon. About mountains of golden marigolds and a festival where believers pelt one another with purple, yellow, and red powder.

"Wow," Millie says, all rapt and crushed out. "Listening to you reminds me of when I was sick with strep throat and my aunt bought me a coloring book that I splashed with plain water and invisible colors magically appeared. It's as if my image of religion had always been just the black-and-white outline and now you've filled it in with color."

None of this is adding up to any big data bonanza for me as far as figuring out how to sway Sanjeev's vote. So, after a quick check to make sure that Sanjeev and Millie are completely occupied paddling around the "ocean of nectar," I zip upstairs for a peek at Sanjeev's room.

It's as if an ops team has scrubbed it for all signs of human life. A bed, twin, neatly made. A nightstand with a goosenecked reading lamp, a glass of water, and a small alarm clock. Is Sanjeev liberal? Conservative? Mammal? Reptile? There are no clues. Not a poster, not a CD, not an ironic T-shirt. The single solitary compass heading I get from Sanjeev's internal landscape is a little altar tucked away in his closet. Burnt sticks of incense poke up in front of many-armed Shiva, the destroyer, Ganesh, elephant-headed remover of obstacles, and a couple others. I have already gleaned, though, that Bindi Boy is awash in subcontinental idol worship, so the altar discovery is not much help. In spite of the incense and blue gods, my greatest fear is that Sanjeev might be a pure datahead. Someone who actually listens to reason.

That would be fatal to my cause. If I have any hope at all of pandering to Sanjeev's baser instincts, I must find out what they are. I am leafing through his Jockey shorts when I hear Sanjeev and Millie coming up the stairs. I slip out of his room. It is time to do something I truly excel at: shopping.

Like Cells in a Body

WE ARE AN INTENTIONAL community here." Juniper is my Torquemada, my Grand Inquisitor, addressing the house meeting on why Seneca House must be cleansed of my heretical presence. She stabs a withering glance in my direction. "We *chose* to live together. *She* is the antithesis of all that we are."

As Juniper enumerates my crimes against humanity, I peer up at the gathered. Per my predictions, Presto and Clancy, the computer phantoms, and the ganja twins, are no-shows. I study the remaining eight residents, my judge and jurors.

Jerome is using the edge of his student ID and thumbnail to pluck ingrown hairs from his weedy beard. Lute is fingering an invisible guitar and working out chord progressions to accompany lyrics he is mouthing to himself. I know I can get these two. My former employees, Doug, Olga, and Sergio, are all sitting together. That is not a voting bloc I want to see. Still, I have some ideas for turning at least one of their votes. Which would mean that with Millie I'd have the four votes I need, since house rules stipulate that a tie goes to the guest.

Of course, I worry about Sanjeev. His dreary insistence upon facts could screw my entire marketing plan. Facts are not my friends. When I tune back in, Juniper is still droning on. "The very cornerstone of our intentional community is that we all ascribe to certain principles. I mean, there are reasons we didn't pledge Kappa Alpha Theta."

Jenna Bush's sorority? Dream effing on!

On the best day of any of their lives, the Kappa Alpha Thetas would never have taken a single one of these losers. The mere mention of UT's premier sorority triggers a delicious memory. During its heyday, Wretched Xcess coordinated the chapter's big anniversary bash. Rather than roach spray and mildew, their house smelled of Jo Malone cologne, lilies, and the estrual funk of a couple dozen synchronized menstrual cycles. A bass note of roast beef coming from the kitchen added a comforting smell of home, of the daddy bucks that nourished every squeal and giggle bubbling through the house. The help, black butlers in white gloves, maids in starched aprons, all moved silently, invisible as Bunraku puppeteers that convention has trained the eye not to see.

Oh, to have partied with Jenna. Oh, to have been a Kappa Alpha Theta legacy with my place in the world assured from birth. Oh, to have been so certain of that place that, well in advance of my twenty-first birthday, I wouldn't slink into a bar and timidly proffer the fake ID. Instead, I would have demanded—demanded!—to be served. And not once but on two separate occasions. How different my life would have been with that level of confidence. That and the media team to back it up.

Sigh.

"Blythe? Blythe?"

Millie's voice breaks into my fantasy.

"Huh? Yes!" I snap to. All eyes are on me.

"Did you want to say a few words?"

I jump to my feet so that the jury can fully soak in my outfit designed to suck up to every tendency—hipster and non—that I have uncovered. I rub a gnarly knit cap against hair that I have prepped with a little baby oil for the very winning not-washed-in-two-weeks look. Next I wind a twelve-foot muffler a bit tighter about my neck, then unbutton my blue polyester Pep Boys short-sleeved shirt with BOB stitched over the pocket to reveal a vintage *Smokey and the Bandit* T-shirt underneath. Finally, I adjust my Hello Kitty stretch bracelet and make sure the fake nose stud I pasted on is still in place. (Amazing what a person can find at Goodwill. Even more amazing what a person can simply put on and walk out wearing without paying for. I consider my shoplifted items to be a loan. One I will pay back with generous interest the moment I am back on my feet.)

Feeling the room warming a bit, I open with an all-purpose, "Mistakes were made. I'm not denying that."

"'Mistakes??'" Juniper sputters. "A 'mistake' is using the wrong fork at dinner. A 'mistake' is not writing your aunt a thank-you note. Not paying your workers and feeding unsuspecting party guests a date rape drug are not 'mistakes.'"

"Point taken," I admit. "Guilty on all charges." There is no way I am going to win by arguing "facts" with Juniper. My one slender hope is visuals, sound bites, hot buttons, and random digressions. I turn to Lute and Jerome and bombard them with an asteroid of a non sequitur: "I have no excuse for my actions except that I just love Daniel Johnston and Roky Erickson so much that I don't know what I'm doing."

Lute and Jerome turn to each other and their mouths drop open in unison.

Eureka!

Daniel J. and Roky are Austin's premier burnout music legends. What could be more authentic, more unquestionably *not* sellout than guys who ended up gobbling Thorazine in Austin State Hospital? And how both heart-meltingly sincere *and* fashion-forward ironic to worship musicians who live in their mom's garage? Did it take a genius to deduce that these cult gods would be Jerome and Lute's idols and points of absolute intersection? Probably.

"Huh? What the hell are you talking about?" Juniper asks, as earnest a little nerd as her favorite candidate of all time, Ralph Nader. "You're not making any sense."

Sense, I have no interest in making sense. I am making points. Big ones, judging by the warm bath of eye contact I am enjoying from both members of THE Fresh 'n' Fruity. As Juniper blathers on about Seneca House being "an interwoven, interdependent community" I evaluate my po sition. I am getting the blatant pandering portion of my program under control. Even better, I catch Sanjeev in an unguarded moment, staring at Millie while her attention is elsewhere. For the first time, I see clearly what I can't believe I missed earlier: Millie's crush on Sanjeev is reciprocated. Adoration beams from his sacred-cow brown eyes as he gazes upon her. It is written on every curry-soaked pore.

This is great. Sanjeev's gaze is googly-eyed enough that I'm pretty sure he will vote me in just to please Millie. This prospect cheers me so much I can barely pay attention to Juniper as she drones on. "You may think that this is just some dumb hippie platitude, but I believe that we are all one. Like cells in a body. And Blythe Young is a cancer."

I sneak a peek at Millie. Surely she will object. She doesn't. In fact, she's giving me a look that actually seems to be judgmental. I didn't think liberals were allowed to do judgmental. Has someone changed the code on me? Panic stabs me with the fear that, like Al Gore, in my rush to be all things to all people, I might have lost my home state.

I run into the kitchen and reappear a moment later with the snacks I'd genetically engineered earlier in the day to appeal to my target constituency: chocolate-chip Rice Krispies Treats. They have retro-dork coolness for the hipsters who can only enjoy food they can laugh at or express political stances through. Plus there is chocolate, which all females require.

Juniper objects to this rank electioneering, but no one can hear her over the plague-of-locusts-level crunching. More and more, Juniper's whiny stridency and appeals to reason are making her seem like someone it would not be fun to have a beer with. And since *Fun to have a beer with?* is the single most important question the American electorate asks, Juniper is currently losing this campaign.

"Anyway, y'all," I snivel. "It's too bad I probably won't be hanging with all y'all anymore, cuz when I was mixing up these Krispies deals, it really made me want to try out some of my fancier recipes. I have this killer crème brûlée I would have loved to do for you. This awesome Chocolate Intemperance. An amazing vindaloo. An incredible meat pie and Vegemite on toast. A veganalicious grilled tofu cutlet with pesto–pumpkin seed sauce. Did I mention the Chocolate Intemperance?" Indian, Australian, vegan, and female, I pander to as many culinary demographics as I can identify.

For a bunch fed on groats and lentils this is crack cocaine. They look up at me with longing so unrestrained it is like staring at eight Homer Simpsons all thinking about doughnuts. Framing. Framing is all. I choose my words carefully, waiting until the last chocolate-drenched Krispie is gone and they are facing a future devoid of succulent goodies before I offer them the veil issue. "Of course, if you want to *let someone else tell you* what you can and cannot eat that's fine. If you want to *give up your freedom to choose,* to control your own bodies, that's cool."

With any luck, I have made a vote for Chocolate Intemperance into a vote for individual rights, for the hearty free-range American pioneer spirit with a little pro-choice tucked in as well. I can feel a consensus building. No, I can *smell* it building and it smells like the Aztecs' gift to me. It smells like cocoa.

"That is *so* not what this meeting is about," Juniper says in a dismissive, high-handed way. High-handed and dismissive, that is good. That is *so* not fun to have a beer with.

Olga wipes chocolate from her hands, then tears up strips of notebook paper. "We are voting now, *da?*"

When, without so much as a glance in my direction, Millie asks, "Blythe, will you wait outside?" I know I am in a new and unforeseen pickle. Anytime the jury won't look you in the eye, the only choice left is top or bottom bunk.

I must take drastic corrective measures. "Y'all," I whimper. "You know what? You don't need to have a secret vote. I've made a lot of mistakes and all I want now is to know how I can be a better person. I just want to learn from y'all. Every single one of all y'all."

What I want to learn is that Millie and Bindi Boy aren't going to bounce my ass back to Dog Crap Lane. There is no way on God's green earth that Millie Ott of Waco, Texas, will ever vote me, Charles Manson, or Idi Amin out if she has to do it to our faces.

Period. Nonnegotiable. Make nice is embedded too deeply in an Old School Texas girl like Millie. Secret ballot, no question, I'm gone. But to my face, never happen.

I have to get the rabble behind an open vote. I need to invoke some Christians/lions bloodlust. I know that, secretly, they all want their very own home version of *Survivor*. They want a gruesome nine-person ego pileup to rubberneck. They just don't want to admit they want it. I have to give them a smoke screen, make them take the veil.

"It will be, like, a learning experience for me to hear what y'all have to say."

Learning experience. What good little liberal can resist a learning experience?

"Hand count for an open vote," Jerome proposes.

Millie and Juniper are the only ones who don't shoot a paw high into the air, fingers waggling greedily.

Juniper surrenders. "Okay, whatever, we'll go around the room. Everyone say how they're voting and, if you want, tell why."

Lute and Jerome are up first. I hum "You're Gonna Miss Me." The boys join in on Roky Erickson's masterwork from the 13th Floor Elevators with a little air guitar and drum work, shrug, and vote me in. Their exit-polling data consist of two words, "Why not?"

Not surprisingly, Juniper gives me a gigando thumbs-down. "Where do I begin?" is all she will say by way of explanation.

As predicted, Olga follows suit, offering the very succinct, "I hate the bitch."

"Sergio?"

With a world-weary shrug Sergio votes against me, citing his own personal life philosophy, "Sometimes you get the elebator, sometimes you get the shaft."

"Doug?"

Not wanting to make this any harder than it has to be for Doug, who did, after all, try to pay me back, I look away and don't turn back until Juniper asks, "Doug, why is your thumb up?"

"It's okay with me if she stays."

"What? This is not what we talked about."

"I know, but I've been where she's at."

"Exactly. And you sold everything you owned, moved into a co-op boardinghouse, and tried to pay everyone back."

"That's me. We all went a little crazy. Got greedy. Everyone handled it differently." Doug keeps his thumb up until Juniper very reluctantly records his vote.

For a moment I am stunned by Doug's magnaminity. And then I want to jump up and down screaming with joy because *I am in!* As soon as Millie, who is next in the batting lineup, votes for me I will have my four votes and I am in. Thank God, Sanjeev isn't the next voter.

Juniper speaks. "As decided in the House Chaplain Open Voting Rule, so as not to sway anyone by force of moral authority, Millie will go last. Sanjeev?"

"What?" I demand. "*Robert's Rules of Order!* Millie is the next voter."

"Can someone shut her up?" Juniper inquires. "Sanjeev?"

I interrupt, "I just have one question before Sanjeev votes."

"What?" Juniper asks, her usual tone of peevishness spiking dangerously.

I ignore her and face Sanjeev. "I am just wondering, Sanjeev, do you hate the Pakistanis as much as I do?"

From the looks that Sanjeev and Millie exchange—exasperated, sad to be proved right—I see that if I ever had any kind of hand, I have just seriously overplayed it.

"That," Sanjeev says, his accent suddenly tilting more toward the England of boarding school canings than his melodious homeland. "That question is exactly what I find so objectionable about *this person*. That is demagoguery of the rankest order and I cannot countenance it. I vote no."

Okay, faulty intelligence. The guy is Gandhi and I missed the diaper. Four against. Three in favor. One vote to go.

I am most definitely in a clinch now, the very place where I once believed myself to be so good. I have to have Millie's vote to stay. I

lock Millie in a gaze of sisterly pleading that speaks of our long history together.

She looks away and says, "In my work, my life, the house has to
come first. Not me, not my friendships, what is best for the house.
Which is why I will have to—"

No! No! No!

"—abstain."

Abstain? Did not see that one coming.

Four want me out. Three want me in. One won't say. Millie
hasn't actually voted me out, but I am gone anyway. I can't speak.
Wind out of the sails. Horse latitudes. Utterly becalmed.

"Yeah, well . . ." Juniper starts to say something, but a morning-
after embarrassment overtakes her and the rest of the group. The
show is over. They look away, stand, and begin to shuffle out.

"Fuck it!" Juniper stops everyone in their tracks. "Shit, I can't
have this on my conscience. If she really doesn't have anyplace else
to go, I change my vote. She can stay."

Huh?

Millie jumps up and wraps her arms around Juniper. "Oh,
Juniper, that is wonderful! Thank you so much." I am baffled, not
only by Juniper changing her vote but by Millie's reaction. She is
genuinely, truly happy. "Blythe, I hope you appreciate Juniper's
incredible generosity."

I nod, too puzzled by Juniper's action, too absorbed in trying to
figure out what her secret agenda might be, to speak.

"Of course," Sanjeev says, "if she is to stay, appropriate boundaries must be set."

"Of course," I croak out. Usually there is only one word I like
less than "appropriate" and that is "boundaries." Normally, both of
them in the same sentence give me cramps. But next to the words
"Sterno" and "hobo," they make me positively ebullient. I will say
anything, do anything, agree to anything, to keep from being
thrown out.

"Of course, there will be penance," Millie says.

I snort a bray of laughter, relieved that even Millie can mock the ridiculous Grand Inquisitorial aspect of this tribunal. She had me worried for a second. *Penance?*

Too late, I notice that no one else is smiling. I stop laughing. I'll have to keep the charade up for a bit longer. "Penance. Yes, of course, I agree."

I am proud of how sincere I sound.

A Fallen Woman

I scrub lasagna pans the size of wading pools encrusted with galvanized soy cheese and lacquered with whole wheat noodles and wonder two things: First, why did NASA ever have heat shield problems when they simply could have shellacked their pods with Juniper's foundry-fired vegan lasagna? Second, and much more troubling, is the question of why I wanted, no, why I *struggled*, to remain at Seneca House. Steam from the lava-hot water frizzes my hair until it resembles the Chore Boy in my hand. My fingers prune in the grease- and skin-dissolving acid-bath detergent. I feel as if I entered and won a contest where first prize is . . . A YEAR ON A CHAIN GANG!

How much worse than a chain gang could life on Dog Crap Lane be?

The answer keeps me scrubbing. It also keeps me sweeping, mopping, washing windows, vacuuming, disinfecting, and all the other "House Love" that Labor Czar Sanjeev piles on. I tried the corner-cutting technique popularized by all your more profitable maid services: Never use water when a swipe of baby oil will coat dirt and microbes much more efficiently. Some of the true waterless wizards can "mop" a kitchen with a moist towelette.

Sanjeev does not turn out to be an admirer of efficiency. Nor was he taken in by my Pine-Sol in the teakettle trick. Son of a reformer-doctor, he swabbed and cultured the kitchen floor after I mist-mopped it. When strains of an Ebola-like virus appeared, he insisted that I use actual H_2O.

The one purely happy result of my labor is that I have scrubbed my way back into Millie's heart. "Your boyfriend is a sadist," I inform her, dropping onto my bed at the end of week three of my sentence.

Startled, Millie looks up from her book, *The Gospel of Judas.* "Do you mean Sanjeev? He's not my boyfriend." She puts the book aside. "Why? Did he say something?"

"No, but every time he looks at you he blinks out 'I want to drink your bathwater' in Morse code."

"He does? Really?"

"I don't know. Maybe he's mentally dressing you in a sari."

Millie shakes her head, and says sternly, "That is not appropriate."

"Whatever, he's a sadist. Look at my hands!" I hold up mitts an oyster shucker would have envied.

"That was our agreement. If you stayed in the house, you had to make reparations."

"Yes, reparations, fine, but it's not as if I bombed Pearl Harbor. Don't you think my sentence or penance or whatever this is is a bit excessive? I feel like a fallen woman in a nunnery."

"That's not a bad metaphor. Admit it, this *is* good for your soul."

"Look, metaphors don't give a person dishpan hands and whatever else this might be it is *not* good for my soul."

"We don't require belief. Just labor. The heart will follow where the hands lead."

Who is "we"? I want to ask, but, as usual, exhaustion overtakes me so suddenly that I don't even have time to remember that I can't fall asleep without a few of my friends from the Schedule IV controlled-drugs portion of the program.

Millie is gone the next morning by the time I wake up reflecting upon how wonderful unaided sleep is. I slump back onto my little single bed, as virginal a plank as any novice ever rested upon between the evening self-flagellation and popping on the hair shirt the next morning before scuttling off to wash everyone's feet in the convent refectory. Just as I am snuggling in, though, Sanjeev pounds at the door. He sticks a paint scraper in my flayed hand and points to the approximately three billion windows in the house. All of them painted shut by past residents.

Sanjeev outlines my Sisyphean task: "Make them open."

Several mugs of powdered coffee slurry later, I stand in a bed of lantana frilled with newly blossomed yellow flowers. As I scrape away various geologic strata of paint, the house's entire history is laid bare. Top coat is a ghastly Greenpeace sage applied by the current eco-warrior residents. Beneath that, my scraper uncovers the soul-scouring greed gray of the late nineties. A flash of tan appears, then it is on to the early nineties, where I hit the years of my earlier residency.

Butterflies flutter into the air as Millie steps through the banks of golden yellow lantana and joins me. She plucks off the rubbery ribbon of violet that curls up over my scraper. "Oh my gosh, do you remember when we painted that?" The color is as fresh and vivid as the day we applied it.

"We were such rebels."

"Purple trim. The house was abuzz. I loved it."

"Loved it for a week or so before Robin ordered us to paint over it with that hideous peanut butter color."

"She could be a bit of a martinet."

"'Could be'? Oh, Dr. Dr. Robin can still handle a riding crop."

"Do you remember how we tied plastic bags filled with ice cubes to our heads?"

Before I can process and contain the memory, a pang constricts my heart. I put it down to overconsumption of lentils, electrolyte imbalance, and a dangerous Code Warrior deficiency which I would have done anything at that moment to correct. I am certainly not going to connect the pang to its true source.

Millie does it for me. "Actually, it was Danny's idea. Remember?"

Remember Danny Escovedo? Oh yes, I remember.

Millie continues, "Then we started telling each other our Coldest Ever stories. Danny won, didn't he?"

"Yeah, Danny won."

"He told that hilarious story about the time his band got stranded hitchhiking outside of that little town in North Dakota."

"I believe Danny said it was Witch's Tit, North Dakota."

"And he was in a heavy metal—"

"Speed metal."

"—band and their van broke down and the whole band was wearing their ridiculous stage outfits."

"Spandex leggings, ladies' rabbit fur jackets, platform boots. I think he called their look 'hooker who's watched *Spinal Tap* one too many times.'"

Millie stops and looks at me. "That's the first time I've heard you really laugh since you got here."

"It is?"

"Danny could always make you laugh. Whatever happened with you and Danny?"

Me and Danny?

Before I can answer, Sanjeev appears. "Millie, a moment, if you will."

Millie hastens to the side of His Priggishness, and I go back to scraping and thinking about Danny. We met when I was working at the Kinko's near the law school. Danny took a part-time job there, since being the reigning god of Austin's indie rock scene, while highly remunerative romantically, didn't actually pay his bills. In looking back, I realize that, from the first moment, we had chemistry to burn. Pipettes, beakers, volumetric flasks of chemistry. Our relationship was built on jokes, and the jokes were always about sex. Danny was three years younger than me, a gap that seemed unbreachable back in the days when three years represented roughly one-seventh of my entire life span. Now that it covers only one-eleventh of the too-rapidly-mounting total, I wonder why I ever cared.

But back then, I was off-limits, hence safe, for many reasons. Because of the age difference. Because we worked together. Because Danny was fully booked tending to the flocks of groupie skanks who swarmed around him. For all those reasons, we could both pretend that the jokes were jokes.

At work Danny constructed a parallel universe in which I was the sex slave of our manager, Templeton, a punctilious little fellow with tiny hands, tiny feet, and an unfortunate habit of twitching his nose when offended. In Danny's alternate world, Templeton pawed me with those tiny hands in squeaking pink and gray frenzies of depraved mouse couplings.

Danny grew quite elaborate in his tales of our forbidden, interspecies love: Templeton wooing me with nibbles of the potted-meat-product sandwiches he brought for lunch, holding them out to me in his wee mousie paws. Me, succumbing to the erotic twitching, then being forced to satisfy his depraved rodent desires.

As a therapist might have said, Danny and I "led with sex." It occurs to me that, in the beginning, Trey and I had the same sort of joking, frothy relationship. The instant I start thinking about Trey, a dozen fire ants bite my feet. I scream, jump out of the lantana bushes, and swat at the ants, but pearly blisters are already puffing up. Needle pricks continue until I dig the ants out from between my toes.

I search through the lantana bushes for the paint scraper. At close range, the flower-frilled bushes smell like insecticide and sting like nettles. Also the "butterflies" looping above the flowers turn out to be creepy, bat-faced moths with the bodies of garden slugs.

For the next week, I stay out of range of the fire ants and gouge at the paint, barely noticing as I strip away the layers of the house's evolving identity. Midseventies avocado gives way to sixties psychedelic orange. Hours later, I reach all the way back to a time when people didn't feel compelled to share their inner essence with the world via house-trim color. I arrive at white. Plain white. Decades and decades of just plain white follow until I am down to the bare wood hammered into place a century ago.

The windows slide up and down. All three billion of them. And then I paint. Using the house's vast store of leftover paint, I create a batch of a buttery cream color that glows like candlelight in the fading sun. It is the best color that has ever been applied to Seneca House and, day after day, I paint until there is not enough light left to see.

At night, I take five Advil, drop like a stone into bed, and have whatever a girl's equivalent of a wet dream is about Danny. The Merry Maid version, I suppose, since no fluids are involved. I wake up bemused by the novelty of sexual feeling. It is such a welcome change from brooding about precisely which inadequacies caused Peggy to dismiss me as summarily as a servant caught pocketing the family silver that I spend the next day thinking about Danny. And the next. And the one after that.

The Transitoriness
of Life

With a chartreuse furze of new growth feathering the trees, Austin wakes and remembers that it is a city of flip-flops and tank tops. Its brief flirtation with temperatures low enough to justify striped mufflers and knit caps is long over. Street gutters fill with a spongy mass of fallen live oak tassels. Outside our open window, a pair of hummingbirds darts about the coral vine twining there. A scent like old-lady talcum powder wafts in from the pale lilac blooms of the chinaberry tree reaching branches up to our second-story window. The blossoms' sweet fragrance mingles with an even sweeter aroma exhaled by the banks of honeysuckle lying collapsed beside the house. The sweetest of them all, though, the mimosa trees, haven't yet blossomed into pink clouds of candied blooms that can send a person into diabetic shock just from breathing. I love the extravagant excess of mimosas. I'm pretty sure that if I can hold on until the mimosas bloom, I will be all right.

It has been weeks since I imbibed anything stronger than those Advil, and all visible twitching has stopped. Minutes, hours, maybe an entire day can pass without my thinking once about Code Warrior. Master Sanjeev, however, continues to display a thin-lipped missionary disdain toward me as he hands over jugs of bleach and sics me on the battalions of mildew occupying the bathrooms.

At the end of week four, I step into the kitchen, which is now Ebola free thanks to me and Sanjeev's petri dishes, and make a surprising discovery: I am hungry. My gut, tightened by Code Warrior, betrayal, divorce, bankruptcy, the IRS, and general existential terror, has repelled food for so long that it takes a minute or two for me to recognize the churning sensations as hunger along with its accompanying desire to do something tasty to remedy the situation.

I inventory the comestibles and accept that the only possible way to disguise the disgusting collection of whole grains and soy abominations will be to go ethnic. I recall the contribution I made to the house when I lived here before and step into the backyard. The herb garden has survived. Every leaf I pinch—basil, thyme, parsley, cilantro, rosemary—releases the smell of summer. When I have filled a bag with the most tender leaves, I glance over at the co-op next door, New Guild, the mother ship. They seem to have, of all things, a freezer handily located on their back porch. Their *unlocked* back porch.

That night we eat whole wheat capellini made edible by a pesto that contains as much olive oil and butter as I can incorporate into it accompanied by a carnivore's platter of grilled sausages, pork chops, and T-bones topped with bacon for those who indulge. The viands are gone before Sanjeev and the vegans can protest the appearance of meat on Seneca's high-minded table. Further questions about the source of all the inhaled animal protein are lost in the sounds of furious mastication as residents snorkel down the Chocolate Intemperance I place before them.

The next night, it is on to a giant Jamaican hoedown, which, in spite of the country's reliance upon jerked meats, turns out to be highly amenable to a vegetarian ornamentation. Of course, the Saperstein girls, Yay Bombah and Nazarite, are ecstatic about the gungo pea patties, johnnycakes, bammy, and callaloo, declaring each dish more "boonoonoonous" than the last. The dreadlocked duo's two-fisted shoveling technique and the way their red, green, and gold stretch-waist pants strain around their middles are a testament to the appetite-stimulating properties of marijuana.

The night after that, just because I am tired of Sanjeev treating me like an Untouchable, I make *mangsho jhol, murgir jhol, Kosha*

Mangsho, Channa Dhal pulao, and several other unpronounceable dishes swarming with turmeric and curry, cardamom and cumin. They bring tears to his velvety brown eyes, which makes Millie beam like a mother at a Christmas pageant. Everyone else is feeling so warm and tingly and pleased with themselves for accepting a dingy Third World cuisine that I think it best when vegans Presto and Clancy inquire about the wonderful, unplaceable flavor of the *mattarwalli kheema* to tell them that it is, yum-yum, fermented soybeans rather than, oops, ground lamb.

As Yay Bombah and Nazarite are helping themselves to seconds and everyone else is finishing firsts, Millie jumps up and announces, "Oh, dear, I'm late!" Then, just as she does every evening, she rushes into the kitchen and emerges a few moments later carrying a clattering assortment of pots. Sanjeev pops up to help her and his hand brushes against hers. Millie blushes an atomic red at his touch. Sanjeev jerks his hand away as if he'd been burned.

I am trying to puzzle out what is up with these crazy kids when Doug raises his glass of iced tea, clinks the rim with a spoon until all the other residents look up from the trough. "I would like to propose a toast to Blythe for the finest meals we've eaten since I've lived here." Even Juniper clinks Doug's glass.

After dinner, feeling fairly certain that the young people of the tribe won't be shoving me onto an ice floe, at least until they've finished digesting, I risk a public appearance in the living room. Sanjeev sits at the dining room table working on house accounts. Jerome sprawls on the armchair reading the *Daily Texan*. Doug stares into the homey glow of his laptop, taps a few keys, and music, very pleasant music, issues forth. From the kitchen come the soothing sounds of someone else cleaning up as Presto and Clancy clatter about.

For one second, I feel I am exactly where I was intended to be. I am drug free, actually sleeping, and doing things for others. Atoning for past missteps. Paying my debt to society. Successfully evading the IRS. As if summoned simply by my thinking about the letters *IRS*, the ancient house phone rings for the first time since my arrival. A black film-noir-style instrument, it is wired, not plugged, into the wall. The phone was here when I moved into the house the first time and seems to have been preserved as a museum piece ever since. The receiver is actually dusty, since everyone owns a cell.

It rings a second time. I panic.

The IRS planted an electrode in my brain and they're monitoring my thoughts. The future is here.

It rings a third time.

I am closest to the phone. When I don't move, Sanjeev gives a grumpy sigh, slaps his mechanical pencil down onto the ledger book, answers the phone, then repeats the caller's request: "You're calling for Blythe Young?"

In spite of my frantically waving my arms in front of my face as I shake my head *No! No! And hell no!* Mr. Social Contract volunteers in a stern tone, "Why, yes, Blythe Young is right here."

Sanjeev holds the phone out. "You have a phone call."

"Male or female?"

"Why is that pertinent?"

Since I can't tell Mr. Social Contract that it is pertinent because the IRS agent hunting me is male, hence I prefer not to communicate with that half of the world's population, I settle for, "Would it be possible to tell whoever it is that I'm not in right now?"

Sanjeev blinks, as baffled as a toddler by the concept of the white lie. "But you are. You are in right now."

"Technically, yes, but don't you abhor the invasion of privacy that today's modern devices afford?"

"No. If you don't want to speak to him, tell him yourself."

"So, 'him,' male then. How would you describe his voice? Punctilious? Bureaucratic?"

Sanjeev glares and jabs the phone at me until I take it. It is heavy as a brick in my hand. After Sanjeev disappears upstairs, I say in a bouncy Kolkata accent, "Hello, I regret to inform you that the party you are seeking does not reside at this address. Good-bye."

"Blythe Young, that is the worst Indian accent I have ever heard."

"Danny?"

"Millie told me you were back at the Seneca."

"She did?"

"Yeah, I've been looking for a minute to talk to you ever since she called. And, oh, shit, it suddenly doesn't look like it's going to be this one, either. Fuck, they're calling me. Listen, Younghole, I'm in the studio now and this prima donna I'm working with is finally ready. I'm coming to Austin soon, okay? If I call will you promise to do that really bad Indian accent again? That is so hot. Maybe we can round Templeton up for a little three-way action."

"Only if you bring the deviled ham."

"Deal. All right, Mistress Younghole, it's a date." Without moving his mouth away from the phone, Danny yells, "Calm the fuck down, I'm coming." To me, he says, "The next Avril Lavigne is coming unglued, I've gotta go." Before he hangs up, Danny chitters into the phone and I remember him back at Kinko's, a line of un-amused law students waiting for their copies, while he curled his hands under his chin, poked out his front teeth, twitched the imaginary whiskers on his upper lip, and imitated what he maintained was Templeton's frenzied mating call.

I am chittering back when I realize that Danny has hung up and I am making a beaver face at Juniper. I dart upstairs like a dog with a bone that I want to gnaw on in private before the rest of the pack can take it from me. When I reach Millie's room, however, the door is open, and Sanjeev, his back to me, is inside. Something about his posture causes me to stop dead. He hovers over Millie's small desk, touching her pen, running his long, artistic fingers over her date book. He uncaps her ChapStick, rubs the tube against his lips, closes his eyes, and presses his lips together, kissing the pomade that has touched Millie's lips, then he slips the tube into his pocket. It is both the creepiest and most romantic thing I have ever seen. I back silently away. Whatever is between Millie and Sanjeev, it goes way beyond a simple crush.

Downstairs, I wait until Sanjeev scuttles past, heading for his room at the rear of the house, before I go back upstairs. Which is where I am a couple of hours later when Millie returns. As soon as she enters, I pounce. "What did you tell Danny?"

"He called? Well, he certainly took his own sweet time."

"What did you tell him? About me?"

"Only that you were back in the house."

"You didn't tell him why . . . you know, what happened?"

"You mean that you've been through a difficult divorce?"

"Yeah, right, that." No need to bring up the difficult bankruptcy and difficult drug withdrawal.

"He did ask if you were quote, unquote, 'involved.'"

"He did? What did you tell him?"

"I told him you aren't. We didn't go into details. He's in the middle of producing a record and is super, super busy. Are they still called records? Albums? CDs?"

"Danny is a producer?" I imagine a garage with egg cartons stapled to the walls. "I can't believe you called him."

"Oh, we've . . . stayed in touch." Millie giggles like an animated woodland creature. "All right, I called him because I knew you wanted to talk to him. And because I am certain he would want to talk to you."

"Quite the little matchmaker."

"Guilty as charged. So tell me everything."

"Not much to tell, really. We barely spoke at all. He wants to get together next time he's in Austin. Which will probably be never."

"Don't be pessimistic. Great loves always find ways to work themselves out." Making that statement causes her giddiness to suddenly leak away. She plops down onto the chair in front of the desk where Sanjeev had been caressing her writing utensils earlier.

"What's between you and Sanjeev?"

She is alert again. "Why? Did he say something?"

"No. But it's clear, *very* clear, that he has feelings."

"That's not true. Why? What makes you say that?"

I can't tell her about Sanjeev making out with her ChapStick.

In any case, Millie holds up her hand and stops me before I can speak. "No. Don't say anything. What is between Sanjeev and me is all that can ever be."

"What exactly *is* between you two?"

Millie considers the question for far too long before answering, "Mutual respect, I suppose. We also share a certain sensibility. An awareness that life is both short and significant in ways that are not always immediately apparent. Sanjeev has said that it is rare for a Western woman to have such an awareness of the transitoriness of life."

"Ooh, la, la, 'transitoriness of life,' that is so hot. Well, he is clearly smitten."

"He is? How do you know?"

"The way he looks at you."

"He does? How does he look at me?" Millie is on her knees on the bed. Then, abruptly, the excitement vanishes and she sinks down. "No, don't answer that. It's not possible. It will never be possible. I knew that from the start."

"Oh, Millie, I'm so sorry. It's so obvious now. Sanjeev is gay."

"Please, shut up."

"Did you just tell me to shut up?"

"Yes, I'm sorry, but you really can't talk about this anymore."

"Millie, it's okay. I fell for this guy once who was gay. I don't know how I missed that he was gay. He actually even looked a little like Sanjeev. Same great eyelashes. That lanky, slithery sexiness. In retrospect he was so obviously gay that I don't—"

"Sanjeev is not gay! He's engaged." Millie gasps and slaps her hand across her mouth as if she can stuff the words back in. "I can't believe I said that. I swore to him that I would never talk about this. To anyone. I haven't even put it in my journal."

"Sanjeev is engaged?"

"His parents have chosen a bride for him."

"Does that still happen?"

"Ninety-five percent of all Indian marriages are arranged."

"Why? Don't they have Match.com in India?"

"Marriage is not a joking matter in India."

"Sorry."

"It's all right. I didn't really understand either until Sanjeev explained it to me." Millie gets a sad, faraway look in her eyes. "According to Hinduism, marriage is a sacred relationship that extends across seven or more lives. Two souls come together to help each other progress spiritually so that they may find salvation. They have to marry because their karmas are intertwined." Millie sighs. "It is destiny."

"It is also the twenty-first century."

"Sanjeev's parents are very traditional. His bride-to-be, Bhavani Mukherjee, is Bengali Brahman from Kolkata, as is Sanjeev's family. They have already consulted astrologers who studied the heavens to determine the most auspicious day of the entire year for the ceremony. It will take place in one month. A week after the semester has ended."

"Nice of the heavens to accommodate finals."

"They have already selected the seven married ladies to portray the seven forms of God. One for each day of the week. They will use red powder to make the clockwise swastika on a pot of crystallized sugar to ask Ganesh to bless the couple and make the ceremony run well. They have engaged artisans to construct the *mandap,* the wedding canopy, on the grounds of the bride's family estate. They've booked the priest and pared the guest list down to eight hundred relatives, business associates, and friends."

"Do they have an event coordinator? No, forget I said that. Can't Sanjeev just tell his parents that he's having second thoughts?"

Millie smiles ruefully and shakes her head at my ignorance. "To change his mind at this point would cause his parents, himself, and Bhavani Mukherjee to be cast out of society. Bhavani would suffer the worst. No decent family would ever have her once she's been rejected. Her life would be ruined. All their lives would be ruined."

"Couldn't he do it in a way that wouldn't impugn this Bhavani Mukherjee? He could tell them he's converted to Scientology. They'd never want him then."

"Sanjeev is far too honorable to attempt such a subterfuge. He wouldn't be the person I admire if he did. He was very clear from the beginning: He is here in America only to learn enough so that he can return and help with his father's work. He has nothing but contempt for his countrymen who come here and are seduced by Western ways. His parents are still reeling from the shock of learning that Sanjeev's brother, Vijay, has switched his major from molecular biology to video game design. No, Sanjeev will never betray his parents or who he is. He will return to India and marry Bhavani Mukherjee. And that is that."

"Does Sanjeev even know how you feel?"

"No! And you must never tell him. Ever. Do you promise?"

"Okay, yeah, sure."

"No, really, Blythe, you have to promise me. If you told him that I have, uh, feelings it would destroy our friendship and I don't think I could go on without at least that. So promise."

"I promise."

"No, really, really, really promise."

"All right, all right. I really, really, really promise."

Millie nods her head sternly. "Good. The case is closed. Forever. Let's move on. Danny called."

"Yeah, he called. That's all. Doesn't mean anything."

"But after all these years? It means he's still carrying a torch."

"There was never a torch."

"In his heart. There was a torch in his heart. A love all the purer for remaining unspoken."

"Millie, you just might be the most romantic person I know."

"Me? You're the one who's been carrying a torch for all these years."

Millie turns off the light, and in the twilight moment between sleep and waking I see Sanjeev pocketing Millie's ChapStick. But when he turns around, it is Danny, and the ChapStick is mine.

You Never Turn a Stranger Out

OVER THE NEXT FEW DAYS, I notice how being a nitwit with a crush opens me up to things I've previously blocked out. Lying in bed, thinking about Danny, I hear, really hear, music again for the first time in almost a decade. From every corner of the house, a Babel of musical genres beams in, and every song reminds me of Danny, the musical chameleon who changed bands and styles as often as he switched girlfriends. The music transports me and I wonder why I unplugged from what had once been a major power source in my life. When had I gotten to the point that the last time and place I'd moved to music was "It's Raining Men" at an aerobics studio?

All those years of making, then losing, money, I hadn't noticed that music had disappeared from my life any more than I noticed that friends, movies, ethics, sex, and Snickers bars had vanished as well. When had a Snickers bar from the freezer stopped being a treat? When had all my friends mutated into connections who slowly, then swiftly, dropped me after the divorce?

The music flows in from every room in the house. It streams over parched aural passages and soaks into desiccated synaptic pathways. Reggae from Nazarite and Yay Bombah, of course. Presto and Clancy beam in lugubrious, indie stuff. Korean hip-hop floats up from one of the computer wizards downstairs. Sanjeev occasionally cuts loose with a hit from the eighties taken from the blander side of the charts. My favorites, though, filter in from a surprising source: Juniper's room. The stuff Juniper plays fills the air with haunting female voices that seem to have bounced off of the Appalachians, Dollywood, and the moon on their way to my ears.

Just as one of my particular favorites starts up, Millie walks in. I ask her, "What is that song?"

Millie cocks her head, listening intently as the female singer yowls and gargles lyrics to a kerplunking banjo and tinkling mandolin accompaniment.

It mesmerizes me. Now that I have reactivated my atrophied music muscle, it won't stop flexing. "I love that song. I have to know who that band is." I strain to make out the melancholy words that drift through the air and catch a few words. "Did they say, 'Legs of punch a train'?"

Millie shrugs. "I couldn't understand. Let's go ask Juniper."

"Uh, me and Juniper . . ." I mime trying to force two magnets together.

"Jerome, Jerome will know; he's a music genius."

Millie leaves and returns almost immediately with Jerome in tow. "Listen," she commands him.

After only a few seconds, the song ends, but Jerome has heard enough. He taps away on Millie's laptop. "Might the song you are seeking sound a little like this?" He punches a key and plinking banjo notes patter down like fat silver raindrops on the dust.

"That's it! That's my song!"

An angelic voice yowls and slurs. *We never turn a stranger out from the lakes of Pontchartrain.*

"'The Lakes of Pontchartrain,'" I yell, happier to possess the name of this song than any furs or designer frocks I once owned. Okay, maybe not the striped sable. Or the Jean-Paul Gaultier cocktail dress with the garnet piping.

"You want me to download it?" Jerome asks.

I jerk my eyebrows in Millie's direction and scowl at Jerome, but it is too late.

"Download?" Millie asks. "Are you talking about illegally downloading music? Don't do that on my computer."

"Don't worry," Jerome says. "You're thinking of Napster. That's all over now. This is just an intrahouse music-sharing network. Choi Soon Yong and Elmootazbellah Kamolvilassitian hooked the house into the university's system so that they could run their programs."

"So this system is sanctioned by the university?"

"Oh, completely," Jerome assures Millie. "It's just us students sharing our music."

I may have little interest and less expertise in the technicalities of file sharing, but I can recognize the sound of a moral corner being cut when I hear one.

"Why don't you just have a listen?" I say, snapping headphones over Millie's ears and turning up the volume so she can't hear when I ask Jerome, "That 'sanctioned by the university,' that's bullshit, isn't it?"

"Total crock. But not to worry. An adorable side effect of being a self-contained module sheltered by the university's computer system is that it makes the house invisible to RIAA bots out trolling for music pirates."

"So you all run this swap meet with total impunity? There's no chance of anyone, of Millie, being caught?"

"None."

Millie takes the headphones off and asks me, "Blythe, are you certain this is totally on the up and up?"

Jerome, his fingers hovering above Millie's laptop, waits for my reply. Not wanting Millie's moral persnicketiness to get between me and something I crave intensely, I answer, "Totally."

The album is downloaded onto Millie's laptop by the time Jerome steps out the door. Then Millie and I listen to the kind of Appalachian fiddle playing that saws directly into the most tender part of your heart and makes a person yearn for all that is lost, and I could not care less where this music came from, only that it is here. The elegiac tone makes me slump into a comfy mournful mode.

Millie brightens when the next song plays. "Oh my gosh! Is that 'Oh, Susanna'?" We listen to:

I come from Alabama with my banjo on my knee.
I'm going to Loozeeana my true love for to see.
It rained all night the day I left, the weather was bone dry.
Sun so hot, I froze to death. Susanna, don't you cry.

Millie joins in on the refrain.

Oh, Susanna, don't you cry for me.
I come from Alabama with a banjo on my knee.

On the second verse, she drags me off the bed and we swoop through a jokey, joyful waltz.

I had a dream the other night
When everything was still
I dreamed I saw Susanna
A-comin' down the hill

A buckwheat cake was in her mouth
A tear was in her eye.
I said I'm coming from the south
Susanna, don't you cry.

As we whirl around the room, pounding century-old dust out of the floorboards, I catch a glimpse of the shimmering Zac Posen jacket, my suit of lights. It is a ghostly blur, a streak of past motion on a photograph. I did have a lot of sublime things in my old life, but I didn't have this, a friend to dance with.

"Millie," I huff out as we launch into the fifth replay of "Oh, Susanna." All the bounding about has joggled loose a question that I cannot believe I've never asked. "What exactly is it you do all day?"

Millie stops dead and her smile turns sly. "I thought you'd never ask."

Nipples Pucker

Miss millie! Miss Millie!" The cries reach us over the screeching of brakes as Millie brings the recumbent bike to a stop. The half dozen tin pots in the trailer clang and clatter even more loudly than they had with every bump on the ride down. I am back on Dog Crap Lane and the 'bos are starting to swarm down out of the hills.

Piles of blankets and grimy sleeping bags sprout legs and walk toward us. A dog with one blue eye and one brown, bandanna around his neck, leads the way. Then it is beards and sunburns, missing teeth and body odor.

Body odor?

Body odor is far too close for comfort. I am reaching for the button to raise an automatic window, to put a thick pane of impact-resistant glass between myself and the vagrants, when I remember that I am not sitting high above them all in the Escalade. I recall that I am no longer, either figuratively or literally, looking down on the men. That I myself am one vote away from working for food. And, splayed out on the front seat of a tandem recumbent bike, staring at roughly zipper level, that gap seems to be closing rapidly. I spring off the bike and scurry away as the pack closes in.

"Well, look who's here," Millie calls out with unforced delight as the first man reaches us. "Joe, look at you. You got a haircut!"

"Cut 'em all, Miss Millie." Joe, a bullet-headed guy with the build of a bouncer, answers in a thick Cajun accent as he rubs a meaty hand over his shaved head.

Millie laughs at the old joke. "Does the Loozeeana Man want his usual Pickapeppa sauce?"

"You know what I always say, 'A day without Pickapeppa is like'"—Millie chimes in on what is obviously a familiar line—"'a day without sunshine'!" She splashes a couple of tortillas with the thick, brown sauce. From one aluminum pot she produces a couple of hard-boiled eggs; from another, an orange.

Joe, grinning, takes eggs and orange, lumbers away, and the next man steps up.

"Curtis! I thought you'd gone back to Kansas City."

Curtis is a spindly African American guy with twigs and dead grass in his hair and a smile that stars pay thousands for. "You know I couldn't stay away too long from you, Miss Millie."

"The usual for you, Curtis? Stubb's Bar-B-Q sauce and two tortillas?"

"You read me like a book."

"One of the classics, Curtis. A book no one ever gets tired of."

Curtis beams as Millie hands him a couple of tortillas. He holds them in his horny palms while Millie squirts puddles of sauce on each one; then he slips the two eggs she gives him into the pocket of his grimy brown hoodie.

"And your vitamin C, good sir."

Curtis takes an orange from Millie's hand with a courtly bow, sweeping a pretend hat from his head. "I am in your debt, kind lady."

The other homeless men wait patiently until Curtis has his turn; then the next one ambles forward. Millie knows each man's name and something about him.

"Carl, how's that hand?"

"I told you I coulda done them stitches myself."

"Carl, that was a horrible gash. Thank you for letting me take you to the clinic."

"Lotta motherfuckin' trouble for a little motherfuckin' scratch."

All right, that's more like it. The snarling sociopath lurking beneath all this Capraesque clowning emerges. To my surprise, however, the other 'bos immediately turn on Carl. They badger and insult him until he apologizes.

"Uh, sorry for the language, Miss Millie."

"Thank you for the apology, Carl," Millie says, as if her entire world hangs on how Carl the Hobo treats her. "You're a Hellmann's man, right?"

"I'm a hell of a man, all right, but I'll take a little dab of that mayo."

Carl leaves and another bum takes his place. "Jesse, are you drunk already?"

A wino, maybe a beero, some lifelong fan of all things fermented, Jesse is glassy eyed and putting off a stench that has even his buddies on Dog Crap Lane giving him a wide berth. Only Millie stands her ground, smiling as if the Jesse she sees and smells is the one who once came from the maternity ward wrapped in a powder blue receiving blanket, all pink and clean and smelling brand-new. Jesse is as toothless as a newborn and works his lips for a few seconds before getting a collection of grunts and wheezes out, "Yes, ma'am. Sure am."

"Starting awfully early, Jesse. Should I just splash a little bourbon on your tortillas?"

The last gets a big laugh from Jesse, and he perks up enough to offer the riposte: "Jim Beam, if you got 'er, ma'am."

Still chortling, pleased with his sally, Jesse takes his tortillas with ketchup, claims a couple of eggs, an orange, and shuffles away.

Each succeeding man is issued the same fare along with his choice of condiments: pickled jalapeño, squirt of mustard, Pickapeppa, mayo, ketchup, mustard. No bourbon. No Jim Beam. Each one takes the food, but what he really lines up and waits patiently for is to hear Millie say his name and speak to him in a kindly manner. To have a woman acknowledge his existence in some way other than by raising a thick pane of impact-resistant glass.

I have always suspected that Millie is the most purely good person I've ever met. It is now clear that her goodness is of a Mother

Teresa quality. In a million years, I could never dive into that mosh pit of microbial horror, scraggly beards, and WILL WORK FOR BEER signs. Backing even farther away, I keep one eye on the hobo mob, alert for any sign of a psychotic break or Vietnam flashback, while searching the trail for a possible rescuer. Where *are* all the annoying twits broadcasting into cell phones when you need them?

When the last vagabond has been issued his tortillas, eggs, and orange, and flapped back into the hills from whence he'd come, Millie hops onto the bike, rings the bell jauntily, and calls out, "All aboard for the next stop!"

Instead of huffing back up Twenty-fourth Street to the house as I expected, Millie heads south on Lamar. We breeze past Pease Park as it winds along Shoal Creek, where a new crew of bare-chested young men hurl Frisbees with the grace of Greek discus throwers.

"Millie," I yell back over my shoulder, "I read an article that says the organizations that work with the homeless advise against giving them money."

"Did you see me giving anyone any money?" Her question has a giggly lilt that says she's had this discussion before and is pleased and prepared to be having it again.

"Well, you know, you're not supposed to do things that will discourage them from getting into programs."

"I don't think a couple of tortillas are going to stop anyone who really wants it from getting help. Might even give him or her enough strength to stand in lines and fill out a lot of forms."

"You know what I mean."

"Sort of. But this, what I do, it's just between me and them. Between friends. In those programs you're talking about who's going to know that Curtis likes Stubb's barbecue sauce or that Carl prefers Hellmann's?"

We turn east on César Chávez. The Colorado River sparkles beside us. Pink and white clouds of blossoms fuzz the trees lining the bank. A slender scull with eight rowers torpedoes through the silver water. The scenery grows less pastoral the farther east we go. Soon we are in a neighborhood where houses are painted lime

green and hot pink. Here and there an old bathtub shelters a shrine
to Our Lady of Guadalupe. We zigzag through vacant lots and convenience stores that sell *barbacoa* tacos and phone cards for prepaid
calls to Mexico. A warehouse next to the railroad tracks overflows
with used office furniture. Several battered Aeron chairs and Herman Miller workstations are piled up outside. I have located the
dot-com burial ground.

A few blocks later we come upon a vacant lot where day laborers of the undocumented variety mill about. A pickup truck with a
magnetic sign on the driver's door that reads AKINS LANDSCAPING
pulls up, and the men swarm around the driver's window. The
driver, wearing a gray sweatshirt with the sleeves cut off and a
gimme cap with a picture of a fish and the word BASSWIPE on the
front, yells a few rudimentary questions in construction site Spanish. Four men hop into the bed of the pickup and settle themselves
beside an overturned wheelbarrow and a load of manure covered
by a blue tarp.

The rejected men left behind at the day labor lot are downcast
until they catch sight of Millie. Everyone lights up and begins hail-
ing her in excited Spanish. Millie answers with equal enthusiasm.

"Heriberto! Chuy! Alejandro! *Que está pasando, hombres?*" Then
she is hauling out her condiment assortment, the palette of self-
expression that is her gift to these strangers in a strange land.

"*Salsa fresca, sí?*"

"Jes, Mees Meelie."

"Tomas, *te gusta el salsa tomatillo, verdad?*"

"*Sí, me gusta mucho.*"

"*Chipotle para usted, señor?*"

"*Muchisimas gracias, señorita.*"

Each man is served his eggs, tortillas, his moment of recognition. Each one comes away nourished.

On the long pull uphill, back to the university, Millie detours
over to the Drag. But the shops and restaurants along the stretch of
Guadalupe across from the campus are not what interest her. The
empty aluminum pots and pans in the trailer clatter as we come to

a halt next to the Baptist church on the corner of Twenty-second and Guadalupe. A tribe of street kids lounging on the front steps take turns harrying passersby. Their pleas for spare change range from the ingratiating—"Please, mister, I just need two dollars and fifty-three cents more for a phone card to call home"—to the insulting—"Come on, you fat-ass sorority bitch, gimme your money; you don't need another cheeseburger."

They light up instantly upon spotting Millie and then, just as quickly, bury their enthusiasm behind masks of adolescent sullenness. After we stop, they wait for several minutes, then saunter over desultorily as if they were headed in that direction anyway. Millie greets each one of the street kids like a celebrity.

"Spood! Look at you! I like the hair beads." A lanky kid hiding beneath an oversize army jacket, cheeks spangled with acne, touches the beads braided into his long, lank hair and dips his head to hide his pleasure at the compliment.

"Kat? Is that you? Kat, where have you been? I've missed seeing you." A pudgy girl, her low-slung jeans exposing a puppy tummy of baby fat, rushes up and tells Millie a long, convoluted story about staying with her aunt in Dripping Springs and going to school there until the aunt's boyfriend took off in the middle of the night and stole her aunt's car and how somehow that all led to her being back here on the street with her "real friends."

Kat has a cute Betty Boop voice which sounds funny when she tells Millie about "all them hos and bee-yotches back in Dripping."

An emaciated boy tattooed from the top of his shaved head to his toes approaches shyly. "Hag War!" Millie calls out to him. As he gets closer, I can see that the tattoos are leopard spots and that what Millie has called him is "Jaguar" with a Spanish pronunciation.

"Jaguar, you got some new tats."

He claws the air with a slow-motion feline grace, but doesn't answer.

"You still have those wild contacts?" Millie asks.

The boy opens his eyes wide to display amber irises with vertical black slits for pupils, more like a demonic goat than a jaguar but distinctly not human, which seems to be the idea. I try to calculate how many thousands of dollars' worth of body modification the young man is sporting, give up, and move on to the larger question of why "adults" are aiding and abetting him in this process.

I also wonder why Millie is not handing out grub to this crew. Then I notice the crumpled McDonald's bags and Starbucks Venti-size cups littering the church steps; these kids aren't interested in hard-boiled eggs and tortillas.

The only member of the tribe who doesn't congregate around Millie is a girl in her late teens, pale as steam. She huddles in the shadow of the church. Her eyes are caked in black liner; she wears leather bondage pants, motorcycle boots, and a muscle shirt that displays ropy biceps ringed with a bracelet of thorn tattoos. She gives off a sexy dangerous androgynous vibe like both the coolest bad boy and hottest bad girl in high school. She sidles over and shoots me a look so icy my nipples pucker.

I nod her way and try to project Millie's saintliness but end up giving the girl a tight, tucked-lip Protestant smile.

The girl returns my smile with a jolly "Fuck you, bitch."

I invite her to do the same.

Millie comes over. "Oh, good, you met Nikki."

Nikki flips us both off and skulks back to the front steps of the church.

Millie watches her depart, concern dimpling her features. "Nikki seems a little down today."

"Nikki seems a little homicidal today."

"I'll just go and check on her."

Somehow Millie is not repelled by the girl's shield of steely disdain and plops down next to her. Nikki looks away. Kat hovers beside me, watching Nikki intently.

A Prius honks. The driver leans out of his window, points at the recumbent bike parked in the street, and yells at me to "Move that monstrosity!" I wave for him to go around the bike with an outstretched middle finger. He squeals past, purposely scraping the side of the bike. Sanjeev's lead pipe construction does a lot more damage to his Prius than the Prius does to the bike. By the time I take my thumbs out of my ears, stop waggling my fingers at the car swerving out of sight, and check back on Millie, Nikki is sobbing in her arms.

The cute, chubby Kat, watching her friend, leans toward me and explains in a whisper, "Nikki's dog, Zebra Dog, run off."

"Oh."

"She's been waiting for Millie to come so she could talk to her."

"Uh-huh."

As Nikki dries her tears, Kat asks me, "Are you an old girl?"

I shrug and smile amiably the way you do when you're in a foreign country and have no idea what anyone is saying, so you end up grinning and nodding your way into a three-way with a henna vendor and a camel.

When Millie brings Nikki over to us, Millie's shirt is streaked with inky puddles of eyeliner from where Nikki has cried on her. Nikki is still scowling, but she looks even better with the Marilyn Manson makeup washed off.

"I see you've met my buddy Kat," Millie says, putting her arm around the pudgy girl. Kat bounces worshipful beams between Millie and Nikki. "And you know my friend Nikki." Somehow Millie manages to get her arm over Nikki's shoulders even though the girl is half a foot taller than she is. "Girls, this is one of my best friends, Blythe Young. Blythe is hanging with me for a while. A long while, I hope."

I nudge Millie. "We should probably head back. I need to soak garbanzo beans or scrub grout with a toothbrush or one of the other fun activities I get to do while hanging with you."

Nikki cuts a wary glance my way. Like me, Nikki receives on the cynical, sarcastic frequencies otherwise known as reality, which Millie and Kat both seem blissfully oblivious to. Nikki narrows her eyes and I feel as if the girl can see right through me and thinks that Millie needs to be protected from me.

Millie answers, "Oh, we don't have to leave quite yet."

"If we don't, your boyfriend is going to get grumpy."

"Boyfriend!" Kat pops her eyes at Millie. "You have a boyfriend! And you didn't tell us!"

Millie glares at me. "That's just Blythe imagining things."

"Details! Details! Details!" Kat squeals.

Millie used to squeal that exact word at me when we lived together and she wanted to know more about my romantic encounters. But Millie is not in a details mood. In fact, she is plainly pissed off. "Blythe was making a joke. Not a particularly funny joke."

On the way back to Seneca, Millie gives me the silent treatment.

"Millie, I'm sorry, but those kids will never meet Sanjeev."

"That's not the point. I asked you never to mention Sanjeev and me."

"I'm sorry, Millie. I am a jerk."

"You are a jerk."

"I just said that."

"Blythe, I'm not kidding. A promise is a promise and I must have your word on this."

"You have it, Millie. I'm sorry. Really truly sorry. I screwed up and I won't ever do it again."

Millie nods but doesn't say anything, and I make a note to myself to seriously never *ever* say anything, to anyone, ever again about Sanjeev. Then, as we pass the Pi Phi sorority house, Tara-like with its Greek pillars and Old South plantation style, I recall an event Wretched Xcess coordinated there when a former sister married a young tech baron rich enough to rent the place for his bride's dream wedding. The ice cherub sculpture with handmade vodka flowing through his plumbing would have kept Millie and her boys in eggs, tortillas, and condiments for a year. This realization causes me to ponder yet another significant question: "So, you don't actually have a job. Who pays your rent and buys the eggs and stuff?"

"Another question I thought you'd never ask. Wow, Sleeping Beauty, you are really starting to wake up."

Penance for Our Sins

Exfoliate.

That is all I can think as I glance around at the women packed into the living room for this meeting of the Old Girls. Millie, who is at the center of the gathering, has made a sign reading WELCOME SENECA HOUSE ALUMNI ASSOCIATION. I recognize a few faces, since many of the women lived in the house during my first tenure.

The room is aswirl in more formless flax, hemp, linen, nubby cotton tunics, rebozos, and stretch-waist pants than a yoga instructors' conference.

Stretch-waist pants? Why not simply wear a giant sign that reads I HAVE GIVEN UP?

I remind myself to keep a cyanide pellet handy for the moment I ever find myself in Chico's or any store that sells clothes in sizes 1, 2, and 3. Only Cokes and condoms should come in just three sizes. The human body requires a bit more calibration. And shoes? Not just clogs, *Birkenstock* clogs. All the color, shape, and style of pinto beans. I'm glad I wore the Zac Posen and my Louboutins.

The major issue, though, has to be diet. What parallel universe do these women inhabit where there is no South Beach, Zone, WW, Pritikin? Low carb, high carb. Pick one, ladies, any one. I am not saying that everyone has to be a twig like Nancy Reagan, but even our own hometown dumpling Laura Bush will do. We don't all have to go for Eleanor Roosevelt, do we?

And speaking of sanctimonious overachievers, my old nemesis,

Dr. Dr. Robin, from my thwarted Pap smear, is here. Thankfully, Robin is making a point of ignoring me, which I infinitely prefer to the good doctor bringing me up on identity theft charges.

I recognize a few familiar faces. High school reunion in hell, if that is not too redundant. I am trying to avoid eye contact when a stocky Asian woman thrusts herself upon me.

"Blighta Yoong!"

"Oh, my God! Byung Chao Soo, is that you?"

"Thas my name, don wear it out. But now I am Bunny."

"Bunny. That's the perfect name for you." It is. BCS never walked when she could bounce and her sunny disposition was one of the bright spots in a house dominated by women whose lives revolved around scathing critiques of the social order and erratic menstrual cycles. "You were in computer science, right? No, no, violin. Weren't you studying the violin?"

"Piano. But I am so ober that. Too Korean, know what I'm saying?"

"Your English has gotten really good."

"Roger that. Habba to hab the good English when you a please dish splasher."

There are one, two, three seconds of dead air as I puzzle out what a "please dish splasher" might be. Then, *click.* "You're a police dispatcher!"

"Better fit for me with my pea poles kills."

One, two, three.

"Yes! Yes, *people skills,* you always had great people skills."

"Whuz you gum?"

"Well, my game is event coordination. But I'm currently . . . currently, I'm working on a documentary about housing co-ops. University housing cooperatives. Like this one. In fact, I'm actually living here at the moment. For research purposes."

"You! You!" Bunny grins and stabs me with her index finger. "You got it going on! You all that *and* a bag of chips!"

"Blythe? Blythe Young, is that you?"

"Jen! Alli! Wow, you guys look great!" I greet the house's resident dueling dykes, infamous for all-night dissections of their tumultuous relationship. A toddler tugs on Jen's hand, which sports a goliath diamond engagement ring and wedding band. I have a vision of a "commitment ceremony" with both parties in tuxes and then the turkey baster.

"Is this your"—*boy? girl?* I can't make out the sex of the toddler hanging on to Jen's hand and discard "hermaphrodite" as a guess not likely to warm the hearts of many parents—"child?"

"He's Jen's," Alli answers. "I'm just Aunt Al. Right, slugger?" Alli scoops the child up and begins tissuing away some of the leakage pouring from every available duct and orifice.

"So, you two?" I seesaw a questioning hand back and forth between them, praying they will leap in and fill in the blanks.

"Not together anymore. Not as lovers anyway," Jen answers in the forthright, too-much-information way that is the curse of the therapized.

Her attention still on mopping up toddler effluvia, Alli adds cheerily, "Yep, Jen got her LUG and moved on."

Jen leans in to provide unsought clarification. "Lesbian Until Graduation." Jen and Alli laugh self-consciously frank, open laughs.

Still there is a bit of a tone when Alli adds, "Yeah, Jen's just a giant het now." She sticks the gooey Kleenex in the pocket of her formless jacket.

Jen's son starts tugging ferociously at her and grunting, "Pup-pup! Pup-pup!" He points to Big Lou the cat eating from a bowl on the side porch.

"Yes, Simba," Jen tells her son, pretending that her patience is strained even as she glows with mom pride. "We'll go see the pup-pup. But Mom is going to have to hold you because that can be a very dangerous pup-pup."

They leave and Alli says, "He calls anything with fur a pup-pup. How cute is that?"

"His name is Simba?"

"That's just what Jen calls him, Simba, the Elephant Boy. She says she feels like an elephant hauling this tiny creature around all day. That he's like the mahout who whacks her on the trunk to pick him up and take him where he wants to go."

Alli watches Jen and her son with such obvious longing and adoration that I have to ask, "So there's no . . ."

"Bitterness? Hard feelings? Homicidal rage? At first, yeah, I was demented. Once she went skipping off back to boys—a total has-bian!—I was making wax dolls and sticking pins in them. I keyed her car. Can't believe I did that. Actually, it was Millie who got us speaking again. Got me to start coming to these meetings. I didn't even know that Jen had named her son after me."

"She named him Allison?"

"Well, Alex. They call him Al." Her voice grows wistful. "That's what she used to call me when we were . . . Okay, I promised my therapist that I would maintain a forward, outward focus. What are you doing now?"

I unspool the whole documentary fantasy for Alli, adding that the Bass brothers are funding me, but that has to be kept a secret, explaining, "It hasn't been announced yet. What about you?"

"I'm program coordinator for the Platinum Longhorns."

"Really? You?" That last question mark could have been considered insulting, but Alli and UT alums who've given in excess of fifty thousand dollars to the alma mater are a highly unlikely pair. The plushiest of the plush Pee Heights princesses were always talking about trips they'd taken with the Plat Longs. Jaunts to Tuscany for a plein air sketching holiday. Excursions to Bali to study temple art. Private cooking lessons in London with Nigella Lawson. The Platinum Longhorns' trips were, mostly, a pretext to allow Kippie Lee and her coven to hang out and gossip about one another while pretending to study art and culture in deluxe, five-star settings where there was guaranteed to be great shopping and purified ice in the drinks.

"I know." Alli shakes her head at the absurdity of her career. "Strange that I should end up spending my days with Republicans." She takes in my jacket and shoes and adds quickly, "Not that there's anything wrong with that. I mean, seriously, if you are, Republican, that is, that's fine. At least we're all here doing penance for our sins, right? Helping Millie to buy off our guilt for not doing more ourselves. I guess that's part of your reason for coming back. That and the, uh, documentary."

She turns toward the porch where little Al is trying to eat out of Big Lou's bowl. "Oh, that is too cute!" She pulls a digital camera hardly bigger than a credit card out of her pocket. "Auntie Al has *got* to get a picture of that."

" 'Penance for our sins'? What does *that* mean?" I ask, but Alli is already rushing away.

"God's eyes! As I live and breathe, it's our own Blythe Young."

Ariadne grabs me. She doesn't seem to have aged a day since I first met her, probably because when I first met Ariadne she both *looked* middle-aged and *existed in* the Middle Ages. As a mead-making, heraldry-designing, wench-in-glasses member of the Society for Creative Anachronism, she delights in all things medieval.

"Ariadne, hey. You're looking well. How are things in the society? Still making mead and doing your heraldry stuff?"

"By the rood, no. I've moved on to something far more arcane than that." She leans in, her eyes twinkling, and whispers, "The law. I'm an attorney, but don't tell anyone." She lowers her voice for even more pretend secrecy. "My mother thinks I play piano in a house of ill repute."

I feel sorry for the poor saps who end up with Lady Guinevere representing them in court.

Ting! Ting! Ting!

At the front of the room, Robin taps on a glass with a fork. Conversations trail off and the group begins to coagulate into meeting mode. I search for an escape route and notice a knot of vegan residents at the refreshment table shoving mini ham quiches and spicy chicken wings into their mouths with both hands.

Dr. Dr. Robin waits until everyone is quiet before she sweeps a hand in Millie's direction. "I give you our very own Mother Teresa, our conscience, our touchstone . . ."

While Robin goes on with the introduction, Sanjeev appears at the back of the crowd. His eyes are riveted on Millie. Emotions play across his face: admiration, yearning, hope, desire. In one clouded instant, however, they are all washed away and replaced by despair. The same hopelessness flashes across Millie's face as she glances at him. Then she slaps a fake grin on and bounds to the front of the room. For some reason, she is wearing a derby hat. "Oh my gosh, Robin," Millie says. "Was that an introduction or a eulogy? I'm not dead yet."

The house phone rings and Sanjeev answers. He catches my eye and waves me over. I reel the anvil of a phone out onto the front porch.

"So, Younghole, where are you taking me for our date next time I'm in Austin? And don't think I'm gonna put out for some cheap-ass dinner at Olive Garden either. No action unless I see fabric on the tabletop."

"I don't know, Escovedo, I may need some references here. Referrals from satisfied customers."

"Hey, I'll do better than that. I'll come over there right now and give you a free sample. Money-back guarantee."

It is so juvenile. Kidding, teasing like a couple of high school boys in gym class, but that is our language and we are speaking it again. I barely notice the meeting taking place on the other side of the glass front door while I talk to Danny. My divided attention is why it takes me a few minutes to figure out what is happening when Millie takes the derby hat off her head and the Old Girls start chunking in bills and checks while Robin runs credit cards in the corner.

Even as Danny and I banter back and forth I process this new information: The Old Girls are supporting Millie.

What You Love on This Earth

So, are you completely lacking in a life too?" Nikki asks me as we watch Millie trying to talk to Jaguar.

Millie and Jaguar squat on the sidewalk beside the Baptist church. Millie is having a hard time making contact as the tattooed boy's attention seems to be focused on some imaginary howler monkey or parrot squawking in his mental jungle. The other street kids bound after passersby, shaking plastic cups, begging for spare change. When anyone well dressed passes by without tossing something in the cups, the kids pretend to cough and hack, "Die, yuppie scum!" into their hands.

Nikki dangles a forty-ounce bottle of malt liquor in a brown paper bag off her jutted hip just below a motorcycle-chain belt. She brings the bottle to her lips and tilts her head up for a big chug. Sunlight catches on the rings above her brow and glints off a tiny diamond in her left nostril. "I take silence to be consent." Nikki tugs again on the bottle and holds it out to me.

It is nine o'clock in the morning and a runaway teen, already drunk, panhandling on the Drag has concluded that I am completely lacking in a life. Not much point in trotting out the documentary story for this audience. In fact, I have no reason to work Nikki at all; there is nothing she can do for me or to me. That knowledge makes me feel unencumbered, weightless. I take the bottle and answer, "Pretty much, yeah."

The sweet Kool Aid–flavored liquor leaves me woozy, nauseated, and deeply nostalgic for Code Warrior.

Nikki nods approvingly. "All right. Millie would be all, 'Drinking's bad for you. Get an education.' For a fucktard dee bag, you're pretty cool."

This is the funniest thing I have ever heard.

"Me? Cool? I am not cool. I'm a gigantic washout freeloading off of a friend I dumped years ago so I could claw my way *up to* becoming a fucktard dee bag by using, sucking up to, or cheating everyone who crossed my path."

This admission makes me feel so giddily light that I try a few more. "The IRS is hunting me. Probably DEA; Alcohol, Tobacco, and Firearms; and the INS as well. I defaulted on my college loans, so someone will be coming after me for that, too. I'm thirty-three years old and I've got a roommate. I'm sharing a bathroom with six college kids, three of whom have very bad aim. Yeah, I'm cool."

"Could be worse."

We both drink to that. The malt liquor buzz lets me see past Nikki's piercings and tattoos and hostility long enough to ask, "What do you want to do?"

Nikki hefts the bottle. "Besides finish this and get another one?"

"Yeah. Besides that."

"What? Are you going to be all, 'Get an education'?"

"Right, like mine really helped me. Where I ended up, I would have been better off working at Burger King. Any kind of cost-effective mass-feeding outfit."

"Maybe in the olden days you didn't need an education to work there, but you do now."

"That's probably true."

"Oh, it is. Trust me. Burger King won't even let you near the Fryolator without one."

"I doubt that."

Nikki shoots me a sideways glance out of slitted eyes and asks warily, "Not that I give a shit, but what do you think I ought to do?"

"You'd have to be a whole lot worse off than you are to take career advice from me."

"Duh, I know that."

"What do *you* think you ought to do?"

Nikki rolls her eyes.

"No, seriously. What does Nikki want to do with her life?"

She shrugs.

"What do you love on this earth? What are you good at?"

"Me? Like what was my favorite subject in school?"

"No. Forget that bullshit. What are you *good* at? What's the thing that when you do it, you forget about time the way you used to when you were a kid and really got into something?"

Nikki takes a big swallow and holds the bottle up high. "Getting fucked up."

After years spent intuiting, then exploiting the desires of rich women, tapping into the dreams of the well-to-do and making myself into whoever could deliver them, Nikki is an easy read. Her hair is magenta today and done in haphazardly artful arcs and swirls. Her makeup is a self-portrait, a fantasy painted on skin. "You're living on the street. How do you keep your hair and makeup looking so good?"

"Young pussy. I can always get inside, use a bathroom, when I need to."

"So you 'need to' do your hair and makeup."

"No. I just like to, that's all."

"Nikki, you're an artist. You are a cosmetic artist. You are a colorist and a hair designer. You need to go to beauty school and get the bullshit piece of paper that says you can practice the art you were put on earth to create."

Nikki doesn't shrug or roll her eyes. "Yeah, like that'll ever happen."

"Why not? What's stopping you?"

"Uh, look around. You see a car? You see a beauty school I can walk to even if one would let me in the door?" She snorts at the ridiculousness of the whole idea.

It suddenly becomes desperately important to me to solve this one problem, to convince this girl to do what I want her to do. "I can get you in the door. I can get anyone in the door anywhere. That is not a problem. And here . . ." I fish out the keys to the minivan and hand them to Nikki. "Transportation problem solved. Skip a few lattes and you can put gas in the thing. It's the piece of crap parked behind Seneca House."

"You're letting me use your car?"

"Minivan. Sorry. But, consider this, you can sleep in it. You and Kat. Seats come out. All the soccer mom features. I'll try to figure something out about tuition for beauty school."

Nikki holds the keys away as if they were oozing slime. "Why?"

"Gift horse. Don't look it in the mouth."

I am trying to figure out why I feel so bizarrely elated because I've made someone take my only source of transportation when Millie drags a highly agitated Jaguar over to us. "Blythe, look!" She holds out the scrawny cat boy's arm. Above the inside of his wrist is a new patch of tattooed jaguar spots beneath a quilt of raw scabs. A streak of red crawls up the pale, undyed part of his inner arm.

"He's got a massive infection. I can't let go of him or he'll run away. We've got to get him to the People's Clinic up in north Austin. Go get your van."

"Millie, it's empty. Out of gas."

"Okay, we'll have to take a cab." Maintaining her hold on a struggling Jaguar, Millie tosses me a giant Taco Bell cup and orders, "Panhandle."

"What? Me? Panhandle? Isn't this what the Old Girls give you money for?"

Millie is shocked at the suggestion. "Not for this. Those donations are specifically earmarked for eggs, tortillas, condiments, and my living expenses. There is no line item for cab rides in my budget."

Hissing more like an alley than a jungle cat, Jaguar pulls away from Millie. His speed is reduced considerably by an insistence upon quadrupedal locomotion. Down on all fours, Jaguar doesn't cover much ground. Millie runs after him.

Nikki holds up her own cup. "Well? Shall we?"

"I'm not going to beg."

"Here." Nikki plunks a quarter and three pennies into my cup, then shakes hers. "Get that whole alms vibe going. A female who has most of her teeth doesn't need to do much more than shake the cup. Go. Get him." She shoves me in the direction of an older man, probably an English professor, judging from his fleeciness—fleecy beard, fleecy hair, fleecy corduroy pants.

I catch a glimpse of Millie wrangling Jaguar. He shrieks in real human pain when Millie accidentally grabs his infected arm. I clink the coins in my cup and tell the professor, "It's for my friend." I point to Jaguar. "He has an infected tattoo."

The professor stops and listens as if I were one of his favorite students.

"We need money for a taxi to the People's Clinic. That boy thinks he's a jaguar and some bastard keeps giving him tattoos that he can't take care of."

"Oh. Okay." The professor stuffs three dollars into the cup just like he is asked every day for money to treat infected jaguar tattoos.

I don't have time to lower my cup before the next three passersby toss change into it.

If I'd had any idea.

"Get them! Get them!" Nikki whirls me around and thrusts me toward three women hurrying past. From the lack of student denim or faculty fleece on the tailored trio, I peg them as visiting professors in international finance. Maybe architecture but nothing more down-market than that. Giddy from my surprising successes, I decide to wrap this mission up in a hurry with a surefire appeal to female solidarity. I rattle the change and yell, "Help a sistah?"

As the three women stop, I notice two things simultaneously: One, across the street, a huge banner flaps on the side of the mono-lithic Harry Ransom Center reading, WELCOME, PLATINUM LONG-HORNS! SUPPORTING A CELEBRATION OF TEXAS WOMEN OF LETTERS.

Streaming into the center are all the key members of the Pee Heights Mafia: Cherise Tatum, Missy Quisinberry, Paige Oglesby, Morgan Whitlow, and the rest of the inner circle. The second thing I notice is that the three women I have just begged for spare change are Kippie Lee Teeter, Bamsie Beiver, and Cookie Mehan.

The instant they see me, Kippie Lee and Bamsie step back, their desire to beat me with tire irons momentarily paralyzed by Southern-girl niceness. Cookie Mehan, with her more Western roots in ranching, however, is only too willing to take off the velvet glove and flex the iron hand. Luckily, she is too surprised to immediately call the police and instead demands, "Blythe Young, what the hell are you doing out here? Are you begging?"

"No. This? Begging? No. I was just bringing this over to . . . to you! To see if y'all need any change! For parking. Whatever. Help yourself." I hold out the cup, noticing far too late that it is emblazoned with a leering Chihuahua holding a femur in its mouth and asking, WANNA BONE?

"God, you guys look great. Have you lost weight? Bamsie, you still doing Zone? Cookie, what is it? South Beach. You look incredible. Incredible. Kippie Lee, love those shoes. God, I'd love to catch up with all y'all," I glance at my bare wrist, "but I'm meeting my crew in five minutes. This"—I wave at the cup, the street kids, my nails, hair, entire squalid existence—"it's all research. Working on a major documentary on homeless youth. I'll make sure and put y'all on the list for the preview screening. Comped. Y'all are comped."

Kippie Lee pulls out her cell phone and begins punching in numbers.

Police or IRS, I'm not hanging around to find out who she is calling. Cursing the damnable shooting schedule that is pulling me away, I beat a hasty retreat and duck into the nearest dark alley. About to infarct from humiliation beyond anything I've already experienced, I slump against a Dumpster and try to catch my breath. I smell before I notice the presence of someone sweating off a lifetime of fermented grains. It is Jesse, the beero from Dog Crap

Lane. Clutching a grubby pink blanket around his shoulders, he grins his toothless grin at me as he stuffs a dollar into the Taco Bell cup I'm still gripping. "Don't worry, Chief. Things'll get better."

"I hope you're right, Jess," I say as he shuffles away. "I hope to hell you're right."

Psycho Porker

NIKKI AND KAT move into the minivan. No one in the house protests because Millie goes to each resident and lobbies for the girls and because she keeps my involvement a secret. There are no complaints even when the girls swipe containers of yogurt and monopolize the bathrooms. Nikki and Kat panhandle for a few hours in the morning to raise money for gas, then spend the rest of the day either using up the gas or holed away in the van, painting toe- and fingernails and doing elaborate makeup jobs on each other. Nikki doesn't mention beauty school again. This annoys me. Intensely.

On the fourth evening of their stay, I pile two dinner plates with salad from the giant bowl someone has made for dinner and a couple of pieces of chicken from the pans cooking in the oven. I add squares of chocolate cake also nabbed from the house dinner.

In the backyard, my little minivan seems happier now that it is occupied. I tap on the door. Kat slides it open and takes one of the plates. "Chocolate cake. Awesome."

Nikki, sitting cross-legged on the floor of the van, watches me like an animal in its lair.

"You want this?" When Nikki doesn't answer, I put down the plate and a piece of paper next to it. "That's the number of the closest beauty college, Académie de Beauté. They've got classes starting next week. They have this deal with a couple of salons in town where you can work as a shampoo girl to pay for tuition. Call them or get out of the van."

Nikki doesn't touch the number. "I know why you're helping me."

"Really?"

"It makes you feel good to help someone *you think* is a bigger loser than you are."

"You could be right."

"Well, fuck you very much, but I can go to cosmetology school on my own without help from you or anyone else."

"I told them you'd come in tomorrow at ten for an interview."

"I already talked to that place. You can only do the shampoo girl thing if you have previous experience. So forget that."

"Gosh, Nikki, a girl like you, I'm sure you could just walk in there and charm them with your bright and positive sunny attitude."

"Fuck you."

"No, fuck *you,* bitch." I want to punch Nikki in the face. Instead, I shove the plate of food toward her. "You should eat this before the chicken gets cold."

"Blythe!" Millie rushes up, waving a note. "Look what I found taped to our door!"

I recognize Juniper's printing. Product of the Texas public school system, she never learned cursive.

Before I can take it, Millie reads out loud, "'Blythe—'"

"Not 'Drug-addled Cunt'? I must be making progress."

Millie shushes me and goes on, "'Danny Somebody called.'" She presses the note to her chest and squeals, "Danny called!"

"Could you just read the note?"

"Okay, okay. 'Be in town next Friday. In studio right now. Can't call. Will send car—'" More squealing. "He's sending a car!"

Nikki interrupts this time. "Read the fucking note!"

"'Will send car to pick you up at seven.'"

"Friday?" I am stunned. "That's less than a week away? That is not possible."

"A week? Why is that not possible?"

Millie's question is touchingly innocent. Nikki and I both ignore her. Nikki stares at me, taking in hair, skin, clothes, and calculates. "You're right, one week is not possible. You need two weeks. Minimum."

Nikki's ER-serious tone convinces me that the girl understands the true dimensions of the looming disaster. "We don't have two weeks," I wail.

Nikki touches my hair and winces. "It's hopeless."

"No, not hopeless," I plead. "You've got to help me." I am panicking and imploring Nikki to save me: The girl is showing impressive natural Swami talent.

"Okay, first, I'll do a cut on you that's not so Junior Leaguey."

"My hair has never been Junior Leaguey!"

Nikki drops my limp strands. "Have it your way." She puts the earbuds of her iPod in.

I grab her hand. "No, fine. You're right. What about makeup?"

She tilts her head from side to side, looking me over. "Is this guy at all hip or is he like you?"

"Like me? What's that supposed to mean?"

"He's a record producer," Millie informs her proudly.

"Right. What kind of music? Classical? Accordion? *Polka?*"

"Blythe's friend works for a company called Archive Records."

"Archive?" Nikki repeats, incredulous, and turns to me. "You're crazy. There is no way someone with a label that hip is calling you."

"Notify Ripley's, because, apparently, that's who he works for."

"Oh, wow. We have *a lot* of work to do."

"That's what I'm saying." It is a relief to have someone truly understand. "I need at least two weeks for hair reconstruction alone—"

"Three unless he likes straw."

"Then my face. Oh God, my face—"

"Elephant Man."

"Shut up! You're supposed to disagree. The dream, of course, would be a series of peels. Some microdermabrasion, a little bit of laser work. Photo facials. Loads of fill. Botox or whatever the latest neurotoxin is. Failing the preferred, yet impossibly high-priced options, I need a full month for the complete facial series, starting with serious exfoliation. Three weeks of extractions. Cool mist and deep cleansing ten days before. And, of course, the nails." I hold my hands up. Not a single nail has survived my stint as Sanjeev's scullery maid. I drop my hands. They land on my stomach and make a hideous discovery:

"Flab! I have a stomach!" I pinch and poke the roll of fat mushrooming over the waist of Olga's jeans.

"Yeah, I wondered if you realized what a porker you're turning into."

"Nikki, stop that!" Millie orders. "Blythe is still far too thin. She's just not dangerously emaciated anymore."

"Even if I have my stomach stapled tomorrow, there's not enough time to lose this, this . . ." I jiggle the micrometers of alien flab. "That's it. I can't do this."

"Stop freaking out," Nikki barks. "If you're gonna be a porker at least don't be a psycho porker. Go upstairs and wait for me."

Up in Millie's room, I study myself in the mirror. Nikki is right. My hair *is* Junior Leaguey. I have to figure out a way to get a really good cut. Nikki barges in carrying towels and beauty products. I recognize Juniper's face scrub, Doug's volumizing conditioner, and a tube of something with Cyrillic writing on it that must belong to Olga. Kat follows with a steaming teakettle.

"We'll begin with a moisturizing facial." Nikki dampens the towels with hot water and wraps my face like an old-time barber with only the tip of my nose sticking out, then starts brushing my hair.

"Leave my hair alone," I yell. Muffled by a wet towel, my words come out, *Ree muh rair aroe.*

"Don't worry. I'm just going to trim off some of the split ends. Now shut up and moisturize."

Some snipping ensues. Then some more. Then still more. Too

much snipping. I start to rip the towel off my face. "What are you doing?"

Nikki grabs my hand. "Relax. It only sounds like I'm cutting a lot. I'm just being really, really careful to only trim the very, very ends."

I ease back into the chair. "Okay. But just the ends."

Kat starts rubbing olive oil into my cuticles and hands and I drift off. The towel is gone when I wake up and it feels as if my face has vacationed in some soft and dewy land. It is velvety and has a slight minty tingle. My nails shimmer with a rosy glow they haven't had since grade school.

"Wow. Let me see."

Nikki presses the hand mirror against her chest and crosses her arms over it. This makes me so nervous that I lunge forward and rip the mirror from her hands. I take one look, grab Nikki by the arm, drag her downstairs, and shove her in the passenger seat of the van.

Kat gets in the back. "I think it looks good," she squeaks.

I stick my hand out. "Give me the keys." Nikki tries to sull up on me. "Give me the keys!" I thunder, and she hands them over.

We drive in stony silence. The atmosphere inside the van could have been measured barometrically, like an approaching storm.

"I think it looks good," Kat tries again.

"You. Shut up." To Nikki, "You did not have permission to cut my hair." I park in front of the Académie de Beauté and order both girls inside. Nikki responds surprisingly well to murderous rage.

The "académie" is like an alternative high school, a place for all the oddballs who couldn't make it on a regular campus: the chubbies, the gays, the transgendered, the terminally alienated, the too cool for school. They all wear white smocks and are giving haircuts to the senior citizens who patronize the place for the discount rates. The old ladies, draped in plastic capes, clutch plastic handbags on their knees. An instructor, a six-foot redhead with dyed hair ratted high into an impossible updo, a pink chiffon scarf over her Adam's apple, and a charm bracelet clanking against a man wrist, moves from chair to chair, critiquing each student's work. A cloud of hair spray and happy chatter hangs over everything. Kat and Nikki start to edge away, but I yank them back.

A woman who is about ten months pregnant comes to the front, holding a half-eaten container of blueberry yogurt with a spoon sticking out of it. The name tag on her blue smock reads, MRS. BRIDWELL.

"Are you the manager?"

"Why?"

I point to my head. "Do you see my hair?"

Mrs. Bridwell takes a small step back.

"She cut it." I push Nikki forward.

"We have no liability. She isn't one of our students."

"Well, she should be. Although she did not have my permission, this is the best haircut I have ever received. Do you see this?" I swing my head around and feathers of hair tickle across my face. "My hair has never done this. And see all these little flippy deals?" I touch the places where my hair arcs up in perky curves. "It's never done that either. I didn't even know it could do that. No mousse, no gel, no rollers. She just cut it and made it do that."

"Your old cut was just so sucky, it killed your natural wave," Nikki says.

"See? No one ever found my natural wave before. So, I'm telling you, you should let this girl take classes and you should put her on your work/study program."

Mrs. Bridwell rakes her fingers through my hair, pulling strands up, and watching the way they fall. "Nice cut. Who did you study with?"

"No one," Nikki answers. "I just always watched when I got my hair cut and copied what worked."

"She also does nails and makeup," Kat adds.

"So, both of you want to enroll?" Mrs. Bridwell asks.

"Yes!" Kat answers. "We have our own transportation."

"I'm not making any promises, but Kindest Cut of All is looking for someone to sweep up. Maybe shampoo. Come back tomorrow and I'll check you out before I send you over. We'll talk about classes then, too." She holds up the yogurt. "I've got to finish this and get back on the floor." As she walks back through the big room she calls out to the instructor, "Jackie, these girls are coming in tomorrow. Girls, tell Jackie your names."

The girls look at each other. Nikki submerges her excitement beneath a mask of cool, but Kat is openly euphoric. Jackie takes their names, then twiddles her fingers at us as we leave. "Hasta lumbago, girls!"

"Hasta lumbago!" both Nikki and Kat trill back.

For the next few days, Nikki slathers me in sunscreen before I go out with Millie, and my burn turns into the first tan I have had in a decade. That combined with Nikki's daily facials leaves me with a plumped-up glow that no amount of professional ministration has been able to achieve in the past. I look better than I have for a very long time. Considering that I am drug free, sleeping, eating, and exercising regularly for the first time in nearly a decade, I can only chalk the effect up to health.

Health—if I'd known what a beauty bonus it is, I might have tried it earlier.

By Thursday hair, skin, and nails are as good as they are going to get, but wardrobe remains a major concern. Millie says I am welcome to any of her cotton shirts and stretch-waist jeans, but I don't think Scrapbooking Mom is the exact right note to hit with Danny. I try various combinations of Olga's jeans and my Zac Posen jacket. Buttoned, unbuttoned, sleeves up, sleeves down. All the variations call *Miami Vice* to mind. Besides, the shiny intimidation jacket doesn't go with my feathery new haircut.

I am trying to build up my courage to wheedle something wearable out of Olga when Nikki bangs into my room. The salon has made her remove most of her less savory piercings and cut way back on the makeup. There is nothing now to cover up how flat-out beautiful she is.

"No, please, Nikki," I say as she bursts in. "Don't even consider knocking. I insist that you just barge right in. Why are you taking your clothes off?"

Nikki sheds a pair of gigantic homeboy jeans and a sloppy top. Beneath them, she has on a silk ensemble of low-rise pants with a matching top that is a cat's cradle of loops and ties. The color is somewhere between bluish silver and dove gray.

"God, that's a beautiful outfit. You should be on a runway somewhere. Seriously."

Nikki strips the outfit off and hands it to me. "Here, this'll look good with your tan and it complements your coloring."

The outfit floats into my hand, feathery as my new haircut. Tags with the name of an exclusive shop on the Drag dangle from the armpit. "Did you shoplift this? I can't let you shoplift."

"Okay. No worries. I'll take it back right now."

I try to give the silvery fantasy back to Nikki, but something has frozen my extensor muscles, and the outfit remains clutched to my bosom. "Or you could take it back Saturday?"

"I could do that. Try it on."

Nikki adjusts the ties. "Check it out."

I step in front of the mirror on Millie's closet door and wonder how I could have spent so much money and so many hours procuring clothes and never found anything that looked half as good as something a street kid shoplifted.

"Nikki, it's amazing. *You're* amazing."

Nikki cocks her head from side to side, sizing me up. "I guess you're the least sucky you're gonna be."

"I am. I'm the least sucky I'm gonna be."

The Socialite's Oath

AND THEN IT IS FRIDAY, 18:59 hours. Showtime.

I peer down from the second-story window and prepare to soak in the full impact of having a car and driver pick me up. Alternating surges of humiliation and prom-date thrills course through me when the longest, whitest stretch limo I have ever laid eyes on rounds the corner and halts in front of Seneca House. I wonder whether I should hide and disclaim any knowledge of the embarrassingly ostentatious vehicle or if I should ask to be borne down to the car by the house's six most muscular residents?

In the end, I wait in the room until everyone in the house is fully aware that the Moby Dick of all stretch limos has beached outside. One by one, all the forms of music that have been streaming into my room for the past weeks fall silent as everyone rushes downstairs to find out who the car is for.

A second later, there is pounding on my door. "Blythe! Blythe! Open up."

I crack the door to find Lute and Jerome hyperventilating. "The driver says Danny Escovedo sent the limo to pick you up!"

Jerome's excitement takes the form of belligerent heartiness. "I can't believe you know Danny Fucking Escovedo. Why didn't you tell us you know Danny Fucking Escovedo?"

"Did you say Danny Fucking Escovedo? No, no. There's been a mistake. Danny *Copulating* Escovedo is the one I know. Distant cousin. Whole other wing of the family."

"Hah fucking hah. Blythe, listen, you have got to, got to, got to, nonnegotiable, you absolutely have to get Danny E. over here to listen to us. By the way, you look hot."

"Mos def," Lute agrees enthusiastically, making his ringlets sproing up and down.

"I'm not kidding," Jerome growls. "Get him over here. Period. End of discussion."

When I meet Jerome's hostile glare with one of my own, Lute pushes him aside. "Ignore this wanker. He graduated from the Dick Cheney School of Charm. What he's trying to say is that we would esteem it a great personal favor if you would be so kind as to put us in touch with Mr. Escovedo. It has long been our dream to record with Archive Records."

"Yeah," Jerome interjects. "This in spite of the label's well-known abuses including, but not limited to, charging artists hundreds of dollars against royalties for chicken sandwiches from their cafeteria."

"Oh, yes. Appalling outrages," Lute agrees. "Any one of which I would kill to be subjected to."

"I'll mention it," I say. "I don't know how far it will go. Danny just works for this company."

"I wouldn't say 'works for' as much as 'is,'" Lute corrects me.

"Really?" This is interesting information.

Jerome gasps with exasperation. "The guy is sending a limo for you and you don't know that?"

"Not my world, blowhole. Fill me in."

Jerome delivers a minicolloquium as we head downstairs. "Your Mr. Escovedo made a fortune exploiting the indie scene. Then Archive hired him to produce. Everything he produced went platinum. He put Archive on the map. He could have ended up owning the company, but he wanted to stay in the field. So he's the highest-profile A-and-R man in the business."

"And that would be . . . ?"

"Artists and repetoire," Lute supplies.

"God!" Jerome explodes. "People always say 'repetoire.' Firstly, the word is 're-PER-toire.' PER. Secondly, it's *artiste et répertoire.* From the French."

"Bite me," Lute advises him. "From the Latin."

Downstairs, the entire house has congregated. Everyone pretends to have reasons for being there that have nothing to do with gawking at me. Millie and Sanjeev make a show of reviewing the house's books. Millie glances up as I descend—the silvery gray-blue outfit floating about me like wisps of fog—and her face melts into the fond expression of a mother seeing her daughter off to prom.

"Be home by eleven, young lady," Lute calls out as I leave.

"With your panties on, you little trollop," Jerome snarls.

Outside, the driver opens the back door, and the first thing I learn about stretch limos is how ridiculously uncomfortable they are. The seats are so low it is like riding in a canoe. All the smoked glass makes it impossible to see out so that it is more like a submarine than a canoe. As Moby Dick glides silently through the night, I hike up to the front seat and ask the driver where we are headed.

"The Four Seasons."

This is good. The Four Seasons Hotel is the coolest place in Austin since the people who are too cool to be Austinites stay there. Brad and Jennifer and Ethan and Uma are regulars. I take the endorsement of these solid celebrity couples to be a very good omen.

The limo docks in front of the hotel and a doorman leaps forward to help me out. "Mr. Escovedo is waiting for you in the bar," he informs me in a way that is smooth and sophisticated even if he is a college kid in khaki shorts.

The lobby bar sports low tables and plush settees. Just the spot for checking out either a million Mexican bats leaving their home beneath the Congress Avenue bridge to stream in a dark ribbon above the river or who Benicio del Toro is meeting for drinks.

I attempt a slow, devastating entrance. My plan is to slink slowly over to Danny's table, giving him ample time to absorb the full impact of the shoplifted skankwear. This doesn't come off quite as hoped because Danny is not amid the robber barons populating the small tables.

I finally spy Danny in an exclusive corner, hidden by an admir-
ing throng of music hipsters, a sultan accepting the tributes of subjects from the far-flung corners of his empire. I almost don't
recognize him. I expect the lanky lad of years ago. Instead, Danny
appears to have spent the past few years at Krispy Kreme. In short,
he has gone down Alec Baldwin Lane. Which only means that
Danny has put on weight while remaining criminally handsome.

Every eye in the place is riveted on him. Except for the three
pairs that flicker away and settle on me when I enter. Tragically,
those eyes belong to Kippie Lee Teeter, Bamsie Beiver, and Cookie
Mehan. The ladies occupy a darkened corner, slugging down moji-
tos, checking out whose husband is out with whose secretary, and,
no doubt, bonding further over their hatred of Blythe Young. Bamsie spots me and immediately reaches into the Birkin bag at her
side, whips out her cell phone, and begins stabbing in numbers. I
assume that those numbers belong to either IRS agents or police
officers and am backing slowly away when Danny spots me and
booms out, "Younghole! Get the hell over here!"

Bamsie's hand freezes as she watches the sultan stand, throw his
arms open wide, wrap me in a *Godfather* hug, then push me away to
take in the hoochwear.

"Jesus, God, look at you. Shit, Elly Mae, you's all growed up."

The crowd around him laughs with the hebephrenic giddiness
of sycophants currying favor. I know the laugh well. In my prime,
no one curried better than me. I glance back at the triumvirate.
Their finely tuned social synapses are visibly snarling. The desire to
drop an anvil on my head collides with the socialite's oath: First, do
no harm—to anyone higher up on the seating chart, that is.

Safe for the moment, I turn my attention to Danny. He no
longer seems younger than me the way he did when we were copy-
ing briefs at Kinko's. He has a heft to him that goes far beyond
weight; he has the tonnage that comes only with success. It is clear
from the mob of young women fawning on him that Danny has
executed a jujitsu on time and performed the move that allows a

man to subtract a year of age for every million or so he's got in liquid assets, until a top CEO can run away with his grandchildren's
nanny and no one thinks much of it. So, once again, I figure, I am
too old for Danny.

"Hey!" Danny claps his hand, and the chattering crew falls silent.
"Disperse. Office hours are officially over as of"—he studies his
watch, holds up a finger, drops it like he is starting a race—"now!"

With a rustle of leather from their identical jackets, the four
young men in the group leave, flagging studiedly casual waves and
calling over their shoulders, "Laters, Danny." "Catch you, mañana,
hombre."

The young—statutorily young—women don't shoo so easily.
One holds a CD against her breasts, so that Danny is forced to cop a
handy feel as he takes it from her. She looks like a taller, thinner
Vanessa Williams, which is to say the woman is an android composed of spare parts left lying around at the Supermodel Factory.

"Yes, yes, I promise I'll listen to it," Danny says, dismissing her
with a seignorial wave.

Another lingerer is wearing a mesmerizing pair of jeans that are
literally only legs held up with an intricate rigging of straps and
thong bikini. She presses against Danny, whispering in his ear and
shooting kittenish glances my way.

"Thanks for the offer, Shaundra," Danny booms out. "But I
doubt that my 'date' is interested in a three-way. Though I could be
wrong. Younghole, how about it? You up for a three-way with
Shaundra here?"

"Maybe a rain check."

" 'Nother time, Shaun."

Shaundra doesn't so much leave as she is reabsorbed into the
ether of male fantasies from whence she materialized. I am feeling
about eighty-five years old by the time the last of the hangers-on
melts away.

"So, you're the hip-hop Donald Trump."

"Oh no, Younghole, you're starting in on me already. If that's the way it's going to be you are going to need a drink." He wipes lipstick off one of the snifters littering the table, grabs a half-empty bottle of Courvoisier, and pours. "In fact, you're going to need *lots* of drinks to drown that bug in your ass. I love that line."

"Jack Nicholson. *Terms of Endearment*," I supply.

"Hallelujah! A woman with a brain. We are drinking to that." He fills the snifter, hands it to me, then takes it back. "Don't drink out of that. Too many ho-crobes."

He flags a waiter over, and fresh glasses are produced. "Sorry about this." He waves at the Courvoisier. "And the stretch monstrosity. You've got to fulfill expectations, you know what I'm saying?"

"Word," I answer dryly.

Grinning, he taps my shoulder. "You, you. You were always very light on your feet, could dance around. Now, Sister Mary Younghole, remind me, why didn't we have a mad, passionate affair?"

"The line was too long."

"Hah. Because I had a thing for you, you know."

"You did not."

"You led me around by the nose. The sophisticated older woman. First you had that sad-sack boyfriend, Edgar—"

"James."

"Same difference. Then that gigolo, that tango instructor from Argentina."

"Fencing champion from Hungary."

"Again, details. You always had the mens buzzin' 'round you. God, you look good. What do you do? Zone? South Beach? Personal trainer? You're a rail. But in a good way. Cameron Diaz would kill to have your figure. Kill."

It flabbergasts me to hear Danny Escovedo doing the weight-bonding routine as well as I ever did in my prime.

Danny holds his arms out wide to clear the view of the Escovedo girth. "Have you noticed what a hog I've turned into?"

"You could never be a hog."

"And yet, I am."

In that instant, the reedy boy I knew disappears, and I can't imagine Danny ever looking any other way. Or ever being sexier. I bring the snifter to my nose. The Courvoisier smells like a distillation of every extravagance from my lost paradise. By the second snifter, I've told Danny the entire tale of my divorce, preceded by my rise on the swamp gas of the Internet bubble and subsequent fall with bumps along the way against every branch of Austin's social tree.

"In fact," I whisper, enjoying the necessity of leaning in close to Danny, who leans toward me in return until our heads touch and his brandy-warmed breath puffs against my cheek, "the three socialites most likely to lead a lynch mob are right over there."

"Where? Show me. Who's messing with my girl, huh? You mess with my girl, you go down, bitches."

I get an atavistic thrill from his joke-vendetta routine. Even kidding, though, I can't remember the last time a man stood up for me. Certainly Trey didn't. Trey rolled over on me the instant his mother told him to.

"What do the bitches like to drink?"

"Kir Royales."

Danny waves the waiter over, scribbles a note on the back of his card, sends him off, and tells me to watch.

A moment later, the waiter reappears at Bamsie, Kippie Lee, and Cookie's table with three flutes effervescing brightly.

As the waiter leans in toward the women, Danny whispers, "And now he tells them who I am."

The waiter points to Danny and hands them his note. The women huddle up, read the note, then flash astonished gazes.

"Don't look." Danny nods and winks at the ladies.

"What did you write in that note?"

"Nothing much. I told them that my dear, dear friend Blythe Young has informed me that they are all incredibly talented and would they consider a private audition."

"They will never fall for that."

"You're right. What they will fall for, though, is the much bigger, much more irresistible illusion that I'm so hot for their bony asses that I would work such an obvious scam. Why, have a look now."

Danny twiddles his fingers at the ladies and I turn, bracing myself to be sliced by three socialites glaring daggers. Instead I find Kippie Lee Teeter, that pillar of Austin society, has undone the top three buttons of her blouse and is sloshing the full bounty of her implants forward. My Pemberton Heights landlady and mother of little Chance and Daphne, Bamsie Beiver, is flipping her hair from side to side, head thrown back, laughing gales of tawny laughter. Cookie Mehan, gardening maven and no-nonsense ranch girl, is licking her lips and shooting Danny the kinds of expressions found above 900 numbers.

Danny puts his arm around me. "Your worries are over. You are golden. You are their new best friend. But, just to be sure, let's seal the deal."

There is only a second or two when I think that kissing Danny Escovedo in the middle of the Four Seasons lobby in front of Kippie Lee Teeter, Bamsie Beiver, and Cookie Mehan is a bad idea. Then I taste his mouth, all warm from the brandy, spiced with tobacco, marijuana, and coffee, and the kiss seems far and away the best idea anyone has ever had. By the time his mouth moves from mine, I can't recall who might be watching or why I ever cared.

"I wanted to do that from the first minute I met you. It was a young lad's simple dream."

"Wasn't your dream to die playing with your band at some crappy bar?"

"Dream? Shit, that was me looking into a crystal ball."

"Okay, you've already heard my pathetic tale. How did you get from local rock god to music mogul? Tell me a story that has a happy ending."

"At least one that doesn't conclude with my getting beaten to death by a biker because I won't play 'Freebird' nineteen times. Which is how my story would have ended if I'd stayed in the band.

No, I had my come-to-Jesus moment the winter I ended up wearing a Hawaiian shirt, playing Jimmy Buffett covers on some booze cruise abomination.

"We were up on deck, banging out 'Wasted Away Again in Margaritaville' for about the eight hundredth fucking time. The wives were taking their tops off and shaking their tits at anyone they weren't married to and it suddenly starts raining. Fine. We unplug and we're packing up. But, oh no. These shitfaced boomers are having so much fun that they demand—demand—that we keep playing.

"So there I am looking at all these horny geezers who don't give a fuck if the music monkeys die. Electrocuted playing bad covers of bad songs was not the death I signed up for. Running into the side of a mountain in a small plane, choking on my own vomit, groupies putting too much of the wrong shit up my nose, sure. That, *that,* is what I signed up for. Cool rock 'n' roll deaths. But fried on a booze cruise? Uh-uh. That was not the obituary I was going for. I jumped ship as soon as we hit Puerto Vallarta and hopped the next plane to LA. Took the first production job I could swing."

"But you are such a great musician."

"That and a quarter, huh? Music is a crap business. You can be a seriously mediocre writer and make a living, right? Get some job doing the annual reports for Rape the Land, Inc. But a musician? Doesn't matter if you have the greatest chops in the world and charisma to burn, you'll still end up playing the Ramada Inn or teaching guitar at a strip mall. Musical talent is a curse. Speaking of which, I've got to get to work. Check out a couple of bands. You coming with me?"

I pass on the opportunity to hang out at a smoky club while underage hoochies in bondage getups drape themselves over Danny. Besides, my evening is officially complete the moment he escorts me past Bamsie, Cookie, and Kippie Lee. Suddenly, I rate the official high-pitched, Texas-girl salutation audible only to dogs and sorority sisters. "Blythe! Lookatchew!"

Danny gets into the limo with me, and my appreciation of the stretch increases as we head back to Seneca House. Making out in the backseat of a moving vehicle is a new dimension in transportation. At the house, Danny insists on coming in. "Stroll down Memory Lane. But only for a few minutes. I have a breakfast meeting with a group I signed in San Antonio last month; then I've got to spend some serious time in Houston. Amazing rap scene there."

"I think I should warn you—" I start to say as we cross the threshold. I never get to finish warning him that he will probably be besieged by desperate musicians because he is immediately besieged by desperate musicians. Jerome and Lute press copies of their demos on him. Yay Bombah and Nazarite casually break into a reggae version of "I Fought the Law." Olga undulates her snaky body and drenches Danny in smoky Balkan gazes. Presto and Clancy, in high event-coordinator mode, dart about like Chihuahuas on crack.

Danny searches the crowd pressing in on him. "Where's Millie?"

"Right here," Millie, standing unrecognized directly in front of him, answers.

"God, another one who got even more beautiful behind my back." Danny wraps his arms around Millie and the laptop she is holding.

"I must be some kind of incredible beauty secret. As soon as I go away, the girls get supermodel gorgeous."

"Maybe," Millie says as Danny loosens his hold, "that's because it's too dangerous for pretty girls when you're around."

"You!" Danny yells. "You! I'm gonna write you another fat check right now. How's the work going?"

"Danny supports you, too?" I ask.

"Oh, all the cool people do. The work is going well. Really well. I used part of your last donation to buy Jesse some special shoes after he cut his right toe off when he was showing Carl how to use a chain saw."

Danny holds his hand up. "Good, good. No details required." He points at the laptop Millie holds. "Any reason you're clutching that thing like Moses with the tablets?"

Millie, wearing a smile of secret delight, opens her laptop and proudly holds it out to Danny.

"What's this?" Danny studies the screen. His eyes narrow, his brow wrinkles, his mouth drops open. "What the . . . ? Is that my—"

"Yes! It's Archive's latest album . . . Or is it called a CD now? Anyway, it's your latest release, and it's far and away the most popular selection in the house!"

Danny studies the screen. Behind his back, Jerome presses his palms against his forehead, squeezes his eyes shut, and mouths the word "no." Watching Jerome is like studying the stewardess on a plane flying through an electrical storm. His expression tells me that we are going down.

Danny leans in farther. "Someone's downloading it right now. Hay-sus Kreesto. They sucked that down in what? Ten seconds? What kind of bandwidth do you all have here? This is like NORAD or something."

Just then Doug, headphones clamped over his ears, comes downstairs singing, "'Gimme, I'm gonna take it. Gimme, I'm gonna take it . . . You feel me . . . You feel me . . . Gimme, I'm gonna take it'" from the title track of Archive's latest release, "Gimme, I'm Gonna Take It" by Li'l CheeZ.

Doug, noticing that everyone is watching him, stops on the stairs, bites his lower lip, and drops it like it is hot, executing some not-bad dance moves.

Millie beams at Danny. "See? What did I tell you? Everyone in the house loves your new release!"

"Oh, I can see that."

"You can tell Little Cheesy that the homeboys and homegirls of Seneca House"—Millie pauses to bite back a giggle at her urban outrageousness—"love his work."

Danny nods thoughtfully. I consider diving in to do some damage control, but am not sure what the damage is or how to control it. Danny closes the laptop, hands it back to Millie, and requests that we both join him on the porch.

Outside, he asks one question: "Have either of you downloaded music through this house network?"

Millie, still suffering under the delusion that pirating music is a gigantic artistic tribute, answers first. "Danny, please don't be offended, but I haven't ever downloaded any music. If I ever do, however, yours will be the first."

"What about you, Younghole?"

"Not so much as one phat beat," I assure him.

He gathers us both into his arms and kisses the tops of our heads. "That's my girls."

I snuggle against him and breathe deeply. With just one white lie, the crisis has been averted. At least for me and Millie. And, really? Who else is there?

The Dogs of Law

OVER THE NEXT FEW DAYS, Danny calls from all around the state, always shouting above the roar of live music. I want to ask him about the downloading incident, but since he usually can't hear a word I say, I let it go.

The call I get early Friday afternoon, though, is not from Danny. "Blythe, hey, it's Alli. Listen, quick question, can you recommend a good, no, a great caterer?"

"Yeah. Me. Though, actually, I'm more of an event coordinator."

"Oh. Well, you see, it's for a Platinum Longhorns program and . . ."

"Your ladies would stab me to death with their black AmEx cards."

"Something like that, yeah."

"What's the program?"

"You know how I do these fund-raiser trips?"

"Right. Tuscany. Provence. The Greek Islands." These were the Plat Longs' big annual trips where the society ladies would dress up for one another and gossip about their friends while they were supposed to be soaking up culture. If it was Florence, they would do a quick check-in at the Uffizi, brief run-through of the Duomo, then zip over to the Ponte Vecchio to start the main event: shopping. Same deal in Bali, half an hour for temple art, then a day of buying batiked evening gowns. "So why do you need a caterer? You're not going to take one with you to some foreign country, are you?"

"We're not going to any foreign country this year. The dollar is so bad that we wouldn't make any money at all, and, thanks to your big buddy in the White House, everyone in the world wants to kill us."

"Why is he my big buddy?"

"The jacket. The shoes. I've learned how to spot the signs. Anyway, the ladies are too freaked out about terrorists to leave the country, which is why Kippie Lee came up with her brainstorm. Without checking with me first, she decided that the thing to do is rent out the Pi Phi house, where many of the women spent the happiest days of their lives, and have the culture brought to them. They're going to have big-name profs lecture while the maids and butlers bustle around attending to their every need. Compared with Bali, the price is an incredible bargain. Our profit margin is going to be very healthy."

Alli gets specific with figures that cause me a moment of intense professional envy. "Healthy? I couldn't have made that much off an event with a sawed-off shotgun. Mazel tov, my friend."

"Oh, thanks. This one trip will float the Plat Longs and give me complete job security for at least a year. But I do need a caterer who can work with all the ladies'—"

"Insane demands?"

"Something like that."

I recommend Antoinette, at Let Them Eat Cake; I owe her one for stealing Sergio. And most of her clients. The instant I hang up, the phone rings again. It's Danny.

"Do you want to come to the Grammys with me? I know it's a ways off, but you've got wardrobe to think about, right?"

"Are you kidding? The Grammys?"

"You'll be sick of me by then. You and Jerome will be married. First kid on the way. He'll have a job selling egg rolls on the Drag."

"They shut the egg roll vendors down. Cockroaches."

"Jeez, no egg roll vendors? I existed on those things. Wow, end of an era. Okay, your boy Jerome will be a lifeguard at Deep Eddy. No, a shuttle-bus driver. Or maybe making sandwiches at Thundercloud Subs. They haven't shut Thundercloud down for cockroaches, have they?"

"No, in fact, I think it's this week's special."

As Danny goes on free-associating about the perfect Austin fantasy life Jerome and I will be living, I do mental jumping jacks about the hint of a future he is holding out to me. Then Lute edges over and begins singing about the burden of being adorable. "I'm your mirror and you love what you see. But turn it over cuz that ain't me. I ain't your toy. I'm a real live boy."

Lute nudges me until I tell Danny, "Uh, here's Lute," and surrender the phone.

As Lute goes into the bridge, Millie trundles upstairs and Sanjeev watches her disappear with sorrowful brown eyes.

Just as Lute is lamenting, "I know you're one of them girls. All you see is the curls," I notice a brown car glide to a stop in front of the house. It has the seal of the state of Texas on the door. My heart is thumping madly even before I read, TRAVIS COUNTY SHERIFF'S DEPARTMENT. A bulky deputy in a khaki shirt gets out, surveys the house, cranes his neck over to one side, and talks into the microphone clipped to the epaulet on his shoulder.

I grab the phone back. "Danny, I gotta go."

Before I can scamper off to the backyard and make a run for the border, a young woman sprints across the front lawn to catch the sheriff. I recognize her but can't think of the name. Blond, petite, wearing a peach-colored suit and too much makeup, she would have been my sorority sister had I ever been in a sorority. But I definitely remember having drinks with the woman. Lots and lots of drinks.

When Blondie corners the sheriff and sticks a microphone in his face—activities all being filmed by a cameraman—it comes to me that my "old friend" is Amy Truelove, Channel 7 *News at 10* newsgal. Many indeed were the drinks Amy and I shared. Entire bottles of Chardonnay polished off in front of the television set as I watched her thrust microphones into the faces of various miscreants in orange jumpsuits.

Orange jumpsuit.

Me + orange jumpsuit.

This equation propels me decisively toward the front door. In full view of the sheriff, who is pounding hard enough to rattle the panes of glass between us, I turn the key in the lock, slam the dead bolt home, pocket the key, and beeline for the back door. My plan is to run down to Dog Crap Lane, where I will hide out among Millie's egg people until such time as I can regain possession of the van, then embark upon a crime spree. Crime Spree seems the next step up on my career ladder.

I am sprinting through the dining room when shouts of, "Who has the front door key?" ring out.

Tragically, Millie pipes up, "No worries, I've got an extra one!"

The door is unlocked before I reach the kitchen. The sheriff booms out, "I have John Doe subpoenas for the following IP addresses." He reads off strings of digits.

Sanjeev recognizes one of the numbers and asks, "Why is Millie being subpoenaed?"

My ears are so prepared to be bludgeoned with either the phrase "aiding and abetting a fugitive from the law" or "accomplice to fraud, drug delivery, and tax evasion," that the sheriff's answer, "Copyright infringement," leaves me puzzled. Then, with banjos playing "Oh, Susanna" in a creepy-ominous *Deliverance* way in my head, I remember the songs I downloaded onto Millie's laptop.

In the living room, the entire house is swarming around the sheriff. Jerome gets the last subpoena.

Invisible? I want to scream at Jerome. *You said the house was invisible. What happened to invisible?* But of course, I already know what happened to invisible: *I* happened to invisible. I brought Danny into the house. I put downloaded music onto Millie's laptop.

Channel 7's Amy Truelove sticks a microphone in Yay Bombah's face and asks, "How does it feel to be part of the latest round of test cases filed by the Recording Industry Association of America for copyright infringement?"

Yay Bombah shakes her dreadlocks. Before she can answer, Jerome grabs the microphone. "What a joke that is. The biggest infringer upon copyright, upon the rights of artists, *is* the recording industry. The RIAA's concern for artists is a cynical smoke screen. The only thing they're concerned about is the bottom line."

While Jerome rants on, Amy furiously scans her cheat sheet of questions. She yanks her head back up before the cameraman turns on her and is ready with a cross-examination. "The RIAA accuses you and most of the other residents of running a file-sharing network designed to promote widespread music piracy."

"'Piracy'?" Jerome yells. "The pirates who plundered the musical legacy of everyone from Robert Johnson and Bo Diddley to Android Peacekeepers and Used Rubbers are calling *me* a pirate?"

Out of view of the camera, Amy's cell phone rings. The newswoman whispers furiously into it as Jerome rails on. "This is hilarious. The record companies have been manipulating copyright laws for years, and all the manipulations were designed to steal everything they could from the actual creators of the work. You know what they are really worried about?"

"We gotta roll," Amy announces to her cameraman. "A protest at the Capitol. Something about telling the governor that 'gay is okay.'" Amy snatches the mike out of Jerome's hand. Even when the lights flicker off and the sheriff and news team vanish, Jerome bloviates on, as impassioned as ever. "The record companies aren't worried about 'lost sales.' They're worried about artists discovering that we don't need them. They're worried about—"

A shriek halts Jerome's screed. The shriekers are the house's computer phantoms. Juniper interprets for them. "Choi Soon Yong and Elmootaz are worried about losing their student visas. Two of those subpoenas have their IP addresses on them. Choi Soon Yong says that the only way the RIAA could have found out about LANs like ours is if someone told them. Elmootaz says someone would have had to practically invite a record executive in and show them the system for them to find us."

With the single-mindedness that makes lynch mobs so successful, the residents turn as one and face me. Before that moment I believed that they couldn't hate me any more than they already did.

I was wrong. There are as-yet-untapped reservoirs of vitriol reserved exclusively for "parasite whores" such as myself who invite record company executives in to witness their Jolly Roger levels of piracy.

"God, we are so screwed," Yay Bombah informs Nazarite, matching the numbers on two of the subpoenas to their IP addresses.

"Daddy is going to kill us," adds Nazarite, both of them having abandoned the Lion of Judah and reverted decisively to their original identities. "I read that they've sued people for, like, one hundred twenty thousand dollars for every song on their computers. We've got how many songs?"

"About a million," sister Saperstein answers.

"God, we are so screwed."

"Don't worry," Jerome says. "These things never go to court. The companies always intimidate their victims into settling."

"How much they pay?" Elmootaz asks.

"I don't know," Jerome answers. "A few thousand. I'd be happy to spend that much just to expose their hypocrisy."

"And you've got a few grand stashed away?" Juniper asks.

"No, but—"

The house sinks into a stunned silence as we contemplate how impossible it will be to pay even the smallest settlement.

"Look," I say, "this has got to be a mistake. Danny is just not that kind of person."

Jerome snorts loudly. "Yeah, right."

"I'll talk to him and get him to call the dogs off. It'll be okay. Really. Trust me."

Perhaps the "trust me" is ill-advised. At least it lightens the mood, since Juniper breaks into hyena convulsions of laughter.

I call Danny and he answers before the second ring. "Younghole, you bitch, why did you let that Aussie torture me? If I want to listen to blond airheads sing, I'll call Britney. So, have you figured out what you're wearing to the Grammys?"

"An orange jumpsuit."

"No, I think Beyoncé already has dibs on the orange jumpsuit."

"Danny, the sheriff was here."

"Subpoena time, huh? Bet that made your boyfriend Jerome happy. Answer to a martyr's prayer."

"You did this? You turned the house in? You couldn't have done this on purpose."

"No, you're right, I *accidentally* called the RIAA and reported egregious criminal activity."

"Danny, how could you do that? To me? To the house?"

"What do you mean, 'you'? I specifically asked you if you had downloaded any music and you specifically told me you had not. You and Millie. No music. That's what you told me."

"Okay, there might have been a song or two that I downloaded onto Millie's laptop."

"You lied? To me? Why?"

"I didn't think it mattered."

"God, Younghole, you thoroughly porked the pooch on this one. I never in a million years would have turned the house in if I thought it would hurt you or Millie."

"I never in a million years would have believed you would do this."

"And I can't believe you would think I'd do anything else. What do you imagine Henry Ford would do if he walked into a chop shop filled with stolen Thunderbirds? You think—"

"Yeah, but you aren't Henry Ford and this isn't a chop shop. This is a house filled with people who have no money, who took me in and helped me. Danny, this is Millie's—"

Danny ignores my interruption. "—you think Henry Ford *might* mention it to someone in the company? You don't think Henry wouldn't be derelict in his duty to that company if he *didn't* mention it? Look, there aren't any kindergartners over there who have no idea what they're doing. No quadriplegics who can't haul themselves to a record store. You've got a full-blown file-sharing network. Now, whatever you or your friends might think about the industry I work in, it's what we've got. We spend millions developing new artists, rolling out new product, and if we go down, well, I hope your Herman's Hermits albums are in good shape, cuz there ain't gonna be no new music."

"Please, Danny, for me, call off the dogs."

"For you, Sister Mary Younghole, anything. If I could I would, but I can't. It's out of my hands. They've already let slip the dogs of law. As your little buddies, the music pirates, are so fond of saying, the genie is out of the bottle."

Guilty as Sin

I SIT IN the deep leather hush of the waiting room of the best intellectual property rights law firm in town. Which just so happens to be Teeter, Tawter, and Deaux. I have no worries that I will run into Hunt Teeter, Kippie Lee's philandering asshole of a husband. Since he is a founding partner our case rests safely below his radar. Next to me are Doug and Juniper, representing the house, and Dr. Dr. Robin, who insisted on coming to look after the interests of the Old Girls.

It turns out that we, the residents of Seneca House, are the Great White and Unpopular Minorities test case the RIAA has been dreaming of. Overprivileged college kids, one Middle Eastern, one Chinese, no children or widows. They couldn't have put together better defendants in a lab.

"Waiting room" is not quite the right term for where we are. Not with its connotations of ancient copies of *Field & Stream* and screaming children. No, we have been supplied with Evian by a solicitous intern named Chloe who has the manners, clothes, and teeth of someone with roots in the Ivy League. The reading material on the carved rosewood coffee table is an art book about Victorian snuffboxes. And screaming children? Not on Planet Billables.

Robin has barely begun enumerating all my moral failings when Chloe returns and announces softly, "Mr. Dix will see you now."

Dix?

Fighting shock as we follow Chloe down a hall, I tell the others to go on ahead without me, then pull Chloe aside. "Did you say 'Dix'? Which Dix?"

"You will be seeing Mr. Henry Dix the Third."

"Tree-Tree? What is Tree-Tree doing here?"

"Mr. Dix is our client contact. We are very fortunate to have him assisting us in an interface capacity where his unique talents as both a lobbyist with significant legislative contacts and—"

I cut Chloe off with a brusque, "Yeah, right." I don't have time for the full wanka-wanka. I already know that anytime a Dix is involved, the answer to "What is he doing here?" is, "Extending the grip of my mother's blood-sucking tentacles." I mention a tiny detail: "Trey doesn't have a law degree."

Chloe loosens the death grip I have obtained upon the sleeve of her bespoke jacket. She indicates with a subtle sweep of her hand toward the open door of Trey's office down the hall that this is not her problem. Through the open door, I see that Tree-Tree's office has its own entryway which features a large aquarium atop a half wall that functions as a sort of divider. Hidden from view by masses of rippling algae, I slip inside the office and Chloe shuts the door behind me.

Concealed by the aquarium, I peek into the wobbly, underwater scene unfolding in Trey's office. This is the first time I've glimpsed my ex-husband since his family air-evacked him out of our marriage. He is pulling out chairs for Juniper and Robin. The aquarium rippling lends the scene a wobbly flashback quality. It could have been me in that chair being tended to by Henry "Trey" Dix.

Doug pivots in his chair. I fade farther into the underwater foliage as he searches the office. "Where is—"

Thankfully, the reliably testy Juniper cuts Doug off with a curt, "Pit stop," before he can reveal my name.

Trey is trotting out his best country club manners, the ones reserved for parents of important friends, college admission directors, people who can do things for a presentable lad. He helps everyone settle in, patting hands, shoulders, leaning in to ask, "You okay there? My girl take good care of you? What can we get you? One of them French fizzy waters?"

Trey points to each person in turn and asks, "You good?" He massages Doug's shoulders. "You work out, don't you? You do!" He stabs a finger into Doug's chest as if he'd caught him in some scampish prank. "You're a monster gym rat, aren't you?"

Doug shrugs. "Not really."

"You're not gonna tell the boss on me if I take my jacket off, are you?" Trey asks Doug. "Cuz you look like trouble."

Doug, who is wearing his most formal outfit, a guayabera and clean jeans, shrugs. "Be my guest."

Trey winks at Doug as he shucks his jacket. "I like you. You're trouble."

He moves on to Juniper. Cupping her hand in both of his as if it were a baby chick, he soaks her in and announces, "You're a tall drink of water. I'm gonna call you Slim."

Slim was my *nickname.*

Juniper, who is actually fairly broad in the beam, does not object. He moves on to Robin. I can't wait for this die-hard feminist to read Trey the Seneca Falls Convention Act. I can tell from the annoyed quirk of her eyebrow and peptic seam of her lips that she sees right through his unctuous bonhomie and is ready to uncork.

Before she can open her mouth, however, Trey asks, "Darlin', where did you get those eyelashes?" Robin does have great eyelashes. "You, you are Bambi. Case closed."

Trey shifts his attention back to Doug. He shakes his hand in a manly fashion while thumping his shoulder. "And now we've got Trouble. What am I gonna do with you . . ."

"Doug."

"Doug? That's what you'd like me to think, isn't it?" Trey fixes Doug with a bad-boy grin as if they were both in on the most inside of inside jokes. "You are one bad hombre. I'm gonna have to call you Drug, cuz . . ." He looks around and leans in to whisper, "You smoke the herb, am I right, mon?"

"No."

Trey mimes sucking on a joint, complete with jerky inhalations, eyes squeezed shut against the curl of imaginary smoke, then a coughing exhalation. "We all smoke the herb, right, mon?"

Trey wears a silly, stoned grin as he returns to the overlord side of the desk. "So, tell me," he asks, folding up the monogrammed cuffs of his custom-tailored shirt in a ritualized display of folksiness. "What problems can I make disappear for y'all today?"

As Doug outlines our case, Trey mutters, "Sons of bitches." "Assholes." "Jerkwads." Such are his considered legal opinions, delivered while shaking his head in righteous disgust and anger.

"How do you feel about some of the more aggressive defenses?" Doug asks. "Countersuing for racketeering, First Amendment protection against the chilling effect of—"

"Oh yes. Oh *hell* yes," Trey answers with a ringing bellicosity that calls his renegade grandfather Uno to mind. "You do not mess with me and you do not mess with my people and y'all are now, officially, my people. We'll countersue the bastards back to the Stone Age is what we'll do. Racketeering, tax evasion, pedophilia. Are you asking me what we'll countersue with? Is that what you're asking? Cuz my answer is, 'Whatta you got?'"

"So you're proposing—" Doug begins.

"Are you asking me what I'm proposing?"

"Yes."

"Because if you're asking me what I'm proposing, is that what you're asking?"

Doug doesn't bother to answer.

"Okay, just want to get that straight, because what I propose is this: I propose that we rain a shitstorm down on them that'll make 'em sorry they ever crossed paths with Slim, Bambi, and Drug. You wanna know what I say to the R fucking IAA? You wanna know what I say?"

Three pairs of eyes glow with the throwback glee of having the biggest sumbitch in the jungle taking up the cudgel on their behalf.

"I say, bring it on! Cuz we will not only wipe you off the map, we'll make you pay us a fortune in damages for the pleasure." Trey glances from Juniper and Robin—who are making tiny fist-pumping gestures—to Doug, who is, thankfully, withholding judgment.

"Looks like we got us a quorum. First thing we're gonna need is all the documentation you've got. We have to see just how much of a case the RIAA has. Drug, buddy, you look like the tech wizard in the group; maybe you could just step over here to my computer and send a big ol' group message to everyone in the house and tell them to forward all their files and pertinent documentation to me so I can get the brain boys working on making this all disappear."

Disaster! That cannot happen. I don't know what angle Trey is working, just that he is certain to have one. I pray for Doug to jump up and storm out.

"Drug? We're waiting."

"I'm thinking."

Thinking? No! Storm out. Yes!

They cannot even consider getting involved with Trey. Though it is the last thing on earth I want to do, I step out from behind the aquarium. "Don't listen to him."

Trey greets me with a casual, "Blythe, I was wondering when you were going to join the party." Ever the perfect host, perfect rush chairman, perfect lobbyist, ever the guy who always makes sure everyone has a drink in their hands, and that it is a double, Trey offers a graceful, "I assume y'all know my ex-wife."

Though distracted by the impressive sight of three jaws dropping in perfect synchronization, Trey gives me his patented twinkly grin as I belatedly notice the video camera on the ceiling above the aquarium and the small monitor on Trey's desk that have been displaying my hiding place from the moment I stepped into the office. "You should know by now that folks in my family don't like surprises."

"Seriously, don't listen to him."

"Slim One, are you ridin' in here to warn your compañeros all about me? Tell 'em what a bad hombre I am? Maybe mention that I'm not *technically* a lawyer?"

Trey's affable admission worries me. "Well, you're not. You're not a lawyer."

"And damn lucky for you I'm not, either. Y'all don't want a lawyer. Spot y'all are in, lawyer's gonna hurt you a hell of a lot more than he'll help. You get a lawyer, you're playing their game. And, my friends, that is a game you are gonna lose. You know why?"

"Don't listen to him," I warn yet again as I try to figure out what Trey is up to.

Robin ignores me and asks, "Why?"

"Cuz y'all broke the law!" Trey declares, delighted. "Y'all's guilty as sin. You stole the goods and are in possession of said stolen goods. You get anywhere near a courtroom and they will fry you."

"Don't listen to him. He comes from a family of total users. Liars. Completely without scruples. They're not what they seem. They're—"

"Could you shut up?" Robin, whom I have lied to and tried to use without scruple, requests.

Trey winks at Robin. "Thanks, darlin'. I appreciate the backup, but I don't really think it's necessary. Is it, Blythe? I mean, as far as someone not being what they seem and lies and all, I doubt Slim One wants to go very far into that."

I say nothing. He is as well acquainted with my fictional embellishments as I am with his.

Trey puts his arm around me. If anything, he smells even better than he did when we first met. "Slim One and Tree-Tree understand each other. Don't we, Buttercup?" He chucks me under the chin, then steps away.

With a wink and a finger gun in my direction, Trey retakes control of the meeting. "What y'all need is a massive preemptive strike. Y'all need a few strings to get pulled so this stinking turd of a case never gets to court. What you need is what I can provide and it sure as shit ain't a law degree. It's connections. Slim One, you care to comment?"

"Yeah," Juniper sneers. "You care to comment?"

"About what? Is he connected? No question, his family is all about connections."

Doug shakes his head. "This has 'bad idea' written all over it."

He stands up. "We need to find a real lawyer and get a real plan." With that, Doug leaves. Robin and Juniper are thrown into turmoil by his defection.

"The deal's falling apart, ladies," Trey observes calmly. "You wanna go and round up your stray?"

They rush after Doug, leaving Trey and me alone.

I stand to leave. "Well, my work here is done." Trey lunges out of his chair, grabbing my arm. "Blythe, please, don't go. I've wanted to talk to you for a long time."

"Where did your accent go?"

"Blythe, this is the sound of me speaking from the heart. Not being the family jester, happy party boy, not playing any of the roles I was forced into playing by my family from the time I was still so young that I never knew how to be anyone else."

"Trey, where was this level of self-awareness when we were married?"

"Blythe, there is so much I am genuinely sorry for. So much I want to make up for. This, helping you and your friends out here, it's one way I can make amends."

"But why? What's in it for you? For your family?"

Again the wink and finger gun, this time to signal that I've caught him. "All right, I'll shoot straight with you." His accent is back. "As you may have guessed, the family is sort of behind this firm. We hire the fancy-pants lawyers and put their names out front so we can keep our brand clear. This is going to be a huge high-profile case, and the firm wants to dominate this business, this intellectual property deal. Internet's changing everything. It's the new oil. Whole new game, music, books, anything you got that can be changed into pixels or whatever the hell it is computers change shit into. Lotta money's changing hands and lawyers are gonna suck up most of it. This is our chance to get in on the action. This is the case we've been waiting for."

From the hallway comes the sound of Robin and Juniper arguing. Trey drops my hand, leans in close, and whispers, "Slim, if you tell anyone, the Chancellor will have you killed."

This is the Tree-Tree I remember.

Robin and Juniper reappear with a reluctant Doug in their wake. "Doug has some reservations," Robin announces. "Doug, you want to share your concerns?"

"Actually, I'd like to hear what Blythe has to say. I mean, obviously, the big question here is, Should we trust Mr. Dix? And Blythe is in a unique position to answer that for us."

"So?" Robin demands.

"Don't ask me. Have I been right about anything yet?"

Doug speaks. "All right, then give us your considered opinion."

"My considered opinion? In my considered opinion you shouldn't trust any member of the Dix family any farther than you can throw the weaselly bastards."

"Blythe, darlin'." Trey shakes his head with fond bafflement. "Are you calling my family weaselly bastards? Is that what you're doing?"

"Yes."

"Well, we're not. You're in the wrong section of the animal kingdom. We Dixes are half hyena and half snake. The whole damn bunch of us!"

I have nothing to say in the face of Trey's grinning exuberance.

"And isn't that exactly what you want now? Aren't a complete lack of moral scruples and utter contempt for the public opinion that we plan to mold like Silly Putty precisely the qualities you need to back the RIAA down? So what if old Tree-Tree doesn't have an actual 'law degree'? He's got legal underlings, lackeys, grinds chained to oars down in the galley to do all that boring stuff. Besides which, if we play our cards right, if we play this the Dix way, your stinking turd of a case will never come to trial."

"And just how do we play our cards right?" Juniper asks.

"There you go, Slim Two, asking the tough questions." He puts an arm around Juniper. "That's why I like smart girls. Married one, didn't I? Slim One, why don't you answer Slim Two's question. Tell 'em about the Family and how good we are at making sure we take care of our own."

I reflect on all the family stories I've heard, all the peccadilloes chuckled over: the teacher fired for daring to flunk a Dix; the waitress bought off before she could press charges when Trey and some frat brothers walked a bar tab and stuck her with a bill that was more than she would make in a week; the transcript full of Cs that was good enough to get Trey into the Ivy League after Uno endowed a new wing; the DUIs that disappeared from police records. And though no one chuckled over this, I'd heard about an illegitimate child who was hushed up, the mother bought off, leaving Trey to drink and snort his way from job to job, and, in the end, to be set up by his family in Pemberton Palace.

It is pointless to warn the others about Tree-Tree's brand of good-old-boy intimidation and his family's behind-the-scenes strong-arm tactics. If I reveal that what Double T has, what has always been enough to get Trey and every Trey like him over in life, are family connections and standing golf dates with all the other silver-spoon string-pullers in town, I will only prove his point.

"Well?" Doug prompts me. "What do you think?"

"What I think is that Henry Dix the Third is *precisely* the person you need."

"All right! That's what I like to hear!" Before anyone can say another word, Trey presses a cabinet door to reveal a minifridge filled with Dom Pérignon. Chloe appears carrying a tray of champagne flutes. They are all clinking them together, toasting victory over the RIAA, toasting their future working relationship, before they've even made a deal. By the time Trey is forcing thirds on everyone, Robin has gotten giggly and is batting her Bambi lashes at Trey from beneath sheepdog bangs.

Trey claps his hands together. "All right, gang, before we all get too buzzed, we got us a little work to do. Drug, you're our computer dude—"

"Actually, I'm not all that good with the technical—"

"So why don't you get cracking on having everyone in the house, all our little co-defendants, shoot their files over to us so we can get the legal drones working on how best to make this all disappear. I'm thinking preemptive strike. A legal blitzkrieg that'll leave the RIAA crapping their pants. But I can't set that in motion until I know what we're dealing with. Doug, can you get those files for us?"

Doug looks at me. I can't formulate a logical objection. Trey does in fact seem to be exactly the right piece of slithering offal for the job. Trey motions Doug to a computer. With a last glance in my direction, he sits down and types in a group message that asks all the residents of Seneca House to forward lists of their purloined music files to Trey Dix and his firm's crack team of intellectual property lawyers. Doug hits SEND and Trey pops open another bottle to top off everyone's glass.

Trey's computer pings merrily as, one by one, all of Seneca House's residents forward evidence of the total scope of our theft to our new legal counsel. As the last ping chirps out, a line from Trey's favorite movie, *Animal House,* runs through my brain. The line was delivered by the smooth frat boy, Otter, to the hapless Flounder after Otter wrecked Flounder's car. "You fucked up," Otter told Flounder. "You trusted us."

Vast Assumptions

"YOU TOLD US WE COULD TRUST THIS EVIL SACK OF SHIT!"

A few days later, I awake to Juniper screeching and smashing a newspaper against my face. I push it away and read the headline: "Local Firm to Handle Landmark Music Theft Case." Of course the firm is Trey's, and of course they are now working for the RIAA.

As far as you can throw him. I am too furious to bother reminding Juniper of the caveats on my endorsement. I grab the cell phone that Juniper holds out and punch in Trey's number.

"Slim, Slim, Slim, you talk to your mama with that mouth?"

Among all the invectives that I hurl, Trey takes umbrage only when I won't stop shrieking that he is a liar.

"Slim, I might be all those other things you claim I am, but I was not lying to you. The scenario I presented was definitely in the mix. But after the legal eagles got a look at the files y'all sent in—shit, files? whole fucking catalog of the history of Western music, more like it—it was 'No way, José.'"

Trey chuckles gently when I screech about legal ethics and client confidentiality since he'd already covered those pesky technicalities by not having a law degree. "Sorry, Slim, just not in the cards for you today."

Though it is pointless to scream at the dial tone after Trey hangs up, I do it anyway. When the blood rushing in my ears settles enough, I hear Millie, who obviously hasn't seen the paper yet, yodeling up to me from the front yard.

"Yoo-hoo, Blybees! Are you awake?"

I poke my head out the open window.

Millie is in the fron t yard, straddling the recumbent bike, ready for an egg run. "I forgot the Tinactin for Heriberto's athlete's foot. Could you toss it down? Also, there's a form up there that Jesse needs to fill out to get into a detox program."

Millie keeps yelling up more items she has forgotten. In the end, I gather everything up and take it all downstairs. I help Millie load up, then watch her set off, the red flag on the back whipping with each thrust of foot against pedal.

The morning is still cool. Surprised at myself for being surprised by Trey and dreading what is to come, I plop down in an ancient rattan chair at the far end of the porch and try to take stock of the catastrophe I have unloosed. A heavy growth of star jasmine exudes a fragrance that would have been sweetly calming if I had not been quietly flipping out. Beyond the jasmine stands a row of crape myrtles. They shadow that corner of the porch and leave it cool and hidden from view.

From inside the house, Sanjeev's phone tinkles out its signature ring, a hectic version of "Rule Britannia." A second later, he bustles across the porch without noticing me on his hurried way to the front yard. As serious as Sanjeev always is, he is twice that serious when he answers the phone. "Hello, Baba." His next words are delivered in rapid high-pitched Bengali. I assume he is discussing plans for his marriage to Bhavani Mukherjee in front of eight hundred friends and relatives.

Shielded by the crape myrtles and the jasmine's lustrous forest-green foliage, I observe Sanjeev undetected. He finishes his call, snaps his cell shut with a flip of the wrist that almost makes him look cool, then paces back and forth across the few sprigs of grass that have managed to survive the scorn which decades of proudly alternative students have for anything that smacks of a lawn. He pauses, glances up and down the street, and takes a pack of cigarettes out of his pants pocket.

Once I get over the shock of seeing the subcontinent's answer to Cotton Mather sucking down a Marlboro, I realize what has been there all along though disguised by a screen of priggishness: Sanjeev is sexy as hell. Back when Sanjeev was just the nit doing bacterial swabs on floors I'd mopped, I had not been able to see Millie's attraction. Perhaps it speaks to my own lack of high-mindedness that it is not until Sanjeev's good looks fully register that I truly believe in Millie's love for this son of India.

"Why are you spying on me?"

Apparently, the jasmine doesn't provide as much of a cloak of invisibility as I'd thought. "I'm not spying on you. I happen to be sitting here enjoying the cool morning air."

The phone call has clearly irritated Sanjeev and he is looking for someone to take it out on. "You promised that this friend of yours, this Danny, would call off the dogs. Well?" Sanjeev demands. "Will the dogs be called off?"

Another one who has not yet heard about the fiasco with Trey. This doesn't seem to be the perfect moment to fill him in. "I didn't promise that Danny would call off the dogs, and no, it doesn't appear that he will."

"So the lawsuit is proceeding?"

"It would seem that it is, yes."

"Do you understand what this means?"

"I think I've got the broad strokes."

"Do you? Because I don't think you have the tiniest inkling of what you've done. Not to the house, not to me, not to Millie."

"I know. I've screwed up and I am reallyreallyreally sorry."

"But you're always screwing up and you're always reallyreally-really sorry, aren't you?"

"Sanjeev, step off, okay? I've admitted to the full range of my character flaws and have been doing nothing but making amends since I set foot in this place. I'm tired of being your whipping boy."

"So, you think that your 'amends' make everything fine?"

"I didn't say that."

"Because they don't. I warned you once about exploiting a person as fine as Millie and you ignored my warning."

"Sanjeev, was it *me* downloading music in front of a record company executive? Was *I* the one rubbing Danny's nose in it?"

"No, but you are the one who misled Millie into believing that stealing music over the Internet was a fine community-building activity."

"Look, I don't need this. You aren't telling me anything I don't know and haven't admitted already. There's only so much groveling a person can do and I've done mine, so get over it."

"Get over it? Are you so blinded by your heedless self-absorption that you still can't see what you've done? How you have imperiled Millie's work, her mission?"

"Me? Blind and self-absorbed? Talk about the kettle calling the pot black."

"What do you mean?"

"Nothing. Forget it."

"No, tell me, I'm interested. What are you talking about?"

"Just drop it, okay?"

"Drop what?"

"Nothing."

"Tell me, precisely what it is you are referring to."

Sanjeev's haughty imperiousness annoys me so much that I blurt out, "I'm sure you can probably guess."

"Guess what?"

I try to leave, but Sanjeev blocks the door. "Sanjeev, please, just get out of my way."

"Not until you tell me what you are talking about."

"Don't pretend."

"Could you mean . . ." He pauses and looks around.

"Millie's gone," I tell him. I am tired of playing their ridiculous little game, pretending I don't know they are obsessed with each other.

"So you're telling me that what I am blind and self-absorbed about is—"

He has so worked my very last nerve that I can't keep myself from snapping, "Millie! Millie Ott! Yes, God, of course, you big dolt. I mean Millie."

He stares, blinking.

"Please, for God's sake, don't be the only person who doesn't know how she feels. I *am* blind and self-absorbed and I know how she feels. Everyone in the house knows. Shit, the paperboy who drives by here at five in the morning knows."

"Knows what?"

"That she loves you, you pompous, high-minded moron. And what's more, it's painfully obvious that you love her, too."

Sanjeev's face drains of color, going from blazing copper to dull pewter as he stares in shocked silence. Disastrously, though, it is not me he is staring at; it is Millie. She has returned for something she has forgotten and is standing behind me.

"Okay, Millie, before you say anything, I'm sorry I broke my promise, but it is obvious that Sanjeev knows and that you know that he knows and that he knows that you know and before anyone gets huffy why don't you both just thank me for getting the obvious out in the open before someone goes off and marries the wrong person?"

Thanks do not appear to be in the offing. In fact, breathing doesn't seem to be happening much. "Could one of you say something?"

They continue to stare without speaking; then, for just a fraction of a second, both their faces lighten and they stop looking as if they're facing a firing squad. I am congratulating myself for breaking through their constipated righteousness when Sanjeev's shoulders abruptly slump and he marches swiftly away.

Millie, stunned, bereft, watches him disappear down the street. Several very long moments go by before Millie speaks. "You have no idea what you've just done." Without another word, without so much as a glance in my direction, Millie bolts upstairs.

Of all the elements of the scene that just played out, one of the most difficult to believe is that Millie would leave her fully loaded bike abandoned in the front yard. Knowing that I have screwed up, but not yet appreciating how badly, I set about trying to patch things up and, as best I can, make the run for Millie.

As soon as I finish deliveries to the hoboes and day laborers, I zip upstairs, certain I will be able to smooth things over. I reach the door to Millie's room and find it locked. A blanket, a pillow, and my few belongings are piled outside. I pound on the door.

"Millie, please, let me in." No answer. "Talk to me. Tell me what I did that was so wrong." No answer. "Millie, I'm begging you. Don't just cut me off like this. All I did was speak the truth. At least I deserve an explanation."

Millie unlocks the door and lets me in. When she finally speaks it is in a scarily controlled tone of voice and with a complete lack of eye contact. "You don't deserve anything. Not an explanation, nothing. But I'll give you one. Sanjeev is engaged. I knew that from the very beginning. It is the foundation upon which our friendship was based. Sanjeev and I could be friends only so long as we both pretended, even to ourselves, that there was nothing more. Because we both knew that there could never be anything more. Now you have taken that pretense away from us. In taking away the foundation for our friendship, you have taken away our friendship. Sanjeev's sense of honor will no longer permit him to be in my presence."

I try to protest, but Millie silences me. "You are spoiled. As spoiled and oblivious as the rich people you complain about, the ones you claim ruined your life. You ruined your own life with your greed. Like them you make such vast assumptions. You have so much that your empathy and imagination stop tragically short. You can't even conceive of what it is to have so little. Of what it means that a simple friendship with a man is the most precious thing in your life. The one thing you cannot imagine living without. You took that away from me. You took away my one thing."

CAST OUT

A Hunger That Has
Nothing to Do with Food

AFTER A FEW HOURS of futile pleading and pounding, I gather up my things and take them to the minivan. Kat is not thrilled that I am taking Nikki's place, but she can hardly object.

"I guess it's still yours. Technically," she admits. "Just move that stuff out of the way. And that. You can take that to the Dumpster if you want. Ew, is that what was stinking? Toss that out."

For the rest of the week, Millie refuses to come out of her room. I bring up trays and leave them at the door. Sometimes they disappear. Most of the time they don't. I stand outside the door and listen to Millie cry. I imagine breaking down the door with a metal ramrod like SWAT teams use.

Instead, I talk Kat into helping me do Millie's egg runs. Kat refuses to sit in the front of the bike. So, once again, utter lack of moral character, motivation, and financing end with me splayed out on the front seat of the recumbent bike. Still, a few hours of pressing tortillas into hands caked with dirt, cement, axle grease, fertilizer, putty, and grout always give me a new perspective on the ultimately effete nature of my problems.

By the third day, I am an old hand at running Millie's show. Kat and I finish with the Pease Park gang and the day laborers, then we pedal back uphill toward the university. Foot traffic is light on the Drag. Finals are in full swing, and the student population is hunkered down in carrels or coffee shops cramming most of a semester into a couple of days. The sky is overcast from agricultural fires burning out of control in Mexico that send clouds of smoke north. The street kids slouching in front of the Baptist church pass a Game Boy around. They seem tougher, more urban, in the gray light.

They glance up at the sound of the Dorkocycle's rattling, clanking approach and turn as one toward Kat and me, their faces, for just a split second, as open as flowers tracking the sun in time-lapse photography. For that instant, they look like the kids they are, eager, expectant, waiting for something good to happen. Then they see that, once again, Millie is not with us, and the armor of coolness slams back into place, leaving them even more aimless and fumbling than before. Even the hyperkinetic Jaguar is subdued, though he is the first to break from the gang of street kids and saunter over in a modified cat spring.

"Jaguar, let me have a look at that arm," I call out just as Millie would have, and the tattooed boy offers his arm for me to examine. My stomach heaves at the sight of the dirty piece of gauze taped over the infected tatoos, and I have to force myself to lift the pad and peek underneath. Fortunately the wound is healing well. "You're a good cat, Jaguar. You're keeping yourself clean. The infection is almost gone." I pull out the first-aid kit Millie keeps strapped to the cart, cover a new square of gauze with antibiotic ointment, and tape it on.

Jaguar growls out his gratitude, then grooms himself, rubbing his head up and down against a curled-over hand held stationary in front of his face before he scampers away to the nest he's made with his dirty orange sleeping bag. He kneads and fluffs the bag up before settling onto it.

A girl who looks about fifteen with strawberry-blond hair and a babyish voice that sounds like Kat's comes forward and points to the tortillas. "Can I have one of those? Things are slow out here today." A tiny bell tinkles on a ring on her pinkie finger as she takes a flabby tortilla from Kat. Flakes of pearlized blue polish cling to her nails. She wads the tortilla up, stuffs it in her mouth, and chews with the mechanized ferocity of someone trying to feed a hunger that has nothing to do with food. My pulse gallops as I think about what waits for her on the street. Her flip-flops are worn to wafer thinness. I take mine off and trade with her.

The rest of the tribe gradually gathers around. They want news of Nikki more than they want eggs and oranges. Kat holds them spellbound with her update. "I just talked to Nikki this morning and she was all, 'I *love* cosmetology school.' Plus, she's like this amazing natural talent."

"Well, duh," Spood says.

"She's working on manicure technique now? Proper hygiene, shit like that. You can get mad wicked infections from manicures. The school gave her this little room to stay in? That's why I can't stay with her yet? After she finishes her training, she'll actually start cutting hair. That's when she's going to get her own place and I'll move in with her."

Spood straightens himself up within the army jacket. "Tell her not to forget the little people when she's styling J.Lo's hair."

"She's working on it," Kat says. Then, as if convincing herself, she murmurs, "Nikki's working on it."

For the last few days, I have overheard Kat *not* talking to Nikki. Just leaving her messages that Nikki never returns. I need to warn Kat about Charisma Girls like Nikki, tell her not to trust them. Not to expect too much, not to expect anything, in fact. I'll caution her that she will only be disappointed if she depends on Nikki. For anything. That she needs to start making alternate plans to take care of herself because Charisma Girls watch out for one person and one person alone: themselves.

Spood entertains the kids by chewing wads of tortilla, then tilting his head back and shaking Tabasco sauce into his mouth. They are so enthralled that it startles them when Kat breaks away and bellows in a scary Darth Vader voice, "Put that down, motherfucker!"

A clump of frat guys is dragging Jaguar's sleeping bag away from him. Jaguar is defending his territory by hissing and pawing at the air. The frat boys find this hilarious and jerk at the bag all the harder.

Kat gets in the face of the biggest, brawniest boy. "Yo, homo, whatcha need his bag for!" She slices her hand above her head like a rapper warming up and, with as much urban spin as she can pump up, asks, "You gonna go fuck your boyfriend!? Huh? That what you need the bag for?" With a mighty tug, she yanks the bag away, then, head bobbing from side to side, crows, "Yeah, I did it, bitch! I took it! Uh-huh! Oh, yes, I *did*!"

The frat boys look at one another, consider annihilating the gnat taunting them, shrug, and walk away. Kat follows for half a block, calling them bitches, then returns the bag to Jaguar and helps him fluff his nest back up.

The tribe gathers around their conquering heroine. "You so pwned their gay nooblet frat asses!" Spood exults. "Nikki couldn'ta pwned no better!"

Kat brushes off the compliments with a coolness I wouldn't have thought she possessed. "Whatever."

I decide not to warn Kat about Nikki.

A Free-range Buccaneer

FOR THE FIFTH straight morning, ever since Millie banished me and I have been sleeping in the little van with Kat, Sanjeev awakens me shortly after dawn with a chaotic conversation in Bengali. Each day the conversations have increased in pitch and volume. And I can't utter a word of complaint.

Though Millie hasn't spoken to me since she threw me out, she passed the word that I was to be allowed to use the kitchen and the bathrooms. I am not sure that sleeping crammed up next to Kat is any better than straight hobo life on Dog Crap Lane, but I don't want to test the premise by letting Sanjeev know I am huddled in the van.

The sun and Sanjeev's voice rise. Forcefully, he addresses someone whom I assume is his father as "Baba." In a less forceful, more wheedling tone, he pleads with "Ma." All the conversations, though, end with Sanjeev muttering resigned "hyas" interspersed with dispirited "okays." Each day, his family beats him down a bit more, and today, as usual, he hangs up and stands outside sighing for a long time. By the time he finally goes in, the sun is fully up and there is no hope of my going back to sleep.

I stare at the molded gray plastic of the van's interior and contemplate this new rung of hell I have descended to. Oddly, though, it is no longer the lost paradise of Pemberton Palace that I pine for; it is a paradise of an entirely different nature. Probably because of Millie's freakish saintliness, I recall some distant vacation Bible school teacher talking about how the worst part of getting tossed out of the Garden of Eden was Adam and Eve's pain at being separated from God.

Ick, did I just think that? All that "Kumbaya" Christianity of Millie's, it's getting to me.

That thought flickers away and is replaced by the memory of a creepy old engraving of Adam and Eve being cast out into a dark storm. The dark part sticks with me. I close my eyes, and it's dark. I open them and it's still dark. This is new. And not pleasant. During the Bubble Years, then the Society Years, Millie was always there in the darkness like a night-light. Or a low-fuel light. Some really irritating reminder that I was running on empty. But that maybe, if I just ignored the light, pretended it didn't exist, I could keep going for a few more miles.

That's what's missing now. That annoying blinking light. All those years of believing I was a free-range buccaneer, proud of making it on my own with no help from anyone, with no one caring, were a mental disorder. Millie cared. Millie always cared.

I miss her. It is not like missing anyone else I have ever known. It is like missing a country, a way of life. And, I remind myself repeatedly, not even a country or a way of life that had much to recommend it.

"Your foot is in my face."

"Oh, sorry." I remove my foot.

"No worries." Kat wriggles into a sitting position. "I have to get up anyway. Millie needs me to help her get the house ready for the emergency meeting today. Haul in chairs, make coffee, stuff like that."

"What emergency meeting? It's Saturday morning." Since I have been forced to maintain a subterranean profile after Millie kicked me out, and since conversations now stop dead on my rare trips into the house, I am a little out of the loop.

"The board of directors of the Old Girls called it. They're all coming. All the old residents, everyone who's been contributing to help Millie. They're totally freaked about the lawsuits and shit.

They could really all get sued. So, okay, all the residents, everyone here at the house who got a subpoena, they're all like 'Oh, we're poor, poverty-stricken students. We don't have any money. Stupid to sue us.' And the RI-whatever, the record company fuckheads, are all 'Yeah, okay, so we'll sue these rich lawyers and doctors and shit on this board of directors deal.'"

"Oh, Jesus."

"What? It's not like they're gonna sue you."

"They'll get the house. Millie won't be able to continue her work."

"Is that what she's buggin' about? I thought you guys had a thing and you broke up and that's why Millie is all whacked out."

"There was never a thing. What's wrong with Millie?"

"All sorts of weird shit. She doesn't hear when you ask her something. She's got that brain-fry look in her eyes like Jaguar. I caught her crying the other day." Kat's teen bravado disappears. "I've never seen Millie cry before. Never even really ever seen her sad. God, why are *you* crying now? I didn't think you were a crier."

"I'm not. But I've done something really, really bad to someone who really, really doesn't deserve it and I don't know how to make it better."

"What'd you do? Steal her stash? No, Millie doesn't even drink. Talk smack behind her back? You snaked her boyfriend! That's it. You totally two-elevened her man-ho. Is it that Sandy guy she's all crushed out on?"

"You know about Sanjeev?"

"Well, duh, she gets like she's on crank around him. All super, super peppy and happy. Or she used to. So you tapped that, huh?"

"Sanjeev? Sanjeev thinks I'm scum."

"So why is Millie mad at you?"

"I don't really want to talk about it."

"Oh, okay, but you want to make up?"

"It might not be possible."

"It's totally possible. Remember that one time when Zebra Dog run away and Nikki was all sad? Well, I used my natural talents and beading skills and made her this really cool necklace and that cheered her up majorly. So what are your natural talents and skills?"

"I don't have any natural talents or skills that Millie has any use for."

"Maybe I can teach you how to bead. It's mostly just knowing what colors look good next to each other."

"Maybe."

Kat stretches and her pink top rides up, exposing the cute puppy tummy beneath. She pats my hand and says, "Don't cry, okay?"

Her sweetness reminds me of Millie and makes me sadder.

"Kat, I'm down. Really down. I wish I could be a role model for you, but if there were drugs here right now, I'd take every one of them. I don't know how much longer I can stand this."

"I feel you, believe me I do."

We sit in the van for a minute and listen to traffic rumble past. Kat finally says, "You could come in and help me move chairs into the living room. Maybe that'd get Millie to stop being mad at you."

"It's going to take more than that."

"Well, then just move chairs to not be a lazy bitch, bitch."

These seem to be words to live by, so I follow her into the house.

The Salty, Wet Ones

I AM IN THE KITCHEN making muffins and not being a lazy bitch when the Old Girls start trickling in. I can hear them talking in the living room—their greetings, whoops of delight when they spot old friends—but I can't see them and, far better, they can't see me. Which means that I am the major topic of discussion. I can't identify the first speaker who blurts out, "I hear that not even Millie is speaking to her anymore."

Someone mumbles a response. I fantasize that one of my old housemates is springing to my defense. No need to imagine Robin's response, however; it rings out loud and clear. "Well, she couldn't have fucked up any more if she'd systematically set out to utterly destroy the house and everything Millie has been trying to accomplish."

Another female voice chimes in, "At this point, I don't see what good an emergency session is going to do. I mean, why the hell didn't anyone ever mention that all the board members are liable?"

There are more aggrieved murmurs; then Robin bursts out again, "Hell yes, I'm pissed off. I'm furious. It's like my grandfather always told me, 'No good deed goes unpunished.'"

"You are so focked." Olga's lugubrious tones echo for a second until they are absorbed by a cacophony of shrieking imprecations, most of which feature colorful modifiers attached to my name.

The next question catches me off guard. "Hey, anyone seen Millie?"

Millie is not out there?

I'd assumed she was already at the meeting. Horror movie scenes unspool in my head: Millie hanging from a rafter, Millie blue from an overdose.

Juniper answers. "I haven't seen her. Anyone seen Millie?"

I hold my breath. When no one replies, I drop the muffin tin and race out of the kitchen.

The scene in the living room resembles the end-of-the-year sale at CP Shades, a jumble of natural fibers and barely restrained female aggression. The enraged and legally exposed Old Girls are blistering whichever current residents are closest to hand. Alpha females Robin and Juniper are in each other's faces. Ariadne is squaring off with Yay Bombah and Nazarite. Byung Chao Soo and Olga are going at it. Dozens of other females I don't recognize cluster about. The instant they catch sight of me darting past, hostilities cease. I am the invading Martian who brings all the earthlings together. I race on.

Upstairs, I halt outside Millie's partially open door, heart thudding, and steel myself for the worst, then nearly collapse with relief when I hear Millie saying, "Surely it's not that disastrous."

Between sobs, Alli answers, "It's worse, Millie. From day one, those Plat Longs have been looking for a reason to fire me. I didn't exactly hide my orientation from them at the interview; they were just so clueless they didn't pick up on it until after I started work. But, Millie, I can't lose this job. I haven't told anyone this yet, but . . ." More sobs. Millie murmurs words of comfort until Alli pulls herself together and goes on. "Millie, my whole life I've dreamed of being a mother and I'm finally in the process of doing it. I'm going to adopt a little girl. Her name is Ming Mei. Here, I have her picture already and everything."

"Oh, Alli, she's beautiful."

"They sent that after I was approved. But they do a last-minute check to make sure nothing has changed, and they won't let me have her if I don't have a job. And I won't have a job if this event falls through. Millie, I love my baby already. I've never loved anyone the way I love this child."

"Alli, Al, sweetie, don't cry. It's going to be okay. They can't stop you from getting Ming Mei. It's going to be okay."

Alli blows her nose. "It's her, it's that damn Kippie Lee Teeter who got the board to sign off on this trip without ever checking with me. *Me!* The person who's supposed to implement the whole impossible thing. And now it's completely subscribed. Every single wife of every single one of our largest donors signed up."

"I'm not sure I understand exactly what this trip is."

"It's not actually a trip. For the first time ever, the Platinum Longhorns are going to stay in Austin. Kippie Lee even came up with a name: Think Thin: A Week of Learning and Leaning. The idea is that we are going to have gourmet food for every insane diet these women are on, plus, *plus*, a series of quote, unquote, 'stimulating lectures by UT's finest.' I rented the Pi Phi house right around the corner, had everything set up. That one program would have kept my job safe for another whole year. Long enough for me to bring Ming Mei home. But then . . ." Alli breaks into sobs.

"Then what, Al?"

"Mold remediation! I just found out this morning that the Pi Phi house is oozing with Stachybotrys mold and they have to close it for six months for mold remediation. I have been on the phone all day trying to locate another site. But there's nothing available at this late date. God, I wish I had passed organic chemistry. I'd be a vet right now. If this falls apart it will totally, totally crash the budget. I told you they've been looking for a reason to fire me. This is it!"

"Millie! Millie!" Robin's voice booms up the stairway. "You up there? The natives are getting restless!"

Millie, holding Alli's hand, steps out. I wouldn't have believed that in only five days a person could become gaunt, but Millie has. Always before she'd had a bursting-with-home-baked-goodness fullness about her. Now she is all hollows and shadows. Millie's eyes meet mine and register nothing. She dips her head and steps around me without a word. I feel like crumpling to the floor and crying. But why bother? Millie is the single, solitary person on earth who ever truly cared about me leaking the salty, wet ones.

I take a seat at the top of the stairwell and listen to Robin pound her gavel, calling the meeting to order. Then she outlines the catastrophe. I am referred to repeatedly as "the individual in question."

The instant she is finished, the meeting disintegrates into squabbling chaos until Robin announces, "We'll hear from Millie now."

The house falls so silent that I can easily hear Millie's voice, hear how flat and emotionless it is. "Thank you, Robin. Thank you all for your help over the years. I think it is clear from Robin's very thorough report that, even if we could find a firm willing to represent the house, the minimum cost for any sort of defense would bankrupt us. I have drawn up a statement claiming that I deliberately withheld information from board members about their personal liability."

"But you didn't," Robin protests.

Millie ignores her. "Of course this means that my work is over."

A clamor follows this announcement. Several of the women protest that they will continue to support Millie whether the house survives or not. But it is clear from Millie's monotone response that her heart is broken. Less obvious is that it is my fault. I can't undo the damage I've done. I can't give Millie back the relationship with Sanjeev that I have taken from her. But I might be able to help her hang on to the one other thing that makes her life worth living: There is an exceedingly remote possibility that I can save Millie's work. I stand up, dust off my butt, and head downstairs.

That Which Is Truly Right and Truly Proper

A FRAT BROTHER selling baby seal steaks and NRA memberships would have gotten a warmer reception than the one I receive from the Old Girls. It doesn't matter; I am on a mission for Millie and lose no time in wresting the podium from Robin so I can get on with it: "I can save the house."

The residents, past and present, greet this announcement with an exchange of rolled eyes and arched brows signaling that the complete mental collapse they had long expected to follow my total moral decay has occurred.

Again, I don't care. The only person I care about is Millie. But her expression doesn't change except when she glances at Sanjeev on the front porch. Then it goes from despairing to agonized. As inert and unstrung as Millie is, Sanjeev is energized to the same degree. Electrified, actually. He paces, puffs openly on a cigarette, gnaws at his nails, fidgets, and twitches. The veins at his temples throb, and he is sweating profusely. Sanjeev doesn't appear so much heartbroken as on the verge of a massive coronary.

I lay out my plan using the ultrasane manner and tone I once employed to convince clients that pitching a big top on the front lawn and hiring Cirque du Soleil would be an entirely reasonable way to celebrate Junior's eighth birthday. The rancor and spleen which greeted my appearance turn into gape-jawed bafflement as I explain my idea. When I finish, Alli jumps out of her chair, eyes glistening. She rushes up to clutch my hand and proclaim, "Do you really think you could pull it off? Do you really think we could hold the Platinum Longhorns event here?"

My answer, a stirring "I do," is undercut somewhat by Juniper's hearty guffaws. Her buddies, Olga, Doug, and Sergio, join in. "You really had us going there for a minute," Juniper says, wiping tears from her eyes. "Have the Platinum Longhorns stay here for a week? That's a good one." She glances around at her buddies and asks, "Can't you just see Kippie Lee Teeter chowing down on a big plate of soy-chorizo *migas* while perusing a flyer about a Transgendered Vegans for Peace rally?"

Even Olga thinks this is hilarious. "Or thet other silly bitch, Boomsie Bivver, sharink shithole bathroom with boys what are peeink everywhere."

That vision causes Alli's enthusiasm to dim, and she sits down. Millie barely glances up, but when she does her expression is dead. Sanjeev comes in from the porch and joins the meeting. His symptoms have accelerated so alarmingly that he now seems on the verge of a full-blown case of Tourette's.

I address the group. "I'm serious. I really think we can pull this off. With this one event, we can make enough to deal with the RIAA long enough to hang on to the house, and Millie can continue her work."

Juniper peers skeptically at me. "Did you get the Code Warrior refilled?"

I ignore the question. "Look, there's not much I can do to improve this situation. I can't go back in time and not bring a record executive into the house, I can't bead necklaces, I can't, apparently, lead a decent life, but I can do this."

Juniper shakes her head as if trying to shed a bad dream. "God, she's serious. Wow, there are so many levels on which this is demented that I don't know where to start. But just, okay, just for the psychedelically deranged fun of it, let's imagine that we do let those women have their thing here. To begin with, you are aware, aren't you, that you are talking about the most pathologically particular humans on earth? Humans who have enshrined their tastes, their needs, their quirks, their every minuscule desire, into a religion? Into the central focus of their lives? These are humans who call Amnesty International when thread counts dip below four hundred. Who won't put a molecule of food into their mouths unless it is carb-free, organic, and blessed by the pope. Who believe that hardwood floors coated in polyurethane instead of waxed to a natural gloss by minimum-wage hands are a violation of the Geneva Conventions. How do you propose that we transform this flophouse into a place where the cream of Tee Town will spend one *minute,* much less one week?"

The silence that follows Juniper's question is filled with the sounds of a house on life support: deep groans from the plumbing of its ruined alimentary canals, clanks and wheezes from the window units of its diseased pulmonary system, incessant dripping from the incompetent renal circuitry. And the smells. Don't mention the smells.

"Okay, admittedly, there might be a few wrinkles. But, Juniper, you've worked with me before. You've witnessed the transformations I've wrought. That *Dangerous Liaisons* event where we turned a Cape Cod saltbox into a neoclassical French country château? And remember the Deb Ball in Tuscany when we treated all the walls to make them look like they were crumbling. Look!" I gesture expansively toward our own cracked and peeling interiors. "We've got crumbling!"

"It's not the right kind of crumbling. It's not the crumble of old money. This is plain old squalor."

Seneca House's turn-of-the-century plumbing continues to groan and rumble in the background as I recall other transformations. "The West Lake adobe we did over as Studio 54? Disco balls, smoke machines, platform heels. The Pemberton Heights Tudor we mutated into an Ottoman Empire harem? Veils, scarves, eunuchs with scimitars. But those were nothing. You should have seen the extravaganzas I staged back in the dot-com days. A Japanese pachinko parlor, a Borneo longhouse, the catacombs."

"Blythe, those transformations were all smoke and mirrors. Changing the icing on a basically sound cake. They were completely different from what you would be trying to do here."

"How so?"

"Oh, let's see." Juniper taps her chin as if she were seriously thinking. "Gosh, I guess, if I had to single out just one subtly nuanced difference, just one teensy, tiny distinction, it might be . . . hmmm? What might it be? Oh, yes, now I remember . . . *money!* Buckets and buckets of money. Whereas we have buckets and buckets of what? Groats?"

Juniper is right. In the past I could have spun this somehow, usually with outright lies. But some essential component in the machinery that used to keep me running seems to be missing. I no longer have the special energy required to connive. It is time for me to hang it up.

"You're right," I admit. "Forget it."

Alli bursts into sobs. Very little probing is required before the story of Ming Mei pours forth. "I don't know if Blythe's plan will work," she tells the group damply, "but what other choice do we have? For me? For the house? I'd think all of you living here now would especially want to save it. I mean, where else are you going to live?"

In this, the second decade of Austin's housing boom, with ever taller, ever pricier condo developments crowding West Campus, that is a very good point. Anyone who has the means moved out long ago. Lute, Presto, Clancy, Jerome, Doug, Sergio, Olga, even Juniper, weigh their options.

Yay Bombah speaks up and says something about not wanting the "boderation" of moving.

Nazarite, just as devoted as her sister to the fantasy that they are living in a Kingston slum, seconds the motion. "Seen, sistah."

"So," Juniper asks, her eyes narrowed into slits of hard suspicion, "what exactly would be involved?"

Nothing, really. A little Pledge, some Windex, we're good to go.

That's how I should answer. That's how I would have answered in the past. I was the mistress of the lowball quote that I ooched up only after the commitment had been made; after money, lots of it, had been spent. Then came the "extras." *Oh you want actual napkins? The price quoted is for the basic package which comes with a very service- able handful of leaves for each guest. But if you want actual napkins that will be extra.* But I just can't do it anymore. I can't scam them.

"Again, Juniper is right. This idea is insane and I can't begin to pull it off." I abandon the podium.

"Wait!" Sanjeev leaps forward to stop me. His eyes are bugging out of his handsome head as they ricochet from me to Millie and back again. This is it. Sanjeev appears primed to get in some major licks. I brace myself for his attack, for the thorough psychic, spiri- tual, and moral pummeling he is about to deliver. Fair enough.

"Blythe's plan is our only chance," he states unequivocally.

Sanjeev's death grip on my arm makes me wonder if he might be referring to their only chance to lynch me. But he is not directing his comment to the group. His gaze bores into Millie.

"Sometimes it is necessary to step beyond rigid ideas of what is right and proper in order to do that which is *truly* right and *truly* proper."

Millie lifts her head, and all of Sanjeev's twitches and tics are stilled. Calmly he speaks to her and her alone. "When that which is most precious in our lives, that which makes our very lives worth living, is threatened, then it becomes necessary to take bold and unprecedented action. Don't you agree, Millie?"

Millie chews on her lower lip as her nostrils flare and her cheeks redden. Finally she says, "The answer to that question is that it depends on who the action taken will affect. Who will be hurt? We can never place our own desires above others."

"Bosh!" Sanjeev explodes. "Never? You told me that your mother's fondest desire was for you to live at home with her for the rest of your life. Did you not place your desire to live your own life above hers?"

"Yes, but her desire was unreasonable."

"And so is that of my parents."

Dr. Dr. Robin calls upon her years of training as a therapist to get the discussion back on track. "Huh?"

Staring at Millie with the heat of banked passion, Sanjeev makes his plea. "I believe in Blythe's proposal. I believe that, with our help, it can succeed, and we can save our future here together. But are you ready to join me, Millie? Do you promise to stand by my side and declare what you want in this life and to fight for it?"

They all wait to hear what Millie, our moral arbiter, will say. "I don't know, Sanjeev." Then, for the first time in five long days, Millie's gaze engages mine. "Do you really think this is possible?"

No one else besides Sanjeev knows what Millie is really asking. Not just is it possible to save the house, but is her love for Sanjeev possible. I take a moment before I answer, because I can never disappoint Millie again. Ever. "Yes, Millie, I really do."

"And everything will be aboveboard? No corners cut? No playing fast and loose?"

They wait expectantly, all of them, for my response. I am the gunslinger forced out of retirement by the terrified townsfolk. In order to do the right thing, I will have to, once again, do the wrong thing. The first wrong thing I have to do is tell the terrified townsfolk the lie they need to hear. And so, I strap the trusty six-shooter back on and answer Millie in a dead-level voice, "Absolutely not. Everything will be perfectly aboveboard."

"In that case, yes, Sanjeev, I promise to stand by your side and declare what I want in this life. I promise to fight for it. Yes, Sanjeev, I propose that with Blythe's help we fight to save the house."

Millie's proposal is seconded and put up for a vote. The Old Girl board members who don't want to be sued vote for it. The residents who have no place else to move vote for it. Only Jerome, who is always against everything, votes against it.

The proposal passes and I stop thinking of myself as a gunslinger in Western movies. Instead, I remember the *Lethal Weapon* movies. The ones where Danny Glover is always declaring that he is too old for this shit, then is dragged back into the fray the day before he is supposed to retire.

I try to recall if Danny gets killed in the end.

The Tee Town Trifecta

W<small>HAT THE HELL</small> is going on?" Kippie Lee asks as she stands on the walk in front of the Pi Phi house and beholds the devastation. The gracious Tara-like sorority house is completely wrapped in plastic. Workers in white hazmat suits, goggles, and respirators rip out slimy chunks of blackened wood. Alien invasion is not the vibe that the ladies had in mind when they signed on for the Platinum Longhorns Think Thin: A Week of Learning and Leaning.

"We can't stay here."

The princesses gather around Kippie Lee and mumble stunned agreement. Everyone on Alli's list has shown up: Kippie Lee Teeter, Bamsie Beiver, Cookie Mehan, Blitz Lord, Missy Quisinberry, Paige Oglesby, Morgan Whitlow, Cherise Tatum, Mimi McNaughton, Lulie Bingle, Fitzie Upchurch, and Noodle Tiner.

I detect the hand of wardrobe consultant Willow O'Connor in the ladies' attire. Willow seems to have settled on a Ranch Weekend theme. Kippie Lee is wearing a strapless goatskin minidress by Galliano. The getup is belted at the top and has three more belts at the hip that add some junk to the skeletal Teeter trunk. The rest of the ant colony wears some version of this leather-and-buckles prairie-bondage motif.

Alli scurries around them like a collie with ADD trying to herd sheep.

I take all this in from a hiding place in the Pi Phi shrubbery, since it was agreed that mine might not be the most welcome face

242 HOW PERFECT IS THAT

when the ladies discovered that their Think Thin hideaway has turned into Area 51. It is unfortunate that I can't be out there right now mind-controlling Kippie Lee & Co. into walking around the corner to Seneca House. I pray that Alli is up to that task. I worked for a long time with her on a script that combined elements of used-car sales and Scientology with heavy emphasis on closing the deal.

All Alli has to do is deliver the lines I've given her. It is essential that we get the ladies across the threshold and into Seneca House. Oh sure, the Plat Longs have an ironclad refund policy that requires sixty days' advance notice in writing for even a fifty percent refund. But having been on the wrong end of a couple—okay, five—lawsuits with clients demanding refunds, I know that the Plat Longs' contract won't hold up in court. Not when you are baiting and switching down from a stately antebellum manse to a tenement crack house. Because I've looked a few judges in the eye, I know that when our case goes to trial—and to trial it most certainly will go—it will be considerably stronger if we can get the Pemberton Princesses into the house for at least one night. Though two would be much better.

Alli bounces to the front of the group. I told her that the vibe she has to establish is haughty concierge. For reasons I can't fathom, she translated my directive into a denim jumper. Consequently, she looks like a kindergarten teacher on the verge of a nervous breakdown.

"Hello, I'm Alli, program coordinator for the Platinum Longhorns, and I've got some good news and some better news!"

I could have sold that line, but Alli's tense, high-pitched enthusiasm tries too hard. The women eye her suspiciously, mouths struggling against bone matrix filler to seam into tight lines of sales resistance as she continues, "The Pi Phi house is experiencing a sudden, literally overnight outbreak of the Ebola virus."

The group levitates as one in their haste to move away from the house. Ebola might have been overkill, but I did want to both introduce the overnight aspect and preempt any further discussion.

"As you've probably guessed, we won't be staying here." Alli's laugh is too hollow, begs too much for approval. She needs to be liked, and allowing the rich to know you need to be liked is fatal. I itch to get out there and show her what haughty looks like.

Alli lets the uncomfortable silence go on too long before diving in again. "Anyway, the great news is that we've found a fantastic venue just around the corner. Our valet staff is ready to help you with your bags."

Alli executes a stilted Vanna White calling attention to the "valet staff": Lute, Sergio, Jerome, and Doug, all dressed in matching shorts like the bellboys at the Four Seasons. The boys spring forward, grabbing suitcases and doing what I had ordered them to: fluff up the ladies.

Lute doesn't have to do much more than look gorgeous and say anything in his Australian accent and he is charming.

Charm, however, is not Jerome's strong suit. He grunts as he tries to lift Bamsie's matching Vuitton cases. "What the hell you got in here? Anvils?"

"Why?" Bamsie snarls back. "You a blacksmith?"

"No, but I know where I'd stick a red-hot poker if I had one right now."

I am making a note to myself to reassign Jerome to a noninterface position when Bamsie starts giggling and swatting at Jerome's shoulder. "And just exactly where *would* you stick your red-hot poker, mister?"

I recall that Jimmy Beiver, Bams's husband, is a legendarily gruff—okay, borderline psychotic—owner of a national franchise that sucks used grease out of restaurant grease traps, then recycles it into something unspeakable. Chicken nuggets, maybe. Prickly Jerome is a pussycat compared with the Komodo dragon at home.

Doug is the big surprise, though. As directed, he flirts with Blitz Lord, hottie trophy wife and recently admitted delegate from the scary New Austin beyond the Zero Three zip code. The surprise is that Blitz flirts back.

This is going well, I observe from my hiding spot. The ladies are responding as planned to attention from young males with more hair on the top of their heads than sprouting from their ears.

I had assigned Sergio to focus on Kippie Lee. Kippie is our bell sheep. Where she goes, the rest of the flock will follow. Sergio, of course, is a pro. He takes off his sunglasses, bats his lashes a couple of times, and I assume that his work is done. I am wrong. Kippie Lee is proving resistant to Sergio's gigolo charm. She is actually attempting to wrest her Vuitton—from the new Marc Jacobs collection with the gold clasps—out of Sergio's grasp.

I had coached Alli on what to do should supple young flesh fail. If only she doesn't panic and forget the magic words I've drilled into her. But, alas, Alli is panicking.

Say the words, I send my telepathic message. Alli's eyes only open wider in dismay as the rest of the ladies follow K.L.'s lead and try to reclaim their luggage. Just as a couple of strays begin heading for the Rovers and the Lexi, Alli finally croaks out, "Gift bags."

The stampede halts.

Yes!

"Complimentary gift bags for everyone! Please, let's just adjourn to the new site and we'll all collect our *complimentary gift bags.* It's just around the corner. Okay?"

Start walking, Alli. That's it. Good. Good. Don't look back. Don't wait for accession. And . . . we have liftoff!

As the ladies follow Alli, I cut through the alley and sprint into the house, bellowing, "Places, everyone! They're coming!"

My "staff" bustles out to the porch and hits their marks like the trained actors I pray they can imitate long enough to get the women inside.

As far as the house itself, we've done what we could with the place: paint, throws, hosing the rugs down with muriatic acid. The plumbing still groans, and Seneca House is still, essentially, a pit, but there is no way around that. I had to borrow heavily just to stock the kind of food Tee Town women will eat. Expensive food: high-dollar protein, berries, no carbs, no filler, no additives, no antibiotics, no hormones.

"Millie, hit the smell machine!"

Millie dashes upstairs to crank up the fragrance blower my surprise supporter, Sanjeev, cobbled together. A fog of eucalyptus,
bergamot, and lavender blankets the house, puffing out onto the
front porch, where one shimmering gift bag, tongues of tissue poking out like spikes on an agave, waits.

I check my to-do list:

1. Get Hansel and Gretel into the candy house.
2. Avoid being shoved into the oven.

As the group rounds the corner, I install myself in the shrubbery. Alli leads the group up the walkway and they stop in front of
our new sign, reading SENECA FALLS SPA CLINIC. When Tribe Tee
Town realizes that they might actually be expected to enter the
only tenement slum any of them has ever beheld in person, stupe-
faction quickly gives way to the all-too-familiar mutinous murmurs. Fortunately, I have the A-team prepped and ready to go on.

Olga saunters forward, a study in supermodel lankiness, all
cheekbones and disdain. "Hello, lay tease." Olga is so languorous
she could make a tree sloth seem manic. She is my fantasy creation
in a naughty nurse outfit that displays everything Tribe Tee Town
dreams of: body fat in the single digits, baby blond hair, Slavic
cheekbones, skin tight enough to bounce a quarter off of, acres of
leg, and youth.

"Welcome to Spa Clinuck. I am mastair aesthetician. I am born
in Moscow. My father work at Lenin's Tomb. From him I learn all
secret of presarvation. Every two month we are soakink Lenin in
secret solution of glycerol and potassium acetate to mantan pliancy
and freshness.

"You see me? Forty-two year old." The group buzzes because,
although Olga is really twenty-four, she doesn't look a day over
twenty-two. "For Platinoom Lonkhorn, I tell all secret of presarvation. Also, I leckchair on mastairpiece of Hermitage Museum in
Sent Petersburk.

"Only one bat news. Because of clerical fock op, we overbook. One pairson has to leaf. You decide who cannut get in. We put hair on waitink list."

The words "waiting list" conjure up all the ladies yearn for most, from the right schools for their children to an Hermès Birkin handbag. Those cursed mutinous murmurs stop dead once the ladies learn that they might not be able to have what they don't want.

What genius to cast Olga as the doorman, the person to work the velvet rope, the one to create the illusion of exclusivity that is the very cornerstone of Tee Town life. Olga is perfect because she honestly doesn't care if anyone comes or goes, lives or dies. This is a quality that can't be faked, and these ladies can sense it like dogs sense fear. The princesses' interest is piqued. A deal-with-the-devil beauty secret *plus* an art history lecture *plus* the opportunity to blackball a close friend? It is the Tee Town Trifecta.

"I introduce clinuck director, Sanjeev Chowdhury. Duktor C."

Sanjeev steps forward. In another bit of inspired typecasting, I have made the prim, judgmental, officious Sanjeev Chowdhury into the prim, judgmental, officious *Dr.* Sanjeev Chowdhury. His manner goes perfectly with the stethoscope around his neck, clipboard in his hand, and calipers peeking out of the pocket of his lab coat. I have done him up in all white like a cross between a plantation owner and Dr. Brinkley, 1920s creator of the goat gland operation.

I still can't figure out why Sanjeev supported me. At first it seemed it was all about Millie. But they remain as distant as they've been since the day on the porch when I stated the obvious and blew their cover. Whatever Sanjeev's reasons, though, I can't pull this off without him.

Millie, standing next to him, looks smart in the outfit I concocted for her: the backward collar and chaplain's stole embroidered with golden doves over one of DKNY's signature jersey wraparounds that reveal her knockout figure. She is not a leggy android like Olga, but all that pining-for-lost-love gauntness, plus her milkmaid complexion, makes Millie one dishy minister. As Sanjeev begins speaking, she cannot hide her Nancy Reagan, spanielesque adoration.

Most of Sanjeev's welcoming remarks have to do with agrarian reform in the Indian state of Karnataka. It doesn't matter; it all sounds so smart in his high British-Brahman accent. He comes through at the end, though, and very clearly enunciates the vital words I scripted for him: "As most of you know, Seneca Falls Spa Clinic is renowned for being in the forefront of aesthetic technique. We work with Clinique d'Artagnan in Paris and the Instituten Krünk in Copenhagen. During your stay here we will have available several *off-label* uses of products not yet approved by the FDA which my colleagues in Europe have used safely *off label* and effectively *off label* for years. Again, I must emphasize that these uses are"— Sanjeev looks over at where I am rustling in the shrubbery, and his face pinches in disgust as he forces out the words I insisted he use as many times as possible—"*off label.*"

"Off label" is the Holy Grail in the world where mascara wand meets scalpel. Botox's original official purpose was fixing crossed eyes. Calming migraines, stanching torrential sweating, paralyzing uncontrollable facial tics, and—*eureka!*—demobilizing pesky wrinkles were all off-label advances. The ladies perk up at the possibility of getting the jump on an entire continent and discovering another off-label Fountain of Youth.

This is the exact moment when, ideally, I would have taken the floor, closed the deal, and had the ladies streaming in the front door. But since I am currently unavailable, I have lined up a secret weapon: Out onto the front porch steps the closest thing Austin has to a celebrity-socialite, Lynn Sydney Locke.

Lynn Sydney is a vision. Her sexy little Miu Miu summer frock shimmers, her luxurious titian tresses glint, her "fun" art jewelry— sproinging Alexander Calder twists of copper—positively dazzles. I cannot suppress a surge of pride on seeing the ladies' reaction to Lynn Sydney's appearance, since roping her into this fandango was a triumph of timing and packaging.

Lynn Sydney was the first person I called after the house voted to host the Plat Longs. I had a little ace up my sleeve in that regard; I knew that shortly after Lynn Sydney began her conquest of Austin she applied to be a member of the Platinum Longhorn board of directors and that Kippie Lee, backed up by the henchbitches, in a doomed attempt to block the newcomer's inevitable rise to power, had blackballed her. I also knew that Lynn Sydney knew since her information may have been obtained through my personally telling the rising star; I could always spot a comer. So, although a smacking symphony of air kisses had since passed between the two divas, along with mad exclamations about the gorgeousness of the "pieces" the other was wearing, hostilities simmered. Hostilities I was hoping to ratchet up to a full, rolling boil when I called Lynn Sydney.

Before I had finished uttering my name, Lynn Sydney was shrieking, "Blythe Young, no! I heard the most amazing story. Did you really feed K.L. and her crew Roofies? Tell me it's true."

"It's true."

"That is beyond beyond. I would give up all my minutes on my ex's private jet to have seen that. And now they've totally banished you, right?"

"I am officially beyond beyond."

"No, seriously, Blythe, I mean totally, no-going-back, Witness Protection banished."

"Permanent social Siberia. They're trying to send me to prison."

This seemed enough evidence that I wouldn't suck up and then roll over on her for Lynn Sydney to open up about her deep enmity for the princesses, stemming from the blackballing. "Can you believe they tried a ridiculous cock block like that? I mean, please, Blythe, you were like the third person to tell me every detail of that 'secret meeting.' Now it's to the point that they're knocking one another over to see who can get to me first with the dirt. Anyway, the Plat Longs are so Old Austin. I never remotely needed them, did I?"

"Not remotely."

"Not that it matters anymore anyway. I am so over Austin. A girl can't even put together a decent gay entourage in this city. I'm trying to decide: New York or London? Paris is out, the plumbing sucks. My agent found this really really cute flat in Mayfair. Right around the corner from Sotheby's, so that would be fun. Anyway, Blythe, tell me, what's up with you?"

I thanked whatever lucky stars had delivered Austin's hottest social commodity into my hands at the exact moment when she would be most open to being part of—as I packaged it on the spur of the moment—a "really fun guerrilla theater farewell to Austin."

And here she is now, stepping onto the front porch, causing consternation and homicidal envy among the princesses gathered beneath her. With a ringmaster's arm extended toward the star attraction, Alli announces, "Spa Seneca is honored and delighted to present Lynn Sydney Locke as our opening speaker." As I directed, Alli allows plenty of time for Lynn Sydney's radiant presence to sink in before she speaks again. "Lynn Sydney's topic will be 'My House, My Self.'"

Lynn Sydney smiles a little smile that is somewhere between personable and poisonous. "Congratulations to all of you for choosing such a wildly creative, out-of-the-box site for this event. Friends in London tell me they had the most marvelous time recently in a squatter's flat. Very avant-garde. Tiny carbon footprint, all that. Charles and Camilla adored it. I will begin my presentation in five minutes. See you inside."

Lynn Sydney steps into the house and after a few seconds of consternation, Kippie Lee leads what is a very restrained charge up the stairs. The ladies do an admirable job of pretending that avant-garde and tiny carbon footprint had been their intention all along. Only when all the ladies are on the porch, about to enter the house, do I feel it is safe to step forward and nudge Millie into action.

"Oh, everyone, wait a sec, I'm house chaplain Millie Ott and I would like to present to you Spa Seneca's nutritionist, Fatima Sarowa."

That is my cue to place my carefully hennaed hands together over my heart, and bow to the group. My new look—covered from head to toe by a burka, little grille completely hiding my face and identity—seems to be going over well with my former friends.

I gargle something indecipherable, then bow again.

"Fatima is still working on her English, but I want all you ladies to know that having been trained in a culture where serving *haram*, 'forbidden,' food could get your hand cut off, Fatima will honor your individual preferences with a, literally, religious zeal."

This then is to be my real penance: catering to the insane diet specifications of a dozen hysterically finicky women. With a silent wave of Fatima's elaborately curlicued hand, I gesture wordlessly for the women to enter.

Then, buried in the burka, I stop breathing and don't start again until all twelve of my Gretels have crossed the threshold and are inside the house. Now I just have to work on the second big item on my to-do list: Avoid being shoved into the oven.

Find Your Path

As our country's greatest art and culture critic, Renaissance man Dave Hickey, says in his seminal collection of essays, *Air Guitar*, 'Bad taste is real taste and good taste is nothing but the residue of someone else's privilege.'" Lynn Sydney lectures to a dozen women with their feet soaking in tubs, basins, a pair of loaf pans, an old tofu container, and Big Lou's water bowl.

I once coordinated an affair at Laguna Gloria Art Museum where Dave Hickey spoke, so I had observed his mesmeric effect on my ladies. It was the year he won a MacArthur genius grant. That combined with the fact that none of the ladies understood a single word he said lent his every utterance an invincible air of infallibility. I pray that invoking his name now will convince key Pemberton Princesses that, once again, they are part of an "art" experience they must pretend to understand.

Nikki and Kat both look crisply professional in white lab coats. A few weeks of cosmetology school have transformed Nikki, and worshipful Kat is doing her best to emulate her idol. They are abrading Bamsie's and Blitz's feet with a salt scrub. The Seneca crew relieved the ladies of their footwear as quickly as possible. In fact, Nikki and Kat were unbuckling and slipping shoes off even as Kippie and crew stood frozen, gaping in horror at the interior of the house. Although we had cleaned, deodorized, and sanitized, it is still a freak show which only the presence of Lynn Sydney Locke could have made not just acceptable but fashionable in a way that, thankfully, the princesses believe they can't fully understand. All they know for sure is that if Lynn Sydney Locke is here, it has to be cool.

So, instead of gagging on the smell of insecticide, the ladies study Lynn Sydney Locke. They try to figure out how many inches of leg they'd have to have transplanted to look as good as she does in a Miu Miu frock. "Look around," she orders. "You will never again be in a space so free from the tyranny of taste."

Hypnotized, none of the women can turn her eyes away from Lynn's glittering personage until she repeats her command, "Look around."

The women gawk at furnishings scavenged from Goodwill and off the street on Bulky Item Pickup Day, furnishings that were ancient before they ever washed ashore at Seneca House. The full horror of the dump hits Kippie Lee and she starts to stand. I nod at Lute so vigorously that the burka bounces.

Lute, golden ringlets trembling, leaps to station himself at Kippie Lee's feet. Before another thought of escape has time to cross her mind, Lute is massaging K.L.'s arches and metatarsals with a level of ardor she has not experienced since her honeymoon. Or, more precisely, not since her sayonara screw with Cotton Donahue, the passed-out groom's best man. I know that Miss Kip is still struggling with her philandering asshole of a husband getting his plaque scraped in an extramarital format. My bet that she will be up for a little grudge action seems to be paying off, judging from the way she melts back into her chair as Lute applies himself to her instep. That is good. That is very good. As long as we can keep Kippie Lee neutralized, we might be able to hold off a walkout.

I snap fingers filigreed with henna tattoos, and my "staff" disperses among the ladies. Nikki and Kat start painting toenails. Jerome reattaches himself to Bamsie. Missy Quisinberry refuses Sergio's offer of a shoulder massage. Sergio gives her one anyway.

"As you can see," Lynn Sydney continues airily, "this space has been designed to be as free of taste as is humanly possible. Spa Seneca accomplished such an unprecedented degree of taste-freedom through intensive research and analyses of the homes of computer programmers and clog-dancing aficionados. And why? Why do they go to this extreme effort? Because research has revealed that true, *true*, relaxation is impossible in settings that trigger the competitive decorating response. What we are doing is momentarily relieving you of the burden of taste so that you may all experience the ultimate intoxication: the weightlessness of moving about in a zero-gravity taste environment."

I can almost see the air around the princesses' heads growing wavy as it heats up from the effort required to perceive such a dump as the ultimate intoxication. But if Lynn Sydney Locke, occupant of one of *Architectural Digest*'s "Ten Most Influential Homes of 2002," says it is, who are they to argue?

Lynn Sydney returns her listeners' rapt gazes. "During your stay at Seneca Falls Spa Clinic you will be given permission to lay down the burden of connoisseurship. To unharness the yoke of discernment, cut off the shackles of refinement, and experience the freedom of tastelessness."

I peer through the grille in front of my face and study the women's expressions. Are they buying this? Do they care enough about being perceived as discerning, refined connoisseurs to lay that theoretical load down here in Trashy Town?

"Haven't we all agonized over whether hammered pewter or brushed nickel is the fullest expression of who we are?"

Heads nod.

"Whether stained concrete is over? Whether we should have bought out at the lake before all the movie stars moved in and prices skyrocketed? How long are leather floors going to be au courant? Where do we hang the Larry Rivers?"

Bamsie, whom I'd once watched fretting about where to place her R. C. Gorman poster, nods at their shared burden.

As Lynn Sydney goes on, I circulate with a tray of Raspberry Razzers. Every Razzer that I, as Fatima, the shuffling pile of sheets, serve comes with a recipe card listing protein powder, Splenda, and low-glycemic-index fruits. The one ingredient not mentioned is tasteless, odorless, 190-proof grain alcohol. Though not ideal in the moral choice department, it is absolutely necessary and a distinct improvement over Rohypnol.

I have sternly resisted the temptation to take the far lower road and customize each drink to correct the various psychic deficits of the individual guest. A pinch of crystal meth for the lethargic. The barest smidgen of Xanax for the temperamentally tense. And who among this chronically insecure bunch of strivers could not have benefited from the general boost in fellow feeling that only the most judicious administration of Ecstasy could have provided? But even when Sergio volunteered to bring those hollow-heeled boots out of retirement for me, I refused. I made a solemn promise to myself that I was going to do this the old-fashioned way: all liquored up.

Which is exactly the state I pray the women are in when Lynn Sydney makes her announcement. "Well, ladies, I am so jealous of you all. I would give just anything to be able to stay, but"—she is gathering up her Hermès Birkin bag in orange crocodile with the palladium hardware—"it's wheels up in . . ." She checks her Patek Philippe Calatrava for the time. "Shoot! Is it that late? I have to be at the FBO in ten minutes. Thank God there's no security for private jets, right?"

The ladies beam expressions of sympathetic understanding toward Lynn Sydney, and a desperate dream takes root in each of their souls: Never fly commercial again. She bends over and kisses each one in turn, and they breathe in Lynn Sydney's unidentifiable fragrance. It makes them feel as if they had walked out onto the terrazzo of their Italian lover's palazzo high above the Amalfi coast and are drinking in the scent of rosemary, sunshine, and sex. They each feel a palpable pang of yearning when Lynn Sydney heads for the door. She salves that sweet ache, however, with her parting comment: "I can't wait to hear about the amazing experience y'all are going to have here. You have to remember every single detail, and then, when I get back from Bono's thing, I'll have y'all out to the ranch and we'll debrief."

I am dazzled by how well and deeply Lynn Sydney has set the hook. There is no way now that I will lose the ladies. They would have endured trench warfare for the opportunity to "debrief" at Lynn Sydney's ranch. I understand revenge, but what Lynn Sydney has just done for me goes way beyond that. I bustle my burka to rush after my benefactress before she steps into her waiting car.

Outside, safely beyond my guests' hearing, I whisper a word of thanks.

Astonished, Lynn Sydney whispers back, "Blythe, is that you under there?"

"Yes, I thought a low profile might be advisable."

Lynn Sydney's laugh is warm and earthy. One might even have said down-home and redneck. "So, you are really, truly, and permanently out."

"'Out' doesn't begin to describe what I am."

"In that case, don't you remember me?"

When I wag my burka in the negative, Lynn Sydney leans over and screeches in my ear like an eagle.

"You're an Abilene High Eagle?"

The celebrity-socialite holds up circled thumb and forefinger glasses in front of her eyes, gives a bucktoothed, hick grin, and hundreds of thousands of dollars of orthodontia, cosmetic surgery, and the best Swami-tending money can buy fall away, leaving behind "Jo Rae Strunk? But you—"

"Were a scrawny, semiliterate piece of white trash just like you? Yeah, that was me. One year behind you in school. I was always inspired by you changing your name. Can't tell you how surprised and edified I was to rediscover you. Especially since you didn't remember me. I don't plan on coming out of the blue-collar closet until the next divorce is final. At that point, I'll be set and can afford to own anything I want." Lynn Sydney Locke slides into the backseat of the waiting car, pauses, and glances up at me. "Even a trailer-trash girlhood." She closes the door, and the car glides away.

Back inside the house, I find the women finishing a fourth round of Razzers. Kippie Lee is informing Lute of just how much of an honor she would consider it if he'd allow her to finance the recording of his demo. Blitz Lord is letting Kat paint her toenails Hematoma Heather. Missy Quisinberry's eyes are rolling back in her head as Sergio gets after her tense trapezia. Cookie Mehan is receiving detailed instruction from Olga on how to give the perfect blow job. Bamsie and Jerome are arguing in the feverish way of couples one step away from ripping each other's clothes off. And Morgan Whitlow is telling Paige Oglesby how really, really, no, *really* cute she has always thought she is.

I pull Millie aside and whisper to her, "Deploy."

Millie nods uncertainly, picks up one of the giant menus of services I have put together, and goes to Kippie Lee.

"Here are our services," Millie says, holding the menu open so that Kippie Lee can peruse it while Lute rubs shea butter into her cuticles and gives her a breakdown of what it might cost to put the Fresh 'n' Fruity on the road to tour behind an album. The services are another one of my fantasy creations, a dessert cart of indulgences: pomegranate-cream body wrap; French-vanilla sugar scrub; Thai lemongrass-coconut cuticle rejuvenation; peppermint cleansing facial. But it is Millie's own free service that she pushes the hardest.

Millie directs Kippie Lee's attention away from Lute's ringlets and to the last line on the menu:

FIND YOUR PATH. Consult with a nondenominational pastoral counselor about the meaning of your life.

I edge in a little closer for maximum eavesdropping and see Millie studying Kippie Lee's face with an otherworldly intensity that makes Kippie Lee pull back and ask, "What are you staring at?"

"You are sad. You are very, very sad. You are sad in a way that even the best figure and biggest house in the world will not make any better."

Kippie Lee looks spooked.

Perfect! Millie is coming through. She was highly resistant to the whole idea of me prepping her for some maximally effective pastoral counseling sessions. I argued that, given how little time she had with the ladies, wouldn't it help to know their deepest, darkest secrets? Millie had ethical questions with this approach, but I went ahead and gave her the scoop on all the ladies anyway. She listened to their backstories with the proviso that she would not use any of my intel unless she felt the "tingles" that meant a person needed her help. I told her not to worry about tingles; these gals needed so much spiritual healing, she was going to think she'd been electrocuted.

And, obviously, that is exactly what is happening.

"Could you give us a moment alone?" Kippie Lee removes her foot from Lute's lusty grasp and rereads the description of Millie's service:

FIND YOUR PATH. Consult with a nondenominational pastoral counselor about the meaning of your life.

Perhaps it is the grain alcohol. Maybe it is the virtual certainty that she is losing her husband to a dental hygienist named Marigold. Possibly it is accepting that not only will she never have Becca Cason Thrash's thirteen powder rooms, but that the upstart Lynn Sydney Locke has rendered her Xanadu and her entire way of life obsolete that does her in. Whatever the mix of reality with regret, exhaustion with starvation, tears puddle in Kippie Lee's eyes as she looks down at Millie's kind face and asks, "You could find meaning in *my* life?"

Millie leans in closer. "No, but you could."

"Nondenominational?"

"Completely."

"Because I'm Episcopalian."

"We won't let that get in our way."

"And privacy?"

"Of course. Absolutely. Everything we discuss will be held in the strictest confidence."

"Everything?" K.L. asks.

"I took an oath," Millie assures her. "Kippie Lee, whenever you're ready, I can help you."

"How about right now?"

Millie escorts Kippie Lee upstairs to the small bedroom she's converted into her office/confessional.

The princesses fall silent as they watch Kippie Lee follow Millie upstairs. Once it is clear that their leader is staying, it is no longer safe for anyone to leave. Women in bare feet scamper over to Olga to sign up for as many services as they can so they won't be put on the "voloonteer" list.

After Kippie Lee comes down two hours later, beaming, drying reddened eyes, and giving off a postcoital radiance, all of Millie's pastoral counseling sessions book up, along with most of the other services.

Still, that first night is rough, with several walkouts threatened. All by staff outraged at demands for down pillows, nondown pillows, wheat-hull and organic-spelt-husk pillows. Sergio calms the waters by delivering mugs of Sleepytime to each of the ladies. Only when they are dozing soundly does Sergio confirm my suspicion that, yes, he had made Sleepytime into Comatose Time with some extra boot-heel-flavored additives that gave all of our guests the magic ability to doze off with a brick for a pillow.

"All right," I tell Sergio, "but from now on there are to be no further additives. I'm going to play this hand without stacking the deck."

"You hab changed," he says.

"I hope so," I answer.

Hump the
Ancient Shag

THE FIRST ORDER of business the next morning is weigh-in. Fatima takes on this chore. The ladies would rather have given out their ATM numbers than their weight, but revealing the digits to silent, shrouded Fatima is somehow acceptable.

Weigh-in takes place in Millie's ultraprivate confessional room before anyone has consumed so much as one drop of water or one crumb of nutrition, yet after every microdrop of fluid has been voided. As Kippie Lee steps up, I ache to put a big fat butcher's thumb on the scales. I yearn to tack on a bonus two or three pounds that could miraculously be deducted at checkout. But I have vowed not to stack the deck. Besides, every one of our guests knows her weight down to the ounce. In fact, Kippie Lee knows how many grams a thong adds and usually insists on waxing before stepping on the scales. Even if I had wanted to, there would be no way to cook the books.

Toward the goal of achieving slumber naturally, my staff marches the ladies from one end of the university to the other. I have uncovered Old Girls in every department on campus. The bookish Seneca alums all gravitated toward obscure fields. So the princesses are treated to lectures on the importance of the Chadwyck-Healey humanities collection to scholars of Renaissance literature; advances in quantitative analysis of nucleotide modulation of DNA binding by DnaC protein of *E. coli;* and, the showstopper, adaptations to temperature of the Queensland fruit fly.

Luckily, years of membership in high-minded book clubs have stupefied the ladies into believing that boring means good. The turgid lectures combined with a dozen cross-campus tromps in record-breaking three-digit heat guarantee an early bedtime.

Forced to abandon Seneca House, my helpers and I bivouac next door at New Guild, since our sister co-op is empty until the summer session starts. Unfortunately, all the bedrooms are locked up so we have to make do in the common areas. As spare as the accommodations are, I am looking forward to getting horizontal on the pool table Millie and I claimed. As soon as I shed the burka, however, my team starts unraveling.

Juniper is the first to rip off her white lab coat. "I don't care if I have to eat out of a Dumpster, I can't do another day. Another minute."

"*Da.* Those bitches are focked op."

Even Doug jumps on the dog pile. "The way they quiz you on every molecule of food they put into their mouths. It's insane. I'm with Olga. If I have to do another day of this, I will punch someone."

I don't know how to motivate them; no point in holding out the carrot of a debriefing at Lynn Sydney's ranch to this crew. I stick with the basics. "We have no choice. We have to make at least enough to deal with the RIAA or we'll lose the house."

Far too much laissez-faire shrugging meets this dire prediction. Juniper sums up the general feeling of the group: "Whatever."

"No, not 'whatever,'" I burst out. "Come on. This is not that hard." I dig deep into my arsenal of motivational tools and stumble upon the basic credo all of them learned in public school to the exclusion of dreary rote skills like multiplication tables and spelling: appreciation for diversity.

"You're just not appreciating the fact that these women come from a different culture, a foreign culture. For them, all these dietary observances are, quite literally, religious. Diet is their religion. It is the one thing they truly believe in, and you have to respect it as such. Look, Sanjeev doesn't eat beef. Yay Bombah and

Nazarite won't eat pork. Juniper, you won't eat meat, eggs, cheese. Pretty much anything other than bagels and Mint Milanos—"

"That is so not true!"

"So these gals won't eat a few things."

"Like carbohydrates," Doug says.

"Just give them a tumbler of olive oil. Listen, I'm the one who paid for the berries and basil and bluefin tuna, I'm the one doing all the cooking. I promise, by tomorrow, or the next day at the latest, they will mellow out, okay?"

A buzz of grumbling meets my request.

"Humor them. Just pretend they've all got Alzheimer's. If that doesn't work, then allow me to share my own personal form of motivation. Pretend that if you can't make these women happy for just another day or two, just long enough to give us a leg to stand on in court, you're all going to get thrown out on your asses. Pretend that you'll be down on Dog Crap Lane with me, except Millie won't be showing up with the eggs and tortillas. Huh? How about that for a little visualization exercise?"

The grumbling ceases, and we retire to whatever floor or pool table we have been able to wrest from the cockroaches.

Weigh-in early the next day is an unalloyed triumph. Possibly because of the walking and sweating the day before. Possibly because most of the group fell asleep halfway through dinner. Whatever the reason, the ladies are bubbly when they come down for the morning meal.

I am back in chador and back in the kitchen, where breakfast is another hideous chemistry challenge for Fatima. The punishment is so fitted to the crime that I bow to its perfection. Catering without the aid of pharmaceuticals is hard work. I who passed off Cream of Wheat enlivened with the magic of sunny yellow popcorn seasoning as polenta, who slipped catfish through customs as Copper River salmon, now must use a gram scale to cook real food for real food fanatics.

I whip up a frankly delicious frittata and begin serving. Since I expect a barrage of grumpiness because the food is late, the giddy, sorority atmosphere that greets me in the dining room is a pleasant surprise.

Bamsie and Jerome jabber at each other without even the tiniest hint of conversational pauses. Jerome takes advantage of the rare opportunity to speak to a human female who is not backing rapidly away to list his favorite bands and/or performers by genre: "Okay, in reggae or more accurately dance hall, it's Eek-A-Mouse and, no question, Bob Marley. For punk, I'd have to go with Braindamaged and Massengil."

Bamsie doesn't answer so much as continue her own soliloquy detailing the ways in which her husband does not understand her. "We're just not soul mates," she concludes. "He's afraid of intimacy. He's a sweaterback who refuses to wax. He doesn't ever listen. We never talk. Not like this. Just sit down and discuss how we're feeling. I'm friends with Heather, his first wife. He also refused to do couples counseling with her."

Jerome responds by asking, "Should I put goth/techno/house/synth all in one category or break them down?"

In the midst of this roaring Niagara of gab, Missy Quisinberry tracks Kippie Lee's every move. The instant Miss Kip excuses herself for a potty break, Missy waves the ladies in for a quick huddle, then pronounces the awful words, "Hunt Teeter took the hygienist to Jeffrey's last night."

"No."

"Yes. Jebediah was there with a client. He called me first thing this morning."

The group gasps a communal gasp of mourning because this report from Missy's husband means that Kippie Lee's marriage is history. A union is officially over when the rich and powerful husband or, far more titillating, the rich and powerful wife takes the paramour to Tarrytown's holy of holies, Jeffrey's, for Crispy Oysters on Yucca Root Chips.

No one speaks until straight shooter Cookie Mehan gives voice to the anxiety weighing heavily on all the ladies: "There's a world of women out there who want our jobs. And they're all younger, their boobs are perkier, and they weren't around when the big man flunked Management Fundamentals for the third time back at UT." Cookie has isolated the fear that fuels the trips to the cosmetic surgeon, the hours at spinning class, the lifetime of counting calories, carbs, prestige of children's schools, stylishness of backsplashes.

"This is a hard truth to accept." Cookie looks around the table. The women always listen to Cookie with extra attention, since She Has Her Own Money and, if what she says is true for her, it is doubly so for the non–trust funded. "But accept it every woman must: Men are programmed for novelty, and you can only be new once." It is a bittersweet moment. Especially for Blitz. On the one hand, since Blitz is included in Cookie's searching gaze, it means that Austin society has finally accepted her. On the other, she has to face the sad realization that she began tarnishing the instant she said, "I do."

All the women sigh heavily. Fortunately, this reminder of for whom the bell tolls is quickly forgotten when the more compelling topic of whether or not this season's new pastel lip and nail colors make you look washed-out presents itself.

And then Olga appears to change the subject entirely with the day's first activity: cardio striptease. All the ladies giddily accept one of the feather boas she hands out. To the accompaniment of some languid electro-house music featuring a singer who sounds like Greta Garbo on downers, Olga starts undulating and barking commands.

"Swiffel hips!"

Olga's previous employment at Exposé Gentleman's Club comes to the fore. The ladies, dedicated connoisseurs of excellence, appreciate Olga's obvious mastery of the form as she flips her boa between her legs and rides the pink feathers with heavy-lidded abandon. "Make luf to boa!" she commands before shifting to, "Feekyoor eight! Feekyoor eight!"

The class follows her, swiveling their pelvises in looping figure eights.

"Make luf to floor!"

The class hits the carpet and starts humping the ancient shag.

Morgan Whitlow, on the floor next to Paige Oglesby, simulates the most realistic passion.

A steel beam wedged into the living room to support the sagging second floor is Olga's next object of desire. "Make luf to pole! Loozen up!"

The class twines around the beam like ferrets in a mating frenzy. By the time the women have spent themselves and are patting towels across complexions glowing in a way that no amount of retinol or special time with the European handheld shower has ever been able to achieve, they are pretty certain that it would not be possible for them to get any "loozer."

Queen of
the Stoners

And then Yay Bombah and Nazarite show up bearing a small bale of the best marijuana a furniture magnate's money can buy and inquire in their guileless, weed-to-the-people way, "Who wanna black up, mon?" The twins fire up a Paul Bunyan of a spliff and hold the smoldering trunk out to the ladies.

Ants touch mandibles to trade chemical messages so that all the members of the colony can sync up. Similarly, a dozen gazes bounce from one face to the next as Tribe Tee Town struggles to reach a nonverbal consensus. In the culture war being fought in Austin, Texas, in the year 2003, there are some very interesting casualties. Austin has long been a place where young Tejanas come to get a degree, get a husband, and get wild. And most of the princesses managed to accomplish all three. The problem is, given the tight-assedness of the times, no one knows for sure who has done what, and to come out of the closet as a pothead would be tantamount to admitting to a far, far greater sin: being a liberal.

So Cookie Mehan, who came of age on a ranch in West Texas, blazing up with the help from the time she was fourteen, does not take the blunt. And Blitz Lord, who got her nickname by being queen of the stoners at Immaculate Conception High School, also holds back. As do Noodle and Lulie, who both used to brag about having been Dallas debutantes on acid, though it has been a long time since either one has mentioned the "on acid" part.

It is pretty much a standoff and would have remained nothing more than an amusing story to spread around at the next ballet gala if Kippie Lee, who'd forgone cardio striptease for another session with Millie, hadn't rejoined the group at just that moment and snatched up the proffered joint, saying, "I don't know about all y'all, but there is already too much in my life that I have missed out on." Then Kippie Lee takes a hit that would have done a Grateful Dead roadie proud.

After exhaling into her friends' faces, she explains, "Talking to Millie has helped me see that there is a big beautiful world beyond Pemberton Heights, and if I don't get out and explore it, I'm going to be dead and never have really lived and no one's going to care that I had mother-of-pearl backsplashes. Though, just for the record, I did have them before Lynn Sydney got hers. But that doesn't matter. Not really."

Showing herself to be quite a dab hand with the cannabis, Kippie Lee passes the joint to Cookie. Cookie Mehan's *mota*-smoking youth becomes obvious as she pinches the joint to her lips, sucks in with a hipster's locomotive inhalations, then passes it on to Blitz. The twins' gift makes the rounds with only Missy Quisinberry abstaining.

The Saperstein sisters' generosity turns out to be a mixed blessing. Yes, the visitors are all laughing like lunatics, but the ganja interlude also creates a crisis in the diet department, and Fatima has to wrest a box of dry brownie mix from Paige Oglesby's manicured hands before getting the girls back under control.

The upside of ravenous appetites, however, is a marked falloff in discernment. Suddenly, even those whose diet imams expressly forbid corn in any form are grinding through the bags of popcorn that Fatima heaves at them like sandbags being piled up on the levees of a raging Mississippi.

Another positive aspect of the twins' largesse is that the women find the Saperstein girls' impromptu lecture on the biblical roots of Rastafarianism utterly riveting. They listen spellbound and glassy eyed as Nazarite recites pertinent verses. "'He causeth the grass to grow for the cattle, and *herb* for the service of man.' It's right there in the Bible," Nazarite says, pointing to the passage with fingertips stained a rich ocher. "Psalms one hundred and four, verse fourteen."

"Or try this," Yay Bombah says, offering further biblical endorsement of their hobby. " 'Thou shalt eat of the *herb* of the field.' "

"Yeah," Missy Q. agrees pensively. "And what about Proverbs, chapter fifteen, verse seventeen, 'Better is a dinner of *herbs* where love is, than a stalled ox and hatred therewith'?"

Yay Bombah and Nazarite congratulate Missy on her "dread" knowledge of the Bible. As a devout Southern Baptist brought up on a literal interpretation of the Bible, Missy suddenly understands that Scripture leaves no doubt as to the action she must take. She holds out her hand, and Yay Bombah passes the joint.

Happy Horseshit

THE MOMENT OF MELLOWMENT stretches into the next day, then the next. By day 5, Blitz Lord and Cookie Mehan are the only ones who appear in Millie's crow's nest for weigh-in. After recording their weight, I rush downstairs to start whipping up the usual periodic chart's worth of disparate breakfast orders, only to find the women already gathering pens and notebooks for that morning's lecture to be delivered by everyone's favorite medievalist, Ariadne. Her topic? "Da Vinci De-Coded."

Ariadne was so incensed about all the historical errors in the best seller that she proposed the colloquium as a public service. "How can an author be taken seriously who doesn't know that King Philip the Fair of France, *not* Pope Clement V, crushed the Knights Templars?" Every book club in Tarrytown had read the tome so, for the first time in a thousand years, the rest of the world shares Ariadne's obsessions. The ladies actually want to know the answer to her question.

They all troop out, the house falls silent. After five days of non-stop servitude, I finally have a moment to think. The first topic I begin to wonder about is what has caused the startling changes in almost all of my former friends. Not only are most of them no longer obsessed with their weight, but the demands, complaints, gossiping, competitiveness have all virtually disappeared. Why? I check the sign-in sheets. Nikki and Kat have been busy with manis, pedis, and facials. Juniper has had a few takers for hot-stone massages. Sergio has seen quite a few of the ladies for deep-tissue work. In fact, I note that Missy has made many repeat visits. Several on the same day. But only one staff member's dance card is completely filled, only one person has seen every member of the tribe except for no-nonsense Cookie Mehan, and that person is Millie Ott.

Could Millie be the catalyst? The only way I can account for this sea change is that Millie, slyboots, is using all the secret information I gave her. I have to test this hypothesis. The sign-up sheet reveals that Cookie's first private session with Millie started only minutes ago.

I race up the stairs as fast as a person wearing a circus tent can race and slip into the utility closet conveniently located next to the room where Millie has been conducting her private sessions. The closet roils with ducts twisting out from the fragrance blower Sanjeev cobbled together. All the coils disorient me. I bend down and, as silently as possible, remove the floor-level flexible coil that I think leads to Millie's room. A suffocating cloud of eucalyptus, lavender, and bergamot belches forth. I put my ear to the opening.

"Jew are holding a lot of tenchun in jour pelbis area. For jew I recommend full release." Sergio's silken Latin murmur purrs through the hole in the wall.

"Oh well, if you think so."

Missy Quisinberry?

"Jes, jes, I do. Shall I dim the light?"

I shove the duct back into the opening before I can overhear Missy's response. More careful this time, I locate the coil leading to Millie's room and silently pull it loose.

"Cookie, you have been carrying too much weight for too long." Millie uses a tone I have never heard from her before. Gone is her typical apologetic deference. She speaks with the certitude of someone explaining gravity. "It is not good to carry so much weight."

"Well, I know that," Cookie snaps back, sounding like the tough ranchwoman she was raised to be. "Your damn program here isn't helping me either. I've barely lost a pound and a half. I'm thinking about demanding a refund."

"Cookie, you know we're not talking about that weight. You can put your burden down."

"Don't get mystical. I don't do mystical. I wouldn't have come up here if I thought you were going to get all woo-woo. Of course, no one who's been in here to see you will tell me what you tell them. All they'll give me is some happy horseshit about 'Ooo, she changed my thinking.' 'Ooo, she's got such amazing insights.' I assume that you have some big revelation about what diet worked for you. I know you used to weigh two hundred pounds. That's all anyone will tell me. You had your stomach stapled, right?"

There is a silence and I assume that Millie is shaking her head no.

"Lipo? Weight Watchers, right? You look like a Weight Watchers person. Slow and steady. Church basement full of women cheering when you reach your goal weight. Trading recipes for Bundt cakes made with Splenda."

"Cookie, I have a question for you: Would you marry a man who hated your body?"

"Don't go all Dr. Phil on me."

"Would you work for a boss who constantly criticized you? Who demeaned you? Who continually came up with ever more unattainable goals?"

"I know where you're going with this and it really doesn't interest me."

"If you know, Cookie, why are you such a bad boss to yourself? To your own body? Cookie Mehan, you have been carrying too much weight for too long. Let it go, Cookie. Put it down."

"Oh, please." Cookie's voice crackles with its usual astringency.

"Look at yourself in the mirror, Cookie."

"Listen, I don't know how you buffaloed all the others, but where I grew up we shovel bullshit, we don't buy it."

"Look at yourself and understand that your body is deteriorating."

"Believe me, I don't need you to remind me of that."

"Understand that with each second another grain of sand slips through the neck of the hourglass."

"Take a peek at my rear end. You don't have to tell me that all those grains are heading south."

"Understand that your body is a vehicle that will wear out and die."

"Exactly. That's why I'm trying to do everything I can to keep the miles from showing."

"Whether they show or not, the body records them. Look in the mirror and thank your body for being such a good vessel for your spirit."

"Okay, now you're getting seriously woo-woo and I told you I don't do woo-woo."

"Don't be a bad boss to your own body. To your spirit."

Cookie groans. "Give me a fucking break." But she doesn't get up and walk out. Millie goes on. Her words are hypnotic, insistent in a liquid way, like a stream carving out a canyon, one inevitable, irresistible drop at a time. It is impossible to argue against what amounts to a gentle rain. It will fall whether you agree with it or not.

"Thank your body for serving you well. For moving your mind and spirit through a world more beautiful than any of us has a right to."

"Oh gee, thank you, body, for saddlebag thighs and mosquito-bite tits."

"Thank your body for being strong and for being soft."

"Soft, that's for sure."

"Thank it for allowing you to express love and to receive love."

"Look, this Oprah Lite shit just isn't doing it for me. You're helping me find my path, all right, and it's heading straight out of here."

"I will tell you one sure thing about your path, Cookie."

"About time."

"You will get old and you will die."

"News flash. News flash."

"Cookie, if you know that one thing for sure, why are you putting so many eggs in the wrong basket?"

"Say what?"

"Choose another basket. The basket of your body will crumble. Put those eggs in a basket that will last. Only you know the best container for your own most precious self-worth. I would advise, though, against choosing one favored by eighteen-year-old boys."

"All men are eighteen-year-old boys," Cookie snaps, but a bit of the acerbic tartness has washed out of her voice.

"Cookie, if the ultimate answer in your life is size two, you are asking the wrong question. You are asking the wrong question and you are playing the wrong game. You will die. I will die. We will all die. What do you want on your tombstone? 'My shroud was a size two'? 'I had perfect abs'? We're women, Cookie. Our bodies were created millions of years ago to be round and soft. To give comfort and life. And then to die."

"Stop saying that!"

"It is the most important thing you will ever hear. Maybe we come back. Maybe we float around on clouds and harps. We don't know."

"You are quite the ray of sunshine, aren't you?"

"Yes, I am. I truly am. I am shining a light on a message that is truly worth celebrating: Our time on this earth is a party. It would be churlish to complain because the party ends. But it does. Ask yourself how much of this precious time you have spent worrying about your weight or being unhappy with the way you look. Ask yourself what you could accomplish if you did something else with that time. Maybe it's not anything more than planting a garden, but at least you'd have some homegrown tomatoes. Cookie, on your deathbed, what will you regret most not having done?"

I quickly plug the hose back in. Cookie's answer is private. It's hers alone. I am ashamed of myself for having eavesdropped. More ashamed than I can remember being in a long time.

The ladies return and we make it through the rest of the day without incident. But by the next morning I am beyond exhausted and can barely drag myself off the pool table and plod next door. No one is up yet. None of my little helpers is anywhere to be seen. I haul my aching carcass to the kitchen and try to get into harness. But weariness flattens me. I wilt into a chair, and honestly don't think I have enough strength left to ever get up again. Then, praise Allah, a miracle.

Kippie Lee appears at the top of the stairs and announces, "Y'all! Group session in Millie's room in five minutes. Come on! Fire up, y'all!" Doors fly open, the ladies emerge, rush past Fatima, and head upstairs. A few blessedly quiet hours later, they all emerge from Millie's crow's-nest confessional weeping, their arms looped over one another's shoulders, the miraculous transformation from the finickiest of consumers to handmaidens of the Lord put on earth to serve, complete.

Suddenly all the princesses begin treating their remaining time at Spa Seneca as the sort of volunteer vacation where you pay to repair the Appalachian Trail or build a pump station for a poor Mexican village. They regress back to a summer camp mentality, to a time when they made their own bunks and cooked special dinners in Dutch ovens for their favorite counselors at Camps Mystic and Longhorn. The ladies don't make a single demand. They do everything for themselves. For one another. For Fatima and whichever of the other residents comes out of hiding. Most amazing of all, though, with the end in sight, the ladies begin clamoring to sign up for "next year's event."

"They are totally insane," Juniper whispers to me. I nod from behind my little grille. The past week has shown me that Juniper and I can be fast friends as long as I am shrouded from head to toe and don't utter a single word.

Original Sin

I CANNOT TELL how late it is when I awake that night with my foot in the side pocket of the New Guild pool table. I pat the empty space on the baize beside me where Millie had been when I'd fallen asleep only a few hours earlier, practically giddy from the thought that tomorrow is the ladies' last day.

"Millie," I whisper, trying not to wake any of the sleepers clumped around the pool table, but Millie is not among them. Moonlight suddenly spills in when, at the far end of the large room, the door to the backyard opens, and Millie slips outside.

"Would you kindly shut the fuck up?" Jerome crabs as a board squeaks when I tiptoe past his head.

"Oops, sorry."

Outside, the cool night is one of those rare, early summer gifts to Austin. The light breeze is sweet with the fragrance of new growth. A full moon hangs low and plump, making the leaves of the live oaks sparkle like a thousand silver dimes. The pale limbs of a tall crape myrtle glow in the moonlight. Nighthawks chasing bugs zip in and out of the nimbus of brightness shining around a streetlight. I hear the soft murmur of muted voices and peek around the corner.

Millie's face, radiant as an Irish saint's, is tilted up to Sanjeev. She hangs on his every word as he says, "No, don't argue with me. Seeing you work for what you believe in this past week has given me the courage I needed to finally, truly declare myself. I cannot go through with an arranged marriage. I will call my father tomorrow."

"But, Sanjeev—"

"No, I have decided. I will simply ask him how he can ever expect our country to progress if even he, one of our nation's great reformers, insists upon enslaving his own son to a tradition from the Dark Ages. I will tell him that his position is illogical."

Illogical? Tell her you love her, you sap!

"Oh, Sanjeev," Millie whispers with a doomed romanticism not at all in keeping with Sanjeev's heroic announcement.

Sanjeev's face falls. "What is it? I dared to hope that you would be happy."

Millie speaks so softly I can barely hear her. "How, Sanjeev? How can I be happy?"

"Because I am now free to say what has been in my heart for so long: I love you. I love you, Millie Ott."

Yes!

"No, don't say that, Sanjeev."

"Don't say what? That I love you? It's true. I love everything about you, Millie Ott. I love the way your cheeks turn pink when you see me. I love how your right nostril quivers when you say something daring. I love that your hair is glossy as a seal pup's. I love that you sing 'Barbara Allen' when you start off on your rounds. I love your compassion. I love your honorableness. I love that at this very moment your foremost concerns are probably for a girl in India whom neither one of us has ever met."

"It's true. I can't stop thinking about Bhavani Mukherjee. Imagining how her life will be ruined if you don't go through with the wedding. I've done research. A spurned bride is very likely never to find another suitable marriage partner. But, Sanjeev, it's mostly you I'm thinking about. If you defy your family, you will become an outcast to them, to the entire world you grew up in and love so dearly."

"It doesn't matter."

"Maybe it doesn't matter now. But what about a few years from now? A few decades? What if you were to marry someone whom your family has not selected and you have children with this person?"

"If that person is you, it will be the fulfillment of my fondest dream."

"Yes, but imagine having children and knowing that your beloved father will never see them. Never know them. From the very beginning you told me that your life's goal, your dream, was to return to India and go into practice with your father. To continue his work with the poorest in your country."

"Dreams change."

"Yes, but has the dreamer changed? I don't think so. I think you are still the same son who worships his father, who feels his destiny is to serve the country he loves, whose very soul is fed by his ties to that country. Perhaps you wouldn't immediately regret breaking those ties. But someday, Sanjeev, you would, and when you did, you would come to resent the one who caused that break. I cannot allow you to do this. You must not call your father."

I want Sanjeev to grab Millie in his arms. Then I want him to kiss her until she is too breathless to say another word. But Sanjeev doesn't do that. Instead, he nods his honorable head; then, with the barest touch of his fingertips against Millie's cheek, he leaves.

Sanjeev walks off into the night. I emerge and pull Millie into my arms. "Millie, I'm sorry. I am so sorry for what I've done."

As she cries, I wish I could live my life all over. I wish I could straighten out every crooked turn I have ever taken. I wish I would have chosen any other route in life instead of the one that has ended up here with the best person I've ever known sobbing in my arms because I have caused her heart to be broken.

Millie blows her nose and pulls herself together with a shuddering sigh. "Blythe, you did me a favor, you truly did. From the very beginning, I acted in bad faith with Sanjeev. I pretended a friendship that didn't exist. In my heart of hearts, I always wanted more than friendship, even though he made it crystal clear from the start that he could never give me more. All you did was force my falsehood to the surface."

"I wish I hadn't. No one can make it through life without a lot of falsehoods."

"I understand that, but this one was bound to be exposed in time. You just hastened the process a tiny bit. That's all. It was inevitable. Inevitable that it should end like this."

Millie buries her head in my shoulder and weeps. I pat her back, and the moon sets in the summer sky. She stops suddenly and looks up at me, startled. "Did you just say something?"

"Me? No."

"Blythe, what do you want to say to me?"

"Nothing."

"You do."

"I really don't."

Millie keeps staring at me with her genius retriever stare. I'm certain she's reading my mind and I don't like that. "It's nothing. It's stupid."

"Don't think. Just say it."

"No, really. Forget it."

"Say it. Blurt it out. Whatever thought is in your head at this very moment, just say it."

Millie's otherworldly intensity unsettles me. "I'm not thinking about anything but you."

"But I made you think of something else. Something that disturbs you deeply. What is it? Tell me."

"Why? Why should I?"

"Because you want to. You want to be forgiven. You want to change."

"No, I—"

"Say it. Blurt it out right now. Don't think. Don't lie. Say it. Now."

"Is this that tingles thing?"

"Just say it. Now."

The words pop out of their own volition. "I married Trey for his money."

"Tell me the rest."

"Wow, you're kind of a hard-liner, aren't you? Is this how you transformed the princesses?"

"Tell me. Tell me the important part."

"I fell in love with Trey for his money."

"There. Good. The important part. Now we can start."

"I did love him. But without the monstrous family fortune—I mean, if he'd been a busboy at that wedding—I wouldn't have put up with Trey and his ridiculous shenanigans and his ridiculous family for two seconds."

"And so your intense dislike for your former mother-in-law—"

"Yeah, Peggy. She had the goods on me from the get-go. I guess I hated her so much because she played the game so much better than I ever could. The prenup was her way of forcing my hand. She knew I was marrying her son for money before I even knew it."

"So that was your original sin?"

"Hardly original. Every non-trust-funded princess in the house committed some version of it. The difference is, I knew. They're all goldfish, and marrying for money is the water they've always swum in. I saw the water. I knew it was there. I knew what I was doing. No, my original sin was greed. I wanted more. I wanted wretched excess."

"Do you feel better?"

"No."

"You will. I have to be alone now."

Millie leaves and I stay outside for a long time. In the glow from the streetlight, I notice a few bedraggled pink mimosa blossoms still hanging on the trees. Apparently, the sweetest blooms have all come and gone, and I didn't even smell them once.

An Abrupt Harmonic Convergence

Only the knowledge that the sun is rising on the very last day of my own personal Bataan Death March gives me the strength to open my eyes. Millie is already gone. There is a damp spot on the baize where her head had been. It is hot enough inside New Guild that the spot could have been sweat. I hope it is. I am pretty certain it is not.

I barely have enough energy to struggle into the burka and shuffle over to Seneca House. At least the house is cool and smells good. Best of all, though, with the princesses in their new Serve Mankind Mode, I can default to the caterer's friend: giant packages of microwavables from Sam's.

Fatima slings the edibles onto the table. Thanks to the transformations wrought by Millie, no one seems to notice or care much that breakfast is a hillock of Jimmy Dean sausage biscuits paired with a flight of Capri Sun juice pouches. There is an ease and humanness about all the women that I've never seen before. Kippie Lee has lost the frantic, unhinged look she's had for months. Bamsie has stopped straightening her hair and allowed it to frizz up, transforming her into the ridiculously cute troll doll she was born to be. Cookie Mehan has abandoned the makeup she usually trowels on and looks much better with her face, freckled brown by the South Texas sun, happily exposed. Maybe they are more relaxed. Maybe I just never really looked before.

Driven by hunger from their respective hidey-holes, the actual residents of Seneca House appear and slump into chairs around the table. For the first time, residents and visitors all sit together, noshing and gabbing. The ladies seem to be taking it as a tribute to their newly evolved benevolence that "the staff" is now acting like they own the place.

Jerome and Bamsie filibuster at each other as if words were oxygen and they are filling up their tanks for the very long dive back into their own worlds. Missy tiptoes in on bare feet and proceeds to load up a plate with a lumberjack-size pile of sausage biscuits and microwaved pancakes.

"Girl, what have you been doing to work up such an appetite?" Cookie jokes. "Must have been pretty wild."

Everyone is enjoying a kindly laugh at the impossible image of their Scripture demon doing anything wilder in bed than working a crossword puzzle when Sergio enters. There is a split second of ricocheting glances from Sergio smiling blissfully to Missy looking away quickly, then the laughter stops dead. Lips form into unspoken *oh*s of comprehension and no one will ever think of Missy Quisinberry in quite the same way again.

Olga fills the ensuing silence with tales from the Russian Mafia. "*Da*, when I am with Organizatsiya, we run all uf Moscow. I only leaf after gank boss Solonevich steals icons from Donskoi monastery. Even half a billion rubles is not enough for bribink. Is blut bath. No problem. I come here. Find job in titty bar. But the smuck. I cannot stand to breathe the smuck in titty bar. So I get scholairship for university and because I want to meet rich husband"—the ladies nod approval at this career path—"I get jop workink for queen bitch caterer." Olga glances pointedly at me hidden beneath my burka.

Fatima growls the tiniest bit behind her grille. It is all the protest I dare to make, and Olga knows it. Every bit of the saintly Sunday-school sanctimony that Millie has juiced up would evaporate in seconds if the ladies knew who was really slinging the Jimmy Deans their way. Seconds? It wouldn't take that long. All they'd need would be enough time to whip out a phone and tell the IRS exactly where to find me. Or at least where to come and claim the body, which would be battered beyond recognition after the ladies had finished with me.

No one notices Fatima's whimper of a growl as the women crowd around Olga to find out which husbands and, even more riveting, which wives had been open to her wiles. Olga starts listing the mates known on the circuit as strayers and players. One name in particular gets a huge reaction.

"Jebediah Quisinberry?" Missy shrieks.

Olga blows a languorous smoke ring. "*Da*. Major, major poossy hound."

Missy has one apoplectic moment before Sergio catches her eye, drops his velvety lashes, and smiles in a way that leaves Missy a newly philosophical woman. "Oh well, boys will be boys, I guess."

Kat and Nikki wander in with tackle boxes of manicure tools and styling products and start pushing back cuticles and painting free highlights on any takers. Nikki compliments Kat lavishly on her work. "Mrs. B. is so going to love you. Course, she's out having her baby so Jackie'll be supervising you."

"Supervising? Me?"

"Uh, yeah, duh. What? You think you can get your license without supervision? Or maybe you *like* living in a minivan."

"You mean?"

"Mean what? Did you think I was *not* going to come through?"

"No, but you hadn't really said anything for a while and . . ."

"Well, I signed a lease. It's only got one bedroom but, shit, after living in a minivan—"

The rest of Nikki's comments are lost in Kat's squeals of delight.

"Whoa! Whoa! Whoa! Put the brush down. You're getting highlights all over me."

With Kat still in ecstasy, I nuke another platter of forbidden food, throw it on the table, and consider my work done.

I collapse on the futon couch on the side porch next to the living room, intending only to close my eyes and "check for light leaks," as we used to say back in photo lab. But I am completely exhausted, and the couch is so soft compared with a pool table, and the sooth-ing drone of women's voices whispering in the background is the best white noise machine ever, and, without another thought, I drop into coma-level sleep. Nothing penetrates. I am dimly aware of Big Lou, a blubbery watermelon, landing on my stomach and aggres-sively kneading my flesh, but I can't rouse myself enough to shove her off. Sounds of furniture being moved, pots clattering, a vacuum cleaner whooshing, laughing, all barely intrude.

At one point, the couch jostles beneath me, but even that is absorbed in a sweaty nightmare of being strapped on a gurney and heading either for eyelid surgery or death by lethal injection, I can't make out which. Then, again and again, I watch a white limo driving away. In spite of the prickles of anxiety that slip in—a dream of being unmasked by the princesses, of being stripped of the burka and driven naked to Dog Crap Lane where Agent Jenkins garnishees my tortillas—I sleep on and on.

Finally, a distant tinkling, like the sound of the silver bells that Lakshmi used to ring to call consciousness back to bodies stoned on yoga, intrudes on the dreams. I fight my way out of a nightmare in which my disguise is being torn away by the ravening pack on Dog Crap Lane. I try to run, but the burka swamps me. I wake with a start. It is dark and I am sodden with sweat. My heart doesn't stop pounding until I touch the grille in front of my face. Thank God, the disguise is still in place, I am still safely hidden.

It is the last evening. If I can survive the next couple of hours without the princesses discovering my true identity, we'll have it made. Checks will be deposited and I will have done what I can to save the house and Millie's work. As soon as the ladies are dis-patched, hopefully in a shower of generous tips, I will do what everyone in the house, especially Millie, wants most and leave with-out a word. Kat is moving in with Nikki, so I can reclaim the van. I will sneak away tonight. Whether my mother and Griz like it or not, I am going to move in with them until I get on my feet. In another state. Under another name.

When I am solvent again, I'll settle up with the IRS. But only after I've made amends to Millie. Which will take the rest of this life and probably several more in the future. But I'll try.

I follow the tinkling sound into the living room. It is dark except for a few lit candles flickering amid a bank of unlit ones. Everyone, princesses and staff, is gathered around the candles. The word "coven" flashes through my mind, and I imagine myself staked out on the dining room table with a pentagram painted on my naked belly and Kippie Lee holding a dagger.

In the candlelight, Millie is a Victorian heroine dying of consumption, her beauty a spectral, haunting thing. Unshed tears glisten in her eyes. Sanjeev stares at her like a castaway floating on an endless sea, watching the last light on his sinking ship slip slowly beneath the dark waves.

Kippie Lee speaks. "First of all I want to thank the staff of Seneca Falls Spa for turning the kitchen and the house over to us this evening so we could have this ceremony. The last candlelight ceremony any of us had was probably back at the Kappa house. Or Pi Phi. Maybe Camp Mystic. Anyway, those were all important places to us girls growing up in Texas, but I think everyone here tonight will agree that none of them was as important as this place, this week, has been. There are a lot of reasons why it's been so important, but the main one is Millie Ott."

A huge round of applause from all the princesses and all the residents follows.

Kippie Lee continues, "I know that what she said to each of us is secret. What we said to her is secret. So secret, sometimes, that until we told Millie we didn't know the true things we'd been hiding, even, or maybe especially, from ourselves. I know that I'm not the only one whose life has been changed. Probably saved . . ."

The ladies clap and shout agreement. Sanjeev, however, looks like a man being turned slowly over a spit. He grimaces, bites his lips, hyperventilates. Millie contains her heartbreak beneath a serene smile.

"Millie only agreed to this ceremony on the condition that she not be the center of it. I will honor that promise and instead focus on the one thing that I know all of us learned from her: how important our friends are. We all sort of pay lip service to our girlfriends; that's what I used to do. I talked about how important my friends were, but, until this week, I never understood how really true that is.

"Friends. Our friends exasperate us. They annoy us. They compete with us. They gossip about us. We gossip about them. But we wouldn't be who we are without them. Millie told me that each friend God gives us is sent for a reason. Maybe she was sent to comfort you. Maybe you were sent to comfort her. Maybe she was put in your life to prod you to become more than you think you can be. Maybe she is the aggravation in the oyster that makes you form a pearl. Maybe she was sent to make you laugh or talk or think. Maybe she was the one you told when you got your first period. Maybe she helped you buy your first bra. Maybe she will be the one you tell when you get your first hot flash or shop for falsies after a mastectomy."

Kippie Lee stops, picks up a slender taper, and uses it to light a candle. "I light this first candle in honor of my friend Cookie Mehan. When everyone in town knew my husband was cheating on me, only one person was a good enough friend to step forward and tell me to my face. Cookie came over with a big box of Wom Kim's peach pudding and told me. And for that one evening we forgot about starving ourselves to death and ate that pudding with warm cream poured over it and wondered, 'Who needs men when we have Wom Kim?' This candle is for Cookie, who always lights the way for me."

Cookie's no-bullshit, tough ranchwoman mask falls away, and a glimpse of the vulnerable girl she was, and no doubt still is, peeks through.

Kippie Lee holds out the taper. "Would anyone else like to honor a friendship?"

Cookie takes the candle from her friend. "I would die for Kippie Lee Teeter and I think she knows it, but I should probably tell her. A little Wom Kim because she's getting dumped by an asshole who's not fit to shine her shoes and never learned how to give decent head is nothing. When my son, Jacob, died of leukemia when he was four years old, I went into a really, really dark place that no therapy or religion, comfort or hope, could light. Even my husband at the time could not or would not follow me there. The only person who did was Kippie Lee. I wouldn't let anyone in my house, but Kippie Lee just kept coming back. Again and again and again. She didn't bring flowers or food. And, thank God, she didn't bring advice. Words were empty for me. She just came and listened and let me pour out all the pain that probably would have killed me because I didn't see any way to live with it. This candle is for Kippie Lee Teeter, because I wouldn't be here without her and that's God's honest truth." Cookie lights another candle, then nods her head decisively to signal that the case is closed and holds out the taper. "Anyone else?"

Juniper is the first Seneca House resident to take the taper. "My candle is for Olga. Last semester I mentioned to her that there was a problem with my mammogram. Even though I said it wasn't that big of a deal, Olga showed up when I went in for a needle biopsy. She waited with me and held my hand while they did it. And even though I hate the bitch for being too skinny for me to borrow any of her clothes, I love her anyway."

Olga jabs a finger at Juniper. "You! I luf *you!*"

Kat stands next and, eyes glued to the floor, steps uncertainly to the front of the group. "I'm not like what you call a public speaker or anything. Nikki is the one who's good at that."

Nikki grins and it is hard for me to see the angry street kid I first met.

"Nikki is my best friend. I can tell like a gazillion stories but this one time? These frat jerks were all doing their rush or whatever and they came over and started panhandling *me* like that was so funny or something. They were all, 'Why are you panhandling? You're fat. You should give *us* money.' Then they took everything I had made that day. Which never would have happened if Nikki had been there. I hated myself for letting them take my money. I hated myself for having to ask for it in the first place. I hated that all I could do was sit and cry like some fat stupid baby. But when Nikki got back she just goes, 'Those fucking assholes. Fuck it, we're taking the day off.' And she drags me off to see *LOTR Two* and we sit through it twice even though Nikki is not into *Lord of the Rings*. But I am." Kat's hands float up, trying to express what she can never express. "She did it for me."

Kat lights a candle, sits down, and Nikki leans her head over onto Kat's shoulder and rests it there.

Gruff, grumpy Jerome elbows his way to the front and takes the taper. "This is going to sound so unbelievably gay, so fuck all of you. I don't care. I'm lighting this motherfucker for Lute. The asshole. He is the only one I told when my father had cancer and I had to fly back and forth to New Jersey way more times than I could afford and Lute gave me all his miles which he was saving to go home to Australia. So fuck you all, this one's for my boy, Lute." He lights a candle, shoves the taper back at Kippie Lee, and lumbers back to his chair. Without ever making eye contact, Lute holds his fist up and Jerome taps it.

Kippie Lee holds out the taper. "Anyone else?"

When Millie steps forward, I assume it is to deliver what everyone wants from her, a valedictory. The candlelight burnishes and blurs the faces that turn toward her. It brings out the girl at her first sleepaway camp in all the women present. Millie looks into the eyes of every person gathered before her, collects herself, and, voice strong and clear, begins speaking.

"Thank you all for what you have given me tonight. When I am asked why I was not ordained, I always say that it was because of my lack of speaking ability. That's true. But only half-true. The other half is that I don't believe in heaven and, apparently, that's a problem if you want to be a minister. What I do believe, though, is that we make our heaven on earth, right here, right now, and if we believe anything else, we'll never have our heaven. We'll live and we'll die and we won't have our heaven. You all, every one of you in this house, you are my heaven. But the candle I will light tonight is for the friend who brought us all together."

Everyone beams fond glances at one another as they try to figure which one is the special friend while simultaneously avoiding being trampled by Fatima, who is frantically elbowing her way toward the back.

"We each walk a different path, but thanks to my friend, that path has led us all to shelter here together beneath the same roof. The details of our lives are different. Some of us have husbands. Some of us do not. Some of us have lovers. Some of us do not. Some of us have children. Some of us do not. Some of us have money. Some of us do not. The one thing we all have in common is this: We all have friends. I grew up believing that I was destined to live my life without friends. Then I moved into this house and I made a friend."

A kind of nerved-up resignation grips me. I know as clearly as I've ever known anything in my life what I have to do. I stop running away and begin fumbling with the acres of cloth hiding me.

"The candle I light is for the friend who opened doors for me that I would never have walked through without her. I wouldn't be here right now without her. Wherever she is tonight I want her to know that I love her and will always love her. I light this candle for my friend Blythe Young."

Lost in the burka, I can't see the looks of horror and disgust that I am sure cross the faces of all my former friends, but I clearly hear a collective gasp at the mention of my name.

"Would anyone else like to light a candle?" Millie asks.

I know that facing the music is going to be ugly, but nothing will stop me now from stepping forward. I prepare to throw off my disguise. Unfortunately, this bold gesture is hampered by the feet stepping on Fatima's burka.

Before I can free myself, I hear a voice with the bounce of Bengal ring out. "I would. I would like to light a candle." I stop struggling and reposition the grille over my face in time to see Sanjeev step up and take the taper from Millie's trembling hand.

"For too long I have lived in fear of losing my life on earth when all the time I was with the person who is my heaven. I light this candle for Millie Ott."

The room is so silent that we can hear Millie's candle flaring to life.

"And now, please," Sanjeev requests. "If you all will bear with me for one moment, there is something I must do and I must do it immediately. Here, in front of the community that brought us together."

He presses a key on his cell phone, and a number dials. The room is utterly silent as Sanjeev, speaking in clear, ringing English, declares, "Father, it is Sanjeev. I have something to tell you. Something you won't like and something that I will not change my mind about. Father, I cannot marry Bhavani Mukherjee. You know that I love another. I can live without my family, my caste, my country, but I cannot live without Millie Ott. That is final. Hello? Hello! Father!"

Sanjeev holds the phone away from his ear and stares at it. "I don't know if Baba hung up or if the connection was lost or if he had a—" Before he can say "heart attack," Millie puts her arm around him. They fit together with a kind of inevitability that makes everyone feel obtuse for not having seen it before.

It takes two seconds for me to bid farewell to the last wisp of a shred of a molecule of a hope that I might ever have anything approaching my old life back; then I yank the burka out from under the feet pinning it down, jerk it off, and stride to the front of the room. No matter what will come, it is worth it all just to be able to breathe again.

"Oh God, no! What is *she* doing here?" Kippie Lee speaks for her group in a tone that could have curdled concrete. It is nothing less than I deserve. But I'll deal with all those snarls later. Right now I have a candle to light.

I step to the front of the room. Sanjeev smiles as he hands me a taper. "I don't know why Millie has remained my friend for all these years. I didn't deserve her friendship, but she gave it to me anyway.

From this day forward, I will try to do what I can within my limited capabilities to be worthy of it. The candle I light is for the brightest, purest part of my life. It is for my friendship with Millie Ott."

I wish I could say there was an abrupt harmonic convergence in which all was forgiven and forgotten in the golden glow of the candle I light for Millie. But, in fact, it is a toss-up as to who hates me more: the Pemberton Princesses who believe, rightly, that I have pulled another gigantic fast one on them or the residents who believe, even more rightly, that I have just flushed away all their slave labor efforts of the past week to save the house. There is no way now that even a fraction of those fat checks will remain in our possession.

I regret deeply how rarely the right thing is ever the convenient thing.

There is a second of silence as the two stunned factions regroup before loud—hysterically loud—unpleasantness erupts. I am waiting for the princesses to call dibs on the wishbone before I am ripped limb from limb when Sanjeev's phone tinkles out its trademark version of "Rule Britannia."

"Everyone! Please, silence!" Sanjeev orders. "It is Baba."

We all hold our collective breath to hear every word, but Sanjeev answers in Bengali. A frantic, high-pitched conversation follows. The group scrutinizes Millie's expression as we try to decipher whether what Sanjeev is now yelling into the phone is good or bad, but Millie is as lost as we are. With an abrupt farewell that does not seem to bode well, Sanjeev ends the conversation and snaps his phone shut. He stands, staggered and wordless, before the silent group. For once, we are all united, connected, by a single desire: let Millie be happy.

Cookie sniffs back a hiccuping sob as she interprets the look of devastation on Sanjeev's face.

Millie puts her palm against Sanjeev's cheek. "It's all right. You tried and that means the world to me. The world."

Sanjeev opens his mouth, but instead of his usual imperial rolling tones only a strangled squeak emerges. Then, to everyone's astonishment, Sanjeev, the epitome of controlled rectitude, begins blubbering. He puts his head on Millie's shoulder, and, smiling with beatific stoicism, she wraps him in her arms.

Sanjeev finally lifts his damp face from Millie's damp shoulder, collects himself, and speaks. "No, please, everyone, I'm sorry. The news is good. Too good to believe. My brother and Bhavani Mukherjee have fallen in love. The date for the wedding that was to be mine is even more auspicious for them. Bhavani Mukherjee will marry my brother, and I will marry Millie Ott. If she will have me."

A Natural Affinity
for the Larcenous

D<small>OG, IT'S HOT</small>!"

"Curtis, you ever get tired of stating the obvious?"

"Jesse, you ever get tired of being a drunk asshole?"

"Gentlemen, gentlemen."

"Oh, pardon my French, Miss Blythe."

"It's not the French I object to, Mr. Curtis; it's you calling Mr. Jesse an asshole."

That is good for a laugh. Jesse has been smiling a lot more and drinking a little less since I got him some new front teeth. He uses them now to chomp decisively into a Thai chicken salad wrap donated by one of the restaurants I've recruited.

Carl joins in. "Heat's nothin'. Rather have the heat than that danged old cold. You ever live through a winter in Casper, Wyoming, in the back of a camper, I tell you what, you do that, boy, you ain't never gonna complain about no heat no more."

It's my turn. "Of course, in the cold, you can just keep putting clothes on. In the heat, once you're down to tank tops and flip-flops, there's not much else you can take off."

"We'd like to see you try, though, Miss Blythe."

Even though we've been doing a version of this routine every day for most of the summer, the line still gets giant yuks, and I still have to say, "Mr. Jesse, Miss Millie wouldn't like that kind of talk."

Invoking Millie's name causes the bawdy talk to cease immediately. Like everyone whose life Millie changed, the men miss her. I will never be Millie. I knew that going in. I bring an entirely differ-ent skill set to the arena. For instance? For instance, could Millie have taught Curtis, Carl, Jesse, Joe, and the rest of the rotating gang here on Dog Crap Lane how to function while blasted out of their skulls? I think not. Which is sad, since maintaining is an underrated skill that, if nothing else, will get my guys in the door at the Salva-tion Army mission when the weather turns dangerously cold or even more dangerously hot than it is now.

In fact, my little flock seems to have a natural affinity for the lar-cenous take I bring to the endeavor. Showers, hygiene, the whole water-touching-skin deal, were always a hard sell until I showed the guys how to sneak into swimming pools, dorms, and health clubs to shower. Once they felt like they were pulling a fast one, sticking it to the man, they couldn't suds up fast enough. After that it was a breeze getting them into the subversive fun of underwear and front teeth.

The latter are being provided as part of the reparations package Kippie Lee inflicted upon Philandering Asshole during their di-vorce. I planted the idea of hiring the dentist the second Mrs. Teeter used to work for. K.L. liked the double whammy of not only publi-cizing her new role as Austin's Lady Bountiful, but also spotlighting the second Mrs. Teeter's roots in dental hygiene. The spite and revenge angle is one that Millie would never have thought to work.

The problem with doing good, I have discovered, is that it is too often done by the good.

Curtis sniffs his Thai chicken salad wrap. "Does anyone else think they put too much tarragon in again?"

Carl chews thoughtfully. "I was just about to say that."

Over the months since I came out of chador, I have discovered so many pockets of expertise among the men—Jesse can rebuild lawn-mower motors, Carl can get a squirrel to take a peanut out of his hand, Curtis once taught English and can still recite big chunks of Langston Hughes by heart—that opinions on tarragon no longer surprise me.

"Did you talk to Miss Millie?" Jesse asks hopefully.

"Sorry, Jess, she's still out in the field with Sanjeev and Dr. Chowdhury giving vaccinations."

"Them Chowhounds—"

"Chowdhurys," I remind Carl.

"Anyway, San Joe's family better appreciate what they got there. They don't their turbans is wound a little too tight."

"The Chowdhurys are Brahmans; they don't wear turbans. And of course they're falling in love with Millie."

"How could they not?" Curtis asks.

No one can think of a single reason, and after a long moment, I announce, "All right, clean up." I start the timer on my watch, and the men snap into action, collecting the real plates, silverware, and cloth napkins that we'd used. "A new record," I declare as they stow the last spoon in the Dorkocycle's cart.

"So when does Pease Park Catering get its first gig?" Curtis asks. "We've been practicing all summer."

"We're close, Curtis, very close. If you're all shaved and bathed when I come tomorrow you'll be ahead of fifty percent of the servers I used to hire. We'll print business cards and I'll pitch Pease Park Caterers to the Democrats or one of your other less-discerning groups."

This cheers the guys, and a few of them raise containers in small brown bags in a toast to our new venture. Even though there are fewer brown bags than there used to be and they are hauled out slightly later in the day, I don't entirely believe that any of us, especially me, will ever be in the catering business. But it is good to have a goal, a dream, a total and complete delusion. They all serve to keep us moving forward. And me and the guys, we need that forward propulsion.

I say my good-byes and head on down the road thinking how odd it is that, hard as I struggled to avoid it, as much as I lived in mortal dread of the prospect, I have ended up here on Dog Crap Lane. Odder still, I am pretty happy about it. Very happy, considering the alternatives. My thoughts are snapped sharply back into the present when I cross the dreaded leash-free zone. As usual, I am set upon by dogs whose owners chirp out, "Don't worry! He's friendly!" I know by now that you can never count on "friendly" in a dog. Deep down they're all wolves waiting for the genetic twig to snap. What you have to hope for is "slow."

I make it past the last snarling cur, and my thoughts return to the chain of events that brought me here.

Three months ago, on that fateful final night of the Pemberton Princesses' stay, I knew that my unveiling would be quite the buzz killer. And it was. Once I fumbled my way out of the burka, it was a miracle I didn't end the evening in tar and feathers. My continuing salvation was, of course, Millie. That evening, her white magic was operating on a nuclear level. Whether Kippie Lee, Jerome, Nikki, whether any of us willed it to happen or not, we had all been bonded by our desire to see the one purely good person we had ever known get what she wanted. Then when, after aeons of bad calls, the universe finally did the right thing and totally delivered the goods and Sanjeev asked Millie for her hand, and she said yes, the delight that united us all was so immaculate that it even managed to lap over onto me and my sins.

Once the princesses and residents decided that stringing me up would, as Yay Bombah suggested, "totally harsh the buzz," worlds opened. There was immediate agreement among all parties that Millie's work had to continue. A newly vocal Missy Quisinberry made a strong case for keeping the house open as well. She pointed out that not only was it essential as a base of operations for Millie, but that "If we can save just one girl from becoming a naive, unsuspecting Pi Phi or one boy from becoming a lying, cheating Sig it'll be worth it." Kippie Lee agreed and proposed that the Platinum Longhorns turn all the fat checks the ladies had written over to Millie and the house, and, in exchange, the ladies wouldn't sue the Plat Longs back to the Stone Age.

There was still the little matter of the RIAA's lawsuit, though.

Kippie Lee brushed that annoyance away. "Not a problem. I assume my asshole husband's firm is handling the case. This week has shown me clearly what I have to do in regards to that son of a bitch. I'll have lunch with him Monday and point out what a gigantic crack he put his tail in bringing his hygienist-whore to Jeffrey's. We'll just see how much he likes the idea of living off of what some trollop makes telling people to floss. Don't look so surprised. It's always been my family's money. Hunt gambles away every cent he's ever made. That's how the Dixes got their hooks into his firm. Don't worry, I'll convince Hunt to convince the RIAA to go after the university and leave you little fish alone. The case will be tied up in litigation forever. That should keep all the lawyers happy."

"But what about Trey?" I had to ask. "His family's White House connections? Aren't you worried about alienating him?"

Kippie Lee and Bamsie popped their eyes at each other, then burst out laughing. "Girl, where have you been?"

"Uh, well, pretty much right here."

"'Shock and awe' is turning into 'the crock of it all.' Things are bad over there, and, according to our sources in Aramco, they're only going to get worse. We're distancing ourselves. Last thing anyone wants anymore is 'White House connections.'"

Bamsie agreed. "We never really liked Bush anyway. We liked Laura. Every Southern girl in the country knew a hundred frat guys just like Bush and every one of them was smarter and better-looking."

"Yeah, and even those guys were all dumb and ugly."

That left one item on the agenda: me. Oddly, from the moment I stepped out from under the burka, nothing seemed as terrible anymore as going back into hiding. I was even starting to see the upside of prison. I'd do my time, clear the books, and make a fresh start. But as the group discussed whether or not to turn me over to the IRS, a much better idea popped into my head. More of a vision, actually; I saw clearly and in fairly elaborate detail exactly what I had to do. "You should let me take over Millie's work."

When they hooted derisively, I suggested, "Perhaps one of you ladies would like to take over Millie's work with the homeless men in Pease Park? The street kids on the Drag? How about the day laborers? Be a great opportunity for you to brush up on your Spanish."

Although newly sanctified by their week with Millie, the ladies recoiled as if they had just sucked in a giant, aromatic whiff of Eau de Homeless Guy. Without my putting too fine a point on it, they saw that they could either step into the breach and take over Millie's work themselves after she left for India with Sanjeev or do what they did best and hire good help. I was offering to take on the work they didn't want to do *and* I would be punished in the process. It was a win-win. Instead of turning me in, they decided to pay me minimum wage and deposit my salary directly into an account that would be used to start paying off the IRS.

The surprise was what an innovative and generally good do-gooder I turned out to be. For example, I took my day-labor flock from the site to Goodwill, where I kitted them out in polo shirts, fishing hats, and boat shoes. My *mojados* ended up looking like they were heading to Nantucket. Suddenly the suburban ladies were specifically requesting my guys. They didn't know why exactly, but they just liked having Jesus or Innocencio or Heriberto around. The ladies believed that they did better work than those "other ones."

But I feel my talents are most useful with the street kids. The first thing I did was tap the princesses for a big clothes drive. That was inspired. The ladies got to clean out their closets, make room for the new season, *and* tell their husbands they didn't have a thing to wear because they'd given all their clothes away to the needy. Not that any of the street kids wanted to panhandle in a pink-and-green-flowered Lilly Pulitzer sundress. No, I dressed some of the more promising ones in L.L. Bean and then had them distribute our haul to an assortment of consignment stores where the designer castoffs were received with delight and dollars.

It was good training for the kids to pass in the straight world and to see how much more people liked you right off the bat when your death's head tattoo was covered by a perky Abercrombie blouse. The kids decided to make clothes drives a regular thing. They used some of the proceeds to start a scholarship fund at the beauty college where Kat and Nikki are studying, then spent the rest of the money on dozens of little bottles of hand sanitizer to pass out on the street, rooms for sick kids, and unauthorized purchases of Bacardi Breezers.

My real gift to them, though, is that they know they can never put anything over on me. The ones who've been on the street the longest recognize me for the scammer/grifter I will always be. So they listen when I impart the sort of wisdom Millie never had access to. Like how to charm and flatter when you need to; how to get Mom's boyfriend off you; how to pretend to be a lot better person than you are until you actually become a better person. With the aid of the little dodges and scams I guided them through, they started helping whoever needed it the most.

Jaguar was their first candidate. Unfortunately, he disappeared without a word, or even a growl, before we had a chance to do much for him. I cruise the alleys at night searching for Jaguar, but so far have had no luck. The street kids leave out saucers of milk. Others who've never known Jaguar or his story have been picking up the tradition. The Drag is now dotted with dozens of little saucers of milk, like offerings to the elephant-headed god Ganesh.

After their stay at Seneca House, the ladies' lives changed as well. Kippie Lee gave up on trying to hold her wrecked marriage together and went for the jugular, reclaiming as much of her family money as she could, then quickly became the biggest star among Austin's philanthro-socialites. Cookie Mehan moved out full-time to the family ranch to grow heirloom tomatoes and run an underground railroad for illegals passing through the dangerous country. Her weight remained the same, but she lowered her body fat to seven percent leading *mojados* safely across the border. Morgan Whitlow found a girlfriend, and they raise miniature horses together in Bastrop. Bamsie and Jerome continue a mad monologuing affair via telephone that keeps Bamsie's marriage afloat and Jerome hanging on to the sunny side of sanity.

For most of the ladies, however, their interlude at Seneca House was nothing more than a brief recess, an unexpected vacation from their real lives. For a few days, they enjoyed the weightless feel of not caring. Then they went right back to obsessing over carbs and wrinkles, polished nickel fixtures and powder rooms.

As I grind my way back up the long hill from Pease Park to Seneca House, sweat brims over the dam of my eyebrows and spills across my sunglasses. I hit a bump in the pavement and hard-boiled eggs clank in the tin pans, pots rattle in the metal cart. The terrain flattens when I approach Nuts Street. Drenched and out of breath, I glide to a stop in front of the house.

Three new residents, Amy, Megan, and Joe—I call them the Little Women—are sitting out on the front porch drinking iced tea and smoking cigarettes. They are part of the new crop that moved in after I found decent jobs for Olga, Juniper, Doug, and Sergio at salaries large enough to allow them to vacate Seneca House.

"Hey, Blythe," Joe calls out. "I've got some more designs for you to look at."

"Great," I answer.

Joe, an emo boy with a dyed-black forelock tugged permanently over his right eye, and I are organizing a fashion show/fund-raiser. Joe, a fashion major, is making most of the clothes. We're going to use my street kids as models. Nikki and Kat will do hair and makeup. I'll get my homegirl Lynn Sydney, who still maintains her minimalist toehold in Austin even though she spends most of the year in London, to be the nominal chair of the planning committee. That will guarantee 100 percent Pemberton attendance.

When Lute appears on the front porch, a pair of board shorts barely hanging on to his hip bones, and asks if anyone is interested in going to Barton Springs, all three of the newcomers jump up. Joe springs up fastest.

"Blythe?" Lute asks. "What about you?"

"Naw, I'm good."

I watch the quartet leave and imagine the heartbreaks and poignant songs to come. No doubt Joe will fall hardest. I make a note to myself to keep an eye on him. The mailman appears and hands me a tall stack of mostly bills and flyers, though I am pleased to discover that Megan is a subscriber to *US* magazine and flop down on the porch to enjoy it along with the abandoned iced teas and cigs.

My enjoyment diminishes markedly when I hit an article titled "Indie's Hottest Hunks." There, among the frail man-children in their porkpie hats and nose rings, I am stunned to find a complete grown-up, Danny Escovedo. He was caught walking the red carpet into an awards show where the album he produced with L'il CheeZ would win Emerging Rap Artist Album of the Year. But it's not the sight of his handsome face that ruins my *US* moment so much as it is the emaciated waif on his tuxedoed arm. Alleged to be the "next Avril Lavigne," she is beaming up at Danny in a way that makes me want to scratch the tarry smudges where her eyes are supposed to be right out of her head. It is obvious that she is having sex with Danny. The sex I should be having.

It's been two months since I made the last of many calls to Danny. He didn't respond to any of them unless you consider Archive's decision to start giving away their music online in a format that deletes itself after three plays a response. In spite of Kippie Lee's efforts, the RIAA's lawsuit wasn't going away until Danny's decision put them into a publicity headlock.

I can almost convince myself that Danny did it for me. But we're too much alike for me to believe that for very long; he made the legal unpleasantness vanish because it was a savvy business move and benefited him. I understand this.

Not that any of this clearheadedness has stopped my longing for him, the depth of which still surprises me. Time was, the only reason I would have yearned for a man with such a walloping intensity would have been for his ability to create or buy haute couture for me. I certainly never ached for Tree-Tree this way. It doesn't seem fair that knowing you brought misery on yourself actually makes it hurt more.

My snarled synapses interpret this pain as a problem that needs solving and they start flashing "solutions." Visualizations as clear as a treasure map jump into my head with giant Xs marking spots like the underwear drawer where Amy hides the Percocet she got when she had her wisdom teeth taken out and the scrotal-looking woven bag where Megan keeps her Xanax. The number of the street kids' fund-raiser fashion show's meager bank account also makes an appearance.

I am starting to stray dangerously down this trail when, amid a flurry of cell-phone bills and Peace and Justice Coalition flyers, I spot a letter addressed to me from Waco, Texas. I open the envelope. Inside is a curry-colored invitation with the god Ganesh at the top.

I thank the Remover of Obstacles for sending me an event that I truly care about to coordinate. Millie's wedding just might be the only distraction with enough traction to help me plow over Percocet, Xanax, and embezzlement. As easily as opening an envelope, my thoughts turn to trying to figure out how many tubs of icing and artful scatterings of fresh flowers it will take to "repurpose" a very cost-effective purchase from Sam's Club bakery into a wedding cake. The happy thought of dancing at Millie's wedding causes the song that cost me so dearly to start playing in my head:

> *I had a dream the other night*
> *When everything was still*
> *I thought I saw Susanna*
> *A-comin' down the hill*
>
> *A buckwheat cake was in her mouth*
> *A tear was in her eye.*
> *I said I'm coming from the south*
> *Susanna, don't you cry.*

I catch myself singing out loud and wonder if I am turning into a batty old lady. Or just the person I started out to be. It is too hot for such a burst of excitement, and I settle farther into the old wicker chair. A moment later Big Lou bumps my ankle, demanding attention. As I pat the tub of lard, my eye is drawn to the crape myrtles shading the porch. A few blossoms still cling to the smooth,

Chuck & Ruby Ott
&
Dr. & Mrs. Sanjeev Chowdhury

Request the honor of your presence
at the marriage of our children

Millie Louise Ott
&
Sanjeev Chowdhury

2:00 p.m.
Sunday, October 19
Seneca House
Bengali feast to be served compliments of
Blythe Young's Pease Park Caterers

snaky limbs. The papery flowers are bright pink, gaudy fuchsia, watermelon red. Beautiful though they are, the blossoms are as odorless as tissue; it is too hot for even plants to put up a front and try to smell good. I know the feeling. I am down to tank tops and flip-flops. I can't strip away anything more. Fortunately, in Austin, Texas, if you play your cards right, that is all a person needs.

How perfect is that?

ACKNOWLEDGMENTS

I would like to thank my wonderful friends and informants for their insight, grace, and good humor in helping me create, populate, and decorate the high and low societies of this novel: Brenda Bell, Gracie and Bob Cavnar, Malou Flato, Phil Hudson, Clare Moore, Bettye Nowlin, Quality Quinn, the residents of Seneca House past and present, Helen Thompson, Julie Thornton, Becca and John Thrash, Peggy Weiss, and Anne Elizabeth Wynn.

For crucial ideas and support, I am grateful to my sisters, Kay and Martha Bird, and genius friends Carol Dawson, Gianna LaMorte, Kathleen Orillion, and Evan Smith.

Once again I acknowledge the joy of working with the best in the business: Ann Close, Caroline Zancan, Millicent Bennett, Kristine Dahl, Montana Wojczuk, Nina Bourne, Sarah Gelman, Jason Kincade, Patricia Johnson, Kathryn Zuckerman, Kim Thornton, Kathleen Fridella, Marci Lewis, Robert Olsson, Gabriele Wilson, and Chris Gillespie.

For all of the above and the perfect title, I thank Dave Hickey.

And, as always, for my G-Men, George and Gabriel.

READERS GROUP GUIDE

How Perfect Is That

SARAH BIRD

How Perfect Is That

Sarah Bird

Discussion Questions

1. "Try growing up in a double-wide a block off I-20 with a Dairy Queen for your country club, and the boys' JV football coach for your secret boyfriend when you were barely thirteen. Grit? I have more grit in my craw than a Rhode Island Red" (22). How does Blythe Young's background help her cope, even in the world of the extremely privileged? Does her Dairy Queen background ever show through her revamped façade of Blahniks and Prada?

2. Even though in the course of the novel Blythe never remounts to the top of the Austin social ladder, she finds her way to a much happier ending. What allows her to find her own definition of success? Who helps her most along the way?

3. How does Austin as a setting animate this story? Could Blythe's experience take place anywhere else?

4. Blythe's former mother-in-law, Peggy Biggs-Dix, represents a widely recognized archetype of the upper-class matriarch. What is her role inside her family and in society at large? Do we ever feel sympathy for, or forgive Peggy for ruining Blythe's marriage? Or does her story mirror Blythe's own?

5. What do you make of Lynn Sydney at the beginning of the book when she has a short conversation with Blythe at Kippie Lee's party? Does your opinion of her change when she comes in to save the day at the end of the book? How?

6. Do you, as a reader, relate to Blythe—with her wit, rampant perseverance and creative ways to overcome—even though she can be a scoundrel? If so, how?

7. When imagining being caught by the IRS, Blythe recounts, *"I suffered under the delusion that the not really really rich have about the really really rich: I believed that since they have so much, they wouldn't be so petty."* (40) Do you think Blythe's "delusion" has roots in reality? Discuss how her former social circle behaves in a petty manner.

8. Blythe establishes herself immediately as different than the Pemberton Heights crowd, but she also separates herself from the Seneca hippies, by such comments as: "Cooking aromas heavy on whole grains, tamari, sesame, recomposition of soybeans, Third World staples so beloved of kids who grow up on Pop-Tarts, then go boho the instant that they move away from the automatic sprinkler systems of their youth. Having grown up on hamburger that needed to be helped and with a sprinkler system that consisted of me and a watering can, I never understood the impulse." (65) Is Blythe really as different from both as she believes?

9. When Blythe and Millie discuss the Dix family, Blythe recounts the humiliation suffered by Trey's father, Henry "Junior" Dix the Second, whose own dad enjoyed making him stand in the sun and then would ridicule him with: " 'Well, by damn! The little turd *does* cast a shadow!' " (92) Why do you think Bird includes this detail on the Dix family?

10. While rebuilding her life at Seneca House, Blythe has the impulse to romanticize Trey and demonize Peggy, blaming the dissolution of their marriage on his mother. But when Trey appears back in her life, he hurts her immensely again on his own. What differences do you see in the way Blythe recovers the second time around? Do you think she will ever, or should ever, forgive Trey?

11. At first it seems like the friendship between Blythe and Millie is lopsided: that Blythe benefits from the friendship but does not reciprocate. Does your opinion of their relationship change as the book progresses?

12. How does Blythe ingeniously use the idiosyncrasies of the rich against them to survive another day in their company? Think of when she tried to throw a party for Kippie Lee or find a place to live in the Pyramid House. How does the pervasive humor of this book come out during Blythe's capers?

13. Do you think that Blythe was right in exposing Millie and Sanjeev's love, even though it created a temporary rift in the girls' relationship? Was the action driven by Blythe's usual selfishness, or did she have another motivation?

14. At the "Seneca Falls Spa," a place where everyone reaches a point of self-discovery, Blythe finally admits to Millie that she had fallen in love with Trey partly because of his money. Why is this admission so important at the end of the book? Were you surprised by this fact?

15. Blythe comes to see her own flaws and moral shortcomings that stem from greed and over-indulgence, and as a result, tries to change course. Do you think that similar trends in American culture are capable of a self-correction?

An Interview with Sarah Bird

Q: Why did you write *How Perfect Is That?*

A: To cheer myself up. To make myself laugh. I wrote most of this book in 2003 when I was in despair over what was happening in our country. I needed a way to think about the war; about the stolen election; about toxic, Gilded Age levels of opulence and obliviousness. And I needed to do it without wanting to drink Drano. As always, humor, seemed to be the way out.

During a conversation with a friend who couldn't afford to get a Pap smear, my need to understand collided with a need to laugh. She was the fifth highly-educated friend I'd spoken with in as many weeks who had either just lost a job or had a job with such crappy insurance that basic health care was out of the question. Tired of simply wringing my hands, I suggested that she should move back into the co-op boarding house where we both had lived when we were students at the University of Texas. Why, with the money she saved she'd have enough for that elusive Pap smear in no time!

The absurdity of that prospect—moving back into your old college boarding house—tickled us both and, suddenly, laughing seemed like a lot more fun than hand-wringing and railing and wailing. So, rather than futilely obsess about the fate of America, I created a character who was every bit as oblivious, greedy, and short-sighted as those who had delivered us to our current fate. In an attempt to keep hope alive, I also made this scoundrel redeemable. We'll see if the same holds true for America.

Q: How do you respond to readers who take the novel simply as a comic romp?

A: *Hallelujah!* First and foremost, the book has to work as a novel and, hopefully, one with elements of humor. The political agenda is entirely my own and one need not share it to enjoy the book.

Q: **How did you decide on the title?**

A: Well, actually, I originally called the novel *Weightless*. I meant it ironically since my protagonist, Blythe Young, is excessively weighted down with social aspirations, regret, guilt, schemes, lies, sins of both omission and commission. She is desperate to be a woman who lives to gain material possessions and lose body weight.

As fitting as that title was thematically, it didn't convey that this is basically a comic novel. I was moaning to my friend, the art/pop culture critic, Dave Hickey, that I needed to come up with a title that was less weighty than *Weightless,* and he suggested *How Perfect Is That.* Since Dave is a certified genius with the MacArthur grant to prove it, how could I refuse?

Q: **What aspects of *How Perfect Is That* are close to your own life?**

A: The low society stuff is much more autobiographical for me than the high. I did actually live in a UT co-op boarding house called Seneca House while I was getting my master's at the University of Texas. But in that day and age, it housed female graduate students. It has since morphed into a co-ed, mostly undergraduate, sometimes feminist, mostly vegan, generally activist house which the current residents were kind enough to allow me to visit several times.

Beyond that, there's probably less autobiographical overlap in this novel than almost any of my others. Fortunately, many kind-hearted souls in high places helped me with the high society research by sharing their worlds with me, allowing me to glimpse lives that are a round of charity galas, private jets, and Dom Perignon by the crate.

Q: Your protagonist, Blythe Young—while good-hearted—is not always a likeable character. (Cut to our heroine drugging guests at a party she is hired to cater). What was your inspiration for her?

A: Good-hearted? That remains to be seen. Blythe is a scoundrel! A reprobate! A user and an abuser! The whole question in the book is: Can she be saved? Is she redeemable?

This likeability question intrigues me. It comes up far more often in novels with female protagonists than it does when the hero is a male. The conventional wisdom is that female readers don't like books in which the heroine is not "likeable," "relatable." I may be a complete freak in this, but I loves me a bad girl, a woman with some deep and real characters flaws, as opposed to a protagonist whose major flaw is giving too much or something totally cooked up like that. Blythe was fun to write and, I hope, she's fun to read.

Q: To name a few of the socialites that appear in the book: Kippie Lee Teeter. Missy Quisinberry. Noodle Tiner. Lulie Bingle. You can't just make these names up. Do these ladies (or their likenesses) actually exist in Texas?

A: An early reader in New York told me that the names were just too over the top, too unbelievable. Not that truth is any defense when writing fiction, but I did have to laugh since all those names came from lists of Texas Junior League board members. In fact, I wish I'd read today's newspaper in time to include a couple of names I saw there: Naelynn and Gary Beth. Although Texas likes to think of itself as Western, it manifests a lot of southerness, and, in particular, a lot of rural southerness, in girls' names.

Q: While *How Perfect Is That* can be read as a light read, it also has a serious political undertone. Do you think the political attitude has changed in Texas over the past few years?

A: Night and day. At least in the world where the novel is set.

Austin had always been this happy, liberal blue island in a hostile sea of red. Well, after the 2000 election, that sea threatened to swamp our little island paradise. This period, when to criticize the president was to be a traitor, already feels like history, like the McCarthy Era, something that happened a longtime ago. Or maybe didn't happen at all. A time of madness when politics wasn't the thing you didn't talk about because it bored everyone so much, but because friendships would be ended and concealed handguns drawn.

The whole country went through this calamitous convulsion, but it was particularly rancorous here in Austin since there is a large and influential group that, beginning during the years when Bush was governor, gained tremendous social cachet through personal friendships with the Bushes.

In these circles, politics suddenly became an even more fraught topic than it did in the rest of the country. I was fascinated by the peculiarly personal dimension this discussion took in Austin where, suddenly, friendships that dated back to college hippie days were subjected to political litmus tests, and judgments could be rendered on who did or did not accept invitations to the White House. Seating charts became color-coded with the unreconstructed Blues moved far down the table or out altogether.

I knew that the tide had turned when, during the summer of 2006, I walked in on a conversation and heard one of the Austin inner circle of Bushies say, "We never really liked George. Laura was always the one who was our friend." And now, interestingly, many members of that inner circle are supporting Obama.

Q: **What would you say to people who want to categorize this book as just a book for Texans?**
A: This goes back to the long, ongoing controversy about "regional" literature and the extremely condescending assump-

tion it is based on: that the story set in New York—preferably Manhattan—is universal, anywhere else and it's regional.

Blythe Young is a social climber for the ages. She has an interesting manifestation in Austin, but could have cropped up anywhere in the country. She is a classic American hustler amped up on the steroidal greed of both the dot com era and flavored with the virulent strain of Southern Belle-ism that afflicts a certain type of Texas woman.

Q: Your loyal readers are likely to notice that *How Perfect Is That,* while funny, has a darker brand of humor than some of your previous books. How would you compare this novel to your others?

A: As my husband asked during the 2000 election when I was marching, writing letters to the editor and ranting nonstop, "What happened to that carefree girl who didn't used to know who the governor was?" I guess that carefree girl wrote the earlier books.

Q: How long have you been writing?

A: I have been supporting myself entirely with writing since 1980.

Q: Looking back, did you choose the writing profession or did the profession choose you?

A: I believe it chose me in this way: Growing up, I was pathologically shy, deeply introverted, and driven to make things. I loved creating little worlds. When my Air Force family was stationed in Japan, I made a tiny Japanese village with cotton for snow on the thatched roofs of the little huts that I made out of broom straw. I found that recreating my favorite books by, say, painting horrible little watercolors of Heidi's grandfather's home in the Alps, allowed me to extend the experience of being transported by those books. I once recruited my five brothers and sisters to re-enact *Uncle Tom's Cabin.* Sadly, my older brother got perhaps too carried away being Simon Legree; there was whipping involved. In any case, introversion and a drive to escape into worlds I created predisposed me to the writing life.

Q: When did you "know" you were a writer?

A: Since I grew up in an Air Force family, frequently stationed on overseas bases, I had even less exposure to writers than most children. All the career options I was exposed to growing up involved uniforms and missile silos.

The idea of being a writer never crossed my mind until I discovered a form so, *hmmm,* "approachable," that it occurred to me that human beings might be producing it rather than the gods who wrote the books I loved. This form was the photo-romance. I discovered the photo-romance when I was an au pair in France. Ostensibly, I was in France learning French. Actually, I was fleeing a very bad love affair. In any case, I was a twenty-year-old nitwit and the only person whose French was worse than mine was the three-month-old *bebe* I was taking care. So I started buying photo-romances in a shy person's way of learning to speak a language.

When I returned home, I sought out a comparable market in the United States and discovered true confession magazines. Pulp fiction: *True Love, True Confession, Modern Love.* I believe they have disappeared from the face of the earth. There could be no more ignominious way to begin, yet this was mine, and it fit my timid temperament in a way that no MFA program could have. These publications allowed me to learn how to tell a story in a voice that was not my own, to sink deeply into a character and her world, but, most importantly, since these "confessions" were all anonymous, they allowed me to simply learn how to fill up pages with no thought whatsoever that they would ever be associated with me.

Q: What inspires you?

A: I am inspired by books I love and by worlds that I want to capture and put into books such as the sub-cultures surrounding off-beat rodeos; the hothouse community of flamenco dance and guitar in New Mexico; the nomadic world of the military brat growing up in the Far East.

Q: **Every writer has a method to their writing. On a typical writing day, how do you spend your time?**

A: Get up. Drink way too much tea. Spend far too much time on our mediocre local newspaper. Work too many crossword puzzles. Walk my dogs. Answer email. When I seriously stop and think about my day, I can never quite pinpoint the moments when I actually write. I always seem to be taking the trash out or driving to my son's school to bring him the homework he forgot or trying to decide what color to paint the trim. Just now, tallying up all the books I have published, I had a moment of wondering if I'd made the whole thing up.

Q: **How long does it take for you to complete a book?**

A: The shortest amount of time it's ever taken me to write a book was four months. The longest was fifteen years.

Q: **Do you write straight through, or do you revise as you go along?**

A: I try to get as much down as I can without censoring myself too much, then I go back and revise. Sometimes a lot. I wrote essentially five completely different versions of my previous novel, *The Flamenco Academy*. It took me that many attempts to get the form, the tone, and the setting right. Excruciating.

Q: **When you sit down to write is any thought given to the genre or type of readers?**

A: I find it very inhibiting to think of an actual human reading what I write. While writing *The Flamenco, Academy* I had to put readers farther out of my mind than usual since this was my first book that contained no humor whatsoever and I knew that some readers would be disappointed. And they were.

As far as genre, mostly I write semiliterary novels. Fortunately, almost the only convention in this genre is that the work has to clearly not be genre. But I am familiar with genre conventions. The vast majority of writers support themselves by teaching. I always knew that I was not capable of sustaining the level of extroversion that teaching requires. Instead, I supported myself during the early years of my career by writing romance novels. Like pulp fiction, they were wonderful for learning the mechanics of writing. Since this wasn't the form I aspired to, they served as a sort of out of town tryout where I could fill up pages without torturing myself about every word.

Q: When it comes to plotting, do you write freely or plan everything in advance?

A: I didn't really understand plotting until I spent nine years working as a screenwriter. Writing in film is a group enterprise. Probably too much so. But it requires outlines and presentations, so I was forced to know every tick of a story before I told it. This flattens the work to a degree. With luck, talented actors then go in and reinflate it. Still I prefer to allow novels to unfold as they will, to take the shape they are meant to take without my intervention. The characters guide me through the story. Once I know who they are, they tell me very decisively what they would and would not do. Generally, it helps me *not* to know how a book will end as that keeps me from tipping my hand.

Q: Many of your novels portray very exotic worlds and eras, Civil War Spain in *The Flamenco Academy,* Occupation Japan in *The Yokota Officers Club.* You've also set books in the worlds of romance novels and offbeat rodeos. What was it like, essentially, setting a book in your own backyard?

A: Although the novel is set in Austin, where I live, there was still a fair amount of research involved since *How Perfect Is That* is set in social arenas that I don't belong to. Both Austin's high society and low had their own anthropology and getting the anthropology right is one of my chief joys in writing.

Q: **What kind of research do you do before and during a new book?**

A: I consider research the great reward of the writing life. It is a rabbit hole I tend to go too far down and spend too much time in. The kind of research varies for each book. The book I set in the world of off-beat rodeos began as the thesis I did for a degree in journalism. Photography is a magic way to research. With a camera in front of my face, I could disappear into whatever world I was exploring. Plus the photos were fabulous visual notes and sending prints to subjects I wanted to interview further was a great way to make friends.

The Flamenco Academy was the most fascinating to research. Flamenco in New Mexico has a mesmerizing history that combines the Gypsies thousand-year exile from India; the Moorish Conquest of Spain; the conquistadors in the New World; and lots of substance abuse.

How Perfect Is That involved a different sort of research. In part I found it hilarious imagining what it would be like to have Barbara Bush as your mother-in-law. What a weekend with that whole crew might be like.

Q: **Do you visit the places you write about?**

A: In many cases, I choose to write about places that I can *only* visit by writing about them. Such as the Golden Age of Flamenco in the *cafes cantantes* in turn-of-the-last-century Sevilla and the post-Occupation Japan of my childhood.

Q: Where do your characters come from? How much of yourself and the people you know manifest into your characters?

A: My characters are, generally, composites of dozens of people I know all filtered through me.

Q: Do you ever suffer from writer's block? If yes, what measures do you take to get past it?

A: Early on in my career, I saw that I was the type of person who might latch onto "obstacles" if I allowed that to happen. That I could easily obsess about not having the exact right sort of paper or validation from the outside world. So, I committed to writing no matter what the circumstances, to not believing in writer's block. If I didn't have a desk, I wrote in bed on a legal pad. If I didn't have time, I lived ultra-cheap so I could exist on a half-time job. This was great training as it now enables me to completely ignore my incredibly messy house and just about anything else that would interfere with writing when I need to.

Q: What kind of books do you like to read?

A: I adore great novels with comedic elements and seek them out constantly. Some of the early favorites that formed me as a writer are *Confederacy of Dunces* by John Kennedy Toole, *Lady Oracle* by Margaret Atwood, *Ladies Man* by Richard Price, all the novels of Charles Portiss (*Dog of the South, Norwood, True Grit, Masters of Atlantis, Gringos*), and most of Thomas Berger's, particularly *Little Big Man*. I love every book that Nick Hornby and Tom Perrotta have ever written.

Q: When you're not writing what do you do for fun?

A: Drift through big box stores with a tankard of Diet Coke in my shopping cart. I find Costco to be particularly soothing.

Q: If you weren't a writer what would you be?

A: Psychotic. I say that only half in jest. Temperamentally, I'm really only suited to be sitting alone in a room for ten hours a day making up lies.

Q: What is your favorite word?
A: Is there a more perfect word than "onomatopoeia"? I'm sure I'm not alone in cherishing onomatopoeia as my first "big" word. I remember experiencing this tiny blip of power when I learned, when I "owned," this word. It made me avaricious for other words that were both euphonious and impressive. I was quite the little nerd.

Q: What's next for you?
A: I'm currently writing a film adaptation of my last novel, *The Flamenco Academy.*